UNLIKELY

Match

UNLIKELY
Match

a novel

BEVERLY KING

Covenant Communications, Inc.

Published by Covenant Communications, Inc.
American Fork, Utah

This is a work of fiction. The characters, names, incidents, places, and dialogue are products of the
author's imagination, and are not to be construed as real.

Printed in the United States of America
First Printing: April 2003

10 09 08 07 06 05 04 03   10 9 8 7 6 5 4 3 2 1

ISBN 1-59156-193-0

Dedicated to

Isabelle Buxton, one of the world's best cooks, who always has a pie ready to give to someone and who makes fantastically light hot rolls.

The sisters at Brighton Gardens, who are valiantly enduring to the end, and to the sisters of the Salt Lake thirteenth ward, who are their faithful visiting sisters.

Robert Dunn, who at two years of age was vigorously sweeping, mopping, and mowing—an inspiration to us all!

My biggest fan, Maynard Eiling, who always says, "When's the next book coming?"

The world's greatest best friend, Pat Hanson, who never says "no," and in any crisis is right there pitching in to help.

 *Chapter 1*

". . . so that also rules out aluminum cans." *The perfect line for her book.* Maggie Summers just had to remember it until she got back to her computer.

"Somehow she's never struck me as interested in recycling, so that also rules out aluminum cans," she repeated, pulling her mail out of the mailbox in the lobby of her building. Without looking at the letters and magazines, Maggie returned to the elevator and pushed the button for the fourth floor.

Still repeating the line in her head, Maggie pushed open her door, went straight to her computer, and typed in the elusive sentence before she forgot it.

Then she read the last few lines.

Blanche frowned as she looked at the elderly lady in a fur coat digging through the trash can. "What's the duchess doing?"

Ruby's lips tightened in disgust. "She can't be looking for food, not with all her money."

"Somehow she's never struck me as interested in recycling, so that also rules out aluminum cans," Blanche responded.

Maggie smiled. She loved these two old ladies, and she hoped some editor would like them as much as she did and publish her book. She reached for the mail she'd tossed on the desk and sorted through it. *Junk mail, junk mail, a bill, Mystery, Inc. Publishers!* When her eyes caught the last address, her heart raced. But when she tried to open the envelope, she was all thumbs, unable to get her fingers to work. Finally, she ripped the letter out and read the words, her mind barely comprehending the meaning of them. Then it registered. They wanted to see the completed manuscript of *Murder at the Berkeley*.

She had to call her closest friend, Pat Wilson. Although she knew she'd see her and the rest of the critique group tonight, Maggie couldn't wait until then to tell her. She pushed the automatic dial button.

"Hello?"

Pat's cheerfulness added to Maggie's excitement. "I'm glad you're home, Pat. I've got terrific news! Connie Freed, the senior editor at Mystery, Inc., wants to see the rest of my manuscript. A New York publisher! After submitting dozens of proposals in the last four years, finally someone wants to see the completed manuscript. Can you believe it?"

"Of course I can. You're a darn good writer." Pat's voice was confident. "It's about time you had someone interested in one of your books. I'm thrilled for you. After all the help you've given everyone else, you deserve success."

"Don't get carried away." Filled with elation, Maggie couldn't sit still, and she jumped up, pacing the living room as she talked. "Remember, she only wants to see the completed manuscript. She hasn't offered me a contract."

"Yet!" her friend asserted. "Be positive."

"And if this sells, I owe it all to Janet Dailey." Holding her cordless phone in one hand, Maggie dramatically flung out the other hand.

"Puh-lease. You're the one who's taken a dozen writing classes and worked your head off." Pat apparently considered the idea of crediting the famous romance writer with Maggie's success ridiculous.

"No, but if I hadn't read that newspaper article about her and the *beaucoup* bucks she'd made, I'd never have decided to write." Maggie became serious. "I'd never have met you or the rest of the gang. I have to give her the credit—she really did change my life."

"When you put it like that, I guess you do owe her." Pat made the admission grudgingly.

"I'm on chapter seven, and in three more weeks school will be out. Then I can write full-time, nothing stopping me." Maggie stared out her balcony doors at the condominium grounds, her mind not registering anything but a green blur.

"I hear you. But listen, kiddo, everything will be all right if you'll only quit letting people impose on you." Pat's comments were spoken lightly, but they had a steely quality to them. This was no joking matter to her.

Laughing, Maggie plopped down in the blue club chair and ran her fingers through her chin-length hair, ruffling the blond curls. "You always say that, but I do have some responsibilities. Gram's not getting any younger."

"I'm not worried about Isabelle imposing. At eighty she's so independent it's scary. But don't let your brother-in-law bamboozle you into taking care of his kids." Pat usually disguised her dislike of people, but not this time. Her distaste for Brad came through loud and clear.

"Don't worry. I won't let Brad pull anything. But don't forget, they're Karen's kids too, and now that she's gone, I want to stay close. Besides, they're so smart and cute that I can't resist them." Just thinking of her niece and nephew sent a warm feeling right to her heart. She'd do anything to keep them happy and safe.

"That's just it!" Maggie could visualize Pat shaking her head disgustedly. "You can't say no!" Her friend's words came out as four staccato notes.

"I've never seen *you* ignoring people in crisis." One of the things Maggie admired about Pat was the way she helped others.

"That's different." Pat brushed aside Maggie's comment. "But you tend to go overboard, putting everyone's needs ahead of yours. For once in your life, put yourself first."

"Okay! I get the message." Maggie laughed again. She was so excited about the editor's letter that there was no way she would let Pat's always overly generous advice bother her. "Got to go. See you tonight." They said their good-byes, and Maggie hung up.

The writing group she regularly met with consisted of four other writers: Pat and Bonnie, who were published romance writers; and Jackie, Chris, and herself, who were aspiring mystery writers. She hated the word *aspiring.* There was nothing *aspiring* about her writing. She might not be published, but she spent every evening and every Saturday writing. That made her a *writer,* period.

She knew she had better get busy. Tonight the group was meeting at her place, and since she spent every spare minute writing and none on cleaning, she had a big job ahead of her and little time. When she made it as a writer, the first thing she was going to do was hire a cleaning woman.

Maggie felt as if she glowed with happiness. She just couldn't believe it! After four years and a zillion writes and rewrites, an editor wanted to see her completed manuscript! She could feel her mouth automatically curve into a smile, and she felt a flutter of excitement for summer vacation when she'd be free to write!

She dashed into her bedroom and changed into an old pair of jeans. Then she tied her curly hair back so it wouldn't get in her eyes. Going to the storage room, she hauled out her vacuum. Suddenly the cleaning didn't seem too bad.

At that moment, she felt as if life were looking up after the pall of her sister Karen's sudden death. *Cancer.* Even the word sounded ominous. Maggie thought losing her parents had been difficult, but Karen's death had been even worse. A dozen times a day she would think, "I've got to tell Karen"—and then realize she was no longer there to tell. Her passing had left a large void in Maggie's life, a void that she'd tried to fill with writing.

* * *

The bright Denver sunshine and the clear blue of the sky only intensified the contentment that welled up in Maggie on Thursday. Feeling as though she were walking on air, she made it through the day, eager to be at her computer, writing. But once home, she had to face the work of writing two hundred more pages of *Murder at the Berkeley.* At first she'd attempted to write romances, but since she preferred reading mysteries, she changed to cozies—which had an amateur sleuth and no violent scenes.

She tossed her jacket over the back of her blue chair before going into her bedroom and changing out of her beige linen pants and striped T-shirt and into her favorite robe, which was ablaze with tropical pink and lime-green flowers. Although her school clothes were professional looking, she loved wearing wild colors at home. After grabbing a handful of Bonnie's chocolate chip cookies that were left over from the critique meeting, she was all set.

She brought up the story on her computer and read the last page she'd written. One cookie later, the phone rang. She frowned. Hating to be disturbed but thinking it might be her grandmother, she answered.

"Maggs?" Her brother-in-law's syrupy utterance sent a shiver of irritation through her.

She hated that nickname, and no matter how many times she told Brad to call her Maggie or Margaret, he never did. Suddenly leery of what he wanted, she said cautiously, "Yes, Brad?"

"I need to talk to you. Could the kids and I come over?" He sounded almost pleading, which was a distinct contrast to his usual imperious intonation. She concluded something must be wrong.

"Is there a problem?" Her feelings alternated between concern and wariness.

"I can't discuss it over the phone. I'll be over in about thirty minutes." He hung up.

"Thanks. I'll be waiting," she said to the dial tone, thinking that he'd certainly reverted quickly enough to his old, irksome self. She threw on some jeans and a sweatshirt and returned to her writing, finding it difficult to concentrate on the further adventures of Ruby and Blanche when her mind was on Brad's approaching visit. What did he want?

Karen and Brad had been high school sweethearts, and after he'd returned from his mission they'd married immediately. Somewhere along the line he'd become overbearing, and Karen, to Maggie's chagrin, had never noticed. Or if she had, she'd never mentioned it.

Maggie had only written a paragraph when the security phone rang. She sighed deeply, preparing herself for what lay ahead. She'd known Brad too long to think he had anything to discuss but trouble.

When she answered her door, she was tackled by her niece and nephew, Caitlin and Robert, which made her laugh. Love for them flooded her. She adored these two as if they were her own. She bent down and kissed them, hugging them all the while and relishing the feel of their pudgy little arms around her legs. "What are my two favorite kids in the whole wide world doing?"

"We've come to stay with you while Daddy's gone," Caitlin piped up, squeaking with excitement.

Frowning, Maggie stood up. "What?" Then she noticed that Brad had two large shopping bags filled with clothes. She stiffened. Steeling herself to remain calm, she pointed to the living room. "Come in. I think we do have something to discuss."

She held the door open for them while they filed in. As she closed it, a draft of air caught it, causing it to bang shut, a sound which matched her feelings exactly. Why did Brad always feel her life was so insignificant that she could be imposed upon at will?

Brad made himself at home on the sofa, so Maggie sat in the rocker facing him. Caitlin and Robert immediately jumped in her lap and cuddled against her. As usual, Caitlin reached up and touched Maggie's curly hair to feel its softness.

"What's going on?"

"Oh, Maggs, I'm miserable." He looked as if he were going to start sobbing. "You'll never know how much I miss Karen. I loved her so much." At these words, tears welled up in his eyes. "I'm having a hard time getting along without her. Today I got an offer for a consulting job in Virginia that will last for a week, maybe two, and I need to find a place for Caitlin and Robert to stay." Misery tinged his words.

"I can't leave them with a stranger. They've gone through too much the last few months, and they still miss Karen. I don't want them to feel abandoned." He gazed beseechingly at Maggie. "You're the logical person to take them because they're crazy about you, and they'll feel right at home. You know how they love staying here."

She stared at him, feeling his pain. For Karen's and the kids' sake she wanted to help. And besides, she loved having them stay with her. But he couldn't have picked a more inconvenient time.

"I need this job," Brad continued. "If I don't take some of the jobs that are offered, my consulting business will go down the tubes. The company called just this afternoon and wants me there tomorrow." He acted totally overwhelmed.

"Friday?" She gave him a skeptical look.

He took a deep breath. "The company's had a real foul-up with their computers, and they want me there first thing tomorrow morning." He glanced at his watch. "In fact, my plane leaves in two hours."

She frowned. However much she enjoyed the kids, now was a terrible time. "Brad, did it ever occur to you that I have a job myself?"

"Of course. But you can always get a substitute." He sounded as if her job were inconsequential and her presence wasn't absolutely necessary.

Maggie bristled, and all her feelings of sympathy vanished. "I can't just willy-nilly stay home and tend your kids." She didn't like the way he automatically assumed she'd take care of his children. She could feel the frustration seep through her, and she fought not to show it. Caitlin and Robert, evidently able to sense her feelings, sat straight up and looked pointedly at her as if something were wrong and she was the cause.

"Caitlin goes to preschool in the mornings. Your grandmother could watch Robert," he said patronizingly.

"Why doesn't *your* mother?" she demanded in a sharp voice.

He shrugged. "You know how she is."

Maggie did know how his mother was: supercritical and never happy about anything. She had liked Karen, but then, everybody liked Karen.

Maggie soon learned he had everything worked out so she'd have the responsibility. This aggravated her to no end. The kids watched her intently, obviously wondering if she wanted them. Touching their heads, Maggie pulled them closer to her and forced herself to say pleasantly, "I understand. Have you talked to Gram?" She'd bet money he hadn't. He liked to leave others to do the nitty-gritty stuff.

"No. I thought you'd rather discuss it with her," he said matter-of-factly, and he made no move toward the phone.

"I wouldn't!" She spoke softly but firmly. "She's eighty. Have you forgotten that salient point? And it's not as if Gram has nothing else to do either. She has a schedule that would wear out a person half her age." She worked at the temple on Tuesday mornings, worked on her genealogy daily, was the ward compassionate service leader, and volunteered four hours a week helping in the preemie unit at University Hospital.

"Robert's no problem." Brad stared at her as if he couldn't imagine what all the fuss was about. "She can handle him."

Maggie pointed at the phone. "Then you call her and make the arrangements."

Brad rolled his eyes as if Maggie were acting ridiculous, then picked up the receiver and dialed. "Gram, how are you?"

Maggie cringed at his saccharine tone, but she should have expected it. Gram thought Brad was wonderful, and he wanted to stay on her good side. Maggie had loved her sister dearly, but she had always found Brad to be obnoxious. Love radiated from Karen. No one could meet her and not feel of her luminous spirit. Karen had always looked up to Brad as if the sun rose and set on him. How her sister had never seen through him was beyond Maggie. Whoever said love is blind was certainly right.

"I have a favor to ask you. Maggie has agreed that Caitlin and Robert can stay with her while I'm out of town, but she needs someone to watch Robert tomorrow. Could you do it?" He smiled as he listened to the response.

Maggie couldn't shake her irritation, but she had to give Brad credit for providing for his family. Since Karen's death, he'd worked very little. Financially he was probably starting to feel the pinch, but why did he just assume she would take care of the kids? Probably because she would. Her sister's bout with cancer had been short and deadly, leaving Brad devastated and Caitlin and Robert lost. Maggie hadn't comprehended the amount of pain losing a sister would cause. As the only children in the family, she and Karen had been extremely close, and Karen's death had been like losing a part of herself.

"Oh, thanks, Gram. You're a sweetheart." He hung up and turned to Maggie. "She'd be delighted to take him."

Maggie took a deep breath to keep her voice pleasant. "I'm willing to take them for now." Then she added firmly, "But I've made plans for the summer. So you need to make other arrangements if you're going to be out of town a lot."

Brad glossed over her words, just hearing her agreement. "Oh, thanks, Maggs. I knew I could count on you." He picked up each of the kids, hugged and kissed them, then said good-bye. "I'll call you when I get there and give you the number where I can be reached."

The children happily crawled back into Maggie's lap and waved good-bye.

Maggie closed her eyes and took another deep breath. She'd do anything to help her sister's children, but . . . she had to stay focused on the present and not on what she'd rather be doing. Her plans for writing that night were shot. In fact, she'd probably accomplish little the next week. But she'd devote the entire summer to it. She hated for Pat to find out about Brad leaving Caitlin and Robert with her. Her friend would be livid. Her mouth twisted in a wry smile.

"Aunt Maggie, are you asleep?" Caitlin tugged at her sleeve.

"No, honey, I'm just thinking about your visit. We're going to have a good time while you're here." No matter how inconvenient it might be, she did enjoy these two. Their little faces always radiated happiness, a trait Karen had instilled in them. Her younger sister had been such a happy person—always a joy to be around. She doubted Caitlin and Robert had ever had a harsh word spoken to them.

"I'm hungry," Robert announced. "I want pizza."

Maggie wasn't surprised, since that was his favorite food. She grinned at him. "You're in luck, sweetie. I just happen to have a frozen one."

"Do you have soda?" Caitlin never got soft drinks at home, so she always asked for them when she came to Maggie's.

"Afraid not, honey. I didn't know you were coming, so I didn't buy any. Will you settle for milk?" She wasn't much of a pop drinker, so she never had it on hand.

Caitlin gave her a coy smile. "Can we have chocolate in it?"

"Sure." Maggie moved the kids onto the couch and stood up. "Can you two sit here while Aunt Maggie fixes the pizza?"

"We want to watch." Caitlin took Robert's hand, and they slid off the sofa, following right behind her as she went into the kitchen.

Once there, Caitlin climbed on a bar stool. Robert stepped up on the first rung of another one, and the stool teetered before starting to tip over.

Maggie grabbed him just in time. She swung him in her arms. "Sweetie, you almost had a fall just like Humpty Dumpty." She kissed his nose and sat him on the stool.

"I'll put the pizza in as soon as the oven's hot enough. Caitlin, do you want to help set the table?" Caitlin quickly climbed down, and Robert started to follow her. "No, Robert, sit still." She wrinkled her nose at him. "You might fall like Humpty, and all the king's horses and all the king's men couldn't put Robert back together again."

He squealed with delight. "That won't happen!"

"Well, don't take any chances. I want a whole kid here to eat this pizza."

"Aunt Maggie, what will happen if I fall?" Caitlin obviously wanted to be a part of this fun.

Maggie looked properly horrified and, waving her arms, said dramatically, "I'd lose my very best friend, and my favorite niece, and I'd be sick, sick, sick." She grinned at the little girl, who appeared to be enthralled by this prospect. "And to top everything off, I wouldn't have anyone to set the table, so we couldn't eat tonight."

"Yes we can, because I'm not going to fall." Caitlin sounded absolutely positive on this point.

"Here's the silverware." Maggie handed her some spoons and forks.

Caitlin strutted with importance as she put one at each place, folded the napkins, then took the glasses off the counter and put them on the table. "We need plates," she said.

Maggie handed them to her, and Caitlin finished her task. "Is it good?"

"Fantastic. That's the best job ever!"

Caitlin beamed.

After they'd finished eating, Maggie cleaned up the kitchen with Robert sweeping energetically. She had to laugh every time she saw him working. Ever since he was two years old, he'd loved to scrub and sweep, and he took his job very seriously. When he'd gotten it clean enough to meet his standards, Maggie gave them a bath.

As she helped them out of the tub, Caitlin and Robert looked like they were good for a couple more hours. She groaned. She was hoping she could salvage part of her writing time. Once she had them in their pajamas, she put them in her bed and told them a story, crossing her fingers for the best.

She was delighted that after asking for only two drinks, they fell asleep. Maybe she'd be able to finish the page after all. But she couldn't. In the last two hours, her brain had turned to mush, and she couldn't think of one thing for her intrepid detectives, Blanche and Ruby, to do. Finally she gave up and went into the living room to watch television.

She felt discouraged that she hadn't been able to accomplish more, but then excitement at the editor's letter raced through her. She'd get this book finished no matter what. Nothing was going to stop her—not even the two cutest kids in the world.

On Fridays she only had students until noon. The teachers used the rest of the day for planning, and she was certain that the principal would let her take the afternoon as comp time. She usually never left before 5:00 P.M. on regular days, and he knew it. That would solve her problem about what to do with Caitlin in the afternoon, and her grandmother ought to be able to manage Robert until one o'clock. But that still left the afternoons for the next week.

When the news was over, she checked on Caitlin and Robert and got ready for bed herself. Just as she was falling asleep, Brad called with his phone number.

The next morning, she dropped Robert off at her grandmother's, who was pleased they'd thought of her to care for him. Caitlin's preschool was near Elmwood School, where Maggie taught. When Maggie dropped her off, she noticed some younger children playing in a fenced area.

As she handed her niece over to the charge teacher, she said, "Is there any possibility of Caitlin staying all day for the next week starting Monday?"

The older woman nodded pleasantly. "Two sessions of preschool would be too much, but we do have free play and naptime in the afternoon. It's twenty-five dollars a day, including lunch."

Pleased with that turn of events, Maggie sighed with relief. "That sounds like an answer to my prayers."

The teacher continued, "However, we do like to have the tuition paid in advance."

"No problem." She wrote out the check and kissed Caitlin good-bye. "Have a good day, honey. I'll pick you up at twelve-thirty or one."

Caitlin waved and eagerly entered the preschool room, and Maggie returned to her car feeling as if a weight had been lifted from her shoulders. Now she had to find some place for Robert. She didn't think Gram was up to having him all day.

She hadn't considered how long it would take to drop off Caitlin and Robert, and she barely made it to school on time. The bell had just rung, and her cherubs were lined up at the back door, ready to go in.

"Come in, class." She motioned for them to follow her, and she was quickly caught up in the rhythm of the school day. At recess Maggie checked with the principal, who said it would be fine for her to leave early.

Caitlin was hanging on the preschool door waiting for her when she arrived. The girl clutched all her schoolwork in her hand. Maggie admired it, praising her for all the gold stars she'd received. As she drove to her grandmother's, she only half listened while Caitlin rattled on about her day at preschool.

They were about two blocks away from Gram's house and had just passed a busy intersection when Maggie spied Robert, his blond hair shining in the sunshine, marching down the sidewalk all by himself. Her heart stopped.

Chapter 2

Quickly swerving over to the curb next to Robert, Maggie jumped out of the car and dashed towards him. "Where are you going?"

When he saw her, he started running away. Then, to her relief, he fell, bringing on a rush of crying. She caught him up in her arms before he could go any farther, hugging his little body close to hers. As her heart started beating again, tears filled her eyes, and she gave a silent prayer of thanksgiving for Robert's safety. "Where are you going, honey?"

She didn't notice any scratches, but he continued sobbing. "To get fee fies." He showed her the nickel he held clenched in his hand. "I have money."

"You do. I'll make a deal. You stop crying, and after we check on Gram, we'll get some french fries." She smoothed his hair back.

Instantly his tears stopped, and he gave her an angelic smile. "Okay."

As she carried him back to the car, she asked, "Where's Gram?"

"Home," he said matter-of-factly.

Home! What could have caused Gram to let him outdoors by himself? She'd probably turned her back on him for a moment and he'd disappeared. Gram must be frantic.

When she reached the beige-and-green two-story house, Maggie quickly marshaled the two children inside the front entry hall. "Gram, where are you?"

"In the living room, watching television." A moment later a small, white-haired woman, her shoulders rounded with age, appeared in the archway. "I'm so glad you stopped by Maggie," her grandmother said delightedly, a smile wreathing her face. "And you brought Karen's children. What a pleasant surprise."

The two grabbed her around the legs, shouting, "Grandma! Grandma!"

Stunned at her reaction, Maggie choked out, "Gram, I told you I'd be by a little after one o'clock to pick up Robert."

"You did?" Bewilderment spread across her face, and Gram appeared incapable of absorbing the full impact of Maggie's words.

Alarm grasped her. What had happened to Gram? "Yes. When I dropped him off this morning."

"How could that be?" Gram shook her head, sounding perplexed, and she looked so frightened that Maggie couldn't breathe for a moment. "I haven't seen you or Robert all day until now."

Maggie could tell that not only was she herself scared, but that she was also scaring Gram. Stepping between the kids, she put her arms around Gram's frail shoulders and smoothed back her short, white hair, attempting to comfort her. "It's all right. It's all right." She kept her voice soothing while feeling paralyzed from fear. What was happening to Gram?

The muscles in her face frozen, she attempted to smile down at the lady she loved so deeply. "We're going for french fries."

On hearing those words, Caitlin and Robert tore out the door, singing, "French fries, fee fies . . ."

"We won't go without you, Gram. I'll get your keys, and you can hang onto my arm, and we'll be off." Scooping up the keys from the hall table, she escorted Gram toward the car.

"I'm not an old lady, Maggie. I am perfectly able to walk by myself." Gram started to pull away.

"I know, but I want a chance to hold the arm of my favorite person." She scowled at the dainty little woman at her side and tightened her hold. "Are you going to deny me that?"

Gram laughed. "If you feel that strongly, no."

Caitlin and Robert were all buckled up and waiting for them by the time they made it to the car. Belting her grandmother in, she checked on the kids. "Good job. I can tell you two know what to do."

"I learned this in preschool," Caitlin said proudly.

Robert chimed in, "Me, too."

Maggie's hands were shaking as she seated herself in the car. For a moment she closed her eyes. *Relax. Keep calm.*

When they arrived at the drive-in, she ordered four small-sized hamburgers, french fries, and sodas. "I think we'd better eat this lunch at home." She smiled as she watched the faces of the two in back cloud up. "We'll be at Gram's in a minute or two, and we'll eat at the picnic table. How's that?"

They both brightened up.

Once home, she tied towels around Caitlin's and Robert's necks, and then they all went out the back door to the patio and gathered around the wooden table. Caitlin wanted plenty of ketchup; her brother wanted none. When they had settled down to eat, Maggie found she had no appetite. Her stomach was tied in knots, and her throat felt too tight to swallow. Shoving her plate away from her, she smiled at Gram. "What are your plans for this afternoon?"

"I usually turn on *Matlock* and *Oprah*. You don't have anything to rush home for, do you? Why don't you stay and watch them with me?" She sounded eager for company.

"I'd love to." She had no intention of leaving her grandmother alone. "I'll get these two tigers down for a nap, and then we'll just sit and enjoy ourselves."

The two tigers growled and giggled while they finished eating.

After she had them tucked in, she joined her grandmother, who was stretched out on the sofa in the living room watching *Matlock.*

Gram looked up and, with a smile, she confided, "I'm nuts about that guy."

"I thought you had a crush on Tom Brokaw." Gram was famous for her love of the anchorman.

"I do. He's handsome and such a gentleman. But Matlock is not only good-looking with all that silver hair, he's outrageous in the courtroom— even defying the judge." Her eyes gleamed. "And so much fun to watch."

Maggie was too worried about what had happened to Gram to concentrate on the TV show. After a few minutes, she glanced over and found her asleep. She thought about going into the dining room and calling the doctor for an appointment. What else could she do?

Quietly standing so she wouldn't wake her grandmother, Maggie slipped into the kitchen. She found the telephone number under a magnet on the refrigerator and punched it into the phone.

"Denver Medical Clinic," a no-nonsense voice announced.

Inside, Maggie was a quivering mass of nerves, and she struggled to stay calm. "This is Maggie Summers. I'm calling Dr. Wilson for an appointment for my grandmother, Isabelle Hughes. I'd like to—"

Firmly, the receptionist interrupted, "Dr. Wilson is out of town and won't be back in the office until June tenth. Do you want to make your appointment for then? I have ten o'clock open."

Maggie gritted her teeth. She'd never thought Dr. Wilson was a particularly good doctor, and the cavalier attitude of the people in his office made her furious. But she didn't know what else to do. "Okay."

Feeling dazed, she put the phone down. What should she do next? Apprehension started her hands trembling again. How could Gram have forgotten that Robert was staying with her this morning? She'd forgotten several things recently, but they were minor. Forgetting Robert was a major concern.

She clasped her hands together to stop their shaking. She needed to call Aunt Barbara. Gram's only other daughter lived in Atlanta, Georgia, and with Aunt Barbara living across the country, Maggie had become her grandmother's sole caregiver. Slowly she shook her head and then sighed deeply. Who would have thought that her parents would go salmon fishing in Alaska and their plane would crash in the bush? And Karen die at age twenty-eight? Now only Gram was left. Occasionally, like right now, her longing for her own parents and her sister threatened to overcome her, and she couldn't stop the waves of abandonment that flooded her.

She leaned forward on her elbows and cradled her head. What should she do next? *Heavenly Father, please, please help me,* she begged, tears streaming down her face. *I'm so frightened about Gram, and I don't know what to do. Please help me.*

Maggie remained with her head bowed for a few moments waiting. Gradually the tears stopped, and she lifted her head and took a deep breath. Little by little she started to feel calmer, and her thoughts became clearer. Her grandmother needed more than a general practitioner. As she thought about it, she remembered a pamphlet she'd received at

Relief Society a couple of months ago called *Available Services for the Elderly* that was put out by the Junior League. She figured that might be the best place to find a doctor of geriatrics. She couldn't leave Caitlin and Robert alone with Gram to go get it, but she thought she could get Pat to stay while she ran over to her condo.

Drying her eyes with her fingertips, Maggie steeled herself for Pat's ire when she heard the happenings of the last—she glanced at her watch—eighteen hours.

She dialed. The phone seemed to ring interminably before Pat answered. "Hello?"

Maggie felt relieved just hearing her friend's chipper voice. "I've got a problem and I hope you can help me. Brad's out of town, and he left Caitlin and Robert with me—" Before Maggie could say more, Pat exploded.

"What!" Pat's voice embodied her total feelings of outrage. "Just for today?"

"The next ten days." Maggie said the words reluctantly.

"I might've known it." Now her voice crackled with asperity. "The minute my back is turned, Brad gets you to take the kids. *You* need a caretaker."

"That's right—only not for me, though. Can you come over to Gram's for a few minutes while I run home?" Maggie's emotions were obvious in her tone.

"Sure. What's happened?" Now Pat was all concern.

Maggie filled her in on the details of the day.

"Oh, Maggie. It's starting already. There goes your writing." Pat commiserated with her.

"Only for a week." No matter what, she was determined to finish *Murder at the Berkeley* this summer.

"See you in a minute." Her friend's words came in a rush.

Maggie returned to the living room and found Gram still asleep. Oprah was discussing the "sandwich generation." Maggie's mouth twisted. This minute she fit right in the middle of the sandwich generation. Just call her chicken.

She felt rattled, and she tried to organize her plan of action. She'd get the pamphlet, come back, and start calling doctors. She could also pick up the kids' clothes and her own, and they could all spend the night at Gram's. She didn't dare leave Gram alone, so she planned on at least staying the weekend. Then she'd reassess the situation and decide what to do next.

Maggie gently patted Gram on the shoulder. She woke up slowly, her eyes blinking a couple of times, and when she saw her granddaughter's face, she gave her a beatific smile.

"Do you mind if we spend the weekend with you?" Maggie said softly.

Gram's smile widened. "I'd love it! I don't see enough of either you or the kids. By the way, where's Brad?"

Maggie's heart dropped. *This can't be happening—something else she doesn't remember.* She took a deep breath to steady herself and attempted to smile. "He's away on business, so we get to take care of Caitlin and Robert for the next couple of weeks."

Gram nodded her head. "Lucky us."

"We are, aren't we? I've called Pat, and she's coming over while I go home for our clothes." Unable to relax, she sat down stiffly in the chair next to the couch.

Her grandmother's smile changed to a glare. "She doesn't need to come on my account!"

Maggie laughed. "I might have guessed that would be your reaction. Karen's kids are a handful even for me, and I didn't want you to have to bother with them."

At that comment Gram sat up. "What do you mean 'a handful even for you'? Margaret Summers, you know very well that I can run circles around you."

"I know that's true, but do you have to remind me?" she demanded, a smile lighting up her face.

Gram's eyes narrowed as she gazed at Maggie. "You don't think I'm incapable of looking after those children, do you?"

"Heavens no!" Maggie leaned back in the recliner, acting perfectly at ease. "Relax, Gram, Pat will be here any minute, and you don't want her to think she's not welcome."

Her reply came grudgingly. "No." Stubbornness had replaced beauty on her face.

Pat arrived and gave Maggie a quick hug. Her eyes narrowed as she considered her friend. "Don't look so distressed. You'll get worry lines on that beautiful skin. Right now even your blond curly hair looks frazzled, and when," she smiled teasingly, "frizzy hair looks frazzled, it's too much." Then she said reassuringly, "Everything will be all right."

Maggie closed her eyes for a moment. Pat always knew just the right things to say to lift her spirits. "Thanks."

Giving Maggie's hand a final squeeze, Pat moved into the living room. "You're looking wonderful as usual, Isabelle. I'm glad Maggie called me. I haven't even seen you in ages, and I can't remember the last time we visited."

Maggie heard her grandmother say, "It *has* been a while." Grabbing her purse, she slipped out the door.

Once inside her condo, Maggie leaned against the door and surveyed her light-filled living room, which smelled faintly of cranberry candles. She gazed longingly at the soothing room with the splashes of soft peach and green flowers on the cream-colored couch. The deep hydrangea blue of the easy chairs underscored the creamy white of the carpet and walls. Her eyes lingered on the whimsical tables and lamps. She'd finally worked in all the flea-market finds her mother had left her, and she loved this room. Here she could usually escape from the cares of the world, but not today. Now she felt as if she had the weight of all mankind on her shoulders.

If only she didn't have to go back and instead could bury herself in her writing. For a moment she felt a tinge of resentment that everything fell on her shoulders, and then she brushed it aside. She loved Karen's children, and she certainly loved her grandmother. Their needs came ahead of writing. She'd never forgive herself if she let them down in a time of trouble.

Going into the bedrooms, she quickly gathered up clothes for all of them, packed her overnight bag and, after a diligent search, found the pamphlet. Armed with the necessities of life, she returned to her grandmother's.

Caitlin and Robert were still asleep, and the other two were discussing Pat's latest book. Her grandmother always read a romance novel in bed at night before she fell asleep, and she particularly loved Pat's. In the morning she studied the scriptures. She considered these good ways to begin and end her day.

After saying hello to them, Maggie returned to the dining room and settled down in a straight-back chair at the table and pulled the phone next to her. She frowned when she scanned the list of geriatric doctors. Seven doctors and clinics didn't seem like many for a city the size of Denver. In fact, seven was not nearly enough, she decided thirty minutes later after several phone calls. Either the doctor had left the city, the clinics had moved to the suburbs, or, in one case, had changed to internal medicine. Another time she received a recording that the number had been disconnected.

How much more discouraging could it get? She sighed and picked up the phone book. Somewhere there had to be a geriatrician who could see her grandmother. Looking through the University of Colorado Hospital listings, she came across a geriatric clinic, and she called it.

When the secretary answered, she said, "My name is Maggie Summers. My grandmother, Isabelle Hughes, is eighty years old. She's become forgetful the last little while, and I'm scared. I think she needs to see a specialist. I've called every geriatrician in the handbook I have, and I can't find anyone." She fought back the tears, irritated at herself for becoming emotional. Now her words became jerky. "Is there any possibility I could get an appointment for her?"

"Has she ever seen Dr. Rosenberg before?" the secretary asked pleasantly.

"No." Maggie tensed again, wondering if he took new patients.

"My name is Angie." Lilting was the only way to describe the woman's voice, and immediately Maggie felt hopeful. "Could I call you back Monday?"

Maggie gave her the school number.

"Don't you worry, Maggie. You will get an appointment with Dr. Rosenberg." With that, she ended the conversation.

Placing the phone back in the cradle, Maggie sat there for a moment. Then she pushed the chair away from the table and rose, joining the others in the living room.

Pat smiled up at her. "I've had an idea, kiddo. I'll watch Robert on Monday and call around and find a nursery school that will take him short-term. Then Brad can wrestle with the problems of getting them situated permanently."

"I hate to impose on you . . ." Maggie began, but Pat's response was a relief.

"There's no need to do that." Gram's tone was determined. "I am perfectly capable of taking care of that child for one day."

"A whole day is too long, Gram, and I don't have time to run him to the day-care center during my lunch period. Besides, Brad won't be back for at least a week, and we need a permanent solution. I think we better take Pat up on her suggestion."

Her grandmother looked aggravated.

Maggie ignored her expression. When Pat rose from the chair, she walked her to the front door. "Thanks."

"It's nothing." Pat grinned. "If I know anything, I know you would do the same thing for me!"

* * *

On Monday, Maggie hung up the receiver in the teacher's lounge and pumped her arm. "Yes!"

She slipped into a chair at the table where the fourth-grade team was eating lunch. "I have an appointment for my grandmother with the head of the geriatric clinic at University Hospital next Monday."

"Is she ill?" Cecile, a member of the team, asked anxiously, looking up from her salad.

Although she was close to the other members of the team, Maggie didn't feel like discussing Gram's forgetfulness with them right now. "I'm trying to find a new doctor for her."

"I thought you had to be referred to those clinics," Craig, the only male in the group, said between bites of his sandwich.

"Evidently not. I just called Friday, and they didn't question me." She peeled her orange, feeling nearly as elated as when she'd received the letter from the editor about her manuscript, which right now seemed like a thousand years ago. She sighed. The weekend had gone incredibly well.

"Why the big sigh?" Cecile, who looked like a cool, sophisticated fashion model with her short, black hair slicked back against the sides of her head and her makeup perfect, was instead the motherly type who was always the first one to volunteer her help. "Are Karen's children more of a handful than you'd anticipated?"

"No. I stayed at my grandmother's this weekend. She was her usual, energetic self. Saturday she insisted on going to the zoo. I didn't want to go because, after all, she's nearly eighty-one years old." Maggie grinned at her colleagues. "But she said if I didn't take her, she'd drive herself and take the kids. I knew there was no stopping her, so I gave in and took them. When's the last time any of you have been to the tropical section?" She popped a slice of orange in her mouth and shuddered at its tartness.

They all shook their heads and agreed it had been a while.

"You haven't missed anything but a lot of misting air and exercise. After we'd looked at what seemed like every animal exhibit at the zoo, we went through the rain forest—jungle steam and all. Gram led the way, having far more energy than I did. The kids chased after her, and I brought up the rear. Then they wanted to see the monkeys, but I put my foot down."

"At last!" Beth, who looked as if she overflowed with maternal instinct but never put herself out for anyone if she could help it, was appalled.

"On our way home we stopped for hot dogs, and the two kids were asleep before they'd finished eating them. Can you imagine what seven acres of Primate Panorama would have been like with tired kids?" She gazed around the table at the others, who nodded in sympathy. All of the team had taught at Elmwood for years, and they got along great together, which was a decided plus. Maggie had taught for six years at the school and was the fourth-grade team leader, which meant extra work without extra pay. She loved innovative curriculum and trying new things, so she really didn't mind.

Beth waved her hands helplessly. "Deliver me from tired kids!"

"You'd think Gram would have been worn out. I was. But, no, she wanted to do something 'fun' for the evening." Maggie stared at the sour orange for a moment before wadding it up in a napkin and tossing it into the garbage.

"Don't tell me you ran around all Saturday night!" Craig raised his eyebrows in disbelief. He had three children under the age of ten, and he made his opinion of running around on a Saturday night obvious.

"No," Maggie said innocently. "I suggested popping corn . . ."

Cecile laughed. "Nothing's more 'fun' than that."

"There must be!" Maggie shrugged. "Gram made her disappointment obvious all evening long."

Beth glanced at the large wall clock. "Time to get back to class."

As Maggie walked back to her classroom, she thought about the previous Sunday. They'd all gone to church at Gram's ward. Maggie was a Gospel Doctrine teacher in her own ward, but it hadn't been her Sunday to teach. Before they'd left for Relief Society, Gram had put a roast on to cook and made her famous dinner rolls. After sacrament meeting, the food was ready, and after lunch Maggie had put the kids down for their naps. She'd never realized how valuable naps were for some quiet time. Of course, quiet time was not to be with her grandmother, who was a sports enthusiast.

The first thing Maggie had heard after lunch Sunday was the blare of the televison. She frowned now as she remembered it. Some man was giving the play-by-play of a basketball game. She shook her head in wonder. Basketball in May? The season wasn't over? After all, it was nearly summer, and she'd thought basketball was a winter sport.

She unlocked her classroom door and sat down for her final two minutes before her students charged back in. While Maggie herself preferred no TV on Sunday so she could savor the stillness and work on photo albums and her parents' histories, Gram loved watching sports. She considered them clean entertainment. Yesterday Gram had come up with her usual Sunday statement. "It's the play-offs, and we certainly can't miss them. After all, we went to church this morning. The Lord won't mind if we watch a game this afternoon."

Most Sundays that was a signal for Maggie to go home, and yesterday, as soon as the kids woke up, had been no different. Although Caitlin and Robert had loved being there, after an entire weekend she could tell Gram was getting tired from the antics of the rambunctious three- and five-year-old. She was getting tired from them herself! Since Gram appeared to be back to her usual self, Maggie thought it would be safe to leave her. She wanted to believe Friday's episode had been an aberration, but she had a niggling worry at the back of her mind. Gram had never remembered Friday morning or Brad's phone call.

The noon bell rang, interrupting her thoughts, and class began. After school Maggie called Dr. Wilson's office and canceled the first appointment she had made. She didn't attempt to hide her pleasure as she told the irritating receptionist they wouldn't be coming. She sighed with satisfaction and returned to her classroom to work for another hour.

Pat had found a day-care center close to Elmwood, so Maggie left Caitlin and Robert at their respective schools each morning and then a few minutes later arrived at hers. The first day, Robert cried when she dropped him off, and she was in a quandary. Pangs of guilt flooded her immediately, and for a minute she thought she'd better call a substitute and stay home. Then sanity reasserted itself, and she realized that Robert was a happy little boy who would adjust quickly. In fact, she was barely to the door when he grabbed a broom and began to sweep the playroom.

The next day, Maggie reached school not only on time, but early. Each night she stopped for take-out, and they all ate supper with Gram before she took the children back to her place. She hadn't had time to do any more writing, but everything seemed to be going fine, and she relaxed.

* * *

After school on Monday, Maggie picked up Gram for her appointment with Dr. Rosenberg. When she had told Gram that she had made a doctor's appointment for her, Gram had shrugged it off, saying it wasn't necessary because she was healthy as a horse. In the end, Gram had agreed to go, but she made it plain she was going only to please Maggie.

Early that morning, Maggie had called to find out exactly where the geriatric clinic was located and received fuzzy directions. But once she was at University Hospital, things were clearer. The valet service took her car, and the volunteer at the desk directed them to clinic two.

Once they registered and filled out the forms, they were shown to an examination room where the nurse instructed Gram to change into a flimsy gown for a physical exam. She grimaced, but did it.

When she had the robe on, she sat huddled in a chair, looking old and feeble. Watching her, Maggie slowly shook her head. When had she become old? When had she gotten this thin? In her mind's eye, Gram was young and vigorous, and to see her this way broke Maggie's heart.

Someone knocked on the door, and a cheerful redheaded woman entered. "Hi, I'm Dr. Crandall." She shook hands with them, and continued. "Dr. Rosenberg will be here in a moment. Why are we seeing you today?"

Gram shrugged with exasperation and looked at Maggie.

Maggie hesitated. The doctor needed to know about her grandmother's forgetting about Robert, but she hated to discuss it in front of Gram. On the other hand, how could she get help if she weren't open about her concerns? "She's had some confusion. I'm worried, and I thought she needed to be seen by a geriatrician, not just an internist, to make sure she's all right." She smiled at the doctor and Gram. "She's always zipped around, and I want to keep her in the best possible health, so she can continue."

"You've come to the right place. University Hospital's geriatric department ranks in the top twenty in the United States, and Dr. Rosenberg is the best geriatrician in Denver." She turned to Gram. "Now, let me help you up on the examination table. I want to take your blood pressure and listen to your heart before Dr. Rosenberg comes in."

Pulling out a little stool, she steadied Gram as the elderly woman stepped up and climbed onto the table. After checking her over, Dr. Crandall said, "You've got the blood pressure of a sixteen-year-old, and your heart's still beating. What else can I say? You're in pretty great shape."

Gram nodded in agreement. "For an eighty-year-old woman."

There was another knock at the door. It opened, and a tall, good-looking man came in. Gram immediately turned and smiled knowingly at Maggie.

Chapter 3

Gram looked him up and down. "Are you Dr. Rosenberg?"

"Yes." He glanced at the chart. "And you're Isabelle Hughes."

She nodded, and a quizzical smile lit up her face. "Has anyone told you that you look like the hero in a romance novel?"

He laughed. "Not in the last twenty-four hours."

Maggie made no effort to hide her amusement. She'd known exactly what Gram had been thinking, and if the truth be known, she agreed. Dr. Rosenberg was the type who could make a maiden's heart beat faster.

"You fit the description of one of Pat's heroes perfectly." Gram inspected him closely. "Tall, built like an athlete, ruggedly handsome, dark hair with silver streaks, smoldering hazel eyes with topaz flecks in them, and a dazzling smile that makes my toes curl." She sighed with satisfaction.

Dr. Rosenberg raised his eyebrows and grinned, obviously enjoying Gram. "You read romance novels?"

"Every day." Then she said firmly, "I read the scriptures in the morning and a romance at night."

His eyes gleamed with mischief. "You're my kind of lady." He glanced back at Maggie. "Are you Pat?"

She shook her head. "No, I'm Isabelle's granddaughter, Maggie Summers. Pat's a friend of ours who's a well-known romance writer." Gram had lucked out this time. Dr. Rosenberg seemed to be a terrific doctor. Maggie met his hazel eyes, and for a moment the topaz flecks seemed to pierce her soul like a laser.

He sized up Maggie, giving her an easy smile. "Do you take care of your grandmother?"

"Heavens no!" Maggie shook her head vigorously, her eyes twinkling. "If there's any caretaking to be done, she's doing it!"

Picking up Isabelle's wrist, he took her pulse, then asked, "Do you still drive?"

Annoyance flickered across her face. "Of course. I'm only eighty."

"And a lively eighty at that." He gave her hand an extra squeeze.

Gram beamed. She liked people to be aware of how active she was at her age, and she liked good-looking men. David Rosenberg was far more impressive than Dr. Wilson. In fact, Maggie wished her ward had a few eligible bachelors like him in it, even though she doubted he was a bachelor. She glanced at his ring finger, which was bare—not that it meant anything. She sighed.

"I still mow my own lawn, and I make pies for everyone in the neighborhood and the church. I'm famous for them." Her grandmother exuded her usual self-confidence about her abilities.

"Do you make peach pie? That's my favorite." He tested her reflexes and continued his examination of her while Dr. Crandall stood at his elbow, observing everything he did.

"I'll make you one the next time we come." This was a promise that Gram loved making. She was always thrusting one of her homemade pies into someone's hands.

He bent his head over to listen to her heart with a stethoscope, and then said, "It sounds like a lot of work to me."

Gram brushed his words aside, saying, "Making pie is easy."

"If you're sure it's not too much trouble, I'd love one." He gave her a warm smile, intimating that she was special.

Now Maggie found her toes curling. She grinned. Like any good romance hero, Dr. Rosenberg exuded magnetism.

He went to the door and called the nurse, then faced Gram. "She'll help you get dressed while Dr. Crandall and I talk to your granddaughter."

Maggie gave Gram a questioning glance, but she had only a benign expression on her face. Normally too independent to have help doing anything, now Gram just nodded in agreement. She had become putty in the doctor's hands.

Maggie followed them down the hall to the clinic office. Once inside, Dr. Rosenberg motioned for her to be seated. He leaned against the counter, which made her uncomfortable. She disliked people staring down on her or, on the other hand, having to strain her neck to look up, so she remained standing too. "How's my grandmother doing?"

"Her vital signs are good, but I noticed when you filled out the forms you indicated she'd had some confusion. I wanted to get the facts from you before discussing it with her." He met her eyes. "Tell me about it."

Maggie told him about the incident with Robert, and just mentioning it filled her with worry again.

"Has this happened before?" He appeared concerned.

"I don't know. This is the first time it's happened that I've been aware of. The whole morning being a blank in her mind is what scared me." Worry furrowed her brow. "Do you know what caused it?"

"There are several things it could be. I want to order a CAT scan, but I suspect she probably had what is called a TIA. This is a small stroke. The victim is usually affected for a short time, then recovers. Unfortunately, it could be a precursor of a major stroke, so we need to be on the lookout for symptoms. I'll give you a pamphlet describing what to look for.

"I'm going to have some lab work done to make sure her body is functioning normally. I want to see her in a month, but call if she needs to see me sooner. We'll go over the results of her blood work then. If it shows something serious, we'll call you immediately." He made some notes on the medical chart. "Dr. Crandall, write up an order for a CAT scan, and they can have that done after the lab tests."

He turned to Maggie with a quick glance. "By the way, how did you get this appointment? I'm not taking any new patients until October, and all appointments for new patients have to be cleared through me." He gave her a warm, friendly glance. "I didn't okay Isabelle's appointment. I'm not upset about it, just curious."

"Someone named Angie made it for me. I have no idea why she didn't check with you." Maggie shook her head.

"Angie?" He appeared perplexed. "We don't have an Angie in geriatrics. Are you sure that was her name?"

"Yes." What was going on? "She repeated her name several times."

Dr. Rosenberg shook his head. "I don't know who it could have been."

This *was* strange. Who *had* given her the appointment? Surely he must be mistaken.

"I need to talk to Isabelle again. On your way out, the receptionist will call my secretary and schedule you an appointment." He told the other doctor to write the orders for the lab tests and turned back to Maggie. "Don't worry, we'll take good care of your grandmother." Patting her arm, he left the room.

Dr. Crandall handed two sheets to Maggie. "The lab is just across the hall. Give them this order when you check in, and afterward go on down the hall to the radiology department."

Maggie listened to the directions, but her mind was on what Dr. Rosenberg had said about there being no such person as Angie. There must have been some logical explanation for who had given her the appointment, but she didn't know what it could be.

Dr. Rosenberg escorted Gram out. "She needs to start taking a baby aspirin everyday. See you in a month, Isabelle."

Maggie loved seeing Gram this happy. She had a new gleam in her eyes, and she was beaming. "I'll bring the peach pie." From the attentive way he treated her, Maggie could tell Gram felt as if she were his favorite patient.

After the tests, they walked to the valet parking desk with Gram raving about Dr. Rosenberg nonstop. "He tends to be a little bossy, but I like that in a man. Your grandfather was, but I just did what I wanted to anyway."

Maggie remembered this about her grandfather. He'd been as opinionated as Gram. But they'd been a devoted, loving couple.

"Isn't his hair something? I'm crazy about those silver streaks in it. He's so distinguished looking." As the attendant went for the car, Isabelle chattered on. "I didn't want to embarrass him, but you know how Pat is always describing the hero's lips as firm and eminently kissable? Well, that describes Dr. Rosenberg's exactly. Don't you think?"

Maggie would never admit to Gram that she agreed with her, so she shrugged. "I didn't pay any attention." She had a good idea where this conversation was going, and she wanted to head it off at the pass.

Gram's eyebrows shot up. "Don't give me that. No one could ignore his lips. When's the last time you had a date, Maggie May?"

"Oh, thanks, bring up my lack of dates, make me feel bad," she teased, glancing down at her grandmother. The attendant arrived with the car, and she tipped him before seating herself in the driver's seat. As soon as he helped Gram into the car, she said, "You know, it's been so long, I can't remember my last date."

Gram nodded her head. "Yep. Dr. Rosenberg is the perfect candidate. I asked him if he was single when he came back in."

"You didn't!" How horrifying. She hoped he didn't think Gram was asking on her behalf. Why did elderly people think their age made them free to ask and say the most mortifying things?

Gram cocked her head and gave Maggie a withering look. "I did. There's nothing wrong with finding out the marital status of handsome men."

"*If* you're interested. Are *you* interested?" Maggie retorted.

Her grandmother's voice filled with disgust. "Don't talk foolishness."

"Don't get your hopes up. I've told you before and I'm telling you again, statistically I have a better chance of being kidnapped by terrorists than finding a husband at my age!"

"Lighten up, Maggie. What you need is a matchmaker, and I'm available." Gram's jaw had a stubborn set to it.

* * *

After clinic hours, David Rosenberg returned to his office at the University of Colorado Medical School. As he approached his secretary, he thought of Isabelle Hughes and the mysterious Angie. He stopped at Jane's desk. "Any messages?"

"Just a couple." She grinned at him. "So you'll be able to get out of here early." Jane made all of his appointments, and as he shuffled the message slips, he asked, "By the way, do you remember anyone named Angie covering for you while you were away from your desk?"

"When?" she asked in surprise.

He glanced up. "Find Isabelle Hughes's records and see exactly when the appointment was made." He moved around the desk and peered over her shoulder at the computer screen.

"That was a week ago today." She shook her head and frowned as she tried to remember. "I can't recall anything different about that day. When I leave for lunch, I always put the voice mail on, so no one else would have been answering for me. Why? Is there a problem with the appointment?"

"Not really. I haven't okayed any new patients, and yet today I had one. Her granddaughter said that Angie had made the appointment. I knew we didn't have anyone named Angie in the department." He shrugged. "But I thought someone might have been covering for you."

"That's kind of spooky." Jane frowned again. "I don't actually remember making the appointment, but then I make so many that I don't necessarily remember them all. But only a week ago? If I think of anything unusual that happened that day, I'll tell you."

"My grandfather would have said that Angie was an angel and that God had a message for me." Although David said this lightly, he knew this was exactly what his grandfather would have said and believed with all his heart.

Her eyebrows shot up. "Was he that religious?"

"You could say that." He nodded. "He was a rabbi. Rabbi Jakob Rosenberg. But while Isabelle was a lively eighty-year-old with an attractive granddaughter, she didn't have a message from God for me."

"Like I said, *spooky*."

"Who knows." He shrugged. Picking up his messages, he headed for his office. His grandfather had had a profound influence on him. Warm feelings flooded through him even thinking about what an incredible person the man had been. Because of his influence, David had even considered becoming a rabbi himself. His father was a doctor and his mother a psychiatrist, so he was torn between the professions. When his brother Sam became a rabbi, David had decided on medicine.

David read the messages and laid them on the corner of his large mahogany desk. After taking care of the calls, he relaxed in his black leather chair. Leaning back, he thought about his grandfather, an Orthodox rabbi. This terrific man instilled in all his grandchildren a great love for the Jewish religion. While he lived at home, David had observed the Orthodox dietary laws and the laws pertaining to the *Shabbat*. Once he was in medical school, though, he'd attended a Conservative Congregation, and that's what he considered himself now. He loved the Jewish ritual, and he'd never give up his heritage. At thirty-eight he still said the *sh'ma*—"Hear O Israel, the Lord Our God, the Lord is One,"—each night before he fell asleep. It gave him comfort and closure on his day. Was Angie an angel? He was dubious, but he couldn't get his grandfather's teachings out of his mind.

David glanced at his watch, then decided he'd better get a move on. He loved sports, and to him Monday nights were sacrosanct. Although *Monday Night Football* wasn't on, the NBA finals were. He grimaced at his plans. What he should have been doing was finding a wife. He wanted to marry a nice Jewish woman and to have children. But where could he find one?

Staying home alone and watching sports wasn't getting him very far. He didn't know any Jewish nurses or doctors who were single in Denver. There were none in his mountaineer club or rafting group. He stayed for coffee after Sabbath services, and there he'd met several women who were nice enough, but none of them interested him in anything long-term. His grandmother would have said he was too picky, and by now she would have lined up a matchmaker. He grinned ruefully at the thought. Now that's what he needed—a matchmaker.

Gathering up his keys, he left for home.

* * *

On Wednesday, Maggie had been in bed a couple of hours when the phone rang. She woke with a start, her heart pounding, and reached for the phone. "Hello?"

"Maggie." Gram's words quavered. "Can you help me?"

Scared, Maggie abruptly sat up and swung her feet to the side of the bed. The clock read 12:30 A.M. "What happened?" Her breath caught in her throat, and she could barely squeeze out the words.

"I've fallen," Gram said haltingly.

"I'll call 911 and be right over." Trembling, Maggie propped the phone up to her ear with her shoulder and stood up, reaching for her jeans with one hand and attempting to maneuver herself into them.

"I don't need 911 rescuing me!" Gram's voice was weaker than usual, but just as determined. "I'm perfectly fine. I just can't get up."

"Okay—for now. I'm on my way." No matter the circumstances, her grandmother was running the show. "Just stay calm, Gram. I'll see you in twenty minutes." If she had lived in Gram's neighborhood, it would certainly make everything easier.

Nearly in tears herself from shock, Maggie quickly woke Caitlin and Robert, wrapped quilts around them, and struggled to her car. They were half asleep and not too steady themselves, so she alternately carried and guided them along. By the time she reached her grandmother's, they were asleep again. She parked in the driveway close to the house, locked the car, and, leaving the side door open, ran in to see how her grandmother was.

She found her lying by the dining room table, for once not appearing cheerful but like a worn-out old woman. Maggie's heart sank. Tears filled her eyes as she gently helped her up and half carried the frail body to the bed. "How do you feel, darling Gram? Did you bump your head?" She attempted to keep her tone light so her grandmother wouldn't realize how frightened she was.

"I'll be all right. I just stumbled on the rug. One minute I was standing in the hall, the next I was on the floor." She sounded feeble, as if it took more energy than she had to speak any louder.

Fear surged through Maggie. "What were you doing up so late?" She tucked the blanket around her grandmother.

"It wasn't late." Gram again spoke with great effort. "I always go to bed after the ten o'clock news."

"Gram, that was two hours ago. Have you been on the floor ever since?" Maggie attempted to still the quaver in her own voice.

Gram sighed deeply. "Yes, I couldn't get up. Finally I got strength enough to drag myself a ways, and then I rested. After a while I was able to reach the phone."

Maggie's chest tightened as she pictured what had occurred. "What an awful thing to happen." Love welled up in her. She bent over and kissed the pale cheek. "Just rest a minute, Gram. I'll be right back. I need to bring Caitlin and Robert in from the car and get them settled for the night."

Grabbing her keys, she hurried out and hauled the two kids in one at a time. By this time their weight seemed to have increased threefold, and her strength seemed to have decreased the same amount. If there had been one more step, she'd never have made it to the second floor.

Getting them settled in bed, she pulled the covers up and started to move away from the bed. Caitlin opened her eyes, and, giving Maggie an angelic look, said, "You really love us, Aunt Maggie."

Warmed by her simple statement, Maggie smiled back. "I really do." Turning out the light, she descended the stairs to find that Gram had fallen asleep. She left only the night-light on in the hall, and then she wandered into the living room and sank onto the couch. What was she going to do?

She still had seven school days left. Students were always wild at the end of the school year, anxious to be free for summer vacation. Having a substitute instead of their regular teacher would only incite further misbehavior. She sighed. But for tomorrow, she didn't see that she had any choice. Gram seemed too weak to be alone. At six o'clock in the morning, Maggie would call for a substitute, but right now she was intent on removing every scatter rug on the first floor. There were half a dozen, mostly small rugs, just right for stumbling over. Stowing them in the front closet, she checked to make sure the doors were locked and then returned to the living room.

Thursday was taken care of, but what next? Worry seemed to have lodged permanently in her brain. She couldn't relax. It was like waiting for the other shoe to drop. She knew a calamity would happen, but she just didn't know when. One good thing was that Brad would be back in two days. Then she could concentrate all her efforts on helping Gram.

Maggie fluffed up the sofa pillows and stretched out on the couch. It was nearly two-thirty, and if she didn't get some sleep, she wouldn't be worth anything tomorrow.

The chiming of the grandfather clock in the dining room awakened her at six-fifteen. Still half asleep, she made the call to the district personnel office, checked on Gram, and lay back down. The sofa was no longer as comfortable as it had seemed earlier, but she made do.

An hour later, Caitlin and Robert tore down the stairs and jumped on Maggie.

"Wake up! Aunt Maggie! Wake up!" They tickled her face, their shrill little voices bouncing off the walls.

Maggie sat up, holding on to the two so they wouldn't tumble to the floor. This was a game they played when they stayed with her, but her bed had a lot more room than this couch. "Shhh, we don't want to wake Gram."

Caitlin's brow furrowed in puzzlement, and she whispered, "How did we get here?"

"Gram tripped on the rug. So she called us to come over and stay with her," Maggie whispered back.

"Where is she?" Caitlin gazed around the room.

"In her bedroom, asleep." She emphasized the *sleep* part so they would both be quiet.

"I want to see her." Caitlin's little face scrunched with determination.

"No, Caitlin, we don't want to wake her." Maggie tightened her hold on them.

Caitlin pried her aunt's arms away from her body and managed to get off the couch. Holding her finger to her lips, she reached for Robert's hand. The two tiptoed through the living room doorway, Maggie right behind them. When they reached Gram's open door, they stopped and silently watched her sleep. After a minute or so, Caitlin turned around and whispered, "Gram's asleep."

Not to be left out, Robert whispered, "Gram's asleep."

Maggie nodded and herded them back to the living room. When they were sitting on her lap, she said, "We need clothes for you to wear to school." Their expectant eyes watched her.

"PJs are not for school." Caitlin shook her head, and then Robert did.

"No, they're not." Maggie hugged them close and gave them a shake, which brought on giggles. "I've got to go back to the condo. Maybe Pat could stay with you and Gram while I get your clothes."

"We want to go!" They spoke louder. "We want to go with you!"

"Shhh, that's a good idea." She hugged them and gave them a conspiratorial smile. "We'll all go and leave Pat with Gram."

Maggie was grateful that not only was Pat her best friend, but an early riser as well. Her husband worked at the post office, so when he left for work at 5:00 A.M., she got up and wrote. Maggie wedged her way out from under the kids and called Pat.

When Pat answered, Maggie said, "Who's your best friend?"

"You, of course. But that question makes me suspicious." Pat laughed. "What do you want?"

"Gram fell last night, and the kids and I are at her place." Of all the ridiculous things, her voice quivered when she mentioned Gram. Fighting to sound matter-of-fact, she went on. "I'm staying home today with her, but I need to take the kids over to my place, dress them, and drop them off at their schools."

"Is your grandmother all right?" Pat's concern was obvious.

"She seems to be, but of course, she refused to let me call 911. So I'm just taking her word for it." She took a deep breath to regain her composure.

"Oh, Maggie, what next?" Pat sighed. "I'll be right over."

"Thanks." Tears filled her eyes, and she rubbed them furiously. Why was she getting weepy all of a sudden?

When Pat arrived Gram was still asleep, but she appeared to be breathing regularly, so Maggie grabbed the kids and hustled them out the door. "I should be back in an hour."

"Don't hurry on my account." Pat made herself comfortable at the dining room table. "I'll just work on my manuscript revisions."

Maggie was so rattled she hadn't even noticed Pat had her laptop with her.

Once they were at her condo, Caitlin and Robert were cooperative, so she had them washed, dressed, and delivered to school in no time.

When Maggie arrived back at Gram's, Pat hardly noticed her come in she was so involved in her revisions. Her soft auburn hair fanned her cheeks as she bent over her computer. Then Maggie observed that her face was completely made-up with powder, blush, and lipstick. "Nothing like your best friend making you feel even grungier. Here I am, no makeup, wearing clothes I've slept in, wild curly blond hair badly in need of a brush, and you don't have a hair out of place." She was really starting to feel grubby.

Smiling, Pat glanced up. "Stop it!" She squinted at Maggie, giving her a hard look. "On second thought, I don't want to be in the same room with you."

Maggie grinned back. "Is it because I need a bath?" For the first time in eight hours, she found she could lighten up.

Pat rolled her eyes.

"Could you stay a couple more minutes while I shower? I brought some clothes over." She was scared to leave Gram alone even for the few minutes it took her to shower.

"Sure. As long as I can think, I can revise anywhere. Take your time." She turned back to her computer.

Maggie hurried upstairs. When she came down, she rummaged in her purse for lipstick. She finally found the tube. To her dismay, the lid had come off and the end of the lipstick was covered in assorted fuzzies. "Wonderful!" She went in the downstairs bathroom and took a tissue to the lipstick. Even when she got the lipstick on, it still felt grainy, but at that point she didn't care.

Joining Pat at the table, she ran her fingers through her hair, trying to speed up the drying process. If she used a dryer, she'd have a mass of frizzies—the bane of naturally curly hair.

"How long have you been here?" Pat turned off her computer.

"Gram fell about 10:30 last night, and after dragging herself to the phone, reached me about 12:30." At the thought of Gram's ordeal, her stomach knotted.

"Oh, no." Pat made no effort to hide her worry. "What are you going to do?"

"I don't know yet. For now I'm playing it by ear. We were at the doctor's on Monday and everything was fine." She took a deep breath. "If she doesn't feel well when she wakes up, I'll call him."

"Don't forget, Maggie, I'm here if you need help." Pat shook her head. "There's got to be a solution that doesn't mean giving up your entire life for your family." She zipped the computer bag shut and stood, preparing to leave.

At the door Pat turned. "Just remember, kiddo, 'this too shall pass.'"

"I hope so." Her voice quivered again, and she felt more tears welling up. "I don't know why I'm on the verge of crying this morning."

"You've had more than enough piled on your plate the last two weeks, so you're entitled." Pat gave Maggie a hug. "Chin up, you can handle it."

Maggie wished she had Pat's confidence. She checked on Gram and then slipped upstairs to pray. If ever in her life she needed the

Lord's help, it was now. Kneeling by the side of the bed, she poured out her heart to Heavenly Father. She thanked Him for all the many blessings He'd given her, and told Him how much she loved Him and His Son. Then tears flowed down her face, and she began sobbing, "I love Gram so much, and I am so worried about her. I have a week of school left, and I don't know what to do. Please guide me." She finished her prayer and remained on her knees a few minutes.

When Maggie stood, she still didn't know what she was going to do, but she felt reassured that Heavenly Father had heard her prayer.

Wanting to get downstairs before Gram woke up, she hurriedly made up the bed where the kids had slept. She reached the top of the stairs and saw Gram coming out of her room.

Startled, she said, "Gram, what are you doing up?"

Her grandmother glanced up at her. "Maggie, why aren't you in school?"

"There was no way I was going to let my favorite grandmother wake up alone after she'd spent half the night on the dining room floor." Maggie came on down the stairs.

"Oh, that." Gram looked unconcerned. "I told you then, and I'm telling you now, I'm okay."

"Are you sure? Do you feel dizzy?" She couldn't imagine her grandmother hadn't been affected by the fall. "Or lightheaded?"

"No! I'm perfectly fine." Gram eyed her grimly. "You're not planning on spending the day here to quiz me every five minutes about the state of my health, are you?"

Maggie swallowed hard. "No."

"That *no* doesn't sound very definite to me. I'm telling you, Maggie, I'm perfectly fine. It seems to me that you've hardly had time to write since you heard from that editor. Since you were so foolish as to take this day off from school, go home and write! Now move out of my way. I want to take a bath and get dressed for the day," she said with determination.

"Oh, Gram, you're too much." She patted Gram's smooth cheek tenderly.

Her grandmother smiled. "I mean it, Maggie May. I won't have you hovering over me all day long. How many times do I have to tell you I'm perfectly fine?"

Maggie held up her arm. "I swear I won't hover. I am, however, going to fix breakfast for you. So I'm warning you, don't linger in the tub."

"Just watch my smoke!" Gram hustled into the bathroom, as vigorous as ever.

Breathing a sigh of relief, Maggie went into the kitchen and fixed breakfast. She'd just finished setting it on the table when her grandmother ducked into her bedroom and a few minutes later appeared in lavender pants and top, her favorite color. Bright red lipstick blazed on her lips, and Maggie knew she was well again.

Gram looked at the waffles. "My favorite breakfast!" She seated herself and then peered at her granddaughter. "You're too good to me. I don't deserve all this."

Maggie waved off her comments. "Isabelle Hughes, you've helped everyone who has crossed your path, and you deserve everything you get." She grinned. "Now accept it graciously."

Gram grimaced. "All right, all right!" Without another word, she dug into her food.

By the time they finished eating, the weight on Maggie's heart had lifted, and she found she enjoyed the food as much as Gram. "Let me clear these dishes, and then . . ."

"And then you'll go home and write." Gram's feisty tone brooked no argument.

"I'll agree to that. At five I'll pick up Caitlin and Robert, then we'll come back and eat supper with you." Maggie put the jam and the butter into the refrigerator.

"Fine. I'll see you." Gram made her way energetically into the living room.

Maggie had the kitchen cleaned in a jiffy. She lingered at the doorway, watching her grandmother studiously poring over the scriptures. "Good-bye, darling Gram. I'll see you later."

She glanced up from her Book of Mormon. "See you later." She then went right back to her reading.

To her amazement, Maggie didn't even feel guilty as she wrote. She simply felt free, free to be by herself, free to dream, free to create, and most of all, free to write. Although the previous night had been terrifying, the day had turned out surprisingly well.

After arriving at her condo, she went directly to her computer and turned it on. Opening the *Murder at the Berkeley* file, she scrolled down to her last line:

Skirting some large cans of cement compound, Ruby followed Blanche to the windows. "What a magnificent view! Victor can see from the Wasatch Mountains on the east to the point of the mountain on the south."

Stepping across a hole in the floor, Ruby moved over to a pile of lumber. "Everything's here to start framing the new room, including a pile of rags."

"Rags?"

Ruby looked again and screamed. Then she seemed incapable of stopping as the screams tore up her throat.

Alarmed, Blanche whirled around. "What's the matter?"

Gasping, Ruby pointed. "Th-there's Victor."

Maggie grinned as she wrote more of the adventures of Blanche and Ruby, two eighty-year-old sleuths who were as vigorous and youthful as her own grandmother. She loved these characters. Many of their idiosyncracies she had based on Gram's personality. Finally, two hours later, she stood up and stretched, attempting to get the kinks out from sitting hunched over her computer for so long. She walked briskly around her apartment a few times, then decided to walk down and get her mail and walk back up the four flights, hoping that would do the trick.

Her writer's magazine, along with a lot of junk mail, had been crammed into her mailbox. When she returned to her condo, she poured herself a large glass of water, sliced an apple, and sat down to catch her breath and to glance through the magazine before she went back to her computer. The further adventures of Blanche and Ruby ought to keep her mind off any stiffness.

Three and a half hours later, she glanced at the clock and saw that it was time to pick up the kids. She'd had such a productive afternoon that she felt ready to tackle anything.

When she picked up Robert and Caitlin, her good mood quickly evaporated. Robert was crying. The teacher explained that he'd fought over the broom with another child, and as a result, neither one of them got to sweep. As soon as Robert saw Maggie, he started screaming, "I hate school!" He then made a face at the teacher. "I'm not coming back. I want my daddy! I want my daddy!"

So did Maggie. Brad, not she, needed to be here. She could tell Robert was devastated. He hadn't been this upset the entire time he'd stayed with her. Forcing back the tears that were threatening to slide down her face, she gathered up Robert in her arms and hugged him to her chest. "What an awful day you've had, honey bunny. You didn't even get to sweep. Aunt Maggie's sorry. We'll go to Gram's, and you can sweep there." He stopped crying at her words, but he didn't act happy.

She carried him to her car. "Why don't you sit in front by me until we pick up Caitlin?" He hiccupped and then nodded his head. She fastened him in and slid in herself, grateful that Caitlin's school was only six blocks away. As she parked she could see Caitlin leaning against the door. Maggie waved at her. When she drew closer, she saw that Caitlin's face was splotchy red. Obviously, she'd been crying.

Maggie knelt down beside her and enveloped the little girl in her arms. "What's the matter, honey?"

"I thought you weren't coming." Caitlin burst into tears again, rubbing her eyes with the backs of her hands. "I'm tired of this." She sighed angrily. "My mama better come back soon."

Maggie bit back her tears. What could she say? "I want your mama to come back too. It's no fun without her. Let Aunt Maggie carry you to the car, and you can be my baby." Caitlin usually loved playing this game.

Caitlin nodded, giving her a wan smile.

Maggie swept her up in her arms, cuddling her against her chest. "Rock-a-bye baby in a treetop," she crooned to her beloved niece, gently rocking her back and forth as she carried her to the car. Caitlin burrowed closer, then peeked up at her and in her pretend voice said, "Ma-ma."

"I wish, honey." Maggie kissed the little girl before settling her in the backseat and moving Robert to the back also. She squeezed him and kissed his damp cheek.

Worry over the kids started her stomach churning. Maggie eased into the car and then turned around. "What do you hungry tigers want to eat?"

"Pizza!" came from Robert.

"Tacos!" came from Caitlin.

"Let's stop at the store, and we'll get pizzas, tacos, and sodas." For the first time since she'd picked them up, they both seemed happy.

About two blocks from Gram's house was a supermarket. Maggie pulled in and, taking the children with her, went to get the groceries. They still clung to her as if they were afraid she'd abandon them. She made the trip short, and they quickly returned to the car. She sighed when Gram's two-story green-and-beige house came into view. She hoped nothing had happened while she was home alone.

After she'd turned off the child-lock mechanism, Caitlin and Robert jumped out and scurried up the steps, hollering, "Grandma, we're here!"

Gram opened the door, and they said, "We're having pizza and tacos for supper." Each was trying to outshout the other.

"That sounds delicious," Gram said, ushering them into her house.

Once inside the house, Robert immediately ran to the broom closet. His mind strictly on business, he started sweeping. Maggie watched him industriously sweep the kitchen floor, and she had to laugh at his concentration.

Caitlin watched him for a minute, and then, turning to Gram and her aunt, said in a grown-up voice, "I'm setting the table. Aunt Maggie needs my help, don't you, Aunt Maggie?"

"Yes, I do." She grinned at the little girl. "You're such a good helper I can hardly cook without you." Caitlin followed right behind her as she walked into the house.

After changing the tablecloth, Gram gave Caitlin an amused look. "You can't do everything, young lady. You've got to let an old woman help you."

"Here, you can put the spoons on." Caitlin carefully handed them to her and then demonstrated the precise way to place them. "This is the way you do it."

Maggie lingered awhile after dinner, noting that her grandmother seemed to have made a miraculous recovery. She appeared to be her usual perky self. Finally Gram shooed her out of the house and ordered her home.

When they were back at the condo, Maggie watched television with Caitlin and Robert lying on the floor in front of it while she stretched out on the couch. Her mind wandering, she imagined how wonderful the next week would be. School was nearly out, and her vacation loomed! A respite from her darling niece and nephew! Then full-time writing! She sighed in anticipation.

The phone rang. Caitlin ran to answer it. "Hi, Daddy!" she said exuberantly. "When are you coming home?"

Chapter 4

There was silence. "How long is a week?"

A week! Maggie jumped up and hurried to the phone. "Here, honey, let me talk to your daddy for a minute." She took the receiver out of her hand.

"Brad." Her voice was curt. "When are you coming home?"

"Well, Maggs, I've got another consulting job in Memphis, so I can't see coming home until I'm finished with it. By the time I flew out there and got back by Monday, I wouldn't have any time to spend with the kids anyway." Then he added in an ingratiating tone, "You've only got a few days of school left. I can't see any problem."

Maggie gritted her teeth. "I love your kids, but as I said at the beginning, I have other plans, and you'll need to make other arrangements."

"Now, Maggs," he said condescendingly, "you never travel during the summer. Anyway, you've got three months. You'll have plenty of time for other activities."

"Listen! My summer vacation is exactly nine weeks long. I need to finish my book. I will not baby-sit all summer!" She refused to let him dictate how she spent her time.

"What's the problem? Robert and Caitlin sleep for two hours every day. Write during their naps!"

It was all Maggie could do to keep from stamping her feet and yelling at him, and she'd never done that in her life. Softening her tone because she now had the full attention of the children, she said, "Don't count on me."

"Now, Maggs . . ."

"I know you want to talk to Robert and Caitlin." She briskly said good-bye. Motioning the kids to the phone, she slumped back on the sofa, angry to the core that Brad could be so thoughtless. She'd told him about Gram's problems before and how she had her hands full, but he'd blown it off. Good old Maggie could handle any difficulty. She watched Robert and Caitlin excitedly tell their daddy all the things they'd been doing, but she was so irritated she couldn't force her lips to smile at their antics.

When they finished talking, they ran over to her. Caitlin, her face beaming with happiness, said, "Daddy's bringing me a present!"

"I get a present too!" Robert was so excited he could barely get the words out.

"That's wonderful. You have a nice daddy." *Albeit a thoughtless one,* she mused.

Laughing, they plopped themselves back in front of the television.

Even though she did little writing, Maggie enjoyed Caitlin and Robert immensely, and the next week passed quickly. Gram, her old energetic self, ran around as usual.

School was out on Friday, and Brad arrived home late that night, picking up his kids Saturday morning. They were thrilled to see him, and he was just as delighted as they were. She had to give him his due. He did love his kids.

When the door closed behind them, Maggie sank back into her linen rocker. Alone at last! She took a deep breath, absorbing the peacefulness of the room and feeling liberated after all the problems of the last several weeks. Now she wanted to settle in at the computer. She'd written just a page when she realized the silence in the condo was overwhelming. Already she missed the kids.

* * *

David Rosenberg grabbed his leather jacket as he started out the door to a mountaineer club planning meeting at the community college. His phone rang. He hesitated a moment before answering, then glanced at his watch. If he kept this call short, he could still make the meeting.

"Hello?" His voice was wary.

"David, this is Pete. How're you doing?"

"Pete." He always liked to talk to him. Pete had been his best friend all through training at Johns Hopkins and his post-residency geriatric training at the University of Utah. "It's good to hear from you, man. Everything here's going fine." David sensed this call could take a few minutes, so he settled back in his easy chair. "How're Nikki and the kids?"

"Getting along famously. Nan can't talk about anything but starting school this fall. The baby took his first step a couple of days ago. There's no two ways about it—I love being a dad." Satisfaction filled Pete's voice.

"Those words are making me green with envy. One of these days . . ." David said with a smile.

"One of these days, if you keep hunting for a wife!" Pete laughed. "How's the search coming? Has your mother hired a matchmaker yet?"

"I think she's almost desperate enough! She never loses an opportunity to tell me what I should be doing! All I can say is, 'Where's a nice Jewish girl when you need one?'" David said, laughing easily.

"I can't believe that in a city the size of Denver there isn't one available Jewish woman. Are you sure you're looking in all the right places?" Pete teased.

"I'm not at all sure. Any suggestions?" David recalled that Pete used to always have ideas for meeting women.

"As a matter of fact, no. I'm just thankful I found Nikki. Which brings me to the point of my call." He paused. "I'm being baptized into the Mormon Church Saturday evening."

Shock effectively silenced David. Finally, he found the words to say, "You're getting baptized into the Mormon Church?" He shook his head in disbelief. "When did you decide this? I just talked to you a few weeks ago and you didn't say anything about it then."

"I've been considering it for a while, and today I decided. I don't know why, but I had a strong feeling that I should tell you. You've lived in Salt Lake, and you know what the Mormon Church is like."

He did, and Pete's joining the Mormon Church was definitely wrong. "Have you talked to your rabbi?" He couldn't let his friend leave the Jewish faith.

"Yes. I've discussed it, prayed about it, and discussed it some more. I know what I'm doing." He sounded as though he'd given this matter much thought and had an unshakable belief in what he was doing.

But did he really? "Isn't Nikki Mormon?" Before Pete could answer, David rushed on, "Is she what convinced you? You're doing this for her?"

"Yes, Nikki is LDS, and she introduced me to their beliefs, but she made no effort to force her religion on me or to convert me. This is solely my decision."

"I can't believe it." He said the pain-filled words slowly. "Think of the Holocaust. What our families lost because of who they were, and you're just willy-nilly giving it all up? What about your heritage?" He couldn't hide his bitterness at Pete's decision. "How does your family feel about your decision?"

"My mother is unhappy about it, but my father's greatest concern is that his children be good, ethical people. He believes that I am, so he isn't giving me any static. My grandmother is a different matter. She's ready to recite Kaddish for me." Pain that his grandmother took the news so hard filtered through his voice.

"And the thought that she will be reciting the Mourner's Prayer and cutting you out of her life entirely doesn't give you second thoughts?" How anyone could hurt his family this way was unfathomable to David. How could Pete leave the truth and break his family's hearts in the process?

"Sure it does, but in the final analysis, I have to do what I know is right."

Physical pain at Pete's decision knifed through David. He twisted in the chair, trying to shake it off, but he couldn't. "Pete, don't be taken in by this . . . this church." He'd started to say *cult,* but thought better of it. "You attended Hebrew school the same as I did. You had years of training in the Torah and Jewish rabbinical thinking. You *know* the truth. Don't be deceived." Never had a friend's actions affected David this deeply.

"That's just it. I had studied for years. Like I said, this wasn't an easy decision. I weighed everything I'd ever been taught against what the missionaries—"

"Missionaries!" The word exploded from David's mouth. "I thought you said Nikki didn't try to convert you! How do missionaries come into it?" he demanded. The hurt he felt at Pete's leaving Judaism had turned to anger.

"When I attended services, I could feel something that had been missing, and when I heard members of the congregation bear their testimonies, I knew within me that what they said was true. The Spirit bore witness, but this wasn't enough for me. I needed to read more and pray. I asked the missionaries to come and teach me. No strings attached—I just wanted to know more about the Church.

"I read the Book of Mormon. I prayed. I knew that Joseph Smith was a prophet, not intellectually, but from the feeling that filled my body.

"I know without any doubt that Jesus Christ is the Messiah, that He died that we might be saved and live again with Him and His Father."

Although Pete spoke quietly, his conviction penetrated to the core of David's being.

"I know for myself through the Spirit of God witnessing to me that The Church of Jesus Christ of Latter-day Saints is the true church of God, and that the holy priesthood of God is in the Church. I can't deny it."

Pete's intensity seemed to pierce David, and he had a definite sense that what his friend said was true. He shook his head vehemently. But that couldn't be! "I . . . I can tell that you are thoroughly converted to the Mormon Church." He didn't know what else to say.

"I am, and within me I know that what I am doing is right. I hope you will accept it, because I don't want to lose you as a friend." His statement rang with sincerity.

David couldn't believe the turn Pete's life had taken. Finally, he said, "Good luck, Pete. I hope you've made the right decision."

They hung up. For a few minutes the surety of the truth of what Pete had said enveloped him, and then it slowly disappeared. Attempting to put the entire conversation behind him, he glanced at his watch again and saw that he would be about twenty minutes late for the meeting. If he planned to climb on Sunday, he'd better find out the group's plans. He drove over to Denver Community College, all the while feeling as if he'd been run over by a Mack truck. He couldn't get Pete's call off his mind, and he was aghast that his friend was actually giving up the Jewish religion to become a Mormon.

Afterward, David was glad he'd attended the meeting. Sunday's hike had been postponed to the following Sunday. Once back home, his mind continually strayed to Pete's decision, making it impossible to concentrate on *Law and Order,* which, next to sports, was his favorite TV program.

Pete's leaving Judaism only hardened David's determination to find a Jewish woman to marry. He never had and he never would date a Gentile. That was just asking for trouble. But just being Jewish wasn't enough either. Sarah had taught him that lesson. He'd thought his former wife was the perfect person to marry. They were both Jewish, their families were friends, and they'd grown up in the same neighborhood in New York City. He grimaced. He should have known better. Sarah had hated living in Baltimore and being alone so much while he did his internship at Johns Hopkins. She'd complained unceasingly about his selfishness and her lack of a life. When she said she was leaving, he didn't argue. In some respects, he was just glad to know the whole painful ordeal had ended.

He still wanted to marry again, but this time he wanted it to be to someone more mature than Sarah—with the same goals he had. And Jewish.

He watched the news and then turned in for the night. Once in bed, he covered his eyes with his hand and recited the *sh'ma.* "Hear O Israel, the Lord Our God, the Lord is One." Then he added, "I remember the gifts of the day, the gift of today and give thanks, O God." These prayers renewed his sense of identity. He was a Jew. The uneasy feeling he'd had ever since talking to Peter vanished, and he rolled over on his side and fell asleep.

* * *

School was out! What a wonderful feeling. Ever since her mission, Maggie had studied the scriptures first thing in the morning, so it was nearly ten in the morning when she sat down to write. She'd just put her name at the beginning of a new chapter when the phone rang.

Cradling the receiver between her head and her shoulder, she attempted to type *Chapter 9* while she talked.

"Maggs? Maggs, are you there?" No! She couldn't believe it was the same aggravating, demanding voice.

Quickly shifting the phone to her hand, she said, "Yes, Brad." Was that the hollow sound of the security system? "Are you downstairs?"

"Yes. I need to talk to you. Can I come up?"

The last time she'd said yes, he'd wanted her to baby-sit. Her mouth twisted. "Sure." She buzzed him in and opened the door so they could come right in. Sinking back on the sofa, she waited. One thing she knew—she'd sure be glad to see Caitlin and Robert.

Brad came in alone.

Maggie frowned. "Where are the kids?"

"Sister White, a member of my ward, lives three houses down, and she offered to keep them for the morning." He settled down in an overstuffed chair and smiled. "How's your writing coming?"

"Fine." She didn't quite trust this friendly person. Her eyes narrowed, and her body stiffened. She wondered what was coming next.

"That's great." He sounded enthusiastic.

"It is." Surprised at his fervor, she kept her tone neutral and waited expectantly.

"Gram seems back to normal," he continued as if they were the best of friends with nothing better to do today than discuss the family.

"The doctor says she has a distinct chance of having a stroke, but I'm praying she stays healthy." Her prayers had never been so intense.

He nodded thoughtfully.

"Is there a point to your visit, Brad? I'd started to write, and I need to get back to it." She refused to spend the morning chitchatting with him when there were the adventures of Blanche and Ruby she could be concentrating on.

Confidence oozed from him, and his smile veered towards smugness. "I've given this a great deal of thought, and I've prayed about it. We should get married."

Astounded, she could only gasp, "Married?"

He continued with conviction. "The way I see it, you're thirty-one, and at your age the chances of ever finding a man to marry are practically nonexistent. Did you know the ratio of single women to single men in the Church who are your age and older is like six women to every man? I'll bet that you don't have even one eligible bachelor in your ward."

His air of superiority infuriated Maggie, and she said vehemently, "Yes, we do. Alex Stevens." She didn't mention that he was twenty-one years old and had just returned from a mission to Brazil.

"Maggie, listen to me. I'll never love anyone except Karen, but I need a mother for my children. Can't you see that?" His entire speech sounded as though he were lecturing a two-year-old. "This is the perfect answer."

The perfect answer! He hadn't even asked the question. He just *assumed* she'd want to marry him. Outrage engulfed her. How dare he presume she'd be interested in marrying him! She'd had a difficult time even being pleasant to him over the years. Marry him? She wanted to scream, but she kept calm. "I know you're still grieving over Karen's death, and if you're going to work, you do need someone to care for Caitlin and Robert. But the only time a marriage of convenience works is in fiction, and in case you haven't noticed, this is real life." No matter how adamant he was, she wanted to disabuse him of any notion that she might consent.

"But Maggie . . ." He sounded even more determined.

"I won't marry you even to mother your darling children." Her throat tightened from the anger. "And I resent your thinking—let alone saying—that I'll probably never get married. It's none of your business whether I do or I don't."

He plowed ahead as if she hadn't spoken. "Maggie, you can't reject this outright. Pray about it. I feel certain this is the right thing to do." He had conviction written all over him.

"I don't! And after ten years of asking you not to call me *Maggs,* why are you suddenly calling me *Maggie?*" She stared at him. "Doing that will get you nowhere." Her entire body trembled, and she clutched the sofa with her hands to steady herself.

He had the grace to look sheepish.

She took several deep breaths to regain her composure. "I hope I find someone whom I fall madly in love with and who is madly in love with me. That person isn't you. But if I don't, I'm not going to bemoan my fate and be miserable the rest of my life."

Once again, he had determination written all over his face. "All good active LDS women with a testimony want to be married. You can't get to the celestial kingdom unless you're married in the temple." His tone seemed to dare her to disagree.

"I like my life just the way it is." Maggie shook her head decisively. "I'd never give it up for a business arrangement. It doesn't seem possible to you now, but one of these days you'll meet someone you can love. Maybe not as much as Karen, but you'll love her and she'll love not only you, but Caitlin and Robert."

An obstinate expression covered his face. "You're wrong!"

Her eyes narrowed. "Meanwhile, you'll do what countless other people do—manage your children and your life without a wife."

Brad had a mulish set to his lips. "Well, I can see you can't be reasoned with, so I guess there's no use hanging around here." With anger at her resistance emanating from his body, he rose abruptly. "Good-bye."

"Good-bye." She watched him leave, angrily pulling the door open, but making great effort not to slam it.

The shock of Brad's proposal and their confrontation left Maggie mentally and physically limp. She remained on the couch, staring into space, unable to find the energy to move let alone write.

She'd never felt it was necessary to rush into marriage, and it was a good thing because she hadn't had that many opportunities. She'd spent her freshman year at BYU, and although she'd enjoyed the classes, her social life had been nil. Since she preferred Denver to Provo, she'd transferred to Denver University. Now, thirteen years later, eligible men were as few and far between as dates. Because she found singles activities tedious, she seldom attended them, preferring to write or to be involved with her friends. With them she'd explored all types of classes: writing, gourmet cooking, and literary discussion groups. She considered her life fulfilling, but it sure didn't include many men, single or otherwise.

She had such hopes for her writing. Teaching had been wonderful. But after six years, she was ready to move on to something else, and she wanted that something to be writing. She hoped in the future to earn a doctorate from the University of Oklahoma's writing program, but Gram was a major consideration in any plans. It looked like for now, anyway, she'd stay put in Denver.

* * *

When Maggie woke up on Thursday, she kept waiting for the phone to ring with bad news. It seemed like every Thursday some new problem confronted her.

After she'd written for several hours, she glanced at her watch and read 12:00 straight up. She took a deep breath and smiled. So far, so good. While she deliberated over the developments in the next chapter, she crossed her fingers for luck.

The policeman spoke up. "What makes you think he was murdered?"

The skeptical tone in his voice irked Blanche. "A hole in his forehead gave me the first clue." Did they . . .

The phone rang, breaking the silence of Maggie's office.

 *Chapter 5*

"Maggie! Are you there?"

The terror in Gram's voice sent fear tearing through Maggie. Struggling to keep calm, she said, "Yes, Gram, what's the matter? Did something happen?" By this time her legs were trembling, but she was too scared herself to do anything except lean against the wall.

"Can you come over here?" Hysteria edged Gram's words. "Right now!"

"Are you okay?" She couldn't imagine the catastrophe that would make Gram panic this way.

"I'm all right. Just hurry."

"I'm on my way. Bye." She grabbed her keys and purse and ran to the elevator. When she reached the doors, her hands shook so badly she could barely punch the numbers. Her breath came rapidly, and her heart beat so fast she thought she might be on the verge of hysteria herself. She forced herself to take slow, deep breaths so she wouldn't start hyperventilating.

When she reached her car, Maggie sat behind the wheel a couple of minutes, breathing slowly until she had herself under control enough to drive. If she didn't calm down, she'd just upset Gram more.

It seemed to take forever to drive from University to Monaco. However, when Maggie glanced at her watch, she saw that she'd made it in fourteen minutes. She parked in the driveway and hurried into the house. "Gram? Gram, where are you?"

"In here," came a weak call from the living room.

Throwing her keys and purse on the dining room table, Maggie tried to act casual as she entered the living room. Gram lay on the sofa, so Maggie pulled up the footstool and sat next to her. Gently brushing her grandmother's white hair back with her hand, she said, "What's happened to upset you?"

Gram began crying and clutching Maggie's hands. "The most awful thing happened to me today . . ." Her eyes closed and she sobbed.

"Just relax and tell me at your own pace. I'm in no hurry." She kept her tone soft and soothing. "Would you like a glass of cold water?"

"Please."

Maggie laid the pale wrinkled hands down and hurried into the kitchen. She was used to a feisty, take-charge grandmother, and she hardly knew how to deal with this new person. In the past Gram had always been the one to do the consoling when anything went wrong—not the other way around.

On the kitchen counter she found three sacks of groceries, which raised her level of apprehension. What had transpired that was so upsetting that Gram hadn't even put her groceries away? Her grandmother didn't like warm water or ice cubes, so Maggie turned the faucet on and let the water run while she found a glass. When she returned to the living room, she found Gram had her crying under control. Maggie held the glass while she took several swallows.

Gram struggled to sit up straighter, so Maggie helped her. "Ready to talk now?" She seated herself again on the footstool. "What happened?"

"This morning I decided to go to that new grocery store over on Sixteenth. When I finished shopping, I couldn't remember where I'd parked my car. I pushed my cart up and down the lanes of the parking lot until I finally found it. When I started home, I had only gone a couple of blocks when I realized I didn't know where I was or where I was going." Her eyes welled up with tears. "I've lived in the Park Hill area for the last fifty years, and I didn't know where I was. I drove around and tried to find something I recognized. Finally I saw a police station and asked for help. Oh, Maggie," the sobbing started again, "besides being lost, I didn't even know who I was."

"Oh, Gram." Maggie's heart sank. "What an awful thing to have happen. Did the police help you?" She rubbed her grandmother's cold hands, trying to warm them.

"They found my driver's license and brought me home. They offered to call someone, but I couldn't remember you." The tears flowed faster. "How could I forget my darling Maggie May?"

Reaching over, she smoothed Gram's hair back again. "It's going to be all right." Maggie nodded confidently. "Don't worry. It'll be all right."

"Do you think so?" Her grandmother's eyes begged for reassurance.

The plaintive tone ripped Maggie's heart. "I know so." But for all her apparent composure, Maggie's lips started to tremble, and she willed them not to, knowing if Gram had an inkling of her granddaughter's anxiety, she would be even more alarmed.

"You look starved. Should I fix you something to eat?" She attempted to be cheerful, and hoped she didn't seem phony. In the old days Gram would have seen right through it.

"No, forgetting everything scared me too much to be hungry." Her vulnerability frightened Maggie further, and she vowed to call Aunt Barbara the first chance she got. After all, Gram was Barbara's mother, and she needed to know what was going on. Barbara usually called Gram every Sunday, but since Gram always brushed off any inquiries about her health with an "I'm fine," Maggie was sure Barbara didn't know about her mother's problems. She herself hadn't called her earlier because the problems had seemed minor, but what happened today wasn't.

"Well, I'm ravenous, so why don't I fix us both a chocolate milk shake. You only need to drink as much as you want," Maggie said cheerfully.

Barely moving her head, her grandmother nodded.

Gram liked chocolate ice cream, so she always had it on hand. Maggie put the ingredients into the blender and had the shakes stirred up in no time. She filled two glasses and grabbed some napkins and straws before returning to the living room.

Gram's pillows had worked themselves down the sofa, so Maggie plumped them up and then gave her the milk shake.

Gram took a long swallow, then looked up at her granddaughter and smiled. "This is making me feel better all ready. I didn't realize how weak I'd become." She continued sipping until she made a slurping noise.

Maggie gave her a teasing smile. "Want some more?"

"Sure." Sounding nearly like her old self, Gram held out her glass. "Chocolate always hits the spot."

Maggie returned to the kitchen and poured out the rest of the shake. When she rejoined her grandmother, she was glad to see her sitting up. "Here it is." She handed her the drink.

"I'm sorry I called you sounding so hysterical. You must have been worried to death. But I was so scared to think I'd forgotten my life." She sounded woebegone.

"That would be scary for anyone to go through." Maggie's heart ached at what her beloved Gram had experienced, and she wanted to be able to fix it, to have everything all right. "I'm always glad to come over. Would you like me to stay with you tonight?"

"I hate to impose, but I'm afraid to be alone." Once again, her face was as forlorn as her voice.

Maggie moved over beside Gram and hugged her. "You're not imposing. It's my pleasure. I'm just glad I'm able to stay. What do you think about calling Aunt Barbara later?"

"I hate for her to know, but I guess we'd better." She finished her drink and set the glass on the floor, then looked at Maggie with a sober expression. "What am I going to do? The very thought of driving again scares me to death. What if I wandered off someplace and no one found me?"

"I don't think that will happen, but for the time being, maybe it would be better if I drove you to get groceries and to church. Those are the main places you go. If you need me to run you someplace special, just call." Maggie hesitated. "I also think we should call Dr. Rosenberg and see what he says."

Gram perked right up. "He said to call anytime, and I'm taking him at his word. Go call right now."

Maggie smiled. "Just remember," she ordered, "forget the match-making."

Gram raised her eyebrows at that remark and remained silent.

Maggie found his card on the refrigerator door and phoned. When she told his secretary the problem, she replied that he usually returned calls after clinic hours, and Maggie would definitely hear from him that night.

* * *

On Thursday morning before rising, David put his hand over his eyes and said, "I render thanks to you, everlasting King, who has mercifully restored my soul within me."

When he was ready for work, he placed his prayer shawl over his head and shoulders, then gathered together its four corners and brought them to his lips, reminding himself of God's promise to gather the dispersed Jews from the four corners of the earth. "Here I envelop myself in a prayer shawl of fringes in order to fulfill the commandment of my creator, to recall and to preserve the tradition of the generations and in order to direct my heart, as I clothe myself in prayer."

His *talit* was a large, woolen, blanketlike shawl that he'd inherited from his grandfather. While he was wrapped in it, he could sense his grandfather's and his grandmother's presence and felt connected to them and God. His prayers fortified him for the day against whatever irritations and problems might arise. God was with him.

He removed the shawl and returned it to its place in his dresser, ready to start the day.

Since his patients usually had wonderful stories to tell, clinic hours passed rapidly. Each day the geriatric interns talked to the patients first, and then he met with them. Together they worked out what each person needed in the way of therapy, meds, further tests, or referrals to specialists. His love for his grandparents had drawn him into this specialty of medicine. He'd wanted to improve the quality of his grandparents' lives, and he'd decided then that he wanted his life's work to be among the elderly.

On his return to his office that afternoon, he picked up his messages and went in his office to call. One of them was from Maggie Summers. What a spunky lady her Grandmother Isabelle was. He grinned just thinking about her.

* * *

At 5:30 the phone rang, and Maggie hurried to the dining room, making sure she answered it first, not trusting what Gram might have to say about her.

"Maggie? This is Dr. Rosenberg. Has something happened to Isabelle?" He sounded genuinely concerned. Maggie found this gratifying. She hated to think of her grandmother being only a number to a doctor.

"I appreciate you returning my call. Gram had a scary thing happen to her today, and I wanted your advice on what to do." She related her grandmother's experience.

"At this point I suspect that the periods of forgetfulness may be weeks apart, gradually getting closer together. It's time Isabelle quit driving, even if she is 'only' eighty." She could hear the smile in his voice. "When she regains confidence about staying alone, I think you can leave her and she will be all right."

"I worry about her being here by herself."

"She needs to have control over the things she can do safely. Otherwise her confidence in her abilities will lessen, and she'll become more helpless. This can trigger depression. For you to return to your own home for the time being is probably the sensible thing to do. But you need to start considering alternatives to her staying alone. When is her next appointment?"

"The twenty-fourth."

"Good. I'll see you both then." They hung up.

Sighing a breath of relief, she rejoined her grandmother. "Well, Gram, Dr. Rosenberg says not to worry, but it's a good idea for you not to drive. He also said when you felt up to it, you could stay alone."

"Good." Her eyes gleamed. "How did he sound on the phone, Maggie May?"

She threw her arms out dramatically. "To die for!" Then she fell into the chair.

They both laughed.

A half hour later, Maggie called her Aunt Barbara. After the greetings, she said, "Gram hasn't been doing too well. She wants to tell you about it."

"Good." Her aunt had just one sharp word.

Maggie handed the phone to Gram, listening as Gram told Barbara what had happened, leaving out how scared she'd been and how she didn't want to stay alone in case she had another attack of memory loss.

When she finished talking, Gram gave the receiver back to Maggie. "She wants to talk to you again."

"Yes?" Maggie assumed Barbara was planning on coming out to see Gram.

"That's all that happened?" Barbara sounded unconcerned, as if Gram's experience had been a minor blip of inconvenience.

"More or less." What did it take to make her concerned?

"I can't come out right now, so it's reassuring that you don't have the responsibility of a family. Since you have the summer off, everything will work out well." Then she gushed, "You're such a wonderful person. I don't know what we'd do without you to take care of Mom. If anything else comes up, let me know."

Anger coursed through Maggie, and she stiffened. *This "wonderful person" is getting sick and tired of being dumped on. It reminds me of O. Henry's story of "The Third Ingredient" where he said some backs were made for burdens. Evidently my back is one of them.* With a clenched jaw and a barely civil tone, Maggie said good-bye.

She resigned herself to the fact that her Aunt Barbara wouldn't be any help. After all, her aunt had reasoned, she had a family and Maggie didn't. But Barbara's five children were all married and on their own, with the exception of Jason, who had graduated from high school in June. Still seething, Maggie's mouth twisted. That didn't leave her aunt exactly "tied down." She took a deep breath, trying to get her emotions under control, only partially succeeding. There was no question that she would take care of Gram. She wanted to, but she hated the mindset that some apparently believed: if one was single and didn't appear to have a life, they had all the time in the world. This, she reasoned, was not the 1800s when the *maiden* aunt was always the caregiver. Finally, when she'd calmed down, she returned to the living room.

Settling into the easy chair, Maggie reached for the TV remote. "Want to watch TV?"

The color was returning to Gram's face, and she looked stronger. "We can start with *Jim Lehrer's News Hour.* Later we can watch *Lawrence Welk.* I love his music."

Maggie smiled in amusement, knowing that before the evening was over, Gram would have told her about how she'd danced to Lawrence Welk's band live at the Aragon Ballroom, and that some of his group were members of the Church.

After she had turned the TV on to Jim Lehrer, she reached for the roast beef sandwich she'd made earlier. She was glad to see Gram had eaten nearly half of hers, hoping maybe her appetite was returning. A sense of relief began replacing the anger, and she started to relax.

Paying little attention to the TV, Maggie plotted out some more adventures of Blanche and Ruby. She'd remembered earlier that she'd left her computer on, but she assumed it could run all night without breaking down.

The ten o'clock news ended, and Gram stood. "Time to call it a day. And what a day it's been." She headed for her bedroom. "I've got a nightgown you can wear."

"Since you're five feet three inches tall and I'm five feet six, I doubt I'll fit into it." Maggie grinned at the retreating figure of the petite woman.

"At least try it," Gram insisted from down the hall.

"Okay." Maggie knew it was no use arguing any further. She turned out the lights and followed her into the bedroom.

Gram handed her a filmy purple gown that looked like it might fit. Once upstairs, Maggie shed her clothes and attempted to slip the gown on. She got it pulled down to her bust, but she couldn't get the gown any further without tearing it. When she tried taking it off, she couldn't get it to budge. *Great! What a predicament. Hogtied by a purple nightgown. This is what happens when I attempt to get a size-ten body into a size-four nightgown.* Finally, after slowly inching the material up, she managed to set herself free. She found one of her granddad's old shirts in the closet and put that on.

After praying, she lay on her back and thought of the day. From what she had seen, Thursdays were jinxed. Next week she thought she'd just skip the day altogether.

She decided to eat at least one meal with Gram every day. She didn't feel comfortable not having daily personal contact with her. She frowned. Was this the beginning of her decline? What would Aunt Barbara want to do if Gram could no longer stay alone? Expect

Maggie to take care of her? Or put her in a nursing home? Maggie shook her head against the pillows. She'd never let Gram go to a home.

* * *

Maggie couldn't believe it when the next week passed without any further problems. Gram felt safe enough to stay alone on Friday and urged Maggie to return home. She did, but still ate lunch every day with Gram and spent all day Sunday with her. For the first time, she comprehended just how mortal Gram was. Who knew how much longer she might be with them?

On the twenty-fourth she went over to Gram's to take her to see Dr. Rosenberg. The minute she walked in, she could tell some calamity had happened.

"Maggie! Thank goodness you're here! Where have you been? I've been trying to get ahold of you all morning." Gram frowned at her granddaughter. "I don't have enough peaches to make Dr. Rosenberg's pie." Now she looked horror-stricken. "I can't go without his pie. Run to the store and get some more frozen peaches!"

Her words were coming so fast that Maggie could barely understand her. When what she wanted sank in, Maggie glanced at her watch. Getting the pie baked in time was going to mean taking the doctor a pie right out of the oven.

"Gram, I don't think there's enough time."

Gram responded by gritting her teeth, her body rigid with determination, and her eyes narrowed. Maggie could tell convincing her wouldn't be easy. "He'll understand. You can take him one next time."

"Go get those peaches," she demanded. "A promise is a promise."

"Okay." Maggie knew it would be easier to give in now than after they'd argued about it. She grabbed her purse and ran to the car and into the store. When she returned, Gram made the pie and put it in the oven. Maggie doubted it had time enough to bake, but she remained silent.

Gram finished getting ready, and when she checked the pie, it wasn't done. "What are we going to do now?" She looked at Maggie.

"Let's turn the oven off, and the pie can finish cooking. You can take him one next time. I know he'll understand." She patted Gram's shoulder and lightly rubbed her back.

Her grandmother jerked away from her. "*You* don't understand! I'm not going without that pie!"

Maggie looked at her watch again. They had twenty minutes to get there. Since it took that long to drive to the hospital, and then there was the added time of getting to the clinic, they simply couldn't wait any longer. "Sorry, Gram, but we can't wait for the pie, and you *are* going." The firmness of her voice made it obvious that she would not acquiesce to her grandmother's demands. She reached over and turned the oven off. "Let's go." Putting her arm around Gram, she gently propelled her out the door and into the car.

Her grandmother didn't resist, but she didn't speak to Maggie the entire time it took them to reach the clinic.

When Dr. Rosenberg entered the examination room, he held out his hand and shook the elderly woman's, looking her straight in the eye. "Hi, Isabelle, how are you doing?" Even his warm greeting didn't melt the icy look on her face.

"I've been better." She eyed Maggie indignantly. "Thanks to Maggie, I didn't get your peach pie finished."

"Me!" Maggie was shocked at the accusation, but felt like laughing at the expression on Gram's face. "I'm the one who went to the store for you!"

"Yes, but if you'd been home instead of gallivanting all over creation, you could have gone earlier." She turned back to Dr. Rosenberg. "Blame her that you don't have peach pie to eat tonight. But you'll have one next time I come—that's for sure."

"I look forward to it." His eyes gleamed with mischief. "But don't you think you'd better forgive Maggie? You never know when you might need her to run to the store for you."

She shrugged. "The problem with Maggie is she's been single too long."

"Gram! What does that have to do with peach pie?" She could feel the blood rush to her face, and she didn't know if it was from embarrassment or wrath.

"Nothing," Gram said slyly. "It was just an observation."

"Well, keep them to yourself," Maggie returned, knowing she wasn't likely to. Gram had always said exactly what was on her mind.

Dr. Rosenberg laughed. "Isabelle, you're too much, and I love it!" He continued examining her. At hearing his words, a self-satisfied smile lit her grandmother's face.

"You're doing great. I want you to have some blood work done, but unless it tells us something negative, I'd say you're doing pretty darn well for an eighty-year-old."

His words made Maggie nearly giddy with relief.

Once they were finished and in the car, Isabelle said, "What is wrong with you, Maggie May? Dr. Rosenberg is single and you're single. Make some moves, girl. Don't you know how to flirt?"

Maggie sighed. Gram was back to normal. "No, Gram. You tell me how."

Her grandmother sighed too, but it was more of an expression of her exasperation with Maggie. "Smile, girl, smile! Let him know that you're available! You act like you're only my chauffeur, not a warm-hearted, breathing, exciting woman."

"Most people don't find fourth-grade teachers exciting." She kept her eyes on the road.

"You're right, they don't," Gram said agreeably.

Surprised at her response, Maggie shot Gram a glance.

Gram was staring at her critically. "Why don't you try wearing more makeup? You have beautiful eyes, but you need to put on more eyeshadow and mascara so they stand out. In fact, it wouldn't hurt to do something more with your hair. Are those curly mops still in style?"

"Wow, Gram, is there anything about me that you *do* like?" Maggie meant the question to be rhetorical. She wasn't worried about what her grandmother thought about her. She knew she loved her.

"I like everything about you, Maggie May. But most men don't see beyond the wrapping, and we want Dr. Rosenberg to see that you're something special. You need some flash and dash! Make an appointment with a beautician, and I'll pay for it. Are there people who do makeup?"

"Sure." Her grandmother's machinations amused her.

"Make an appointment with them, and I'll pay for that too." Maggie grinned, knowing that nothing would stop Gram's plans.

"Gram, I will not let you spend your entire social security check on me," Maggie said with a smile. "And that's how much it would take to do me over. I go on the theory that a man has to take me as I am."

"Fine. After you've married him, you can revert back, but for right now you need to make some changes. You need to look like a sophisticated woman who'd be the perfect wife for a doctor." Gram nodded her head, apparently in agreement with herself.

"We'll see." Actually, she admitted, she did need to do something about her hair. Maggie had worn it curly and chin length for years because it looked good and was easy to fix. But somewhere she'd heard that "easy to fix" should never be a criteria for how a woman wore her hair.

"Why don't you get blond streaks in it? I think you'd look good—like a California golden girl."

Maggie's head jerked back in surprise. "Gram, where did you hear a phrase like 'California golden girl'? You're eighty years old."

"There's a lot of life left in the old girl yet," she said dryly. "Where do you think I heard it? *Oprah,* of course. They were discussing Christie Brinkley."

"I'm no Christie Brinkley, so maybe we'll dispense with the sun streaks." More and more she realized there was little in the way of popular culture that her grandmother wasn't aware of, and it was likely due to *Oprah.*

They turned in the drive. Gram quickly got out and practically raced to the house to check on the pie. It was perfect—golden-brown and still warm. She cut them each a slice and put ice cream on it.

"Delicious, Gram. I'm glad Dr. Rosenberg didn't get this and we got to eat it instead," she said, eating her last forkful.

"Me too." Gram laid her fork on the plate. "Now you get busy and get those appointments made."

"I will." Maggie stood. "Anything else I can do for you before I leave?"

"Not a thing, Maggie May. See you tomorrow." Gram smiled happily at her.

After kissing her grandmother, she left.

* * *

At nine o'clock that night, Maggie quit writing and stretched out on her sofa. What a day it had been: the pie, the comment to Dr.

Rosenberg, the suggestion for a makeover. Gram went a little far with her ideas, and while Maggie certainly didn't subscribe to the reason behind them, she had to admit Gram had made some good points. Yet no matter how good-looking or how kind he was, she wasn't interested in marrying a Jewish doctor, despite Gram's nudges. But, she figured, getting a new hairstyle ought to be fun.

The next morning she made an appointment with Cecile's stylist, which meant a three-week wait. She knew Gram probably wouldn't be happy with that.

She kept plugging away each day at her writing. Blanche and Ruby had detected through nine chapters, and they only had six more to go. It wasn't exactly on schedule, but it was better than nothing. She estimated if she completed a chapter a week, she'd have the manuscript finished by the middle of August, just in time to mail it one day and start preparing for school the next. It was the end of June, and already she looked forward to Thanksgiving vacation and a break.

Finally on Wednesday, Maggie was forced to stop her flurry of writing and clean her condo. She tended to lay everything on the hall table as she entered, and she usually never got around to moving anything until she cleaned. Today was the day because the critique group was meeting at her place tonight. Her phone rang just as she finished cleaning. The mere ringing of her phone caused her body to tense. She automatically crossed her fingers before answering.

"Maggie, are you going to be home?"

Brad! The sound of his voice didn't ease her tension. It was the first time she'd heard from him since she'd turned down his proposal, and she would have liked to put it off even longer.

"Are you going to be home? I need to discuss something with you."

She couldn't detect by his tone any crisis, so why did he need to talk in person? "Can't we talk now? I've got a heavy schedule today."

"I guess so." His reluctance was evident. "I just think apologizing is easier face-to-face."

Brad apologizing! That was a first! Stunned, she found it impossible to speak for a moment. "What for?" She could think of several things offhand, but none of them seemed like serious candidates for an apology from Brad.

"I've been thinking about my proposal the other day." His words came slowly and hesitantly. "I've missed Karen more than you'll ever know. I worry about caring for Caitlin and Robert. Without thinking it through, I thought our getting married would be an easy answer. I'd prayed about it, and I felt my own decision was a confirmation from Heavenly Father."

"Having done that myself, I realize how it can happen," Maggie inserted softly. She could understand what had happened, but his dogmatic way of blundering ahead was what she found irritating.

"We've never even liked each other, really."

Trust Brad. Maggie laughed but didn't say anything.

"Anyway, I have been thinking and praying about what I should do. I've decided not to stay in the consulting business. Caitlin and Robert need me home with them so they can have a feeling of stability. Anyway, last Friday, the company I consulted with in Memphis called. The CEO told me they'd liked my ideas, and he offered me a position."

"It sounds like a wonderful opportunity. Are you going to accept their offer?" She dreaded the thought of not having the kids close. They'd been gone less than a month, and she missed having them around.

"I know this is an answer from the Lord, and I'm going." He sounded almost humble.

Maggie couldn't believe her ears! This side of Brad was one she'd never seen before, and for the first time, she almost liked him. She had to admit he'd always been committed to the Church, and he'd always honored his priesthood.

"The company wants me there as soon as possible, preferably Monday. I've listed my house for sale, but I need to find a place for us to live in Memphis and make child-care arrangements. Maggie, I appreciate all you've done for me," he hesitated, "and I wish I didn't have to ask, but would you consider taking Robert and Caitlin for the next little while until I can get settled?"

Thinking of Gram's problems lately, she said, "Could your mother take them part of the time?"

"Mom doesn't want to because they mess up her beautiful house." Animosity edged his words. "You'd think with her only grandchildren moving a long distance away, she'd want them to stay with her, but she doesn't."

That sounded exactly like his mother, always preferring a perfect house to her own precious grandchildren. Maggie considered it ridiculous. "Don't worry, I do. When will you leave?"

"I'm hoping to get out of here Saturday morning. I'm staying at the same hotel as I did last time until I find an apartment."

"You're thinking it will be a month or so?" She'd have to schedule her time or she'd never get anything accomplished.

"I hope not, but it might stretch out that long. The Whites are going to watch the house and keep the yard up. Their yard looks like they have a full-time gardener," he laughed, "so I expect ours will be looking a lot better soon."

"I'll love having the kids again." A thrill at having them again spread through her. "Who knows how often I'll get to see them once you move."

"Thanks."

After the call, Maggie returned to her writing. She planned on writing every minute of every day until her niece and nephew arrived. Once they were with her, she'd spend her time enjoying them. She refused to be torn between her writing and the kids. They'd always come first.

To her surprise, Pat agreed, as did the rest of the group, that the only thing she could do was take Karen's children. But Maggie was determined she'd still find time for Blanche and Ruby to solve the mystery—no matter what.

Friday evening when Brad finished lugging in all the kids' paraphernalia, he looked at Caitlin and Robert playing out on the deck with their toys and turned to Maggie. "I know they'll be loved here, and that's a good feeling. I can't thank you enough." He looked at her solemnly. "I truly don't know what I'd do without you. You've been an angel."

Maggie couldn't help but be taken aback by this new Brad—and a little skeptical as well. She'd known him for nearly twenty years, and he'd never been this mellow. Putting her reservations aside, she smiled and patted his arm. "This gives me a chance to spend time with the kids, so I'm glad to do it."

"Thanks. I've got a dozen things left to do before I leave in the morning, so I'd better say good-bye and go."

Brad spent quite a while hugging and talking to Caitlin and Robert. His expression told Maggie how hard it was for him to leave them. When he finally kissed them one last time and came back into the living room, Maggie could see the moisture in his eyes.

He spoke quietly. "See you in a few weeks."

She walked him to the door. "You be careful. The kids will be fine."

He nodded and left.

This time Brad had brought their sleeping bags, so she stowed them in the already-crowded closet in her office and made room for their clothes. The toys she'd store on the deck, and she was grateful it had been screened in so the kids had someplace to play.

The next couple of days went by quickly. To celebrate the Fourth of July on Thursday, she'd taken Gram and the kids to Primate Panorama at the zoo. They'd had a wonderful time. Gram had gotten tired, but she'd taken a nap with the kids, and Maggie had written ideas for her book on a steno pad. They'd had a backyard barbecue in the evening.

Sunday they spent at church and then had lunch with Gram. After that they went home for naps and to work on memory books. Caitlin and Robert brought a delight to her life that she hadn't realized had been absent. At the thought of them leaving for good, sadness filled her. She'd miss those two when they moved.

On Tuesday, with Caitlin handing her the dishes and Robert sweeping the kitchen floor, Maggie loaded Gram's dishwasher. In an hour the kids would be taking naps, and she'd be at her computer. This was the first opportunity she'd had to do any serious writing since their arrival.

Then she heard a loud sound of something falling, and before she could move, Gram said, "Ow!"

Alarmed, Maggie threw her dishrag into the sink and dashed into the bedroom, Robert and Caitlin right behind her. She found Gram in a small heap facedown near the corner of the bed. Her hands trembling, Maggie reached over to help the frail woman off the floor. "What happened?"

"I don't know." Her voice was weak and tremulous. "I was going into the living room, and all of a sudden I found myself lying here. I don't know if I tripped or what."

Once Gram was situated on the bed, Maggie noticed a large bump on her forehead. "What did your head hit?"

"I don't know." She shook her head. "What really hurts is my foot."

Maggie glanced at her right foot. It was turning red and seemed to be swelling. "You might have hit your head on the cedar chest, but," she examined the floor thoroughly, "I don't know what you could have tripped over."

"Iaza oup eatur." Gram laughed.

Her heart nearly pounding through her chest, Maggie said, "What?"

"Iaza oup eatur." She laughed again.

 *Chapter 6*

Maggie panicked. What was happening to Gram? Her language was unintelligible, and her mouth seemed to sag. Forcing back her fear, Maggie said, "I'm going to call the paramedics. I think we should get Dr. Rosenberg to see you." She attempted to smile, but her facial muscles refused to work.

"Oney excipe." Gram shook her head. "Asur neep yak."

Maggie patted her shoulder. "Just as soon as the paramedics get here, we're going to the hospital." She turned to her niece and nephew.

"You two watch Gram while I call the doctor." Caitlin and Robert nodded solemnly as they stood wide-eyed in the doorway, intently watching the goings-on.

Maggie dialed 911 and explained to the dispatcher what had happened. She was so close to tears and so scared that she felt relieved she could get through the story once. But the woman had her repeat it twice before saying, "Stay on the line." Two minutes later, she told Maggie that the paramedics were on their way.

Hanging up, she went back into the bedroom. "How're you doing, Gram?"

She smiled. "Itsa abas tap."

Maggie's breath caught as she heard the garbled words. What was wrong with Gram's speech? Had she had a stroke? She didn't act like anything was wrong.

Apprehensive about what to do or what would happen next, Maggie seated herself on the side of the bed and stroked Gram's hands, reassuring her in a soothing tone. Nearly ten minutes later they heard the ambulance siren. Caitlin and Robert rushed to the front door to watch, with Maggie right behind them. Shooing them out of the way, Maggie opened the door to admit four paramedics. She directed them to the bedroom, and immediately the one carrying a metal box connected Gram up to a heart monitor while the other one took her vital signs. The last two motioned Maggie out of the room and asked for the details of Gram's fall. After she had repeated the story once again, the man who seemed to be in charge called back to the dispatcher to say they'd arrived and what the situation was.

Meanwhile, Caitlin and Robert had gone into the bedroom so they wouldn't miss anything. Maggie led them into the living room and turned on the TV. "You kids stay in here until we see what's wrong with Gram."

Their attention caught by Big Bird, they only nodded.

When she returned to the bedroom, one of the paramedics said, "We're going to transport her to the hospital. Which one do you want us to take her to?"

"University." University was the hospital Dr. Rosenberg was affiliated with. "I need to find someone to leave the kids with, and then I'll meet you there."

She quickly punched in Pat's number. When she answered, Maggie said, "I hate to bother you, but Gram's fallen and the paramedics are taking her to the hospital. Could I drop off Caitlin and Robert at your place on my way there?"

"Sure. Oh, Maggie, what next?" Her friend commiserated with her.

"I don't know." She sounded as forlorn as she felt. What if her grandmother never regained her speech?

She watched the paramedics load Gram into the ambulance. Not wasting any time, she whisked the kids into her car and left. The sight of Gram's frail body and her garbled speech filled her mind so much that she found it impossible to concentrate on driving. She passed Pat's street, unaware of where they were until three blocks later. She had to be strong. If she didn't get a grip, she would be completely useless to help anyone.

When they arrived, Pat rushed out and gathered up Caitlin and Robert and set them on the grass. Then she leaned in the car window, her arms resting on the door. "I called Mimi. It's her day off, and she said she'd come over and watch the kids. You need someone at the hospital with you, so I'll be up as soon as she gets here."

"Thanks, Pat. I really appreciate your daughter giving up her day off to baby-sit." The prospect of not facing this problem by herself released some of her tension. She'd found the crises of the last few weeks difficult to deal with alone.

"Oh, you know Mimi. She loves kids and plans on having a good time with them. Where are they taking Isabelle?" Pat's everyday tone was reassuring.

"University Hospital." Maggie blinked back her seemingly ever-present tears and made herself sound matter-of-fact, telling herself it was ridiculous to fall apart over the name of the hospital.

"See you in a few minutes." Pat waved and turned toward the house. Caitlin and Robert ran up the sidewalk ahead of her as Maggie drove away.

The hospital was twenty minutes away from Pat's, and on arriving at the emergency room, she found a waiting room full of people. Ignoring them, she went directly to the admittance clerk, who asked her for a Medicare card, which she didn't have. Luckily, because Gram had gone to Dr. Rosenberg, her medical information was already in the computer. Finally getting into the ER itself, Maggie discovered that the ambulance hadn't arrived yet.

She glanced at her watch. It had been nearly thirty minutes since she'd left home to come up here. What could be keeping them? Surely they could make better time than she could. Unable to sit patiently, she paced back and forth while she waited. About two minutes later, the paramedics wheeled her grandmother in, one man carrying some vials of blood. They quickly assigned her a room, and Maggie followed them into it.

The paramedic put the blood on the counter. "We were held up while we drew blood."

Gram seemed more alert, but she didn't say anything. A nurse came in and wrapped a flannel sheet around her and asked her what had happened. Gram remained silent, so Maggie described the fall and the results.

"Her doctor is David Rosenberg. Please call him." Maggie attempted not to sound bossy, but the nurse looked annoyed anyway.

"I'll check with the ER doctor, but first we need to have some blood drawn," she said briskly, leaving the room.

"Just a minute," Maggie spoke up, and the nurse turned toward her. "The paramedics took blood in the ambulance."

She blew off Maggie's response. "We only use blood we've drawn ourselves."

Maggie hated to see Gram stuck some more. She looked so defenseless lying there on the examination table. She clasped her grandmother's cold hands in hers. "Are you warm enough?"

The white head nodded weakly.

A young, good-looking man in a white coat came in and immediately stuck his hand out to shake Maggie's. "I'm Dr. Grant. What seems to be the problem here?"

She told him what had happened.

Dr. Grant seemed to listen intently, and then he moved over to Gram, smiling down at her. "How are you this afternoon? I'm Dr. Grant." He reached over and shook her hand.

Gram roused slightly from her lethargy and attempted a flirty smile, but the side of her mouth drooped, and she hesitated for a long time, trying to get the words out. Then she said, "Fine."

Dr. Grant smiled back at her and continued listening to her heart and taking her pulse. "You'll be glad to know Dr. Rosenberg is in the hospital and will be down in a few minutes."

Maggie sighed a breath of relief.

"I'm going to order some tests so we'll know just exactly what we're looking at here." He smiled reassuringly at both of them and left the room. Pat walked in a moment later. Maggie was so grateful to see her that she burst into tears.

Seeing the tears, her friend asked anxiously, "Is Isabelle all right?"

"I don't know. I can understand her a little better, but her speech isn't normal." She shook her head. "After the scare she gave us, she tried to flirt with the doctor and managed to tell him she was fine."

Pat smiled encouragingly. "Just relax and know that Isabelle must be recovering if she can still perk up when she meets a handsome man." She hugged Maggie to reassure her.

While they were waiting in the doorway of the small cubicle, they saw Dr. Rosenberg get off the elevator and confer with Dr. Grant before greeting them. "I'm sorry about Isabelle. Let's hope this isn't serious and we can send her home." He squeezed Maggie's arm and went on into the room. Pat and Maggie followed him.

His eyes twinkled as he looked down at the elderly lady. "Hi, Isabelle. Did you bring the peach pie?"

"No, but I making one." Her mouth still drooped.

"I can't wait, so we'll have to get you out of here in a hurry so you can." He picked up her arm and asked her to squeeze his hand. She couldn't.

The orderlies arrived and lifted Gram onto the gurney. Dr. Rosenberg reassured her, "They aren't too busy in radiology, so you shouldn't be long."

He watched them wheel her to the elevator and then turned to Maggie. "I've got more rounds to make, so I'll leave you here, and they will call me as soon as they have the test results." He gave Maggie a compassionate look. "I know it's impossible right now, but try not to worry. Your grandmother is feisty and a fighter. I think she'll come through this." After giving her forearm another pat, he left.

Pat and Maggie tried to make themselves comfortable in the waiting room's naugahyde chairs, but since the arms were metal tubes, it was nearly impossible. They ended up just sitting across from each other looking straight ahead.

Pat watched Maggie's face relax. "I'm sure you haven't had a minute to think, but you probably should make some plans."

"As soon as I know what Gram's prognosis is, I'll call Aunt Barbara. I hope she'll be able to come out here." What if she couldn't? Maggie wouldn't even let herself consider that possibility.

"I can take the kids." As busy as she was, Pat actually looked enthused about it.

Right now Maggie felt brain-dead, but she agreed with Pat that some things did need to be decided. She said slowly, "I think I'll put them back in nursery school—for the mornings anyway. If things are tense, maybe you could pick them up at noon and bring them home. Once we know how long Gram will be in the hospital, we'll have a better idea of what we're doing."

Pat spoke decisively. "We'll all pitch in, because some way, somehow, you are taking the time to get your book completed. I don't have another deadline for a couple of months, and I'll help."

Maggie's eyes were brimming with tears. "Thanks, Pat. In our mission the rule was, 'Tell your companions you appreciate them.' I appreciate you. Don't ever forget it!"

Pat brushed her comment aside with a grin. "Thanks. The feeling is mutual."

"Maggie Summers, please report to the admittance desk. Maggie Summers to the admittance desk." The announcement startled Maggie, and her heart leaped as she heard her name. Rushing out of her seat, she hurried to the desk with Pat right behind her.

The woman at the station smiled. "Your grandmother's back from x-ray and in that cubicle right over there." She pointed to another section of the emergency room. "The doctor has been called and should be here any time." She buzzed the door open and they entered. When they reached the curtained room, they found Gram asleep, so they sat on some folding chairs while waiting for Dr. Rosenberg.

He came in holding a sheaf of folders containing x-rays. "It was what we expected. The CAT scan shows that your grandmother suffered a stroke. We've started her on medication that should relieve the symptoms, and while it will be slow, we're hoping for a full recovery."

Maggie had stood when he came in, and while his message made her feel as though a weight had been lifted from her shoulders, oddly enough, the news also left her weak-kneed. Without conscious thought, she sank back down in her chair and looked up at him.

Dr. Rosenberg smiled. "It's a good thing you brought her in so quickly. We were able to start the medicine in time to help her. We're taking her to the neurology unit for tonight. The neurologist will want to run more tests this afternoon and tomorrow. We'll see how she is after that before we decide on a release date."

He patted her shoulder. "Don't worry. We'll take good care of her. I think she'll probably sleep most of the afternoon, so you might want to leave and come back later."

"Thank you, Doctor." At last the strength was returning to her legs.

"See you later." He left them and walked back down the hall.

When the orderlies came to move Gram, Maggie and Pat followed behind to the neurology floor. Once in the room, Maggie stood watching her grandmother sleep for a few minutes. They had put her on oxygen, and fluids ran through tubes into her wrist. Despite the doctor's reassuring words, she was still scared Gram wouldn't recover. What would she do then? She glanced at her watch and then at Pat. "It's after two o'clock. I think I'll go home and call Aunt Barbara."

"Good idea. Why don't I bring the kids back to Isabelle's later tonight? We'll feed them first, et cetera, so you won't have the hassle." Pat retrieved her purse off the nightstand.

"You'd better call first to make sure I'm home, so your trip over won't be a wasted effort." Maggie moved to the edge of the bed and leaned over to kiss Gram's pale cheek.

"Okay." Pat gave Isabelle a sympathetic look, and they left together for the parking lot.

Getting into her car, Maggie sighed, hoping that somehow she'd get through this. She didn't have Aunt Barbara's phone number, so she'd have to go to Gram's and get her address book. It turned out the book contained both Barbara's office and her home phone numbers. When she couldn't reach anyone at home, she tried her aunt's work number.

"Aunt Barbara?" After she acknowledged who she was, Maggie plowed on, "Gram's had a stroke and has been hospitalized."

"Oh no!" Her aunt's shock was obvious. "When did it happen?"

"About noon. She's at University Hospital, and they don't know how long she'll be there. I think you'd better come." Maggie forced herself to speak calmly, although she hoped her aunt would sense how urgent it was.

"Don't worry, I'll be on the first flight I can get. As soon as I know what time I leave, I'll call you."

"If I'm not here, leave a message on the machine. I'll pick you up," Maggie said, already wondering what she was going to do with the kids.

"That's too much trouble. I'll rent a car. I love you, Maggie, and I appreciate all you do for Mom. See you later tonight." She hung up.

A rush of relief flooded Maggie. Now she had someone else to help make the decisions. Gathering up her purse and a book, she left for the hospital again.

When she arrived back at the hospital room, Gram was still asleep. Maggie made herself comfortable and attempted to read, but she found it impossible to concentrate. Her mind drifted, and she wondered what was happening to her grandmother. Gram dozed off and on for the next few hours. She'd wake up for a couple of minutes and then be out again.

A neurologist came by to check on her and told Maggie she might as well go home for the evening. At 8:00 P.M., Maggie left. She decided to pick up Caitlin and Robert on her way to Gram's and save Pat the trip. She found Barbara had left a message that she would be arriving in Denver at 8:45 P.M. Checking her watch, she saw that it was already 9:00 P.M., so if the plane were on time, Barbara should be in Denver. It would take at least an hour for her to get in town from the airport.

The kids made no fuss when she put them to bed. Mimi had taken them to the zoo again, and they were happy but tired and ready for bed.

She changed the sheets on her grandmother's bed and collapsed onto the couch. What a day it had been! Worry about her grandmother gnawed at her. If she didn't recover fully from this stroke, how would they care for her? Would Aunt Barbara want to take her to live with her? Somehow she doubted it. She suspected Gram didn't have enough income to hire someone to stay with her full-time, and what with teaching school all day, Maggie herself would not be there enough to be any real help. She sighed, hoping against hope her aunt would have a plan. She closed her eyes. *Oh Father, please let Gram recover from this stroke.*

She heard a car pull into the driveway, and she guessed it was probably Aunt Barbara. Getting up, she went to the kitchen and looked out the window. Sure enough, Barbara was getting her bag out. Maggie opened the front door just as she walked onto the porch. "Aunt Barbara, I'm glad you're here." Maggie flung her arms around her, and her aunt hugged her back.

Barbara followed Maggie into the living room, where she made herself comfortable on the sofa. Taking a deep breath, she said, "Okay, tell me what's been happening. How's Mom tonight?"

"Well, like they say, 'She's resting comfortably.' Tomorrow they'll probably have a better idea of what's ahead for her. This morning she fell and couldn't get up. She also couldn't speak intelligibly. I called the paramedics, and they rushed her to University Hospital. Her doctor's affiliated there, and he's outstanding."

Barbara looked perplexed. "Did this just come on suddenly?"

"Well, unusual things have been happening to Gram for the last six weeks, culminating in a stroke today." She went on to fill Barbara in on all the disturbing incidents with Gram.

"Why didn't you call me?" Barbara demanded. "I would have come sooner."

"We did call you. Don't you remember?" Maggie refused to let her aunt lay a guilt trip on her.

"Yes, but Mom acted like it was nothing." Barbara looked accusingly at Maggie.

"Of course, and the incidents were mostly worrisome. Do you remember telling me it was good I could handle it since I was single and had the summer off?" That remark still rankled.

Barbara looked flustered. "Well, I'm here now, so we can work things out together. Let's get to bed. I imagine tomorrow is going to be a demanding day."

"I changed the sheets on Gram's bed, and you can sleep in her room if you'd like. Karen's kids and I have kind of staked out the other two bedrooms."

"Karen's kids?" The demanding tone was back in Barbara's voice. "Why on earth do you have them? Where's their dad?"

"It's a long story, and we can go into it tomorrow. Suffice it to say, they'll be with me at least a couple more weeks."

"Maggie, you're too good to people. You shouldn't let them take advantage of you." Barbara still sounded irritated about Maggie having the kids.

"That may be, but it doesn't change things right now. Good night. I'll see you in the morning." Tired beyond belief, Maggie dragged herself up the stairs, anxious to fall into bed. After a lengthy prayer, she did just that. But she was still wound up from the day's events, and sleep didn't come easily. She checked her watch at 1:00 and then turned over, trying to find a spot in the bed that would soothe her to sleep.

* * *

"Aunt Maggie," Caitlin whispered, her mouth against her aunt's ear.

Maggie's eyes shot open, her heart beating furiously. "What?!"

Looking startled, Caitlin continued whispering, "Someone's in Gram's bed." Behind her, Robert nodded.

Feeling as if she hadn't had any rest, let alone sleep, Maggie glanced at the clock and groaned. Seven o'clock. She looked at the kids and whispered, "Could it be Goldilocks?"

Caitlin's eyes grew wider, and she shook her head solemnly. "No."

Robert echoed, "No."

"Then it must be your Aunt Barbara, Gram's daughter. Gram's in the hospital, remember? Aunt Barbara came to visit her."

"Does she have any kids?" Caitlin looked hopeful.

"Five, all big. So you won't have anyone to play with. How about crawling in bed with me, and we'll lie here a few more minutes so I can rest a little bit." She wished they'd drift off to sleep, but she knew the chances were slim.

The two dutifully crawled into the bed, one on either side of Maggie. "How long do we have to stay here?" Caitlin asked, scrunching up her entire face in order to hold her eyes closed.

"Ten minutes." Maggie wished. She closed her eyes.

A second later, Caitlin shook her arm and leaned over her. "Is it time?"

Refusing to open her eyes, she murmured, "No. Now rest."

"I want to get up." Robert slipped out from under the covers and stood at the side of the bed.

"Me too." Caitlin crept out the other side.

Maggie groaned again. "Pretend you're cats and sneak down to the living room, then very softly turn on the TV." They both grinned and stood on tippy toes to slink downstairs. She was usually critical of parents who let the TV baby-sit their children, but what a blessing it had been lately. She turned over, hoping for just a few more minutes to sleep.

Thirty minutes later, Maggie woke up again, and this time she got up. After a shower she felt as if she might be able to make it through the day. She put on some faded jeans, a pink T-shirt, and tied her Nikes, confident she could handle whatever the day presented. Then she went downstairs.

She didn't find any sign of Barbara, so she assumed her aunt was still asleep. She could understand how flying across the country, on top of one's mother having a stroke, would wear a person out.

She smiled as she watched the two towheads intently observing Big Bird and Cookie Monster. "Come on, kids, let's get ready for school." She hoped Caitlin's preschool would readmit them without any fuss.

They whirled around. "School? We get to go to school?"

When Maggie nodded, they jumped up and ran eagerly to her, pulling on her hands to hurry her back to their room. "I love school." Caitlin's eyes gleamed happily.

"I love school. I get to sweep." Robert yanked harder on her arm.

They were so excited that in no time at all she had them ready and at the dining room table. Barbara came out just then. Robert looked at her carefully. "Not Goldilocks." He looked at Maggie and Caitlin. "We not Three Bears."

"Want a blueberry pancake? I'm fixing them for the kids." Maggie gave the batter a final stir.

"Sounds good." She looked at the kids. "My name's Aunt Barbara. Do you know I have some grandkids just your age? What are your names?"

"I'm Caitlin, and I'm this many." She held up five fingers.

"I thought so. My granddaughter's named Missy, and she's exactly that many too. What is your name?" She turned to Robert.

"Robert. I'm three." He held up three fingers.

"Robert. What a great name. My grandson is named Jake." She smiled warmly at the children, and their eyes lit up the smiles on their faces. "Where are you off to this morning?"

"School!" they yelled in unison.

* * *

"I wonder what Dr. Rosenberg will recommend." Maggie leaned against the wall outside Gram's room a week later, trying to read the expression on Barbara's face. She hated to have negative feelings, and she certainly couldn't fault her aunt for her reactions so far, but she kept waiting for something unexpected to happen.

"I haven't a clue, but I would like to get the decisions made so I can return home. I can't stay out here forever," Barbara said firmly.

Instinctively, Maggie smiled at Dr. Rosenberg as he came into the hall. Gram was right—he did have the romantic hero persona, and Maggie wished she weren't aware of the fact. She knew just having him for a doctor would speed up Gram's recovery. "How's she doing?"

"Pretty good. She'll probably be ready to be released tomorrow, but she's going to need therapy. We have no idea how long the aphasia will last or the general weakness of her body, so it would be better if you found a rehabilitation center for her until she's recovered more." His glance included Barbara. "The hospital social worker has a list of ones you might want to check out."

Maggie frowned. However, Barbara looked relieved. "Are you thinking this will be a permanent placement?"

Seething at her aunt's reaction, Maggie said, "No!" She spoke so vehemently that both the doctor and her aunt looked at her in amazement.

"What?" Surprised by her outburst, they practically spoke in unison.

"It would be easier for me to have her at home than to have to visit her every day in a care facility." Her words were terse.

"Why would you have to go every day? I would think two or three times a week would be often enough," Dr. Rosenberg reassured her. "At a rehabilitation center, she could have therapy every day."

"Unless she wants to go, we're not even considering it." Maggie's words were decisive.

Barbara considered Maggie. "I can't stay here and take care of her. You and I both know that she wouldn't be happy in Atlanta. Denver is her home."

Furious at her aunt's attitude, Maggie didn't bother to disguise her feelings. "So what you're saying is just dump her off at a nursing home and forget about her? Oh, yes, I can visit her a couple of times a week." She glared at them both. "That's easy for you two to say because you won't be dealing with her. Denver might be her home, but she won't be happy in a nursing facility. Of course, since you're not here, you won't have to hear her beg to go home every time you visit." Maggie shot them both a stubborn look and clenched her fists. "I'm not going to go through that every day."

"Maggie, your intentions are good, but you have no idea what you're undertaking." Dr. Rosenberg sounded adamant, no longer the warmhearted doctor but rather an authority figure who knew exactly what she should do. "Until she is stronger, it will be like caring for a baby, and a fussy one at that. Strokes often times change the victim's personality." He had an implacable expression on his face. "As a doctor, I'm aware of elderly patients' problems and how hard they are for the family to deal with. You need skilled nursing assistance." Then he added what he obviously thought was the *pièce de résistance,* "Don't forget, you have your own life to lead."

"You can put your family in any kind of home you wish to, Dr. Rosenberg, but I will not put my grandmother in a nursing home." Maggie's words shot out like angry pellets.

Dr. Rosenberg looked startled, and Barbara looked embarrassed.

Maggie continued, "You're right, I do have my own life to lead. So I'm going to do what will be easiest for me." She could tell neither one of them would be any help to her. "How long will she need therapy?"

Dr. Rosenberg shook his head. "At her age, it's unpredictable how much she will recover, but I doubt she will ever be able to live alone again."

"He's the expert, Maggie." Barbara's voice was condescending. "We should follow his advice." She gave him an appreciative smile.

Disregarding her aunt's opinion, she said, "I'll check with the social worker and see what our options are for home care. I'm going to visit Gram for a minute. Coming, Aunt Barbara?" She turned to her grandmother's door.

"Just a minute." Barbara had taken hold of Dr. Rosenberg's arm.

Once inside the room, Maggie took a deep breath in an effort to appear calm. She glanced at the small, white-haired woman, and her breath caught. Poor Gram! She looked lost in the white sheets. "Hi, Gram." She picked up her cold hand and rubbed it, trying to get the blood circulating.

"Maggie." It took great effort on Isabelle's part, but she got the name out. She smiled at her granddaughter, but the left side of her mouth still drooped.

Maggie gave her a wide smile, blinking back the tears. She couldn't stand to think of her beloved Gram in this state. "Hey, we've got some exciting news! You're getting out of here tomorrow!"

Gram's eyes flashed, and her face lit up. "I glad."

"What do you think about going to a rehabilitation center for a few days so you can get therapy?" Maggie perched on the edge of the bed, still massaging her grandmother's hand. "I would be there every day."

Gram's eyes narrowed, and she frowned before shaking her head firmly. "No."

Barbara came in and picked up her mom's other hand. "Mom, you don't have a choice. Dr. Rosenberg thinks you'd get better care and more help in a convalescent center."

"No!" Tears filled Gram's eyes as she continued to shake her head.

"Don't worry, Gram. You don't have to go anywhere you don't want to." Maggie bent over and kissed both of her grandmother's soft cheeks. "I'd like to have you home in your own bed myself. I'm going now, love, so I can check out some other possibilities."

Gram smiled again and nodded. "Y-es."

"Are you coming with me, Aunt Barbara?" Maggie didn't know if it would be better or worse to have her along.

Barbara looked reluctant, but she said, "Okay." Giving her mother a kiss, she followed Maggie.

"We'll see you later, darling Gram." She waved at her, and they left.

As they walked down the hall, Barbara said determinedly, "Personally, Maggie, I think you're insane to even contemplate taking Mom home. We can't afford full-time nursing for her, and you keep reminding me that once school starts, you won't be around. Besides, you've got Karen's children to take care of. Give her time. Once she's settled in, Mom will get used to the nursing home."

Irritated once more at Barbara's attitude, Maggie stiffened. "I doubt it. I had some sisters in a nursing home whom I visit taught, and believe me, they never got used to it. They couldn't understand why they couldn't go home, and if they couldn't go home, they wanted to die. I will *not*—and I repeat, *not*—put Gram through that as long as I'm able to care for her."

"I'm sure you can manage for the summer, but in the fall . . ." Barbara's words trailed off, and she shrugged. "Then what?" She shook her head. "I know I probably sound cold to you, but I have a family to care for myself, so there's no way I can have Mom live with me. Since I'm at work all day, she'd be by herself. You heard what Dr. Rosenberg said. She can't live alone. If we find a nice place for her to live now, everything will be in place when school starts. Eventually Mom will adjust." Her tone was decisive, leaving no room for argument.

Outrage consumed Maggie. She fought to get her emotions under control, then turned to Barbara and said coldly, "Forget it. Gram is not going into a nursing home. We're almost to the social worker's office. Are you coming in with me?" She continued staring at her until finally Barbara nodded.

At the encouraging advice from the social worker, a glimmer of hope permeated the bleak feeling that had consumed Maggie since Gram's stroke. He called a home-nursing agency and set up an appointment for the next day, explained the costs and what Medicare paid, and, at Barbara's insistence, gave her a list of assisted-living facilities. They left his office with information, pamphlets, lists, and phone numbers.

Certain that things could be worked out, Maggie said, "I think this will be manageable."

Barbara had been silent for the most part in the social worker's office, and Maggie thought she'd finally accepted the idea.

Then Barbara stopped her niece and said angrily, "What are you trying to do, Maggie, with your blind determination to keep Mom at home? Make me look like I don't care about her?"

At her words, all the aggravation of the summer burst in Maggie. "*I'm* not doing whatever's expedient so I don't have to be bothered with Gram. You were 'willing' to leave her in my hands for the summer since I had vacation." Her tone was sarcastic. "It's amazing how people are 'willing' to plan my summer so they don't have to put themselves out. Since you aren't moving here, and you don't want your mother living with you—"

"There's no one to stay with her!" Barbara's angry words interrupted Maggie.

"I understand! But since I'm going to have the care of Gram, I'm going to do what's easiest for me, and a nursing home isn't." She forced herself to soften her voice. "I know you love Gram. I'm honestly not trying to make you look bad. If this doesn't work, then we'll have to consider a facility of some kind, but let me give this a try," she pleaded. Having vented her feelings, Maggie's frustration with her aunt lessened.

Barbara nodded her agreement. "I feel torn apart by Mom's stroke. I want to stay here with her, but I just can't. If I did take her home, she'd probably beg every day to come back here." She took a deep breath. "I'll see what I can work out so you won't have to struggle by yourself."

They picked up the kids at day care. Once they were home and Robert and Caitlin were down for naps, Maggie started calling the numbers she'd been given. By supper time she'd had the home-nursing agency coming to evaluate Gram for services, and had physical, occupational, and speech therapists all scheduled. She'd found out in the course of her calls that if a person required skilled nursing care once a week, they were entitled to an aide who would come in as often as needed to bathe them and take care of their needs.

"Yessss!" She pumped her arm. This would work out.

Chapter 7

"Here, let me help you, Gram." Maggie grabbed the side of the wheelchair to help Barbara lift it up the porch steps. They'd kept Gram a day longer than expected in the hospital, and they were just now able to bring her home. "Whee!" Maggie said as they sat the wheelchair down. "This is just like a ride on a roller coaster."

"And scary." Lines pinched Gram's forehead, making her apprehension at being maneuvered up the steps this way apparent.

Once they were inside, Maggie leaned down and asked, "Where do you want to go—the living room or your bedroom?"

"Think I'll lie down for while." She chuckled, but the sound had little humor in it. "Never realize riding in wheelchair be so tiring!"

Barbara wheeled her into the bedroom, and both she and Maggie helped Gram onto the bed. "Lie on top, and I'll put a coverlet over you." She reached over and took a lavender-and-lace print quilt off the rack and gently laid it over her mother.

Maggie leaned against the doorway watching, wondering how this would work out in the end. She could foresee little help from Barbara. There was little she could do from Atlanta, but Maggie wondered about even her moral support. She had a feeling that once Barbara was back home, she'd become immersed in her own life and feel that her mother was in capable hands—thereby assuming she didn't need to give her a second thought. Her heart dropped. She hoped that wouldn't be the case.

"Tanks, you considerate." Tears moistened Gram's eyes. "I glad you came. I getting old. It good to have daughter with me."

Making herself comfortable in a chair covered with large, splashy roses, Barbara gave her a loving smile. "I wish I could stay longer."

Gram lay there, her blue eyes intent on the tropical bird prints hanging on the wall across from the bed. "I jus glad you came. I not be alone when you leave. Maggie be here."

Gram had been working with a speech therapist at the hospital, but she still stumbled over words and forgot others.

"Maggie's a very special person, and we're lucky to have her." Barbara glanced at her niece and smiled.

Maggie returned her smile. "Thanks." She hated to be cynical, but she still doubted Barbara's sincerity, figuring her aunt was just grateful to have Maggie there because it meant she didn't have to stay herself. Maggie shook her head in an effort to dispel her negative feelings, knowing that somehow she had to get over the irritation that Barbara evoked in her.

Gram's eyelids fluttered closed as she murmured, "We are . . ."

They watched her for a few more minutes as she drifted off to sleep, and then both of them quietly left the room. Once they were in the living room, Barbara said, "I am glad you're here. I've been checking Mom's finances, and she doesn't have enough money to last more than three years if we put her in an assisted-living residence. They are so expensive. Of course, we could always sell this house, but I hate to—so many memories. Unfortunately, right now I can't help out financially. We have Jason at BYU this fall, and we promised to help Andrea and Bob with their down payment on a home. It's hard being caught in the middle of generations. Our kids on one side, Mom on the other. Steve wants to retire in five years, but I don't know if we'll be able to or not."

Maggie realized then why Barbara had agreed to bring Gram home. She wanted to retire in five years without having to help support her mother or have her live with them. Maggie felt like rolling her eyes, but she kept her face emotionless.

"I wish I could stay longer, but I have an important report due, so I just have to get back to Atlanta tonight." Barbara sank back against the sofa pillows and sighed. "I'm glad I can leave her in good hands."

"I can understand your feelings, but school starts in a few weeks, and then, unless she gets stronger, we're going to have to have more nursing help." Maggie fought to keep her voice pleasant. She didn't want to be at odds with Barbara.

"I've been thinking about it, and I think you should move in permanently with Mom. That way you wouldn't have any expenses, and we wouldn't need a night nurse." She gave Maggie a satisfied look as if to say all their problems were solved. She probably thought Maggie had nothing else to do with her evenings.

She stiffened. "I have a condo, remember?"

Barbara shrugged. "Rent it. It would be a nice investment for you."

Maggie didn't dismiss the idea entirely, but she didn't know if she was ready to take on her grandmother's complete care. "I'll keep it in mind."

Her aunt nodded. "I know you can work things out." She glanced at her watch. "My plane leaves in a little over four hours, so I'd better finish packing."

Barbara moved in the same graceful way that Maggie's mother had, which sent pangs of her own loss colliding through her body. She blinked back her tears, knowing that today wasn't the day to be cascaded with memories of her own family, her mother in particular. She stood. "I'll go pick up Caitlin and Robert while you pack, and then we won't have to leave Gram alone."

"Good idea. I'll see you later."

Maggie watched her aunt disappear into the hallway, and then, boosting herself out of the recliner, she left for the preschool to pick up Caitlin and Robert.

* * *

A week later David leaned back in his office chair and stretched his arms high over his head. He'd returned his phone calls and was ready to leave the office. He wondered—not for the first time—how Isabelle was doing, and even more, how Maggie was coping. Her reaction to his suggestion of a rehabilitation center for Isabelle had nagged at him for the last week. It was a perfectly sensible suggestion, but he hadn't anticipated her hostility to the idea. Isabelle's daughter seemed eager to find someplace to put her mother so she could rush back to Atlanta and be free of the worry. He shook his head.

Family members certainly reacted differently to aging parents. Maggie would do anything to help Isabelle; Barbara didn't want her life upset. David himself would have done anything to help his grandparents, but then, so would the rest of the family, which gave them a strong support system. He admired Maggie for her stand, but he hated to see her with the entire responsibility for her grandmother.

He decided he'd make a house call to see how everything was going. Looking up Isabelle's name on the computer, he quickly jotted down her address. He stood up and grabbed his keys, turning out the lights as he left his office.

He drove slowly trying to see the addresses. 816 Monaco Street. *It should be along here somewhere.* Finally he found it—a two-story, beige-and-green house, similar to the other homes in the neighborhood, set back from the street on a deep lot. The grass had evidently been cut recently, as a small boy stood sweeping grass off the front walk. Isabelle, looking frail, sat on the front lawn next to the porch in a green adirondack chair, watching the entire proceedings. On her first visit to his office, he'd never considered her size. She was dynamic and lively, with a commanding presence, but not any longer. He couldn't help but feel regret at her condition. His experience told him that she would never be her old vigorous self again. The stroke and the three days in the hospital had sapped the life out of her.

Leaning across his steering wheel, his arms resting on it, he gazed around the yard, shaking his head in wonder. Someone spent a lot of time working out there. The lawn was carefully edged along the walk and around the trees and flowers. Rosebushes bloomed along the sidewalk in front. Maggie and a small girl were planting what looked like petunias around the edge of the flower bed next to the house.

David got out and called over to the elderly lady. "Hi, Isabelle, how're you doing?"

Isabelle's face lit up when she caught sight of him. "Dr. Rosenberg! What are you doing here?"

"Just making a house call to my favorite patient." He approached the porch and dropped down to sit on the steps. "Feeling okay?" A closer view of her only reinforced his feeling of her fragility.

She nodded. "The song is right. 'No place like home.' Wonderful to be back." She gave a long, heartfelt sigh of satisfaction. "Course, Maggie is great." She looked at her granddaughter, who was busy digging. "She manage everything. I have nurse, therapists, aides." She leaned closer and whispered. "I don't need all of them, but Maggie insist."

David grinned. Isabelle would be independent to the end. "She's just following orders."

"That my Maggie May." She looked fondly at her granddaughter.

He looked around the grounds. "Do you have a gardener?"

"You kidding?" She raised her eyebrows, looking at him askance. She spoke slowly and deliberately, as if she had to think of each word. "I love gardening. Next to making pies, it my favorite thing. I'd be out there working now, but Maggie won't let me. Wants me to supervise from chair. So I'm stuck here. Once she makes up her mind, no arguing with her."

David himself had certainly seen that side of Maggie. If he were a betting man, he'd bet she inherited her stubborn streak from Isabelle. He looked up. Maggie was approaching, her hands on her hips, stretching what seemed to be a sore back. Trailing right behind her was the little girl. He decided to act as if Maggie and he had parted as best friends. "Hi. I didn't realize you had so many talents."

She laughed, seeming to have forgiven him. "I'm not like Gram." She held out her left hand, which was covered with dirt. "See that brown thumb? This isn't my favorite job, especially planting petunias, which I consider a member of the weed family, but the boss here," she wrinkled her nose at her grandmother, "thinks they're showy." Maggie put her arm around the small girl's shoulders and drew her close. The child promptly hid her head. "I couldn't have done it without my best helper, Caitlin. Caitlin, this is Dr. Rosenberg, Gram's doctor."

The small girl peeked shyly out from behind Maggie's leg. "You're a doctor?" She looked at him amazed. "Here?"

"I wanted to see your grandmother. I can tell she's the same old Isabelle." Although Caitlin watched him, she still clung to Maggie's leg. "Who's that sweeping the sidewalk?" The boy had swept the sidewalk clean once and was now resweeping it.

"My little brother, Robert. He's three." Then she said proudly, "I'm five."

"Come over here for a minute, Robert, and meet Dr. Rosenberg." Maggie beckoned him over.

He shook his head. "No. I'm busy." He stated this quite firmly, leaving no doubt that he wouldn't let anyone disturb him.

Maggie laughed. "Sweeping and vacuuming are his callings in life. He's aching to mow lawns, but that's out until I find a small mower for him."

"Have you ever considered teaching him golf? With his coordination, you might have another Tiger Woods. That's about the age he was when his dad taught him to play," David said mischeviously.

"Really." She laughed. "That's an idea I'll pass on to his dad. I don't know a club from a driver."

"I think a driver is a club." He found himself enjoying teasing her.

"What did I tell you?" She shrugged, but her eyes twinkled. "I'm a novice when it comes to most sports. The sad thing is, I don't even care." She broke into laughter.

David felt his chest tighten at the sound. Once again, he saw Maggie as an attractive woman, not merely as someone's caring granddaughter, and once again, he wished she were Jewish. He stood up and brushed the dust off the seat of his pants. "I'd better be getting along." He shook Isabelle's hand.

"It good to see you someplace beside your office or the hospital, Dr. Rosenberg." Her words were still slow and deliberate. "I like the way you look on front step. So you come again. What you say tomorrow for supper? I make peach pie." She looked at him eagerly, full of confidence.

Knowing that he could never refuse her, he said, "I'll come, but let's have the pie another day. What time do you eat?"

"We eat six o'clock, but pie will be a snap." She tried to snap her fingers, but failed. She wasn't quite as exuberant as she continued, "I've got pie crust in the refrigerator, and frozen peaches. You in for treat."

"I know I am." He looked at Maggie, who seemed to be in agreement with her grandmother. "I'll see you tomorrow."

When he passed Robert, he said, "Bye, Robert."

Intent on his job, Robert didn't raise his head, and the broom didn't slow down a bit. A mumbled, "Bye" was the only hint that he was aware of David at all.

* * *

Maggie's eyes narrowed as she watched Dr. Rosenberg walk to his car. His visit was strange. No one made house calls anymore, especially not the head of geriatrics at a major hospital. She wondered what his real reason was for coming over. She looked back at Gram. "Ready to go in?"

Gram nodded. Maggie put her arm around her as she helped her grandmother stand and go into the house. "Come on in, kids."

"I telling you, Maggie, he interested in you, even without blond streaks in your hair." Gram's eyes sparkled as her granddaughter led her into the living room, Caitlin and Robert right behind them.

"No way." She shook her head as she helped Gram sit down.

"Why else he come over? He saw me a week ago at the hospital, and he had no need to see this soon." She frowned at Maggie. "You need confidence in yourself."

"It's not that. I just see him as a caring person who wanted to make sure you were all right." Dr. Rosenberg's visit to Gram today had moved him up a few notches in her estimation. He evidently wasn't the unfeeling automaton she'd taken him for at their last meeting. She was relieved that her first impressions of him had been correct.

Today the physical therapist had come to help her grandmother walk with the walker, and Maggie's heart ached to see how unsteady she was. Until Gram could balance herself on it, she couldn't use the walker alone, which Gram found aggravating. Now Maggie's fear was that she would try to get up by herself and have another fall.

Tomorrow the speech therapist would come. She was training Gram to swallow the right way. Maggie sighed. Who knew there'd be so many little things her grandmother would have to learn how to do again? "What do you want to eat?"

Gram sagged against the couch, resting her head against the pillows. "I not hungry. I think I sit here and watch news."

"Oh, there's a method to your madness. You don't want to miss Tom Brokaw!" Maggie teased her as she plumped up the pillows behind her.

Gram gave her a weak smile. "Yes."

"Well, how does a small dish of applesauce and some zucchini bread sound?" Maggie made her voice enthusiastic, hoping some of it would rub off on Gram. A warm feeling always filled her heart when she thought of Gram. She was the best grandmother ever, and right now, Gram needed to eat something badly. If she lost any more weight, she'd disappear entirely. Her wraithlike appearance already scared Maggie.

Isabelle sighed as if she were exhausted. "I think I manage that."

Trying to hide her worry, Maggie took a deep breath and said, "You're going to love eating this because it's your homemade applesauce, and I took one of your frozen loaves of zucchini bread out. You know, Gram, you're the world's best cook!"

Isabelle attempted another smile. "And you world's best granddaughter."

Maggie checked her watch. "We've got five minutes until Tom is on, so why don't I help you into your nightie, and then you can watch him in comfort."

Isabelle nodded.

Maggie grabbed the notorious lavender nightgown out of the drawer and took it into the living room. "Here you are. You're going to look like a million dollars." She slid Gram's clothes off and the nightgown on. It all went smoothly, to her relief. Her grandmother appeared completely worn out, and she hated to tire her any further.

Once in the kitchen, Robert anxiously helped her unwrap the pizza and get it in the oven while Caitlin set the table. Once that was done, she dished up applesauce and bread for her grandmother while the kids settled themselves cross-legged on the floor to watch the oven. She grinned. Evidently they'd never heard that a watched pot never boils.

The news was on, and Gram slumped against the pillows, concentrating on the TV. "Do you want me to feed you?" Maggie asked.

"Would you mind?" she said weakly. "After Dr. Rosenberg left, my strength gone."

Maggie laughed, hoping to revive her a little. "What you really mean is that handsome men enthuse you, and the rest of us are blah."

Gram gave her a slight grin, but made no reply.

Maggie pulled the footstool up to the couch and began feeding her. She finished just as the timer on the stove went off.

Caitlin and Robert raced into the living room both shouting, "Aunt Maggie, Aunt Maggie, the pizza's done!"

"Great! You two get up to the table, and I'll get the pizza." They ran back to the dining room and scooted up to the table, eager anticipation on their faces. She brought the pizza into the dining room, and after Robert said the blessing, she served it.

"Maggie, can you come in here?"

Gram's voice stopped her before she could take her first bite. Pushing back her chair, she hurried into the living room. "What do you need, love?"

"I hate to be such a bother, but could you help me to bed?" Gram held her hand out toward Maggie, who took it in hers and put her other arm around her, helping her to her feet.

Her heart dropped as she realized how much lighter Gram was—only a mere wisp in her arms. They slowly shuffled past the kids in the dining room toward her bedroom. Maggie seated her on the side of the bed and pulled back the covers so Gram could lie down.

"Anything else I can get you?" She pulled the covers up and tucked her in.

"No, darling, I fine. Thank you." Her eyelids drifted shut, transparent against the blue of her eyes.

Maggie watched her for a moment before returning to the dining room table and pizza. She shook her head. The day was turning into a long one, and it wasn't even over yet.

"Want more," Robert demanded, his mouth full of his last bite.

"Okay, kiddo." She gave him some more pizza, and he wasted no time in eating it. Caitlin was a daintier eater, and it took her a few more minutes to finish her first piece. Then she was ready for more. One thing Maggie had noticed about these kids was as long as they had pizza, they were happy.

When they finished eating, Robert said, "I sweep."

"What a great idea." Maggie gave him an appreciative look.

Beaming, Robert slid off his chair, heading for the kitchen.

"Caitlin, let's clean off the table, and then when Robert is finished, we'll get ready for bed and I'll read you a story."

"Read *Angus.*" Caitlin raced up the stairs and came running back down with the book.

"Okay, honey. Put it on the couch."

Caitlin marched happily into the living room and deposited the book. Then she came back to the table and carefully picked up all the silverware and carried it to the kitchen. She pulled herself up to the sink and reached for the dishrag.

"No, that's just for the counters." Maggie laughed as she took the damp cloth from her. "I don't think Gram would like her wooden table wiped off with anything wet." She handed her a dry towel. "Use this. It will make everybody happy."

Caitlin gladly took it and practically danced into the dining room. Maggie grinned, wondering if the kids would be this eager to help clean up when they were teenagers. She watched them from the doorway. Robert swept the dining room carefully, making sure he got every little nook and cranny. He wasn't one to take his job lightly. Caitlin had her little hand cupped to catch any crumbs from the table.

By the time Maggie had bathed them both and gotten their pajamas on them, she felt as limp as a dishrag herself. But she resolutely read *Angus* to them, glad she'd put them in bed before reading it because by the end of the book, they were both sound asleep.

She tiptoed downstairs and checked on Gram before going into the living room and sinking into the recliner. She felt Gram's age instead of forty-nine years younger. The kids would be gone in two weeks, and right now she was too tired to feel sad at being separated from them. Why was she so tired? A day teaching school was no walk in the park, and yet she felt even more fatigued tonight than after a school day. Probably stress. She decided she needed to practice yoga—but not tonight. She took a deep breath. Relaxing in the recliner would have to do.

Gram had been home a week, and Maggie had finally managed to get a routine in their lives. While it had only been ten days since the stroke, Gram didn't seem to be getting stronger, which worried Maggie. In about five weeks school would start. Then what? Like Scarlet O'Hara, she guessed she'd think about that tomorrow. Right now, she needed to figure out what to fix for dinner for Dr. Rosenberg.

Although he hadn't mentioned it, Maggie thought from his name that Dr. Rosenberg might be Jewish, and that brought dietary laws to her mind. She wouldn't serve pork, but chicken ought to be safe. The chef on the news at noon had just made cashew chicken salad and given the recipe. It had looked delicious, and since the kids loved cashews, Maggie hoped the dish would be a winner. She had frozen dough for rolls, so she could also have hot rolls. Gram would make her pie, so they'd be all set.

* * *

After Maggie dropped Caitlin and Robert off at preschool, she swung by the grocery store to pick up the ingredients for the salad. She'd put the chicken on to cook as soon as she got home, and then she'd have nothing left to do until late afternoon.

When she arrived home, she found Isabelle sitting at the dining room table, her walker by her side. "Gram, did you walk by yourself?"

"Of course! Here aren't I?" She sounded put out. "You notice, I not eating anything. How you supposed to carry anything when hands are busy hanging on dear life?" Her words were slow and stilted.

"You just sit right there, and I'll fix you something. What sounds good? Oatmeal, waffles, or Cream of Wheat?" These were Gram's favorite breakfasts, and Maggie hoped she'd choose one of them.

Instead she made a face filled with disgust, as if Maggie had been suggesting fried grasshoppers. "Food too heavy. Just toast, dear, and hot chocolate."

Maggie sighed. Toast and hot chocolate weren't the two most nourishing things Gram could eat, but they were better than nothing. "Coming right up."

She put her groceries on the kitchen counter and started in on the breakfast immediately. She added orange juice to the menu before taking the food into the dining room. "Here you are, toots. I'm going to get the chicken on to cook first thing so I won't be rushed this afternoon."

"Oh, we having fried chicken?" Isabelle said delightedly. "Good. I love fried chicken."

"Actually I thought I'd fix cashew chicken salad. What do you think?" She'd have to get more chicken if she fried it.

Gram nodded. "It sounds good. What else?" She broke a piece of toast off and dipped it in the hot chocolate.

"I thought we'd have hot rolls and your pie."

Her grandmother frowned. "Your rolls? Yours on heavy side. Maybe I make them too."

"No, Gram, I have perfectly good frozen ones, and I'll let them rise a lot so Dr. Rosenberg will think he's eating ones made by your two little hands."

Isabelle shook her head. "No. Frozen rolls never as good as mine, but I think pie is all I can manage. Make a lot of salad. We don't want Dr. Rosenberg to go hungry." She took a sip of her cocoa.

Maggie laughed. "Gotcha." She moved into the kitchen and put the chicken on to cook. Then she turned down the heat, set the timer, and went back to the dining room.

Gram had finished eating, and Maggie picked up the dirty dishes. "We're all set. The aide should be here anytime to help you dress, and I think I'll finish planting your flowers while she's here. I'm anxious to finish that particular job." Tenderly patting Gram's cheek, she helped her into the living room. Then she left for the yard.

Grimacing when she looked at the half-filled flat of petunias, she pulled her gloves on. She'd much rather be planting pansies, or anything else for that matter. She wrinkled her nose in disdain as she knelt down and picked up the trowel.

Maggie had nearly finished when the health aide arrived. She let her into the house and turned off the chicken. Then she returned to the yard to finish her job. She slipped off her gloves, glad to have the chore finished, and rinsed off her hands under the hose before going inside.

Once on the porch, she dropped into the green lawn chair and feasted her eyes on her and Gram's handiwork. Maggie couldn't see a weed growing anywhere and, thanks to Robert, not even an extra blade of grass was evident on the sidewalk. The redbud bush seemed to be alive with chattering finches, although the leaves made them invisible. She took a deep breath of the cool morning air and felt invigorated. Now it was time to get on with her preparations for Dr.

Rosenberg. She rose from the chair and pulled open the screen door, letting it fall shut behind her. What a serene, beautiful day.

The aide was just getting ready to leave. She'd bathed and dressed Gram, and helped her get situated in the living room. Maggie dust mopped the hardwood floor in the dining room, and then polished the furniture. Dusting wasn't one of Gram's favorite jobs, and truth be told, it wasn't one of Maggie's either. However, there was some work involved to get the house looking shipshape. The invigorating breath of fresh air she had enjoyed earlier had almost completely vanished by the time she finished cleaning. She vacuumed during the commercials so her grandmother wouldn't miss any of her soap opera. Now all they had to do tonight was keep Dr. Rosenberg in these two rooms!

The speech therapist came shortly after noon, so Maggie left to pick up Robert and Caitlin at school, brought them home, fed them, and put them down for a nap. After the speech therapist had left, Gram had gone into the kitchen to make the peach pie, so now Maggie joined her. "Anything I can do to help?"

Gram gave her a pitying glance. "You know, Maggie, baking not your long suit. You watch."

"Okay, I'll just sit on this stool and observe the master at work." She didn't remind her grandmother that she had completed a course in French pastry baking and actually was quite good at it.

"Darling, hand me two tins out of cupboard." Gram nodded her head toward the far cupboard.

Anxious to be helpful, she slid off the stool and got them for her.

Once the tins were in front of her, Isabelle gently laid the crust in them. "Please hand me peaches out of fridge. I'll have ready for oven in no time."

Getting up again, Maggie found the frozen peaches and also located the cornstarch. She was rewarded with a smile. Isabelle soon had the pie filling stirred up and poured into the crusts. Then she crimped the edges together and said, "That easy. The oven's hot. You slide the pies in. We be all set."

Maggie put the pies in and checked to make sure the temperature was set correctly. Everything appeared to be fine, so she set the timer. Making the pies might have been easy, but she could see that her grandmother was tired out. "Let me help you into the bedroom, and you can lie down for a while."

Gram turned and grasped her walker. "I'll use my walker."

"Great! I'll walk behind you just in case."

Gram moved slowly out of the kitchen and across the hall to her bedroom, Maggie right behind her ready to catch her if anything went wrong. A few minutes later she had Gram tucked into bed with a quilt over her.

With everyone down for a nap, Maggie decided to go in the living room and watch *Oprah*. Settling in the recliner, she made herself comfortable and turned on the television. Her eyelids felt heavy, and she kept blinking. Before she knew it, she was asleep.

"Maggie! Maggie! Help! Help!" Gram sounded hysterical.

Chapter 8

At the smell of smoke, Maggie's heart started pounding, and she jumped out of the recliner. She ran toward her grandmother's bedroom, but at the kitchen she stopped short. Smoke was billowing out of the oven. She rushed to the stove and gingerly opened the oven door. Then, as flames shot out and up, burning the cabinets on either side of the stove top, she quickly dropped it and jumped back. Grabbing the salt out of the cupboard, she moved back to the stove and threw salt on the base of the flames, hoping to smother them. Finally, after nearly an entire box of salt, the flames died down, and she could see that the pies had caused the problem. They were black, and flames still flared on them. Filling had dripped on the bottom of the oven, and fire continued to burn there. She snatched some pot holders and tossed the pies into the sink, then used the rest of the salt on the burning filling on the oven bottom.

When the fire was under control, she looked around the kitchen and groaned. The paint on the cupboards was scorched. The oven bottom was coated with black ashes, and heat still radiated from the stove. But why had the pies caught fire? She glanced at the temperature gauge. "Five hundred degrees!" With a flick of her wrist, she turned it off. How on earth did it get turned up so high? Gram?

In the bedroom she found Gram perched on the edge of the bed, the walker next to her. Smiling quizzically at her, Maggie said, "Did you happen to turn the oven temperature up?"

Gram shook her head, looking completely innocent. "What happened?"

She sounded completely unaware, but it had to have been her grandmother. The kids were still asleep upstairs. Worry nagged at Maggie, but she kept calm. "Somehow the thermostat on the stove got turned to broil and your pies are now burned to a crisp."

Gram's face fell, and tears came to her eyes. "What we have for supper? Too late to make more pies."

She hugged her grandmother. "I'll invite him for another night. This burned smell would wreck his appetite."

Releasing Gram, she went into the kitchen and checked for Dr. Rosenberg's number. She caught him just as he was returning to his office and explained what had happened.

"What a shame! Except for the pie, was anything or anyone else burned?"

Maggie found Dr. Rosenberg's concern heartening. "The paint on the cupboards is scorched, but everything else is okay." By now the rapid beating of her heart had calmed down.

"Why don't I bring over take-out?" His desire to be useful was evident in his tone.

She shook her head, running her fingers through her blond curls. "That's awfully nice of you, but to be honest, until this place is aired out, the strong smell of charred peaches and paint is permeating every nook and cranny. I don't think we can eat here."

"What about me taking all of you out to eat?"

His warm voice enveloped Maggie, leaving her with a feeling of being cared about. "That's so kind of you, but could we make it a different night? Maybe wait until it's easier for Gram to get around?"

"I'd like to be of help tonight. Are you sure there is nothing I can do?" He sounded determined, but the thought of cleaning the kitchen with him, the kids, and Gram present was too much for Maggie.

"Not tonight. Let me just muddle through the evening alone. Gram will bake another peach pie in a couple of days, and I'll call you."

David laughed. "You're just as stubborn as your grandmother says. Fine. You just say when."

She said good-bye, and hung up the phone.

"Maggie! Maggie!"

"I'm coming." She found Gram still sitting on the edge of the bed, anxious to hear the news. "What did he say? What night he coming?"

She smiled at the elderly lady, so dear to her heart. "He offered to bring us supper, but I turned him down. We can't have visitors until we can breathe clear air in this house again."

She scowled. "Maggie, don't turn down chance to have Dr. Rosenberg right here with us."

"Don't worry. I won't! Now, let me help you into bed again, and you rest while I start cleaning up the kitchen." Maggie lifted her grandmother's legs onto the bed and pulled the coverlet over her. She looked at her sternly. "Don't move from this spot without my help." Moving the walker over against the far wall, she left the room, leaving the door open a crack, hoping the distance to the walker would keep Gram from wandering around the kitchen and turning up the oven.

When she looked at the kitchen again and saw the smoke-covered walls, the blistered paint on the cupboards, and the remnants of the fire in the oven, dismay welled up in her. But it lasted only a moment. Talking to Dr. Rosenberg had lifted her spirits, and she knew she could manage. First, she had to open all the windows, which proved to be easier said than done. The kitchen ones went up easily, but she didn't know how long it had been since the dining room ones had been opened, or if they ever had. She pushed, pulled, and pried, and only when she got a screwdriver was she able to get one of the three raised. Dusting off her hands, she went to the living room. The first two were stuck, and, instead of laboring over them, she decided to try the others first. The last three also didn't go up without a struggle, but finally she had air circulating through the downstairs. As she pulled the sheer curtain back, a white-panel truck drove up. She looked closer. Written on the side in large red letters were the words **A PROFESSIONAL TOUCH CLEANING SERVICE.** Beneath that it read, **Disasters Our Specialty.**

Two white-uniformed men got out and headed for the house. What was going on? She hurried to the door. The two men were distinct contrasts; one was tall, dark, and handsome, while the other was older, short, and bald. Before either one could speak, she said, "Yes?"

"Someone ordered a fire cleanup in the kitchen." The bald one seemed to be in charge.

She frowned. "It wasn't me. Are you sure you have the right address?"

He took out his yellow order pad and checked the address. "This is 716 Monaco Street. Are you Maggie Summers?"

"Yes," she acknowledged, still mystified.

"Well, we've got the right place." He gave her a reassuring smile and stepped forward, forcing Maggie to step backward. "Let us survey the damage and see what we need. Then we'll get our equipment and get right on it."

"Just a minute! Who ordered this done?" Then it dawned on her. She knew exactly who'd decided to be helpful.

"Dr. David Rosenberg ordered a rush job." The dark-haired man sighed. "Now, can we get started?"

She sighed in resignation. Pushing the door open wider, she headed for the kitchen, the men following right behind her. "It's a pretty big mess."

When they glimpsed the kitchen, both men looked startled. "This is all?"

She nodded, and the one in charge said, "This is nothing. We should have it completed in a couple of hours." They went out to the truck and were back in a few minutes with their cleaning supplies.

Then they both put on plastic gloves and started. The older one washed the smoky walls with a long-handled sponge mop while the other sprayed the oven. Maggie snatched Dr. Rosenberg's number off the refrigerator and retreated to the dining room to call him again.

When he answered, she said, "Well, Dr. Rosenberg, the disaster team has arrived! Thanks to you."

He chuckled. "Good. I told them to hurry or you'd have it all finished. By the way, call me David."

"Okay, *David.*" She emphasized his name. "I'd just gotten the last window open when they drove up. Other than being speechless at their arrival, I was glad to see them. Thanks. I hadn't even thought of calling a cleaning service, but I'm glad *you* did. But I insist on paying for it."

"No, my dear Miss Independent," he teased. "This is my gift. I don't want to take any chances on any extra delay before I get my peach pie."

"I might have known—an ulterior motive! But you give us a couple of days, and we'll be ready for guests."

"What caused the fire?" He sounded perplexed.

"The oven was on broil. I suspect Gram. She denies it, but it had to be her." She gave a little laugh. "Anyway, now we know for sure that broiling isn't good for pies."

"What do you plan on doing so it doesn't happen again?" He apparently was taking this seriously.

"Watch her like a hawk and hide her walker!" Her words were light, but she wondered herself what she was going to do.

"I hope that does it." He sounded dubious.

"I do too." She paused, then with heartfelt feeling said, "Thanks again. Your thoughtfulness has been a godsend. I appreciate it and you. If your calendar is open, why not plan on dinner Wednesday night?"

"For Isabelle's pie, I'd cancel any previous engagement. Thanks for the invitation."

She smiled at his enthusiasm. "It's the least we could do."

"Aunt Maggie, someone's in the kitchen," Caitlin whispered, tiptoeing into the dining room with Robert right behind her.

"Sorry," she said into the phone. "The kids are up, and I've got to go." They said good-bye, and Maggie turned to the two children, who were scowling.

Caitlin pulled impatiently at Maggie's pants, her forehead furrowed in a frown. "Who *is* that?"

"Those men are cleaning the kitchen." She didn't want to go into detail in case it scared the kids.

"Why?"

Imitating his sister, Robert said, "Why?"

Without waiting for an answer, Caitlin started pulling her aunt toward the kitchen. Maggie resisted. "No, honey. We don't want to get in their way." Her niece stared at her for a moment but made no further move.

"Let's go in the living room so we won't disturb Gram." She took their hands and guided them to the sofa. With each step, their shoelaces flapped along the floor, since neither child had mastered that skill yet. Once the laces were tied, Maggie hugged each one of the kids and suggested that they all go outside and play. They raced to the front door. Outside on the grass, they chased each other, and when they tired of that, Maggie pushed them in the swings at the back of the house. Nostalgia swept over her. The swing set had been built years ago for her mother and Aunt Barbara. She and Karen had swung there growing up, and now Karen's children were swinging on it. She sighed. But there was a profound difference—her mother and Karen weren't there to watch. Before her spirits could sink, she shook her head. The closest members of her family might be gone, but she still had Karen's children and Gram to love. All in all, life was pretty good.

When they returned to the house, they found the workmen had nearly finished, and Gram was ready to get up. Caitlin efficiently pushed the walker over to the bed so Gram could stand. Maggie braced her back and steadied her as they slowly made their way to the living room. Caitlin and Robert raced ahead, moving chairs out of their great-grandmother's way.

Finally they made it to the living room, and the elderly woman sank onto the sofa. She looked over at Robert. "Turn the TV on, honey. It's time for . . ." She looked frustrated, and staring at Maggie, said, "Who?"

"Tom Brokaw." Her granddaughter smiled down at her. "I don't believe it! The name of your favorite newsman not on the tip of your tongue. You're getting as bad as I am!" Taking a deep breath, she prayed that Gram would recover from the memory loss.

Robert reached for the remote and turned on the television. A second later, Tom Brokaw's authoritative voice filled the room.

"We can't get into the kitchen yet, but are you hungry?" Maggie looked at the others.

"Yes!" they shouted in unison, as if they were afraid they wouldn't be heard. Then Robert added, "Can we have pizza?"

"Not tonight, honey. I don't know what condition our oven is in, and I don't want to turn it on. What about chicken sandwiches with chips?" The expression on his face told her he wasn't overly enthusiastic, but transporting Gram anywhere was a major undertaking, and at this point, she didn't feel like going to all the effort it took to go out to eat. If she had, she'd have taken David up on his offer.

"I love chicken, Aunt Maggie." Caitlin beamed at her.

"What about you, Gram? Is chicken all right?" Her grandmother looked slight and vulnerable, as if a mere breath of air would topple her. Maggie's heart tightened. She'd been naive to never imagine Gram being in this condition—let alone that she, herself, would be her caretaker.

The elder woman seemed to merely go through the motions as she smiled tiredly. "Chicken sounds fine, but don't go to any bother on my account."

Maggie leaned over and gave her a hug. "Of course I'd bother on your account. Who else is as important?" This time Gram's smile seemed to have more energy in it.

A half hour later, the kitchen was spotless. Besides cleaning the stove and the walls, the men had scrubbed the cupboards and mopped the floor. Relief flooded Maggie at the sight of the clean kitchen. After happily signing the invoice, she handed it back to the older man. Their white coveralls were now grimy evidence of their endeavors. "Thank you. You don't know how much I appreciate your hard work."

"This was nothing. You should see some of the jobs we have." He handed her a business card, and the two gathered up their equipment and left.

As soon as she'd seen them to the door, Maggie examined the cupboards closely. When she saw the damage to the finish on them, she groaned. Gram had remodeled her kitchen only a few years ago, copying a magazine picture. She'd changed the original painted cabinets to whitewashed birch ones, and replaced the formica counters and the linoleum-covered floor with a moss-green tile. All these changes had brightened up the kitchen, but now the cupboards around the stove had a definite smoky gray color to them, casting a pall on the entire room.

After Barbara's comments on Gram's finances, spending any unnecessary money worried Maggie. She crossed her fingers, hoping the deductible would be low. She resolved to call the insurance company first thing in the morning.

"I'm hungry. When we eating?" Robert stood at her side, peering up. Caitlin, right behind him, was nodding her head in agreement.

"In just a minute." She removed the ingredients for the sandwiches from the refrigerator.

Caitlin, an eager look on her face, said, "Can I be your helper and set the table?"

"Sure." She smiled at the small girl. "You know you're the best helper ever."

Caitlin hurried to the silverware drawer and carefully counted out four knives, forks, and spoons. The plates were in the cupboard on the other side of the room, so they hadn't been affected by the fire. Maggie got them and some glasses off the shelf and handed everything to her niece, who proudly set the table.

For some reason the chicken had little flavor, so Maggie was glad David hadn't come to supper, although she'd have preferred it to have been for a reason other than the fire. But whenever he did come, chicken salad was definitely off the menu. She wouldn't chance more blah chicken. She'd have to think up something else.

The next day the insurance adjuster told her they would replace the damaged wood on the cupboards and that her grandmother had a five-hundred-dollar deductible. Maggie didn't want to worry her grandmother, so she decided to pay the deductible herself.

By Wednesday, Maggie felt as if she had everything under control. The cabinetmaker said he would come in a week to install new sides on the cupboards, and the burnt smell had disappeared except for faint wafts from the upholstery. So once again, Maggie went to the grocery store, this time while the health aide was helping her grandmother. She'd changed the menu to pot roast with vegetables, and she also bought more frozen rolls. As dinner cooked, she kept one eye and ear on the kitchen when Gram went for her nap, and this time the pies didn't end up in the oven with the heat turned to broil.

At 4:30, she put the meat and vegetables in the oven, and then cleaned up Caitlin and Robert. Once they were ready, she helped Gram put on new lavender pants with a matching top, fluffing up her white hair as a finishing touch.

Maggie left everyone watching *Muppets* while she dashed upstairs and changed to sky-blue linen pants and a blue slub-knit sweater made out of ramie cotton. She fluffed up her own hair so that it was a mass of corkscrew curls. After she put on a touch of makeup, she was ready for the big night, except for one problem—a flutter of excite-ment in her midsection.

She attempted to ease the tremors. If she hadn't known better, she would think she was getting ready for a big date. She took a couple of deep breaths, but it didn't help. The flutters were still there. How irritating! Why should she be all atremble like some heroine in a romance novel? She wasn't nervous! She was determined not to be. Taking another deep breath, she hurried downstairs. After all, it was only her grandmother's doctor coming to sample peach pie.

* * *

Putting down the phone after returning his last call, David glanced at his watch. He had enough time to run home for a quick shower and a change of clothes before going to Isabelle's for supper. He loved homemade peach pie, but he felt bad that her burning up her kitchen made it a little pricey for her. He looked forward to the evening, however, and if the truth be told, to seeing Maggie.

When he pulled into Isabelle's driveway, the two towheaded kids ran to the side of the porch to watch him park, bringing an automatic smile to his face. Getting out of the car, he called, "Hi, you two. What's happening?"

"We're having company for supper, and I'm wearing my best dress." As he stepped onto the porch, Caitlin held out her skirt so he could get a better look at it. "Watch." She twirled around as fast as she could go. "Did you see my skirt?"

Looking at the excited face, David laughed. "I couldn't miss it! Are you going to be a ballerina someday?"

She nodded. "I have a Barbie ballerina."

"You'll make a graceful one." He looked at Robert. "What about you?"

The small boy shrugged and just kept staring at him.

David couldn't stop smiling, noting Robert was obviously a boy of few words. *What engaging kids,* he thought. Except for the blond hair, they reminded him of his own nieces and nephews at that age. He'd always loved children, and he couldn't wait to have some of his own. He grimaced, thinking that at the rate he was going, he could have a long wait.

"Oh, here you are. Waylaid by two kids," an amused voice said from the screen door. "Come in."

When David saw Maggie, his pulse quickened, and he took a deep breath to steady it. She looked beautiful. Her friendly smile lit up her face, generating warmth and kindness. He pulled the screen door open wider. "Thanks."

She looked over at Caitlin and Robert. "I think it's time for you to come in also. Dr. Rosenberg has timed it just right. Dinner is ready to be served." Forgetting their good clothes for a moment, they raced in, nearly pushing him down in their eagerness to be first.

Maggie led him into the living room. "Gram, your favorite doctor has arrived."

She helped Isabelle sit up on the couch. "Dr. Rosenberg, how nice to see you. Sit down." Isabelle motioned to an easy chair next to the sofa.

He made himself comfortable, and Maggie left the room. "Call me David, Isabelle." He smiled admiringly at her. "You look spectacular in lavender."

She gave him a pleased look. "Thanks."

"How have you been feeling?" She seemed so frail that her appearance concerned him.

"Fine. How you?" The liveliness of her voice surprised him.

"Keeping busy." In fact, in the last two weeks he'd been hiking twice and rowing once.

"Are you seriously dating anyone?" Isabelle's tone was matter-of-fact, as if her question wasn't anything out of the ordinary.

He hesitated, then said cautiously, "No. Why do you ask?" He couldn't believe the elderly lady didn't have some ulterior motive for broaching the subject.

"Just wondering." Moving her head to one side, she sized him up. "I find hard to believe that man handsome as you, and a doctor, not involved."

He laughed. "Isabelle, you've been reading too many romances. I don't have time for that." *Or, at the present moment, know an eligible woman, which is the main problem.*

Maggie came into the room. "Dinner is served."

"Just in the nick of time. Your grandmother was trying to ferret out the secrets of my love life." He grinned at Isabelle.

"Doctor, as far as I can tell, you nothing to ferret out." She sounded delighted, which made him doubly suspicious of her motive. His eyes narrowed.

Maggie cringed, and she could feel the blood rush to her face. What was she thinking, leaving him alone with Gram? Why would her grandmother even want to promote a romance between the two of them? She knew how Maggie felt about a temple marriage. And Maggie didn't mean a Jewish temple. She wondered what else Gram had said to him. She took a deep breath. "This is perfect timing. I rescued you before she could ask any more personal questions." Although she spoke lightly, she could have throttled Gram. He'd have to be dense not to see through her. Maggie shrugged, knowing he'd be gone in another hour or so, and since he'd have had Gram's pie, she'd make sure he wasn't invited back. If Maggie had her way, Gram wouldn't have another opportunity to grill him in that house.

David moved the walker into place and helped Isabelle stand up to it. They slowly made their way to the dining room table. Caitlin and Robert were already sitting next to each other. David seated Gram beside Robert, and before Maggie could tell him where to sit, Caitlin said, "The company gets to sit by me." She patted the chair next to her, and with a grin, David sat down. That left Maggie between David and Gram.

Once they were all settled, Gram called on Robert to ask the blessing. He gave a short prayer filled with gratitude and asked Heavenly Father to make Gram well. Afterward, in a solemn tone, he said, "That little prayer made my chin tremble."

Everyone was silent, savoring the sweet spirit his blessing had brought. Maggie knew that little prayer had touched them all. When she glanced at David, his expression lifted her heart. She could tell he'd felt it too.

Gram reached over and squeezed Robert's hand. "Thank you for beautiful words." She nodded her head. "Father heard them."

Caitlin looked at David. "I set the table. I'm Aunt Maggie's best helper."

"You've set the table beautifully, so I can tell you are. I doubt she could do without you." He smiled conspiratorially. "What do you think?"

Caitlin nodded in agreement. "She couldn't."

"I couldn't. I don't know what I'm going to do when you kids move." Maggie's tone might have been light, but her heart was heavy.

Caitlin gave her a fierce look, her voice determined. "You're going with us."

"I wish I could." Maggie left it at that. The thought of their leaving upset her just as much as it did Caitlin. The difference was that the children would be with their father, who they loved and who loved them. In a short time they'd be involved in their own lives and seldom think about her. On the other hand, she had no one to take their place.

"How about some pot roast?" She handed the platter to David.

"Yum. This food looks delicious." After helping himself, he winked at Caitlin. "Can I give you some?"

Caitlin's forehead was still wrinkled in a frown, but she nodded yes. He gave her a small piece of the meat.

"Robert, what about you?"

"Yes." He knotted his fist and pulled his arm down to emphasize his answer. "I love meat and potatoes and gravy."

David chuckled. "I'm convinced!" He gave Robert a slice, and when Maggie passed the potatoes and gravy to David, he helped both kids with that.

Maggie was surprised at his enthusiasm for assisting the kids with their meal. She'd been going to dish up their plates herself, but they were enjoying David's attention.

"Cut my meat up," Robert demanded.

Maggie frowned at him.

He looked at her. "I'm sorry. Please cut my meat up," he meekly asked this time.

"I will, honey." Maggie moved around the table and cut his roast. She helped Caitlin too, before sitting down.

"These rolls aren't good as mine," Gram bragged, "but they're not bad." She passed them to David. "Of course," she gave Maggie a sly look, "they be better with real butter."

"Pretend it is, and you'll never know the difference." Maggie knew her grandmother had orders to go easy on fat to get her cholesterol down. Since Gram had grown up on a farm, she thought nothing beat real butter on rolls.

Maggie wondered what David was thinking. The kids were behaving, which was good. Isabelle had quizzed him about his love life, which was bad. Her shoulders kept tensing, and every few seconds she had to remind herself to relax. She couldn't help but worry about what calamity might happen next.

When they'd finished eating, Maggie gathered up their dinner plates and served Isabelle's pie.

She watched David close his eyes and savor a bite in his mouth. "Isabelle, you've outdone yourself. This is wonderful! I feel like I've died and gone to heaven. How did you learn to make such good peach pie? Neither my mother or grandmothers could make pie."

Gram tried to look modest, but she couldn't hide her pleasure at his compliment. "My mother pies won blue ribbon at state fair, and she taught me. I won prizes at county fair, but I always afraid to enter state fair because mine never good as hers."

Her comments startled Maggie. She'd never heard her grandmother admit that anyone, even her own mother, could make better pies than she could.

David frowned, looking skeptical. "How could hers be better? This is ambrosia. Food for the gods."

Maggie enjoyed watching him eat. He relished every bite as if he were a wine connoisseur tasting a fabulous, rare wine. She glanced at Gram, who appeared just as enthralled.

"There's more if you'd like another piece," Gram offered, a broad smile lighting her face.

"No, thank you. I couldn't eat another bite after Maggie's wonderful pot roast." He grinned at Robert. "I agree with you—those potatoes and gravy weren't to be missed."

"Maggie will wrap up the rest for you to take home." Gram motioned to Maggie to prepare some pie for him. "Do you like pie for breakfast?"

"I do. I don't think anything can beat a good piece of pie to start off the day." He glanced down at the kids. "What do you think?"

"Yes!" They shouted exuberantly.

Maggie thought they were probably more enthusiastic about David than about the pie. He'd certainly hit it off with them.

"I'll help Isabelle to a more comfortable chair, and then I'll help you clear up the dishes." He moved to her grandmother's side and helped her stand.

"No," Maggie said, "I'll do them later."

He grinned at her. "I won't take no for an answer, and besides, I'm looking forward to seeing your kitchen."

He guided Gram into the living room, and Maggie could hear him ask her what she wanted to watch. Then the television snapped on.

When he came in, he gazed around the kitchen. "Not too bad, but I'm sure you'll be happy when all the work is complete." Then he looked at Maggie. "I have to admit, you're an excellent cook." He carried the bread basket and the fruit-salad bowl into the kitchen. Then he gave her a suspicious look. "Or is pot roast the only dish you can make?"

She laughed, finding his sense of humor wonderful. "All I can say is, 'I am my grandmother's granddaughter.'"

"I take it that means you cook as well as she does." His eyes twinkled.

She put her fingers to her lips. "Sh-sh-sh. It certainly *does not* mean that!" she whispered. "You've just committed heresy. No one can cook as well as my grandmother—that is gospel in this family— and *never, never* let her know you ever even considered that *I* could cook as well as she does. She'll be the first to tell you my rolls are heavy and my gravy is lumpy."

He grinned. "Oh, is that what those lumps were? Here I thought you'd added mushrooms."

She poked him in the side with her elbow. "Now you're offending me! I strained the gravy and those *were* mushrooms."

With a laugh, he moved away, protecting his body from her elbow. "Okay, okay. You don't have to batter me. Every family has its secrets, and I'll keep yours—you're a wonderful cook. Now this is the *really* big question. How are you at making peach pie?"

She rolled her eyes. "You would have to ask! I make great filling, but my crust is usually as tough as shoe leather. Gram has shown me how a million times, and I still can't make it. I think I handle it too much and don't keep it cold enough. That's Gram's diagnosis anyway."

When she stood up from loading the dishwasher, she looked at him. He was leaning against the counter watching her, and when her eyes met his, she felt a rush of excitement. Gram was right, as she usually was. He did look like a romance-novel hero. Maggie stopped herself at the inane thought. "I'll just wash off the counters, and we can join the others."

He scowled. "Now I'm offended. I've already wiped them off, and you can't even tell?"

"Sorry." Grinning at him, she deliberately gave them an extra swipe.

He whispered, "I need to pay you back for this outstanding meal. What about going to dinner one night?"

Chapter 9

Maggie's eyes widened. His invitation surprised her, and she found that she very badly wanted to go, to do something different. "It sounds fun, but I'll need to get someone to stay with Gram and the kids."

"Do you know anyone? If not, I'm sure I can find somebody." Once again he was the doctor in charge.

"No, I know someone." Maggie knew that Pat and her husband Craig would be thrilled to see her go out, and she also knew they'd be more than happy to come over. She could feel the edges of her mouth curling into a smile.

"It's all set then. What about Saturday?"

She nodded, caught up in the piercing quality of his hazel eyes. "Saturday should be fine." He gently pushed her toward the dining room door. "Come on, Cinderella, let's go in the living room."

Conscious of his hand on her shoulder, she headed into the other room.

While Maggie made herself comfortable in an easy chair, David seated himself on the sofa next to Isabelle. His eyes twinkled as he patted the elderly lady's hand. "Maggie has graciously consented to go to dinner with me Saturday evening. What do you think?"

"That's a wonderful idea." She gave David a charming smile, and then added, "Maggie needs to go out more."

Maggie groaned. Why did Gram have to tack the final phrase on? It made her sound like an old maid or a wallflower or something! That was Gram all right. She never minced words.

David gave Maggie a conspiratorial smile, obviously aware of her reaction to her grandmother's comment. "And I'm happy to take her."

Then he looked at the weariness in Gram's face. "I think I'm tiring you, so I better be going. Thanks for inviting me. Your pie is out of this world. I wouldn't miss having it for breakfast tomorrow for anything."

Gram beamed at him. "You'll have to come again for more. Maggie, where did you put his pie?"

"On the counter, Gram. I'll get it." She rose from her chair and followed David out of the room. "Just a minute." She returned with half of a peach pie.

"Wow! That's a generous piece, but I won't refuse it." At the front door, he said, "See you Saturday about seven."

"See you." As she locked the door behind him, she leaned against it and sighed. What a turn this evening had taken. Who'd have ever thought Dr. Rosenberg, or *David,* as he preferred to be called, would ever ask her out? She only wished he were LDS and she'd met him at church. But virtually no LDS man got to his late thirties without being married.

She sighed again. If only he were a member of the Church.

* * *

On his way home, David thought about the evening. The food had been great. Isabelle's tart tongue always amused him, and Maggie . . . he shook his head. What was it about her that attracted him? Her smile? It lit up her face, generating a warmth and a kindness that he'd seldom found in other women. He knew from his own practice that not all children or grandchildren wanted to be burdened with caring for an elderly parent, let alone a niece or a nephew. And yet she'd adamantly refused to let her grandmother go to an assisted-living home.

The reality of the situation was that he hardly knew her, and his reaction to seeing her tonight had been ridiculous. Her blue sweater might have emphasized her blue eyes, making them fathomless, and her frizzy blond hair might have looked soft and appealing, but that wasn't enough. She wasn't Jewish. *What am I doing?* he asked himself. He'd sworn never to date a Gentile. Now he was, but he vowed there was no way he'd ever let himself fall in love with someone who didn't share his beliefs.

Turning into the condominium driveway, David buzzed the door of the parking garage open. He felt comfortable with Maggie, and he enjoyed her company. He just had to make sure that they stayed only friends.

* * *

Pat had been as excited as Maggie knew she would be at the idea of her friend going to dinner with the doctor, and she hadn't hesitated a moment in agreeing to stay with Gram and the kids. Since she was concerned about everyone's relationships, Pat made a good romance writer. She'd do anything to foster romance in her friends.

After talking to Pat, Maggie felt excited herself. She didn't know if it was the thought of going out with David or just the thought of going out and doing something different. Between her writing and Gram and the kids, she'd been tied to home for quite a while. Of course, she reminded herself, she had been to the zoo, but that didn't count.

Saturday night David picked her up and they went to La Hacienda, a restaurant that originally had been an old railroad station. Maggie thought it had an authentic Mexican flavor, but she couldn't say for sure. She'd never been south of the border. The music—loud with fast guitar strumming and lyrics all in Spanish—gave it at least a decidedly Mexican ambience. A number of people had apparently decided that Mexican food sounded good, because the place was crowded, and she and David were forced to wait thirty minutes in the entryway to be seated.

Once the hostess found a table for them, their waitress brought menus. She, along with the other waitresses, wore a brightly embroidered, white peasant blouse. The waiters had on embroidered white shirts with sashes. "While you decide, I'll bring some chips and drinks. What would you like to drink?" They both had 7-Up.

Maggie, who loved Mexican food, thought everything sounded good, but her favorite was chili verde with pork, so she decided to go with that.

The waitress returned with chips along with salsa and the drinks. "Ready to order?"

David had enchiladas, and she ordered the pork.

Maggie looked at David. It seemed strange to be going to dinner with him. She knew he'd never have asked her out if Gram hadn't invited him first for pie, but regardless, she intended to enjoy herself. When was the last time she'd gone out with an eligible bachelor? She couldn't remember. David was turning out to be as helpful as he was good-looking, and that was saying something! He was solicitous of Gram and had a real knack with Caitlin and Robert. Plus, she couldn't help but think of his generosity with the fire cleanup. She met his eyes and smiled. "You know what?"

He grinned. "No. What?"

She didn't like that grin because even though she was sitting down, it made her knees weak. "You'd make a wonderful husband." And Maggie had to acknowledge, if she were honest with herself, she wouldn't mind being the wife. But a Jewish husband didn't exactly fit in with her plans. Dropping her gaze, she dipped a chip into the salsa. "You've been a lifesaver." She ate her chip before looking at him again.

He laughed. "Funny you should say that. My former wife thought there was nothing lifesaving about me. More like *life ruining*."

"You've been married?" She'd known that he couldn't have possibly been single all these years. "Why am I not surprised? But what I don't understand is how she let you get away!" Her eyes glinted with amusement.

"We have a meeting of the minds on that. I could never understand her letting me get away either." His tone was light, but she thought his eyes showed hurt.

"Do you have children?" Splitting up a family was difficult for everybody. Many of her students came from broken homes, and she knew how hard it was on them.

"No. We were married young and decided to wait until I was established to have our family. In the end, that turned out to be a good decision. Sarah couldn't take the loneliness of having me at the hospital working all the time." He helped himself to more of the chips. "It was my fault too. I was so wrapped up in my work and being the best possible intern that I didn't make time for her. We worked horrendously long hours at Johns Hopkins, and one day when I came home, she'd moved out. Went back to her family in

New York City. It's a terrible thing to say, but I think the only thing I felt at the time was relief." His eyes clouded for a moment.

"Why haven't you remarried?" She didn't believe for one moment that he'd have any difficulty finding a wife.

His mouth twisted wryly. "For a long time I was simply too busy. I didn't want another failure, so I never even considered it. But getting married isn't easy." Then his eyes twinkled as they met hers. "I want to marry a nice Jewish woman, and they're hard to find once you get out of New York City or L.A."

"I know what you mean. I want to marry a nice Mormon man, and they're not too plentiful either." She kept her tone light, hoping she didn't sound desperate, but if he could admit it, why couldn't she?

"You're a Mormon?" He looked astonished. "I did postdoctorate work at the University of Utah in Salt Lake."

She felt as astonished as he looked. "No kidding! I went to Brigham Young University in Provo for a year." She wondered if he'd ever attended church while he lived there.

"Just a year? Why didn't you stay in that bastion of Mormonism? I would have thought it would have been a wonderful place to find a husband." He chuckled as he picked up his drink.

"Now that I think about it, I probably should have. But it's too late. I'm sure there are no *single* men over the age of twenty-one attending now," she said dryly. "And if there were one, a hundred single women are undoubtedly lying in wait to nab him."

"That bad, huh?" He shook his head in mock amazement.

She laughed. "I am exaggerating. But only slightly."

"It looks to me like you've got a problem. What's your plan? Maybe you've thought of something I can use since I don't seem to be getting very far on my own." He leaned closer, as if waiting for her to impart some secret for finding a mate.

"Don't look at me. I'm not the epitome of success in that area." She laughed. "I've gone to lectures, singles activities at church, and I've taken gourmet cooking classes . . ."

"Me too! What kind did you take?"

"French, Italian, Japanese." She'd loved them all, but now she seldom took the time to fix any of them, since she'd rather be writing.

"I took French and Japanese." He drank some 7-Up.

"At the community ed center?" Even though the place was crowded, she didn't see how she could have missed noticing him.

"The Jewish Community Center." He helped himself to more chips and popped one into his mouth.

"No wonder we never ran into each other. I also took flower arranging, writing, and car mechanics. I thought for sure there would be men in that one, but it was mostly women hoping to meet men. The good part is I can keep my own car running." She wondered if doctors kept their own cars running. She doubted it. They probably didn't want to get their hands dirty.

"What about bonsai? I took a class at the Bonsai Center." He looked at her enthusiastically.

"To meet women?" This news amazed her. Bonsai wasn't your everyday, ordinary class.

"No, to learn how to make bonsai. It's always fascinated me." His eyes shone with amusement.

"So did you learn how?"

"I think so. I got so caught up in it that for a while I spent every spare minute creating bonsai. I even joined the Bonsai Society. You'll have to see my terrace sometime. I've got at least a dozen. All different shapes of plants." He sounded proud of his accomplishment and she could see why. "You ought to take the class," he continued. "There are a lot of men. I don't know how many are single, but it wouldn't hurt to check them out."

"Actually, getting out beating the bushes for husband material is more than I want to do anymore. I'm content with my life just the way it is."

"And how is that?" He looked interested.

"Well, before all this happened with Gram, I spent my free time writing and with my friends, who all happen to be female."

At the word *writing,* he immediately looked up. "What do you write?"

"Mysteries."

"I love mysteries!" His face lit up. "Have you read Elmore Leonard?"

She shook her head. "No, I like mine a little gentler."

"Published anything?"

"No, but I'm finishing a book right now for an editor who has asked to see it." She realized that might not sound like a lot to him, but she couldn't keep the note of satisfaction out of her voice.

He frowned, giving her a hard look. "I can't believe that as busy as Isabelle keeps you, not to mention Caitlin and Robert, you find much time to write."

She nodded. "You're right. But when everything settles down, I'll get back to it. I only have five chapters to go before I'll be finished."

"You really should consider placing Isabelle in an assisted-living center, so you'd have some time for yourself." He placed his hand over hers.

At the touch of his hand on hers, a ripple of yearning spread through her. It would be nice to have someone to share her life with right now. She shook her head slowly. "No, that still isn't an option." She wasn't going to say anything else, and then she decided to be honest, no matter how ridiculous it might sound to him. "I have great faith in God, that He loves me, that He knows what is happening to me, and that He will bless and strengthen me."

David looked at her as if trying to read her innermost thoughts. She was sure she'd blown it this time. *Talk about casting your pearls before swine,* she told herself. Although nothing about David appeared swinish, she shouldn't have said anything to him about faith in God.

"I guess I'd forgotten about God helping. I usually just think how can *I* do something. I looked at you struggling with your problems and wondered how you could possibly get through it all." He gave her a gentle smile. "I still think you're taking on too much. You need to think more about your own life, but you're right." He nodded. "God *will* bless you." Then he squeezed her hand.

Her yearning increased. She savored the warmth of his hand and would have liked to have squeezed it back. But she didn't want to send the wrong message. Why did she have to meet a wonderful man who wanted to get married? The only problems were, one, he wasn't LDS and, two, he wanted a Jewish wife.

Just then the waitress brought their dinners, and they both moved their hands to make way for the steaming plates. The chili verde looked especially good.

"Be careful you don't get burned," the waitress cautioned them. "Can I get you anything else?" Both David and Maggie shook their heads.

David picked up his fork. "This looks delicious!" He took a deep breath. "And the aroma is indescribable."

Maggie took a bite, blowing on it first. "Hmm, good."

He cut through the cheese-filled enchilada with his fork. Then, cutting a smaller piece, he took his first bite. A look of pure pleasure covered his face. "Without a doubt, they have the best Mexican food in town."

They ate a few bites in silence, then David said, "Do you like sports?"

"I prefer spectator sports. In our church we take volleyball seriously. Very seriously. I was playing for fun one night and missed a return, which earned me a yelling at, and when I turned around to look at the guy who was so agitated, I got hit in the head with a spiked ball. After seeing stars for a few minutes, I left the sporting arena—never to return." She laughed. As angry as she'd been then, now she found the entire episode funny.

"But you enjoy watching them?" he persisted, acting as if her answer were very important.

"You've got me confused with my grandmother, who loves sports. I only watch them when I have nothing more interesting to do." She grinned mischievously. "And so far, that has never happened."

He rolled his eyes. "You're such a disappointment." His words dripped with mock anguish.

"Don't tell me you're a sports fan!" She raised her eyebrows in disbelief, but she actually wasn't surprised. He looked athletic and fit to her, more like a doer than a watcher.

He nodded.

"I don't believe it. How can an artistic, bonsai lover and international-gourmet cook be a sports enthusiast? That's a contradiction in terms."

"Gee, are you opinionated!" He laughed at her. "I'm a sensitive, nineties type of guy who spends Sundays at Mile High Stadium in the fall and Monday nights watching football in my den. I have Nuggets tickets too. When it's good weather, I hike and canoe."

"Whew! No wonder you're not married! When do you have time to date? If you want advice from me on getting married, I say forget all the sports!" She cocked her head to one side and narrowed her eyes. "On the other hand, how do you feel about volleyball?"

His eyes glimmered with amusement. "I love it!"

"Then I think you might make a good candidate for our church. In fact, can you spike the ball and play in dead earnest?"

He looked aghast. "Is there any other way?"

"You'll fit right in!"

They both burst into laughter, then continued eating.

On the way home, Maggie couldn't remember when she'd had such a good time. She could barely remember her last date. Then she thought of it. Three years ago a guy in the stake had invited her to a tri-stake singles dance. She'd only gone because everyone always told her, "Oh, it doesn't matter if you don't like your date. You could meet someone else you'd be interested in." Then they'd always go on to illustrate their point, telling her of woman after woman they knew who had met her husband that way. So while she wasn't the most eager of partners that night, she was animated and paid attention to her date.

Two minutes after they arrived, a woman from her ward said, "I love to dance. Loan me Michael for this dance, will you, Maggie?" She'd said sure. When Michael came back, he said, "Look, there are several sisters over there who aren't dancing. I think I'd better dance with them so they won't be wallflowers all evening."

She admired his thoughtfulness, but when he came back five dances later with the same tale, she'd said, "I'm in the same boat. I've sat here all evening while you've danced with everyone else. Now it's my turn." If she'd had any way home she would have gone. It was just the sort of evening she despised, and she wasn't going to spend it holding up the walls.

Michael had looked startled at her response, but when she'd stood up, he'd danced with her. She'd vowed to never again go to a singles dance, and she hadn't.

She took a deep breath. Tonight hadn't been anything like that evening. David wasn't anything like Michael. He focused his attention on her the entire evening, and she relished in how delightful it was to have a man show interest in her for a change. She'd genuinely enjoyed herself, and she had to admit that she'd like to go out with him again.

When they drove up in front of Gram's, David said, "I had a good time tonight. How about checking out some other country's cuisine one of these nights?"

"That sounds like fun. I'm game." She laughed. "But I'd hate to impinge on your sports, and since I'm not Jewish, our going out isn't helping you find a wife." She glanced toward him in the dark. David radiated a goodness that she found appealing, and longing filtered through her. Once again, she wished that he were a member of the Church.

"We both need breaks from our arduous lives, and we might as well take them together." His voice was light, and his eyes gleamed in the reflection of the street light. She could tell he wasn't taking her comments seriously.

Once she closed the front door behind her, Gram called from the living room. "Did you have a good time? Tell us all about it."

"I had a wonderful time." She glanced at Pat, who made it obvious she was just as eager as Gram to hear about her evening. "We had dinner at La Hacienda. They must have the best chili verde in Denver. Have either of you eaten there?"

Gram shook her head, but Pat said, "A couple of times, and you're right—they do have good food. But since I'm trying to avoid chronic heartburn, I don't eat Mexican very often. But we're not interested in a new place to eat. Tell us about David. Are you going out again?"

Maggie nodded. "To check out the various international cuisines."

Pat gave her a thumbs-up. "Now for the important stuff. Is he fun? Did he make your heart beat faster? Is your pulse racing? Are you smitten?" Pat had a wicked gleam in her eye, and Maggie could tell she was in for a lot of ribbing. "Tell me your feelings when you're with him! I need some new adjectives for my writing!"

"Please, my pulse has never been so steady." She thrust out her wrist toward Pat. "Take it." Then she dramatically flung her arm back over her heart. "My heart is barely beating."

Never short for words, Pat said with a grin, "You mean he leaves you faint?"

"No," Maggie said firmly, "he doesn't leave me any way." This wasn't quite the truth. "I'll tell you one thing—he is in the market for a wife."

At this statement, both Gram and Pat's eyes widened.

"A Jewish wife," she added, then gave them a self-deprecating smile. "We spent the evening discussing how to find suitable mates."

"If that isn't the limit," Gram said. "Go out with someone and spend the evening trying to get him married off to someone else."

Maggie shook her head in mock discouragement. "Since we're both still single, neither one of us has any killer ideas."

"So far this has the makings of a great romance novel. You two have to end up together so it'll have a happy ending. I could write this story now and my editor would buy it in a minute. 'Successful career woman takes on sister's children and ailing grandmother.' You can tell right then that she is a *virtuous, lovely, of good report and praiseworthy* woman. Enter the handsome doctor. He is kind, considerate, and looking for a wife. She deserves him." Pat smiled triumphantly. "Right?"

"One tiny flaw in the doctor," Maggie quickly pointed out. "He isn't LDS. He can't be married in the temple. The heroine won't settle for anything else. On the other hand, the heroine is from the tribe of Ephraim, and the hero wants a wife from the tribe of Judah."

"Ah, the book's black moment in chapter eleven. All seems lost. The couple will never end up together. Then, voilà. It all works out."

"I hate to burst your bubble, Pat, but as far as I've noticed, real life seldom is based on a romance novel." She shot Pat a quizzical look. "I stopped believing in Cinderella long ago."

Pat looked at Gram with a twinkle in her eye. "That's where we come in. I'm a writer, and you're a matchmaker. It'll be easy for us to figure out a happy ending for chapter twelve."

Gram beamed. "A snap!"

"I'd better be heading home." Pat stood up and gave Gram a hug. Maggie followed her to the front hall. The teasing of a moment ago was gone, and Pat said seriously, "I'm impressed with David. Too bad he isn't LDS."

"He really is a great guy." Maggie sighed. "If only this were as simple as one of your books."

"If only. The best thing about it is you're getting to have some fun." Pat hugged her. "Don't forget, I'll be happy to stay with Isabelle and the kids anytime you want to go out."

Shutting the door behind her friend, Maggie returned to the living room. "It's getting late, Gram. Why don't we turn in?"

Gram nodded sadly. "I'm such a trial for you, Maggie-girl. I'm sorry you have to take care of me."

She sounded so forlorn that Maggie's heart nearly broke. "Are you kidding? This is my pleasure. I love you." She gave Gram a fierce look. "What could I do that would give me greater joy?"

"You're just trying to cheer me up." Her lips trembled. "But Caitlin and Robert and I are wrecking your life."

Maggie felt the tears stinging her eyes. She put her arms around the frail body and drew her grandmother close. "Everything happens for a reason. Heavenly Father gave me this opportunity to be with you, and I'm happy to have it."

At these words, Gram stiffened. "You know that the three of us are in the way of you finishing your book and having a life."

Maggie twisted her mouth into a semblance of a smile. "Look at it this way. If it hadn't been for you, I'd never have met David."

Her grandmother sniffed. "You met him before you became my keeper."

"Yes, but if he hadn't stopped by and if you hadn't offered him pie, I'd have seldom seen him."

"Maybe," Gram grudgingly admitted. "But, oh, my darling granddaughter, I'd do anything not to be a burden on you." Her body was wracked with tears.

Maggie held her closer and said against her hair, "I know you would. But you're not a burden. You never could be. So never, never, never let the word *burden* enter your mind again, my darling grandmother." She kissed her cheek and helped her up to her walker. Once in the bedroom, she said, "I think you should wear your flamboyant purple nightgown." She pulled it out of the drawer. "This gown can't help but raise your spirits."

Her grandmother barely smiled.

When she had Gram tucked in, Maggie went upstairs to her own room and got ready for bed. What a day it had been. She knelt down for prayer and poured out her heart to her Father in Heaven. What was she going to do about Gram? Her home teachers had administered to her, but tonight Gram's despair was apparent. Maggie felt unbidden tears fill her eyes. She felt so inadequate trying to hold everything together for Caitlin and Robert and Gram. She didn't have the time or the energy for anything else, and she'd had to relegate her book to the bottom of her to-do list. But then a thought came burning into her mind. *Heavenly Father hasn't forgotten you, and He will bless you.* With that reassurance, she drifted off to sleep.

During the next few days, Gram seemed to drift a little further into utter hopelessness. Even though her therapists came, Maggie couldn't see any improvement, and her heart was heavy. She was sure Gram's despondent mood kept her from making progress, but she didn't know what to do about it. She had tried cajoling her, fixing her favorite meals, and spending time with her, but nothing seemed to make a difference.

But Thursday was the hair appointment. Maggie hoped that if she followed Gram's advice and got a makeover, it would cheer Gram up. Dropping Caitlin and Robert off at preschool, she went to the salon. She had booked her appointment with Alexander, the stylist Cecile swore by. Since Cecile herself always looked fantastic, Maggie had faith that he could make her look better—even glamorous.

His salon was in the Cherry Creek Mall, which in and of itself exuded elegance. A shimmer of excitement shot through Maggie as she entered the chic black-and-white room. The walls were a glossy white with black and silver lamps. Shiny white tiles covered the floor. The receptionist sat behind a mirrored, art deco desk, wearing a shiny black jacket, her hair done in the latest straight, flippy style. Maggie thought the girl looked as if she'd tumbled out of bed without time to comb her hair—it was a popular look that she disliked.

The receptionist looked up from her *Elle* magazine and smiled, exhibiting teeth as white as the walls. "Who are you here to see?"

Maggie approached the desk. "Alexander at nine."

The receptionist called him, and almost immediately, a tall, nice-looking man with a long mane of burnished hair strolled out through the doorway from the back room wearing a red shiny jacket, his sleeves pushed up to his elbows.

Maggie shook her head in amazement, noting that these people went in for shiny in a big way.

"Good morning, Maggie." He looked her over and then added, "Cecile's told me all about you, and I can't wait to get started."

His voice sounded more condescending than friendly, and Maggie knew immediately she'd failed the test. She could see he couldn't wait to get his hands on her hair. She hung back nervously, wondering if she really wanted to go through with this.

"Come on," Alexander said, motioning to her to follow him. They passed through a large room filled with red-jacketed beauticians and women in various stages of being beautified. He ushered her into his own private cubicle. Swinging the chair around for her to be seated, he said, "I'll brush your hair, and then Irina will shampoo it." He put a shiny white plastic cape around her neck.

A few minutes later, her hair standing straight up from his brushing, Maggie followed the woman to the next room. Irina washed her hair so thoroughly that she thought a few times she might be losing her scalp.

Then Alexander ran his fingers through her wet, curly locks. "You really do need to do something different with your hair, Maggie. Curls are out. Straight is in. Just leave it to me, and you'll be a new person."

"Okay." The word came out reluctantly. She had to keep reminding herself that Cecile looked great, so she didn't have anything to be afraid of. But her uneasiness didn't leave.

"First of all, we're going to highlight the front of your hair with warm, blond streaks." He got out a number of square-inch foil strips. Then he disappeared, returning a few minutes later with two cups of white, foamy goo. "I've mixed up two different shades of blond for your hair." He painted the mixture here and there with a brush, wrapping each strand in the foil. "You're going to look magnificent."

"Well, my grandmother will be happy," Maggie said. "She wanted me to have the 'California golden girl' look."

He nodded his head in agreement. "You will, just wait." After he'd finished, he said, "Come and sit over here under the dryer so the heat can work its magic."

This gave her a chance to read the latest fashion magazines. The summer styles amazed her. She could tell at a glance they hadn't been designed for real people. No one she knew went around with short, short skirts and see-through tops. Disgusting! She laughed. She sounded just like her mother had when she viewed the popular styles Maggie and Karen had wanted to wear when they were teenagers. She was her mother's daughter after all, and she'd sworn never to be that way. But these clothes were outlandish, and she didn't remember her high school clothes being this daring. Either her memory was getting bad, or styles were getting worse, and she suspected the latter.

"You're ready," Alexander said as he lifted the hood of the dryer.

Once in the chair, he took out all the foil, and she gasped. Here and there were little tufts of chicken-yellow hair! "What have you done?" Her voice was shrill, but she didn't care.

"Relax, Maggie! You want to be a golden girl, and you're going to be!" His calm assurance was as bad as the hair color.

She wanted to scream. Striving for composure, although she didn't know why, she said, "Just hurry. I want to get out of here."

Alexander looked astonished and then peevish. "All right, then." He continued, "Your hair is too thick to hold the style, so I'm going to thin it." He picked up a pair of scissors and proceeded to cut and cut. He tilted his head to the side and looked at her hair, then ran it through his fingers. "It's still too thick." He cut some more. Putting the scissors down, he poured lotion in his hands and rubbed it through her hair. Combing it flat to her head, he said, "This needs to set for a few minutes for it to take effect."

"What to take effect?" Maggie looked at him in the mirror, scared to think what else he might be doing.

"The straightening solution." His smile oozed superiority as he glanced down at her.

"The straightening solution!" She jerked her head away. "I don't think I want it straightened."

"Trust me!"

Those were the two stupidest words she'd ever heard. Could he be serious? "Why? I already look like I have baby chicken feathers in my hair."

"You'll love the style," he persisted, smoothing down her hair as if she hadn't said a word.

One thing Maggie was beginning *not* to love was Alexander. What a pompous jerk. How did Cecile stand him?! What would happen if she just got up and walked out now? She didn't quite have the nerve, and she didn't know what she'd do once she got out of the salon. Traipsing through Cherry Creek Mall with a wet, bright yellow head would make her look anything but super sophisticated. Silenced for the moment, she huddled under the shiny white plastic robe that covered her, clenching her fists.

Alexander went on with his ministrations.

Maggie shut her eyes, unable to watch what he was doing to her. Why didn't she just get up and walk out? She couldn't believe she'd look like anything but a mess. She shuddered.

"Hold still. I won't be much longer now."

What seemed like hours later, Alexander's cheery, confident voice said, "It's finished. What do you think?"

Slowly Maggie looked in the mirror. Some woman with stick-straight, *thin* hair stared back at her. A few bright yellow ends flipped up. She was speechless. In her wildest nightmares she hadn't expected to look this awful. She just continued staring, fascinated by how terrible she looked. *Shower, here I come! I'm going to wash that man right out of my hair, all right. Alexander.* Then a horrible thought hit her. *What if the straightening lotion was permanent and she couldn't wash it out?*

"You look just like a movie star." Alexander looked her over once again. "At least your hair does."

"What horror star did you have in mind?" Standing up, she tore off the plastic robe and looked him straight in the eye. "I'm sure I'll get used to it." *If I live that long.*

He looked shocked. "You don't like it?"

"I'm sure I'll get used to it." She didn't dare say anything else.

Maggie grabbed her purse and stalked out.

The receptionist said, "You look great! Isn't Alexander wonderful?"

"How much?" Maggie knew if she had any nerve, she'd just walk out without paying.

The woman smiled again, flashing her white teeth. "Seventy-five dollars, and Alexander usually gets at least a twenty-dollar tip."

Not from me, he doesn't. Maggie smiled just as broadly at the receptionist, "I don't tip. It's against my principles." Writing out a check for seventy-five dollars, she handed it to the woman and left, vowing never to return.

* * *

All morning Thursday, David had been at a geriatrics conference at the University Medical School. Now on his way back to University Hospital, he realized that he was close to Monaco Street, and he decided to swing by and see how Isabelle was doing. He hadn't had any contact with the family since Maggie and he had gone to dinner last Saturday. He'd had to deliver a paper at the conference this morning, and putting the finishing touches on it had kept him busy. He knew he could assume that no news was good news, but Isabelle had been on his mind, and since he was so close, he thought he'd stop and see her.

When he parked he noticed that Maggie's car wasn't in the driveway, and while the door appeared open, he couldn't imagine everyone going off and not locking the house. He decided he'd better check it out. As he went up the steps to the porch, he could see clearly that the house was open.

He stood at the screen door and called, "Isabelle! Maggie! Anybody home?" When no one responded, he called again, "Isabelle!"

Her frail voice came from inside. "Come in."

He found the screen door unlocked. Letting himself into the house, he made his way to the living room, where Isabelle sat in her recliner with a photograph album in her hands. "Are you all alone?" he asked. Her appearance shocked him. How could she have failed so much in a week? She looked drained of all vitality.

"Yes, for moment. The aide just left, but Maggie should be back anytime." She spoke slowly, as if she could barely force her words out. "I'm glad to see you. Can you stay and visit for a while?" Her listlessness troubled him. While depression was a common side effect of a stroke, he had hoped Isabelle would escape it, but it was obvious she hadn't. He hoped she'd become physically stronger and regain her old enthusiasm.

Giving her a cheerful smile, he settled in the floral easy chair. "How are things today?"

Her face crumbled, and for a moment he thought she was going to cry. Then she shrugged, as though it took all her reserve of energy. "I never thought I'd be in this kind of shape. I can barely stand up alone. I forget things. Words."

Compassion flooded him as he met her beseeching eyes. "I can only imagine how devastating it must be."

She sighed deeply, as if trying to rid herself of her discouragement. She opened a faded rose velvet album. "This is my mother's, and when I look at these pictures, all I can do is mourn that I can no longer work on her genealogy. I just barely discovered that my grandmother's family were French Huguenots. They escaped from France to Germany in order to avoid being killed by Catherine de Medici's men." She sighed again. "Now I'll never get my genealogy completed."

"It's interesting that your ancestors should escape *to* Germany to save their lives and mine escaped *from* Germany to save theirs." David doubted that his family would ever entirely recover from the Holocaust.

At this information Isabelle perked up slightly. "Were your parents in the Holocaust?

"They were six and eight years old when their parents escaped the Nazis. My father's father was a rabbi in a large synagogue in Berlin. My mother's father was not Jewish, but since children were considered Jews if their mother was, the Nazis forced my mother to wear a Star of David armband signifying she was Jewish." Just mentioning it sent a wave of pain through him.

Isabelle looked horror-stricken. "At age six?"

He nodded, thinking of his mother's fear. "Even at age six. Horrible even to think about, isn't it?"

"How did they get out?" Isabelle lay the album back on her lap. He could tell his family's history had caught her attention.

"My grandfather owned a nightclub where my grandmother performed. He knew a number of unsavory characters, and through one of them he was able to get papers falsified so that they could cross the border into Spain. My mother and grandmother went first, and they were to wait for my grandfather in Barcelona. Two weeks later, the Gestapo arrested and shot him. Then they confiscated all his property." David's family history never failed to stir his emotions, and he could feel his throat tightening. "My mother remembers him as a big, loud bear of a man who showered her with attention. His death caused a huge void in her life."

Isabelle looked upset. "Oh, your poor grandmother, to lose her husband that way. How did she manage?"

"Actually, her husband had provided well for her. She crossed the border in worn-out clothes, but paper money and diamonds were sewn into the tattered lining. Several times she had some close calls, but she managed to make it. I'm sure she had worries, but my mother remembers a carefree life once they were settled in Spain. No soldiers marching in the streets. No hiding. No holding her breath from fear. After their money ran out, my grandmother sang in nightclubs to support them.

"Then during the 1940s, the Nazi presence in Spain became more menacing, and my grandmother decided to try to find passage to the United States. It wasn't easy because the ships were full and many people were clamoring to get aboard. Finally she found an old friend of my grandfather's who had connections, and he got her passage."

Isabelle shook her head. "What a terrible ordeal to live through. I don't know if I could have made it. Of course," he saw a flash of the old Isabelle, "I can't sing, so that could have been a problem." She gave him a half smile before going on. "We've had it so safe in this country that I can't even imagine what living in the midst of war would be like. Did she keep a diary?"

"No, but my mother has written down her childhood memories and gathered up the few pictures she has been able to find. A few years ago she had them published into a book for the family." His chest tightened as he thought of the pain of his mother's early life, and he was struck anew with it every time he read her memoirs. In New York City his grandmother had gone on singing in clubs, which had left his mother alone most of the time.

"I'd love to read it." She sounded so interested that David made a mental note to call his mother and have her send a book to Isabelle.

"My mother would be glad to hear that someone wants to read about her childhood. The first thing she did when she was finished with it was send a copy to a Holocaust survivors' library."

"Does she have her genealogy?" Her eyes brightened at the mention of genealogy.

"No. I don't think she's particularly interested, and she has a busy practice."

"She's a doctor?" Isabelle couldn't have been more astonished.

"A psychiatrist." David's mother's own early life had given her great empathy with people, and she was also a warm and caring parent.

Her eyebrows raised in amazement. "A psychiatrist?"

He nodded, smiling at the elderly lady. "I think she's an over-achiever." His mother had been consumed with a passion for education, and he admired everything about her.

"Your dad? Is he a doctor too?"

He nodded again. "Yes. You'll be happy to know that his family has their genealogy back to the 1500s. His father was engrossed with his Jewish heritage and the genealogy of his fathers. I think he would have liked to have had it as far back as Abraham." He smiled gently at her. "But no such luck. When they were escaping Germany, he refused to leave the family records behind."

She shook her head. "I'm jealous. My parents weren't interested in it, and they accumulated few records. My own family took all my time and energy for years, and I just never got around to working on genealogy until my husband died ten years ago. Then I had to start from scratch. Trying to keep up with the research and doing my ancestors' endowments has kept me busy. Now it seems I've run out of time." Her chin quivered. "I know I'll never be able to do anything again if it takes any physical effort. I'm a useless old has-been. Why can't I die?" Her eyes filled with tears. "Why do I have to stay around?"

"Isabelle! Stop it!" He gave her a stern look. "You're the center of your family. Do you think Maggie could get along without you here?"

She sighed dejectedly. "I just hold her back. If she didn't have to take care of me, she could finish her book."

"I'm sure she puts you ahead of any book." David wished he could restore her health so she could be the feisty person he'd first met. That was in God's hands, but he felt he needed to do something himself. Then he had an idea.

Chapter 10

"I'll make a bargain with you," David said. "What if I were to come over and baby-sit Caitlin and Robert and visit with you, and we let Maggie spend that time writing?"

Isabelle slowly shook her head. "It too much bother." Her words quavered. "We can't put you out like that. You busy enough without baby-sitting old lady and two kids." Her dejection seemed to engulf her.

Her response surprised him. He thought she'd be eager to free up time for Maggie to write, but he sensed her worry was being dependent on someone else. "Don't worry about it. I'll be happy to do it just for you."

Before either one of them could say anything else, the front door slammed, and Caitlin and Robert ran into the room.

"Maggie got her hair fixed," Caitlin announced to Isabelle and David.

Their eyes turned to Maggie as she followed the children into the room. "Ta-da! Is this 'golden girl' enough for you, Gram?"

"I love it!" Isabelle perked right up. Then she looked at David. "What do you think, Doctor?"

He shifted the question to Maggie. "What do you think?"

"A diplomat—I might have guessed as much." She patted what was left of her hair. "I think I'm never going to a 'noted hairstylist' again! Call me crazy, but chicken-yellow hair has never been my goal, and neither has wearing it artificially thin and straight."

"You surprise me." David grinned at her. "I thought this might be your latest scheme to attract Mormon men."

She rolled her eyes. "I'd rather die single!"

He loved her facial expressions. Whether they were funny or rueful, they sent a shiver of happiness through him. "If you want to know what a Jewish man thinks, I prefer your curls."

"See, Gram—doctors do like curly mops," Maggie said to Isabelle.

For the first time since he'd arrived, Isabelle looked upbeat and cheerful. He wondered if she'd been behind Maggie's new hairstyle.

Evidently Robert had had enough of the conversation and wanted to get back to food. He ran over to Isabelle carrying a plastic bag with Central Park Hot Dogs on it. "Grandma, we got you a hot dog and fee fies."

Caitlin followed behind, a disdainful look on her face. "Robert, we are eating in the dining room." Then she said to David, "Dr. Rosenberg, we didn't get one for you, but," she gave him a sunny smile, "I'll share."

"Thank you, Caitlin. You're a generous girl, but I have to go back to work." He grinned at what a cutie she was. He regretted he couldn't stay and eat with them.

Maggie grinned. "I might even be persuaded to give you my hot dog and share Caitlin's, if you could stay."

He really did hate to go. "Sorry. I can't today, but I am counting on having hot dogs with you another time. Your grandmother and I have struck a bargain."

He turned to Caitlin and Robert. "Would you let me be your baby-sitter while your Aunt Maggie works on her book?" The kids looked confused.

"What are you talking about?" She turned to him.

He could tell Maggie was startled by his suggestion, and he said in a rush, "You need to finish your book, and I want to help you do it." He silently challenged her to refuse. "Since I can't type, I thought of this."

"Oh, yeah. You've got so much free time." Then she grinned again, her eyes flashing with humor. "Don't tell me you're giving up sports!"

She had him on that. He could never give up sports. "Not entirely," he admitted. "My entire body would go into shock, and I'd have withdrawal symptoms. But I don't think Saturdays would bother me. Maybe one or two nights a week."

Her eyes brimming with mischief, she shook her head. "While I think giving up Saturday sports would be good for you, and I really do appreciate the offer, I can't impose on you."

"Of course you can." He wouldn't let her turn him down. Moreover, he found he actually did want to help her finish her book. "Does this family do anything that they don't bargain for?" He didn't wait for her answer. His eyes glittering with amusement, he said, "You can pay me back. Dedicate your book to me," his smile deepened, "or Elmore Leonard."

She burst out laughing. "You win. How could I turn down such cheap labor? When do you want to start?"

David loved Maggie's infectious laugh. "As soon as possible. What about the day after tomorrow? I can come for most of the day. Would that work for you?"

"Gram always says, 'Don't look a gift horse in the mouth.' Of course it would work for me, but all day?" Maggie sounded skeptical.

"Six or eight hours." He wanted to reassure her. "What do you think?"

"I think you'll need a fix, so," she turned to Gram, "you better have the TV going full blast on tennis or baseball."

"I love baseball." Isabelle had become a little more animated, her eyes brightening at the prospect of David coming over. "I'll have someone to watch it with."

"You sure will." David thought she looked better already. Maybe his plan would work. He glanced at his watch. "Clinic hours start in a few minutes. I'd better go. See you Saturday about ten."

Maggie walked David to the door. "You don't know what you're in for, but thanks."

David reached over and ruffled her hair, which barely budged, and grinned at her. "This *is* straight hair." Warm feelings filled him. He looked forward to Saturday. He felt affection for Isabelle, and it seemed good to be involved with a family again. Although he knew he could be criticized for getting personally involved with a patient, contentment filled him as he drove to the hospital.

* * *

Going into the living room, Maggie said, "Come on kids, let's eat." They rushed to the dining room table while she helped Isabelle up to her walker. "Gram, can't I leave you alone for five minutes without you inviting David over?"

"Now, Maggie-girl, his offer to help was his own idea—not that I don't think it's a good one. When he talks about his family and their suffering, you can tell he's a good man."

"Now don't start on that," Maggie admonished, but her eyes twinkled. "I agree. Not every man I know would volunteer his days off to help someone out, let alone a busy doctor who isn't even related to us. We'll see how it works out. After one Saturday of chasing Caitlin and Robert around, he might change his mind."

Gram shook her head. "No. I can tell he's in for the long haul."

Maggie helped her get settled at the table before taking her own place.

"It's my turn to say the blessing." Caitlin didn't give anyone time to disagree before she'd started and completed the prayer.

They finished eating, and after promising Robert he could sweep after his nap, Maggie put both kids down. Then she helped Gram lay down to rest. If she'd had her computer here, she could have written for an hour or so, but unfortunately, it was one of the things she hadn't moved over from her condo. But she did have a priority—her hair.

Usually she washed her hair when she showered, but today she'd have to make do with the kitchen sink. She borrowed Gram's shampoo and grabbed some towels. She didn't think her scalp was up to another hearty wash, so she hoped the straightening agent came out easily and quickly. After several lathers, she rinsed her hair. After toweling it briskly, she checked in the mirror. Her hair wasn't as curly as it had once been, and it was so much thinner that she could almost see each curl individually. But she had changed her looks all right. She may not have looked like a sophisticated woman anymore, but she was still a 'golden girl.' The next time she was out, she was going to buy hair tint. Although after a second look, she wondered if even black could cover up the yellow! After running her fingers through her hair to try and fluff it up some more, she gave up and wiped away evidence of her shampoo in the sink.

She went into the living room and got comfortable in the easy chair, wondering how she could possibly finish her book this summer. She sighed deeply. It was already the second week of July, and by the second week of August, she would need to start preparing for the opening of school. Even if David did come over a day each week, it wouldn't give her enough time to finish it. She still had five chapters to go, and it was impossible for her to finish a chapter in six hours. She couldn't even type that fast, let alone think of ideas and write that fast.

Brad called. He said he thought he had located a place for them to live in Memphis, and he also had found child care with someone in the ward. He'd know for sure in a week or ten days. If the deal went through, he said he'd be back to move Caitlin and Robert permanently in a couple of weeks. She grimaced. The last several times he'd called, he'd sounded more and more like the old Brad. She didn't mind him going, but just thinking about the kids leaving sent pangs of lonesomeness twisting through her. She wished there were some way she could keep them with her.

* * *

David looked forward to Saturday. When he pulled to a stop in front of Isabelle's, he saw Maggie mowing the lawn with Robert hanging onto her side. Caitlin was playing on the porch, and he didn't see a sign of Isabelle. "Hi, Caitlin, what're you doing?"

She looked up, then ran over and grabbed his hand. "Are you our baby-sitter?" He nodded. "Come and see my Barbies."

She had three dolls spread out on the porch and doll clothes everywhere.

"Wow! That sure looks fun."

"Play with me," she ordered, making room for him to sit down on the porch.

He smiled down at her. "Maybe later, honey. Right now I've got to talk to your Aunt Maggie." As he walked across the front lawn, he heard Robert arguing, "Let me mow by myself."

"It looks like you've got some good help there," David said, noting with a wry grin that it looked as if she really had a stubborn little boy who was definitely in the way. "Hey, your hair is looking good."

Maggie appeared happy to see him. "I've only got half as much, and it's yellow, but give me time. This too shall pass." Touching Robert's head, she continued, "Gram's mower is too big for him to run. I think he needs his own." She glanced down at the little hands that tightly gripped the handles.

David knelt down beside Robert. "I don't know how to run a lawn mower. Could you show me how?"

Robert looked astonished, as though he'd never seen a grown-up so dumb. Then his face gleamed with a smile. "Yes." He tried to yank the lawn mower away from Maggie, who held on firmly.

"You don't?" Maggie looked just as shocked. "I can't believe that anyone could be as old as you and not know how to operate a lawn mower."

Grinning at her surprise, he said, "I'm not quite ready for an old folks' home, but I know what you mean. Try living in an apartment your entire life. Not much call for lawn mowing."

"Well, Robert's only three, and he's a whiz. Of course, he's not your everyday kid either." She grinned at Robert and ran her fingers through his already-tousled blond hair. "Anyway, mowing our lawn isn't one of your duties, so it doesn't really matter."

"Since I won't be hiking on Saturday for a while, I need the exercise." David slanted her a smile. "Besides, do you know how much more meaningful this day will be if I learn something new?"

She laughed. "I wouldn't want to impede your progress, so this is the way it works." She turned the mower off, which left Robert screaming he hadn't had a turn. Then she explained how to operate the mower and demonstrated a couple of times.

"I've got it. Grass, here I come."

"You're too eager. First let me show you where everything is in the house." Robert followed them, but stopped to join Caitlin when he got to the porch.

Once in the kitchen, David looked with interest at the new cabinets. "This room looks as good as new."

"It does, doesn't it? The carpenter came last week, and Gram is thrilled with the results. Thank goodness. She loved her kitchen, and it was painful for her to see the mess. I think all of the burned odor is gone too. Can you smell anything?" She sniffed.

"Only home cooking." He couldn't keep his eyes off the cinnamon rolls on the counter. They reminded him of his childhood and his Grandmother Rosenberg's poppy seed rolls. "Those look good enough to eat."

"Exactly what they're for." Maggie's eyes gleamed. "Anytime you want one or some, help yourself. For lunch I've made peanut butter sandwiches for the kids, and there's cold chicken and salad for you and Gram."

He raised his eyebrows. "Didn't trust me to fix lunch?"

She leaned back against the counter and considered him. "Are you kidding? Of course I trust you. You've graduated from gourmet cooking classes. I just didn't know if you could fix plebeian peanut butter sandwiches."

David leaned against the sink and folded his arms across his chest. "I admit it would be a stretch. But is there anything a doctor and a lawn-mower man can't do?"

She shook her head. "Not that I know of." She moved into the dining room. "Gram's in the living room. The kids take their naps upstairs in the bedrooms." She pointed up the flight of stairs. "There are only two bedrooms, and I'm sure you can find your way. Or did you want additional exercise?"

"No, I'll take your word for it. Somehow I think I'll get my exercise for today." He nodded agreeably, following her on into the living room.

"Gram, here's today's senior companion."

Isabelle looked up excitedly. "Just in time, David. The Giants are playing the Dodgers."

"I can't sit down right now because I promised Maggie I'd mow the lawn first." He glanced at her. "She wants to get all the work she can out of me while I'm here today."

"You've got that right! Bye! See you in a few hours."

He grinned at Maggie. "You don't need to hurry back. We've got everything under control here. Isn't that right, Isabelle?"

"It certainly is."

Waving good-bye, Maggie left.

"I'll come back in here in a little while," he promised. "I'm sure I'll need an early break since I don't mow lawns every day."

Isabelle gave him a dazzling smile. "I'll wait right here."

"Back in a flash." He met Robert on the porch, and, taking his hand, they returned to the mower. "You stand back while I start the mower. Then we'll very carefully mow the lawn." He frowned. It seemed dangerous to have Robert so close to the mower, so he decided he'd better watch him closely. After thirty minutes of starts and stops, he decided he finally had the operation of a lawn mower mastered.

Robert just hung on and stared intently straight ahead, making sure they went in a straight line—or apparently that was his intent. When David looked back, the line they'd mowed looked wavy. He shrugged. Who expected perfection the first time you did something? He could tell that this job was going to take several hours, so about eleven o'clock he stopped to rest and check on Isabelle.

Robert followed him into the house, and they stopped in the kitchen for water before joining Isabelle in the living room. When David dropped down on the couch, Robert sat next to him.

"You're just in time. David, I need assistance standing up." He helped Isabelle, and when he sat back down, Robert sidled even closer to him, leaning his head against David's arm.

David found himself wondering how it would be to have a son and teach him to mow and hike and row—even to watch sports with him. Would he ever be a father himself, or would he always be spending time with someone else's children? If he didn't get a move on it, he'd be too old and crotchety to enjoy them.

Isabelle came back, and he helped her get seated. "What's the score?" he asked.

"When I left, the game was tied." The score flashed on the screen, and the two teams were still tied.

"Who are you rooting for?" he asked, settling back down next to Robert.

"The Giants." Isabelle had a no-nonsense tone. "I've been a Giants fan ever since they were in New York and Leo Durocher coached them. You know he was married to Lorraine Day, don't you?"

He grinned. "Lorraine Day? Before my time. I'm a Yankee fan myself."

"Yankee fan!" She spit the words out as if she had something nasty in her mouth. "If you're going to root for a New York team, you could at least have the decency to support the Mets."

This made him laugh, and Robert laughed with him. It was a forced little sound, but David knew Robert wanted to do whatever he did. He could feel the tugging on his heartstrings, and he hugged the small boy and smiled down at him. Robert's little face returned the look.

David's eyes twinkled. "Now, Isabelle, aren't you a little dogmatic about baseball?"

She looked at him as if he'd lost his mind. "Not at all. Some teams you just cheer for—everybody knows that. The Forty Niners because Steve Young played for them."

He looked askance. "Forty Niners? Not me! I'm a Bronco fan, and in fact, I have season tickets to their games."

"Season tickets?" She had a scheming look in her eyes. "One or two?"

"Two." He wondered what she had in mind. He knew Maggie wouldn't be interested in going. She disliked sports intensely.

"That works out fine. After all, Steve Young's retired, and we do live in Denver. I think we should support the home team."

The home team? From what she'd just said about baseball, David couldn't believe that *home team* was any part of her logic.

She gave him a shy, hesitant glance, which he found phony. Then she said, "I've never gone to a professional football game, and I'd sure like to go to one."

He wouldn't put anything past her. "Isabelle, I'd love to take you. I've got the schedule at home, and I'll bring it to you. All you'll have to do is name the Sunday."

At this she frowned. "What about a Monday night one? I shouldn't go to games on Sunday," she paused, "although, if I go to all my meetings first, it would be okay. Only don't tell Maggie. She doesn't approve of football on Sunday."

"I think she'll know if we go on a Sunday," he countered.

"Yes, but not in advance. I don't want her clucking about it beforehand."

"I can't believe that Maggie has that much influence over you."

She gave him a sly look. "She doesn't, but that doesn't keep her from telling me what I should or should not do, religiously speaking."

He loved this feisty Isabelle. She seemed like her old self.

* * *

When Maggie drove into the parking garage of her condo, she had a sense of relief at being home again. She'd had her mail forwarded, and she hadn't been over to her own place in at least three weeks. She hadn't realized how much she'd missed it, but once she entered her unit, she felt as if she'd found sanctuary from the concerns of the last weeks. It had been so long since she'd been here or even thought about it that she'd forgotten just how soothing and peaceful her living room was. She wondered how a person could forget what her home was like in less than a month. But she knew the answer. It was easy when she had a million other things on her mind twenty-four hours a day. She sank back into her peach easy chair, relaxing and letting all the stress of the last little while drain out of her body.

Her eyelids kept blinking shut and, while it might have been only 10:30 in the morning, she needed a nap before she could think clearly enough to write. She went into her bedroom and lay down, pulling an afghan over her. The next thing she knew, it was twelve o'clock and she was awake and feeling refreshed. Opening the sliding glass doors to the balcony, she stood breathing in the fresh air before heading into her office.

She pulled up the chapter she'd been working on, and reread the last few pages until she again felt at the center of Blanche and Ruby's lives.

Blanche liked the detective's looks. He was tall, and she'd always liked tall men. The gray streaks made him appear to be in his forties. Deep lines emphasized the firmness of his mouth. An aggressive nose and an equally compelling chin highlighted a rather hard face, but it was softened by magnificent green eyes that she realized were staring questioningly at her.

"You two found the body?"

Maggie kept writing, a smile on her face. She loved the character of Blanche probably because she was so much like her own grandmother.

She finally leaned back in her typing chair and stretched. Satisfaction permeated her. She'd written six pages without stopping for even one phone call. Evidently David had managed not only the kids but Gram as well. She printed the chapter to take back to Gram's with her so she could polish it during the week.

Maggie hadn't realized how rejuvenating the day would be until she started back to Gram's. New life and energy lifted her spirits, and she felt as if she could conquer any problem that arose.

She parked in the driveway next to the house and ran in the side door. "I'm home!" Caitlin came running out to meet her, and Maggie knelt down and gave her a hug before going on into the living room. Robert was sitting on David's lap on the couch, and she could tell he had no intention of moving. Gram seemed especially chipper. "Everyone looks so happy, I think I should have taken a day off sooner."

"We've enjoyed ourselves. It's nice to have someone to watch ball games with. And David's the man." Her grandmother beamed as she made this comment.

Maggie felt like beaming too when she looked at him. "You're a miracle worker, David Rosenberg. Robert has a new best friend, Gram and Caitlin are happy, and I feel totally revitalized—a new person. Thank you very much." She settled into the floral chair, feeling comfortable. Caitlin crawled up onto her lap. The room and the people in it exuded an air of love and family. David just added to the feeling, as if he belonged with them.

"So do I. I would equate lawn mowing with mountain climbing any day." He gave a mock groan of exhaustion. "But more importantly, were you able to accomplish anything on your book?"

"Yes. Blanche and Ruby are now in the midst of a murder investigation."

His brow furrowed. "Who?"

"My characters have stumbled upon a body, and now they're investigating the murder. Thanks to you, I've completed six more pages." The feeling of accomplishment radiated so strongly through her that she didn't think she could have felt any better if she'd finished the entire book.

"Only six?" He appeared dumbfounded at the low number.

"When ideas are flowing, it takes me nearly an hour to write a page. If I'm having trouble, it takes even longer. Doesn't sound like much progress, does it?" She found people were always surprised that it took so long and that she couldn't just write five minutes here and ten minutes there until the book was completed. She needed blocks of time instead.

He shook his head. "I'm amazed. I never realized it took so long. How many pages do you still have to write?"

He looked extremely interested in this bit of information, and Maggie thought he was probably wondering how long he was going to have to baby-sit while she wrote. "About seventy." She smiled. "I'm on the home stretch."

"Then I need to come for seventy more hours for you to finish." He looked doubtful.

She sat straight up in her chair, nearly sending Caitlin to the floor. "No!"

"Yes!" He grinned at her.

She couldn't impose on him that much. "I wouldn't ask that of you. Saturdays, as long as you can, are fine."

"The problem is, Saturdays aren't enough. Summer will be over long before seven Saturdays have passed."

"I'll get it finished when I can. I'm not going to worry about it. I just appreciate your offer, David. Furthermore, how are you going to find a wife if you're here all the time?" She attempted to keep her tone light, but she had mixed emotions. She did think that he needed to find a wife, and on the other hand, she hated not to have him be a part of their lives.

David said thoughtfully, "Aren't you the one who said that God knows us and is aware of our problems and will bless us? I believe the same thing. So we'll see."

He was using her own words against her, and Maggie could hardly argue. He sounded as if he weren't willing to drop the matter, and if she looked deep into herself, she had to admit that she preferred having him with them rather than off looking for a Jewish wife. Her stomach twisted. *Remember, Maggie, he's not for you. He's Jewish.* Despite her feelings, she couldn't possibly let him spend all his free time here. It wasn't fair to him.

She nodded. "All right. For the time being, we'll leave it as it is. Saturdays only."

David looked down at a drowsy Robert in his arms. "I hate to go and leave him."

Maggie sat Caitlin on the floor and then went over to take Robert. He came right to her and snuggled against her. "Did he take a nap?"

"No," David said sheepishly, standing up. "I was having too much fun with him. Next time. I promise." He went over to Isabelle and patted her shoulder. "See you next week."

Her eyes sparkled. "I can't wait."

Maggie deposited Robert on the couch, where he curled up and continued sleeping. She thought the normal sounds would soon wake him. At the front door, she touched David's arm. "You've been a lifesaver, and I can't thank you enough."

"I'm grateful for the opportunity." His eyes seemed to pierce her soul, and her heart caught at his obvious sincerity. It would be impossible to find a kinder or more decent man than David, and she felt he deserved to find a wonderful Jewish wife.

Even after David left, the upbeat spirit lingered. Everyone had benefitted from David's generosity.

They didn't go to church on Sunday. Gram didn't feel up to it, and Maggie didn't want to leave her alone. She actually didn't know how she could handle all four of them at church anyway. So they listened to the Tabernacle Choir in the morning, and afterward she read to Caitlin and Robert from a picture version of the Book of Mormon. Then they sang all the Primary songs they knew. Listening to their sweet voices and looking at the Spirit shining in their faces sent a stabbing pain of yearning through her. She hungered to have some children of her own, fresh from the presence of Heavenly Father. Sitting with Caitlin and Robert on either side of her reminded her just how barren her life was without children. Soon she wouldn't even have these two as consolation. Then the comfort of the Spirit filled her, and she knew once again that Heavenly Father knew of her circumstances and that He loved her.

Tuesday she had a chance to tint her hair. She'd put a drab brown on it, which turned out surprisingly well. Now she had golden-brown hair, and she looked like a normal fourth-grade teacher, not some wannabe doctor's wife.

That night, Gram and Maggie were sitting on the front porch enjoying the pleasant July evening while the kids played with Legos when David drove in the driveway. The minute Caitlin and Robert recognized him, they ran over to the car. "Uncle David! Uncle David!"

"Hi." Smiling broadly, he opened the trunk of his car. "Here you two—something to keep you busy." He handed them each a large package. Immediately, Robert tore off the wrappings. His eyes grew big. "A lawn mower." He ran to Maggie. "Look! A lawn mower my size!"

"Did you tell Uncle David thank you?" Maggie couldn't hide a smile. Leave it to David to bring a lawn mower for Robert. He would have probably been just as happy with a less-expensive broom, but for Robert, nothing could be better than this: a bright red, metal lawn mower with all the bells and whistles.

"Thank you, Uncle David." Robert promptly went to the corner of the grass and started mowing.

Caitlin waited until she was back on the porch to unwrap her present. She gasped with delight. "Dishes, Aunt Maggie, just like yours! And silverware! I can set my own table."

"I think there's a wooden stool upstairs that you could use for a table for your dolls. I'll run up and get it." While Maggie went upstairs, Caitlin ran inside for her dolls.

Returning with the stool and a dish towel for a tablecloth, Maggie found David standing on the porch waiting for her. He'd given Gram a tin of nuts, which she was busy opening, and he handed Maggie a leather case.

Hesitantly she opened it, wondering what he was giving her, and she quickly saw a laptop computer. "For me?" When he nodded, she said, "I can't let you do this."

He quickly said, "Relax, Maggie, I'm not *giving* this to you. I'm *loaning* it to you. This is one I got for myself, but I never use it. Now during the week when the kids are napping or you have some free time, you can write. When I come over on Saturdays, you can copy what you've written onto a CD and put it on your own desktop."

She was speechless. She'd thought her own computer was too cumbersome to move when she didn't know how long she'd be at Gram's, but she'd never even considered using a laptop. She put it down and hugged him. "Thanks!"

David smiled as she picked up the laptop again. "Now, while you figure out how to work it, I'll visit with Isabelle and keep an eye on the kids." He grinned at the small girl. "I might even join Caitlin and her dolls for a party."

Still in a state of shock, Maggie returned to the living room. She retrieved the laptop user's manual from a side pocket and started reading. Then she turned the computer on and explored the contents of it. The more she typed, the more excited she became. Running upstairs, she got her latest chapter of *Murder at the Berkeley.* A few minutes later, she began the next chapter.

Spying some empty chairs by a large, wicker flower stand filled with an impressive arrangement of oriental lilies, Blanche said, "Let's sit over there. It'll give us a good view of the room."

They studied the other mourners.

Whew! David sighed with relief as he left Isabelle's and started home. The results of tonight had been exactly what he wanted: Caitlin and Robert happy with their presents, Isabelle cheerful, and best of all, Maggie writing on the laptop. He'd had a close call, though. He knew he should have realized that Maggie would never accept a computer from him, even if he had bought it expressly for her. She was a kindhearted, caring person who always put her family first, and she certainly deserved a good husband. What was wrong with Mormon men? Why hadn't they snapped her up long ago? He shook his head in wonder. She was attractive, with a blazing smile that could melt ice forty feet away. Too bad her husband had to be Mormon. And if she were only Jewish. He couldn't let himself even think about it.

As he entered his condominium, David was still pumped up from the satisfaction that the evening had brought him. Plain and simple, he wanted a family of his own. If he received this much enjoyment from Isabelle's family, he could only imagine how much more enjoyment his own would bring him.

Stretching out on the leather sofa in his study, he watched the news and then went to bed. He put his hand over his eyes and recited the *sh'ma*.

* * *

Rolling over onto her back the next morning, Maggie stretched. Exhilaration flashed through her body, and she felt much more alive this morning than ordinarily. Not that she didn't usually wake up happy, but this morning was different. It was a wonderful day, and all because of David. She recalled what a thoughtful person he'd turned out to be. She was still amazed that he would take time out of his busy life to see to the needs of her family, but she could tell he undoubtedly became a doctor because he was a caring person.

She couldn't wait to get everyone settled for the day and to start writing. Now she knew for certain that she could finish her book in the remaining time before school started. She swung her feet to the floor and stood up, anxious to get breakfast over with. She put on an old pair of faded jeans and her favorite Denver University sweatshirt and headed for the kitchen, stopping by Gram's bedroom on the way.

Although the television was on, Gram appeared to be dozing. Maggie patted her lightly on the shoulder. "Are you okay?"

Slowly, the bright blue eyes opened. "I'm tired this morning, and I think I'll lie here a while longer." Her eyelids closed again.

Maggie frowned. This was totally unlike Gram. She was usually an early riser, and even since her stroke, she had awakened early. Could last night have been too much for her? Gram adored visiting with David, so Maggie thought she would have felt buoyed up by his visit. She went on into the kitchen and got out the cereal and milk for Caitlin and Robert. She, herself, would have to be starving to eat cold cereal, but the kids loved it. They wouldn't even consider eating french toast, which was what she was fixing for herself and Gram. She beat the eggs, added the milk, and put the frying pan on the stove. Then she'd dress the kids.

"Good morning, sunshines," she greeted them as she gently shook them awake. Her throat tightened as she thought how delighted Karen would be to see her children waking up happy. She didn't think she could have dealt with grouches in the morning. "Let's get your faces washed, and then you can pick out what you want to wear." She'd found out the hard way that it was easier to let them choose their own clothes, albeit not faster. "Breakfast is ready."

"Do I get to set the table?" Caitlin asked her this question every morning as she got dressed.

"No one can do it better than my own darling Caitlin." Maggie picked her up and swung her around in her arms. "Get your shoes on and go on downstairs."

"We having puffed wheat and milk?" This was Robert's usual morning question.

"Yes, cold cereal lover, you are."

He grinned at her. "Good." Then he handed her his shoes. "Help, please."

"Ah, my favorite boy is polite." She gave him a kiss and swung him around before setting him on the bed again and putting on his shoes.

"Let's go." He pulled on her hand, and they proceeded downstairs.

A niggle of worry diminished Maggie's elation when she discovered Gram still sleeping. Caitlin had the table set, and after the blessing, they ate. Afterward it was back upstairs to brush teeth and comb hair. She decided to let Gram sleep while she ran the kids to preschool.

When she returned, she found Gram still asleep. Touching her gently on the shoulder, she said, "Are you all right?"

"Oh, Maggie." Gram's eyes blinked open. "I'm just a little weak."

"The physical therapist is due at eleven. Do you want me to call her and postpone her visit?"

"No. I'll get up and get ready. Heavens, I can't lie here all day." She moved her legs to the side of the bed, but when she sat up, she made no further move to stand. Maggie moved her walker over to the bed. Her grandmother grasped the sides, and slowly pulled herself up. Once she was standing, she began to sway.

Maggie grabbed her and helped her sit back down.

"My legs are weak, and I don't think they'll hold me." Gram sat back down on the bed. Her breathing sounded raspy. "I don't know what's wrong with me."

Maggie put her hands under Gram's shoulders to help her stand up. "Let me help you into the bathroom."

"I can do it." Her tone left no question about whether or not she would do it herself.

Despite Gram's words, Maggie continued lifting her. When Gram was standing, she shook herself free and started slowly for the bathroom. "Don't worry," she called over her shoulder. "I'll limber up."

But Maggie had her doubts. The wobbly way her grandmother moved worried her.

A few minutes later Gram called, "Maggie, could you help me stand up?"

She hurried into the other room and lifted her. Once on her feet, Gram clung to Maggie as they made their way the short distance to the bedroom. When she was sitting on the bed again, she looked up at Maggie and said, "I think I might have to go back to using the wheelchair. My legs certainly aren't cooperating today."

"I'll help you dress, and then we'll see what the physical therapist has to say." Maggie pulled a pink pantsuit out of the closet and held it up. "What about this?"

"Yes." Gram smiled. "It's so feminine."

"I'll get a pan of warm water, and you can wash your face and your hands in here. Then I'll help you put on clean clothes." She found a plastic pan in the kitchen, which she filled with soapy water and brought back to her grandmother. "Here, I'll place it on this other chair and you'll be able to reach it. Call me if you need me." She returned to the kitchen and cleared up the breakfast dishes. Then she helped Gram dress and assisted her into the wheelchair for the ride to the dining room, and afterward to the living room.

Maggie still felt eager to write, but some of her earlier joy had dissipated. Was this just a phase Gram was going through or was her strength slowly deteriorating for good?

When the physical therapist came, she had Gram practice standing and sitting, then she told Maggie that she thought Isabelle's leg muscles would get stronger over time, but she wouldn't predict how strong or how soon. As far as Maggie was concerned, that made her diagnosis worthless.

Gram sat in her recliner and dozed off and on all day. She made no effort to come to the dining room to eat, preferring just to stay in her chair.

Once Caitlin and Robert were down for a nap, Maggie went back to her writing. She'd finished four more pages by evening, and she was so happy she thought she might burst. She smiled to herself. She hadn't had this much childlike exuberance in years.

Thursday Isabelle felt stronger, but her spirits were low. Even the thought of David coming didn't cheer her up. "Would you bring me my family history book?" She sighed dejectedly. "I want to read about my ancestors."

"What about Parley P. Pratt's autobiography? Have you read that recently?" Maggie hoped that Gram's great-grandfather's memoirs might encourage her. She hated to see Gram look at her family history book because it just depressed her since she didn't think she'd ever be able to work on it again.

"No. I want to read over the names of the people I've found and whose temple work I've done." She sounded distressed.

Reluctantly, Maggie placed the heavy binder on her lap. "Gram, when I get finished with my book, why don't I redo this binder? I could put these pages in some scrapbooks that would be easier to handle."

Isabelle shrugged. "If you want to, but I don't mind this." She opened the heavy blue cover and started mumbling to herself. "Flower Flora Browne, 1528. Rose Kirby, 1564. Bridget Browne, 1594. These women all have family members that I'm never going to find." She looked as if she would start crying any minute.

The pervasive feeling of Gram's grief settled over both of them, and Maggie realized she had to do something to elevate her mood. "Gram, has the temple work been done for each of them?" She knew it had, but she wanted to remind Gram of it. She pulled a chair over next to the recliner and made herself comfortable in it. Then she placed her arm on Gram's to reassure her.

"Yes." Her voice still sounded woeful.

"Who did it?"

She turned the page. "You know I did."

Gram spoke with a hint of exasperation, which Maggie found encouraging. "You have hundreds of people in that book whose names you found and whose work you've done. They are waiting eagerly on the other side to thank you for what you did for them. Think of it! Hundreds of people!" She pulled her chair in front of Gram and grasped her hands. "So what if you're never able to do genealogy work again? I happen to think you will, but so what if you can't? Think of all the happiness you've brought to your ancestors! Now they have a chance for exaltation."

"But I haven't done enough!" Gram's anguish tore at Maggie.

"Gram, Heavenly Father knows what you have done and what He wants you to do. If He has more genealogy work for you to do, I know the way will be opened." Maggie watched her grandmother wrestle with what she had said.

Finally the pale, wrinkled face perked up slightly. "You're really wise, Maggie. Thanks for reminding me of Heavenly Father's love. I know what you said is true, but oh, my darling, I hope you never have a stroke and go through this." Tears filled her eyes and spilled down her cheeks. "Losing my husband and my daughter and my granddaughter were hard, but being left a useless old woman is the hardest of all. I sometimes think I can't manage any longer. I only wish I could be with them."

Tears filled Maggie's eyes as she felt Gram's heartache. "What would happen to me if you go? I wouldn't have anyone left on this earth who loves me. I don't want to be alone." She cuddled Gram's small, delicate hands against her cheeks. "We need each other."

When David came that evening, Caitlin and Robert ran out to greet him. "Uncle David! Did you bring us anything?" They each grabbed one of his hands.

His eyes lit up and he grinned at them. "How are my two favorite kids this evening?"

Pulling on his arm, Caitlin said, "Fine."

Robert pulled on the other arm. "What you bring us?"

Carrying a computer CD, Maggie came down the steps to meet him on her way to her condo. "What are you kids saying?"

"We want a present." They were still excitedly dancing around him.

Embarrassed at their actions, Maggie frowned at the two. "Never let me hear you ask Uncle David for a present again."

Upon hearing her stern tone, Caitlin and Robert stood completely still and looked up at David, absolutely disgraced.

"Tell him you're sorry for being rude."

"I'm sorry." They spoke in unison, their voices indicating they were thoroughly chastened, but they still clung to his hands and gazed up at him.

He smiled reassuringly at them. "I won't always have presents, but tonight I do have a surprise for you." Their eyes grew wide. "I want to visit with your grandmother for a while, and then we'll open the surprise."

Smiling once again, Robert went back to mowing the lawn, and Caitlin rejoined her dolls on the porch.

"Sorry about that." Maggie gave David a rueful glance. "I guess I'll have to admit that Caitlin and Robert are just like all kids. They shamelessly ask for presents."

"I thought for a minute you were going to scar them for life with your reprimand," he said easily.

His warm expression sent a rush of happiness through her. After Gram's despondency today, nothing had lifted her own spirits until now. "I doubt that irrepressible duo can be kept down for long." She could feel the smile fill her face. "But you can't keep bringing them things. They'll think they're entitled to something every time you come."

"Aren't they?" he rebutted, his face filled with mischief. "Everybody likes presents. Don't you?"

"Well, yes, but . . ." She let the words drift to a stop.

"I know." He held his hands up as if to protect himself. "I know. I won't bring something every time I come. But tonight I brought a book to read to them." He looked at his watch. "See you in a couple of hours?"

"Sure. Thanks again."

"No problem." He bounded on up the porch steps, into the house, and then to the living room.

"Hi, Isabelle. What's happening?" He made himself comfortable on the couch.

Her face lit up when she saw him and then dropped again. "Oh, David, I'm glad you're here. Nothing's happening, and that's what's bad."

He tried to keep his tone light. "You mean Maggie's boring you?"

"Sitting in this house is boring me; going to the porch is boring me; not being able to drive is boring me; not being able to walk is boring me. I can't do a thing but look back on what I've already done. There's no future to look forward to." She shook her head despondently.

"What do you mean you aren't able to walk? You've got your walker." What was happening to her physically?

She shook her head. "My legs are too weak to hold me up, and so I'm using a helper." She motioned towards the wheelchair, which was propped against the wall.

Great. He was hoping that when she regained her physical health her spirits would rise. "The physical therapist is still coming, isn't she?" He hadn't received any report that she wasn't.

"She came today, but she doesn't know if I'll get any stronger or not." Isabelle was completely listless.

He'd hoped that having company would help, but he didn't see much carryover from the other night. His experience had shown him that growing weaker would only exacerbate her depression. "Isabelle, I want you to come into the clinic Monday if your legs haven't gotten any stronger. In the meantime, we've got to do something exciting outside this house. Can you think of anything?"

"What I'd really like to do is go to church Sunday. I haven't been since I had my stroke. I miss it and all my friends." Her tone was wistful.

"That takes care of Sunday. What time shall I pick you up?" he said enthusiastically, hoping some of it would rub off on Isabelle.

She tried to give him an impish grin, but she couldn't quite pull it off. He saw, however, a glimmer of the old Isabelle. "It starts at 9:00 A.M. and is over at noon."

He swallowed. Three hours in church was a little more than he'd bargained for, but at this point, he'd do most anything to cheer her up. "Sounds fine to me."

Now her smile touched her entire face, reaching her eyes. "I keep telling Maggie you're a good man." She paused. "I'm only up to going to sacrament meeting, and that starts at 10:50 and is over at noon."

He gave a silent sigh of relief, then said dramatically, "Your wish is my command, dear lady. But what are we going to do on Saturday? We have all day if you feel up to it."

She slowly shook her head. "I can't think of any place else I want to go."

"Then prepare yourself for a surprise excursion on Saturday, and I'll pick the destination." Now he had to come up with a place that Caitlin and Robert would enjoy too.

David and Isabelle continued to talk for a while. Then Gram saw that Tom Brokaw was on TV, and she wanted to watch him. David went out first to check on the kids. Robert was still contentedly "mowing" the grass, and Caitlin had managed to find water and had filled the cups of her dish set for her dolls. When he looked at the guests, he smiled. Somehow her sophisticated Barbie dolls didn't seem to fit into a kid's party. He returned to the living room, and he and Isabelle watched the news together.

Nearly an hour later, Caitlin, and Robert burst through the living room door. "What's our surprise?"

"I'll get it." David rose from the sofa. "It's out in the car." The kids followed right behind him.

He retrieved the book and brought it back to the porch. "Why don't we read it out here so your grandmother can enjoy the rest of her program in peace?"

They both nodded. He sat in the lawn chair and scooped the kids up on his lap. "This is the story of Max. The title is *Max Sleeps Outside.* Have you ever slept outside at night in a tent?"

Their eyes wide, they solemnly shook their heads and said, "No."

From the look on their faces, David didn't think they were very eager to either. He began reading. "Once upon a time a boy named Max wanted to sleep outside. He was five years old, and his mother said, 'Wait until you're older.' But Max didn't want to wait. Taking hold of his dog, Rassel's, collar, he went out to the backyard."

David began to wonder if this book was a very good idea. The kids were staring intently at the pictures, and he hoped they weren't getting any ideas.

Caitlin pointed at the print. "What does it say?"

He read the words to her and then continued the book. By the time he'd finished it three times, Robert was asleep and Caitlin was drowsy. It looked like the perfect time to get them in bed. Carrying them upstairs to their room, he found that Maggie had laid out their pajamas. Deciding that they were too tired for tooth brushing, he skipped that part and tucked them in bed. Caitlin held out her arms and wrapped them around his neck, saying, "I want hugs and kisses." Making a big production out of it, he gave her several, just grateful that she wanted a hug and kiss from him.

His heart lighter, he returned to the dining room to find Maggie coming through the side door, computer disks in hand. "How'd it go?"

"Wonderful. Do you realize that with your trusty laptop here," she pointed to it next to the table, "I've finished ten pages since Saturday?"

Her enthusiasm made up for Isabelle's dejection. "Great! At the rate you're going, soon I won't have any excuse left to come over anymore."

"Actually, the kids' dad should be home next week sometime, and I think I can manage with just Gram." She blew the curly bangs out of her eyes and fluffed up the sides of her hair with her fingers.

He loved the saucy way she did that, and to his amazement, her smile sent a twinge of excitement through him. He took a deep breath. "No, you can't. You're not getting rid of me that easily. I prefer to think that there isn't any way you can get along without me."

"Never let it be said that I, Maggie Summers, refused any help so willingly given. You can keep coming as long as you want." Secretly, she was beginning to think that for her personally, it might not be such a good idea.

"Now that's a relief to know. By the way, Isabelle wants to go to church on Sunday, and I said I'd take all of you. I don't see how you could manage by yourself."

"I can't. David, as I've said before, and will undoubtedly say again, you're a lifesaver." She patted his arm.

"When did this weakness in her legs develop?" Although he hadn't dwelt on the topic with Isabelle, this was a major concern of his.

"This morning she got up late and complained of not being able to stand. She's spent the entire day in her recliner, not even getting up for meals, only to go to the bathroom. We used her wheelchair to get her back and forth." Worry etched Maggie's face.

"If she isn't better Monday, bring her in and I'll run more tests." They went on into the living room. "We're going on a secret outing on Saturday." He grinned conspiratorially at Isabelle.

"Secret?" Maggie gave them a quizzical look. "What's up?"

"You'll be writing, so the rest of us are going on a secret jaunt. I'm the only one who knows where, and I'm not telling." His eyes gleamed.

"If you're not telling, then I for sure am not asking! So there!" She gave them a mocking glance.

"I'd better run along. See you on Saturday about ten." He hugged her grandmother and put his arm across Maggie's shoulders, giving her the lightest of hugs.

She followed him to the door. "Thanks again. Good night." Locking the door, she returned to the living room. Gram looked pale and drawn, as if she hadn't an ounce of energy left. "Ready for bed?"

She nodded, and Maggie helped her into the wheelchair, then they made their way into her bedroom. A half hour later, her grandmother was in bed, and Maggie was on her way to her own room. She checked on the kids, who were lying crossways asleep in the bed. Straightening them around, she tucked them in again.

Once in her own room, she slipped into her nightgown and then sat on the edge of the bed, wondering what she would do if Gram got any weaker. Gram was light as a feather, and already Maggie had a few aches in her back from lifting her today. She was grateful for David. She thought about calling Gram's former doctor and thanking him for being out of town when she needed him. The best thing that had happened to her in months was meeting Dr. David Rosenberg. The Lord had certainly blessed them all when David came into their lives. But what did she do next? School was starting soon, and Gram wasn't getting any stronger. She sighed deeply. She knew without even asking that Barbara wouldn't be any help. Each time she spoke to her on the phone, her aunt just praised her for handling everything so well. She'd have to leave it up to Heavenly Father to guide her, because her thoughts were a jumble, and she couldn't see anything clearly.

She knelt and prayed about all her concerns, then crawled into bed, turning and twisting, trying to find a comfortable position for what seemed like hours. Finally she slept.

* * *

On Friday night, David went to the synagogue for services. Afterward he gathered with the rest of the congregation for coffee. He always enjoyed socializing with the members. Esther Shapiro, one of his favorite people, sat alone at one of the tables, and when she caught sight of him, she motioned him over. He grinned at her as he sat down. "If you're determined to find me a wife, I wish you'd hurry."

"I've found someone," she whispered confidentially. Then she put her hand in front of her mouth and leaned toward him. "See that redhead over there in the green dress?"

"With the three children hanging on her?" As he watched, the woman ruffled the hair of the smallest boy while she talked to the others in the group.

"That's the one. Her name is Naomi Dickens, and she's divorced. Her husband was a gentile. She's felt like something is missing in her life, and she believes the place to find it is here. She's a buyer at Miriam's."

Miriam's? She looked as if she worked in a place like that. Miriam's was an exclusive dress shop in Cherry Creek Mall. He'd been in it several times looking for a gift for his mother.

He continued to watch her unobtrusively. She seemed friendly enough, yet he didn't consider her smile as warm as Maggie's. But she was Jewish.

Finally, Esther stood up. "Let's go over, and I'll introduce you."

For some strange reason that he didn't understand, David found himself reluctant to meet her. But why? She was attractive, seemed friendly enough, and best of all, she was Jewish. But he didn't say anything to Esther; he just followed her over to the other group. Naomi looked up when they approached and gave him a friendly smile.

Esther spoke right up. "Naomi, I'd like you to meet David Rosenberg. He's a doctor at University Hospital. David, this is Naomi Dickens, and we're hoping she'll become a permanent member of the congregation."

David smiled and held out his hand to shake hers. "It's great to have new people join us. Welcome! Are these your children?" He looked down at the three solemn children.

"They are." Naomi returned his smile. "Nathan's eight and the oldest, then Becca's six, and last of all, Saul, five." Then she said to her children, "This is Dr. Rosenberg."

They gravely said hello, and just as gravely shook hands. These children were extremely self-contained, and he couldn't tell if it was fear or bashfulness. He looked at their mother again to see that she was smiling lovingly at them. The children were nothing like Caitlin and Robert. But this was no time to be comparing children—or smiles, for that matter.

Although Naomi was friendly and attractive, for some reason he couldn't define, David didn't want to ask her out. He ignored Esther's pointed looks as he just stood and chatted with the group. Finally Esther said in a determined voice, "I need to sit down. David, would you keep me company?"

They moved back to the table. "Will you tell me what you're doing? I find a perfectly good woman—attractive, smart, religious— and you just stand there talking to the others. You're not the only single man in this congregation. Before you know it, she'll be taken."

What was wrong with him? He seldom met available Jewish women, so why the hesitation? At this rate, he'd never find a wife.

"I'll tell you what. I'll invite you both to dinner on Sunday, and you'll have a chance to get better acquainted with her. I'll serve my roast leg of lamb, so if meeting Naomi is a total bust, at least you'll have had your favorite dinner."

"Okay, Esther, if Naomi can come, you're on." Naomi was an attractive woman, and if he wanted to get married in this century, he realized he couldn't afford to drag his feet.

"Oh, she'll come. I could tell she was interested in you." She spoke confidently, as if there couldn't possibly be any problem with getting Naomi to her house.

He frowned. "How? I didn't sense any such thing."

Esther shook her head as if David weren't very bright. "I can tell. It's just a sixth sense that God gave me."

Oh, sure, David thought. He, for one, didn't believe it was a sixth sense, figuring it was more like bossiness and a desire to have her own way. He gave her a skeptical look.

Leaving the table, Esther joined Naomi. David saw the older woman pull Naomi aside. Then they were both smiling and nodding. Evidently Naomi hadn't expressed any reservation about coming to dinner.

Esther was smiling as she came back to the table. "She's happy to come. Now, David, I want you to be on your best behavior. Charm her."

He looked surprised. "When am I ever anything other than charming?"

With asperity, she said, "Never, but there's a first time for every-thing, and I didn't want it to be at my dinner party."

Rabbi Weitzman came up to the table. "We have a Torah study group forming on Wednesday nights, David, and I'd like to invite you to join us. We're getting together to study from Genesis, say prayers, and to become better acquainted with each other."

"Let me think about it," David replied. He'd graduated from Hebrew school, so he wondered if attending it would really benefit him.

The rabbi smiled and said, as if he could read David's mind, "Let me know what you decide. Remember though, it's been years since you attended Hebrew school, and everyone needs refresher courses. Just as you attend medical seminars to keep up-to-date, you need spiritual development."

"You'll love it." Esther turned to David. "I attend one with the women on Tuesdays. It has changed my life."

David reconsidered, thinking maybe this was something he needed. "All right, I'll be there."

"Seven o'clock in the synagogue library." The rabbi moved on to another group of men.

A restlessness that was foreign to him seemed to permeate David's body. On his way home, he realized that something was missing from his life—not just a wife and children, but something deeper. How did he rid himself of this strange emptiness? It was an emptiness that he couldn't explain or figure out. He shook his head in an effort to shrug the feeling off, hoping that maybe meeting with the rabbi and the other men on Wednesday would give him a clue about what was troubling him.

The next day, he, Isabelle, Caitlin, and Robert spent time at the botanical gardens in downtown Denver. Robert was enthusiastic because he got to see and touch the garden tools, Caitlin was happy pushing her grandmother in the wheelchair, and Isabelle loved being out of the house and seeing the plants and the magnificent gardens. They spent a little over an hour viewing the plants, and then they stopped for hamburgers and french fries on the way home. Robert would rather have had pizza, but he made do with the "fee fies."

On Sunday David arrived at Isabelle's at 10:15. Maggie had everyone dressed and was just buckling Caitlin's sandals when he pulled up.

"You look pretty nifty in that suit, Doctor. Let me remind you there aren't any Jewish women at church." She seemed to enjoy teasing him.

Looking perplexed, he said, "Can you tell me why I am going then?"

She laughed, a golden sound that rang right through him. "I hate to dampen your spirits, but it's for your manual dexterity. If you'll just help me get Gram to the car, we can leave."

"Sounds good to me. Come on, Isabelle, let's take a joy ride." He wheeled her to the steps, and then Maggie grabbed the other side of the chair and they lifted her down to the ground.

Isabelle's eyes lit up when she spied his car. "I love your car, David." He pushed her over to it and helped her inside. "Maggie, why don't you get a BMW like this one?" Isabelle said. "It's so comfortable and relaxing to ride in it."

David stowed the wheelchair in the trunk.

"Sure, Gram. Just as soon as I sell my book." Maggie fastened in Caitlin and Robert on either side of the backseat, and then she got in the middle between them.

The trip took about twenty minutes, and once she was inside the building, Isabelle refused to use her wheelchair. Clinging to David's arm on one side and Maggie's on the other, she led them down the aisle. Caitlin and Robert followed, hanging on to Maggie's skirt. When they were about halfway to the front, Isabelle motioned to an empty row and slid in after Maggie and the kids. Once seated, she glanced at the ceiling, then whispered to David, "I try to avoid the cold air vents. When you get old, air conditioning is almost too much."

He nodded and patted her hand. Then, looking around the chapel, he was surprised to find there were no crucifixes or stained-glass windows. Although he'd lived in Salt Lake for three years, he'd never attended Mormon services. He'd gone to a friend's wedding in a Catholic church once, and to a Methodist church for another wedding, but that was all.

His grandfather had felt that going to churches with crucifixes and pictures of Jesus Christ was affirming the beliefs of Christians. This church was certainly plain. Other than some crystal chandeliers and the blue upholstered benches, the room was free of ornamentation. He thought, however, he preferred stained-glass windows to plain ones because they added warmth to a room.

David glanced at the program. One side listed announcements, and the other side outlined the program. *Testimonies,* it said. He wondered what they were. Testimonies of what? By the congregation? David thought that ought to be interesting. He was ready to observe and see if he could figure out what had drawn Pete to the Mormon Church.

He relaxed against the pew and listened to the prelude music. He loved music nearly as much as sports. He smiled to himself. Those would be fighting words to his mother, who adored classical music and couldn't stand sports. Although the organ was small, the organist played it vigorously, and the music rang through the building as if it were coming from a large pipe organ. He closed his eyes, savoring the sounds.

The music ended. The bishop introduced himself and started the meeting. David decided that the Mormons called their minister a bishop. After some announcements, a choral conductor stood and led everyone in "Gently Raise the Sacred Strain." The strains of the music seemed to fill David's soul, and he couldn't explain the feeling. Maybe Pete had been converted because of the music. Next, a man opened the meeting with a prayer. David had never heard such an interesting prayer. It was nothing like he was used to. The man seemed to be making it up as he went along.

A baby was blessed, and then two men blessed bread and water, which was served to everyone. The communion turned out to be as plain as the church, and David noticed there were no wine and wafers for these people. The blessing said they took upon them the name of Jesus Christ, and David immediately recognized it was something his grandfather would have objected to. When the trays came to him, David passed them on to Isabelle.

Afterward, people started going up to the microphone and saying they knew the Mormon Church was true. David didn't consider himself cynical, but he wondered how they could *know* such a thing. The Mormons weren't like the Jews, who had seven thousand years of history behind them. He wondered what made some people speak and others just listen. Were they assigned? If so, he thought, they could certainly have chosen better speakers. Also, why all the crying? He wondered if this was what every service was like.

Finally, an elderly gentleman sitting in back walked quietly to the front. Dressed shabbily, he had a thick accent. Humbly he told of how harsh life in Germany had been for him. Then he related how he'd found the true church and what a profound difference it had made in his life. As he listened, David's chest tightened and tears gathered at the back of his eyes. This old German's testimony profoundly moved him, but why? Was it just a reminder of his grandfather? He shook his head in wonder. He'd actually believed the man when he said the Mormon Church was true. That couldn't be. David sat there until the service was over, contemplating the man's words and his own strange reaction to them. What was the meaning of this experience?

Afterward, David, Maggie, and the kids waited until most of the congregation had left the chapel before helping Isabelle up the aisle. To his surprise, people were waiting for them in the foyer, and it seemed as if everyone wanted to meet him. He had to admit, these people were certainly friendly. Maggie and Isabelle explained who he was, and he received a lot of warm smiles as people shook his hand. Finally one of the men who had a determined salesman-type demeanor said, "Brother Rosenberg, are you a member of the Church?"

Out of the corner of his eye he could see Maggie grimace. Before he could answer, she spoke up and said, "No, Fred, Dr. Rosenberg was just good enough to bring us all to church today, and we've got to be getting home." She put her arms on the shoulders of Caitlin and Robert and turned to herd them out.

Fred never hesitated. "Have you read the Book of Mormon?"

"No, I . . ."

Fred patted his shoulder. "Just a minute. I'll get you one." He took off through the crowd.

Caitlin pulled on Maggie's hand. "I'm hungry."

Maggie ignored her and said to David, "Sorry. Fred's a little over-enthusiastic when it comes to the Church."

David could tell she wished the man had kept quiet. "That's okay." He smiled to reassure her.

Fred came bustling back with a blue book. "Here's a copy." He handed it to him.

David read the title. "Is this where your church gets its name?"

"Mormon is just the nickname of the Church. It comes from the prophet who compiled this book, but our actual name is The Church of Jesus Christ of Latter-day Saints." Fred's statement was decisive, and David could tell he wanted to make sure he knew the correct name.

"Thank you for the book. I'll read it." He smiled at the man and took Isabelle's arm to help her into the wheelchair.

By this time, Robert was whining as he jerked on Maggie's arm. "I'm hungry. I'm hungry."

"Come on, let's get home." Maggie's exasperation was obvious. As soon as Isabelle was situated in the wheelchair, she grabbed the children's hands and hustled them out of the church building.

On the return home, the kids exuberantly sang some song about popcorn popping on the apricot tree, laughing delightedly between each verse. For the most part the adults were quiet. David could tell that just an hour and half in church had worn out Isabelle.

When they arrived at Isabelle's, he helped her inside, settling her in the living room. When he started to leave, Isabelle said, "Are you sure you won't stay for Sunday dinner? Maggie's meatloaf is almost as good as mine."

"Not today," he glanced at Maggie, "but I'd like to some other time." He hated to turn down meatloaf, but he wanted to have a good appetite for Esther's lamb tonight.

Maggie nodded. "Anytime, just name the day."

"Uncle David! Uncle David!" The kids ran to him. "We want hugs and kisses!"

He swung each of them up in his arms and gave them a bear hug, then rubbed their noses with his. They giggled excitedly.

"See you tomorrow if you're not feeling well," he said to Isabelle before leaving.

David slowly pulled away from the curb. He took a deep breath. Being with Caitlin and Robert only emphasized how empty his life was without a family to share it with. He wanted children. He'd be glad when Caitlin and Robert's dad returned and he didn't have to see these two so often. Of course, he reminded himself, he'd promised Maggie he'd still stay with Isabelle. But he liked keeping an eye on her, and the truth of the matter was, he found himself attracted to Maggie. His heart always beat faster when he saw her. She was such a tenderhearted person, always putting her family's needs ahead of her own, which wasn't right, but he admired it.

If only she were Jewish. But she wasn't, and she'd made it clear she was only interested in marrying someone of her own faith. So where did that leave him? Each time he saw her he found himself more drawn to her, and the only way this could end was in heartbreak— his! He knew he should probably ask Naomi out. He had to admit that if he had any other woman in his life right now, he wouldn't even be thinking about Maggie. He frowned. Or would he? Well, he was seeing Naomi tonight, and unless she turned out to be totally unlikeable, he *would* ask her out. He pulled into the condo parking garage, and as he started to get out of the car, he noticed the Book of Mormon. He felt sure it could never rival the Bible, but he'd told Fred he'd read it, so he would.

He smiled to himself.

Some night when there wasn't a ball game on.

* * *

Making himself comfortable in his leather chair, David reflected on the evening. He'd had a good time. Esther's lamb had been delicious, as usual, which in and of itself would have been enough, but Naomi had turned out to be funny and witty. She'd kept them laughing with stories of buying trips to New York and customers' idiosyncracies. Her children had been with their father, so David hadn't had a chance to get acquainted with them. He looked forward to doing so.

David smiled as he thought about how he'd asked Naomi to dinner Monday night. He'd found out one positive thing about her: she loved sports. In fact, she'd gotten season tickets for the Nuggets in her recent divorce settlement. Still smiling, he went to bed, carefully reciting the *sh'ma*. He was indeed grateful for this day.

Chapter 12

"So what's happened since I've been gone?" Pat asked, her happy voice brimming with curiosity.

"I'm glad you called. I was beginning to get worried." Maggie propped the phone against her head and shoulder while she flipped the laptop on standby. "The good news is, I've written twenty pages on my book this last week, thanks to David."

"Twenty pages! I knew he would turn out to be handy. Anything more pertinent that I should know involving him?" Her tone was light with good humor. For all her teasing, Maggie knew that Pat wanted to see her happily married.

Maggie laughed. "No. He's still looking for a Jewish wife and I'm still looking for a Mormon man. He did go to church with us Sunday."

"What? Tell me about it. Maybe he'll join," Pat said enthusiastically.

"I doubt it." Maggie saw no use in giving her false hope. "But it won't be for lack of effort on Fred Scott's part. He practically forced a Book of Mormon on him. David promised to read it, but I wonder if he really will." She still cringed at the way Fred had acted.

"Let's hope so. Since you had good news, does that mean you've got bad news too? Or is it all good?"

"Well, partly. Gram's speech is much better, but the bad news is that she's getting weaker and more forgetful. We had her in to the doctor yesterday, but David couldn't find any reason for her deterioration. In just a week, she seems to have gone downhill sharply. The other day when I offered to call Barbara for her, she didn't know who

Barbara was. She only remembered one daughter—my mother—and she thought I was her."

"That ought to be a wake-up call to Barbara that she needs to be part of Isabelle's life. But how do you mean weaker?"

"Her legs are nearly too weak to stand on. She won't use her walker because she's afraid of falling, so she's relegated to her wheelchair." Just thinking about Gram's condition sent a frisson of fear through her.

"What are you going to do? Don't you have to be back at school soon?"

"In about three weeks, and I don't know what I'm going to do then." Now the worry started in earnest.

"Brad's kids are still with you, aren't they?" Pat made no effort to hide her exasperation.

"Of course, Pat, you've only been gone a week. How much do you think could happen?"

"Nothing when it came to Brad, but," Pat chuckled, "I was hoping for more exciting news about David. After all, I am a romance writer, and I certainly hoped for bigger developments in that department."

"Unless you know an eligible man, you might as well give up," Maggie said with a hint of steel in her tone. "But on a lighter note, what did you learn at the writer's conference?"

"As usual, the market's saturated, and no one knows what's going to happen next. Book sales are down period. The advice was 'Don't give up your day job.' I'm glad I've got Craig and the post office to depend on." Her voice was airy, as if she weren't really worried.

Maggie didn't suppose she was. Pat had made plenty of money writing. Investing was also her hobby, and she'd done all right. Maggie's investments were so-so, and she realized now that should have listened to Pat more. "I doubt I'll be giving up my day job anytime soon. Without one I'd be on the street."

"You could always sell your condo," Pat suggested, though she didn't sound really serious.

"Only as a last resort," Maggie said firmly. She wanted somewhere to live when she retired.

"I thought the last resort was moving in with me." Pat's ribbing came through loud and clear.

"Are you kidding? You're first on my list of resorts." She knew that if she were down and out, Pat would be the first to offer her a place to live. But she had no plans to join the ranks of the unemployed.

Now Pat became serious. "I'm between books right now, so why don't I come over at seven in the morning? I'll get Caitlin and Robert ready for preschool and help Isabelle. You, my aspiring author, can spend the time writing, either there or at your condo. I'll just take over for the day."

Maggie felt a buzz of excitement at the thought of another whole day of writing without any interruptions. "I really should turn you down, but instead I'm going to take advantage of you." Maggie blinked back the tears, then ran her finger across her lashes to clear her blurry vision. She wanted so badly to get her book finished this summer, and with all these extraordinary people in her life, it looked as if she might be able to do it.

"Good girl. See you at seven in the morning, and by the way, please try to think of something interesting that's happened between you and David. Or if that isn't possible, *make* something happen." Her banter warmed Maggie's heart.

Squelching a grin, Maggie said, "Only if you're interested in fiction!"

They hung up. Feeling decidedly lighthearted, Maggie went to check on Gram. The home aide was helping her bathe. When Maggie got to her grandmother's room, she found her dressed in her favorite purple pants and more cheerful than she'd been lately. Maggie only hoped this was a forecast of the days to come.

An hour later, the physical therapist came. She turned out to be a new woman, and Gram was not happy at all. Maggie had just turned on her laptop when she heard her grandmother call, "Maggie, Maggie! Help me!"

Her heart pounding, Maggie hurried to the living room to find her grandmother pushing the physical therapist away from her. "What's happening?"

"Your grandmother won't cooperate." The woman practically spit the words out.

Maggie looked straight at Gram. "Why?"

"She doesn't like me." Gram had a determined look on her face.

"For heaven's sakes, Gram, that's not true," Maggie protested.

"Ask her." Gram nodded her head towards the therapist. "Do you?"

Maggie couldn't ever remember hearing her grandmother speak to anyone in such a venomous tone. What had gotten into her?

"Enough's enough. I'm leaving." The therapist collected her things while Maggie watched. "Someone else can come next time."

While the therapist might have started out liking Gram, Maggie could tell that she sure didn't now. Not that she blamed the poor woman. Who wanted to be spoken to like that?

Maggie walked the woman to the door. "Sorry about this."

Her apology didn't mollify the therapist. "I don't envy you with *her* to take care of." Her tone made it obvious the dislike was mutual. With that statement, the therapist stalked up the sidewalk to her car.

Back in the living room, Maggie said, "What was that all about?"

"I didn't want to exercise today, and she wouldn't listen to me. So I called you." Gram acted as though yelling was nothing unusual.

"You didn't just call. It was more like a terror-filled scream."

Gram gave her a self-satisfied smile. "It was a pretty good scream, wasn't it?"

"If you meant to scare me to death, yes." Maggie's nerves still hadn't quieted down.

"Help me sit in my chair," Gram ordered. "I don't want to miss the noon news."

Maggie helped her move from the wheelchair into the recliner. "Don't you want to get stronger?"

"Of course I do." Gram clicked the remote. "Just not with her. Someone else."

"You'll be lucky if they send anyone else after they hear how you treated this therapist. No one wants to be treated rudely."

"I wasn't rude. People just need to listen to me. When I say I don't want to do something, I don't want to do something. Didn't she understand English?" Gram aimed the remote toward the television and started changing channels.

"I think you got your point across. I need to pick up the kids now. Will you be all right?" Maggie never liked to leave her alone, and after the scene she'd just made, she especially didn't want to right now.

"Is that woman gone?" Gram looked around the room and then said slyly, "If she is, I'll be okay."

"Try not to alienate anyone else while I'm gone." Maggie thought that in a way the episode had been funny, but the cunning expression on Gram's face concerned her. It seemed as if she had planned the entire affair.

"I won't." Gram's eyes twinkled merrily. She waved Maggie away. "Go on now."

"Back in a few minutes." Worry nagged at her. *What is Gram up to? Do I dare leave Pat alone with her tomorrow?* Maggie sighed. *What next?*

Caitlin and Robert were excited when she picked them up. One of the other children had celebrated her birthday, and they were still exhilarated from playing Drop the Handkerchief.

She fixed tuna sandwiches for everyone, and an hour later, the kids were down for their naps and *Matlock* was nearly over. As soon as she helped Gram get ready for her rest, she resolved to get back to writing.

But she had no such luck. She absolutely couldn't concentrate. Her mind was a swirl of activity, and all of it concerned her family. She couldn't conjure up even one scene with Blanche and Ruby. Finally she gave up and decided to do something else. Going outside on the grass, she did some jumping jacks, some deep breathing, and some sit-ups. Ten minutes later she felt like a new person, one who was so winded she couldn't think of anything but catching her breath. She knew for a fact that no one would mistake her for an Olympic champion.

Once back at her computer, Maggie was able to push everything else aside and embroil Blanche and Ruby in an adventure. She wrote for the next couple of hours until the household began to stir, then she closed the laptop. She'd finish the scene tonight when David got there. He hadn't been coming for very long, and yet it seemed like a lifetime.

After her nap Gram seemed to be back to normal. She was sitting on the front porch with Maggie, Caitlin, and Robert when David arrived. The kids ran out to meet him, clinging to him as usual. Maggie's heart lifted when he came across the grass and she got a clear look at him. The way his mouth curved into a smile delighted her. She needed to be careful before she found herself more than just fond of him. Fond she could handle—anything more could turn out to be a disaster.

When Maggie thought of what Pat had said, her mouth automatically smiled. "What's happening on the search for a Jewish wife? Anything I can report to Pat? She's eager to know the latest. You know how romance writers are."

His smile deepened. "I do have some news to reveal. We have a new member in our congregation who is single. I met her Friday night during the coffee hour."

Maggie's heart dropped, and for a minute or two she felt as though someone had knocked the wind out of her. The funny thing was, she also felt deceived. She felt the blood drain from her face, and she hoped David hadn't noticed. She'd seen him twice since Friday, and he'd never seen fit to inform her that he'd met a Jewish woman. She'd always assumed he'd tell her immediately. She choked out the request, "Tell us what she's like." Did she really want to know? However, she did need to be polite. The muscles on her face seemed paralyzed, but by sheer willpower she forced them into a semblance of a smile, which she hoped looked like more than a grimace.

"She's good-looking, dresses well if you're interested in the superficial things, and has a wicked sense of humor." He sounded suitably impressed.

Maggie tried to appear interested and not wounded by this turn of events. "Are you going to ask her out?" She endeavored to keep her voice light, but she feared she hadn't succeeded.

He frowned slightly, and now his words weren't so forthcoming. "We went to dinner last night."

Maggie stiffened and then clasped her arms around her body as the devastation from his words permeated her body. Her chest tightened, and she could only breathe little short breaths. She wanted to burst into tears, but she willed her face to remain impassive. Why did this news hurt her? She wanted him to find a Jewish wife, and this woman sounded perfect.

"She's divorced and has three children."

She could feel something inside her start to shrivel. This woman had everything he wanted—she was Jewish and she had a family. Maggie realized she had to say something, and then, as if the words were choked out of her, she said, "Are you going to keep seeing her?"

"I think so." He didn't sound positive.

His tone sent a glimmer of hope through Maggie, and she noted the odd sensations that tripped through her body. She liked David as a friend, but for a few minutes, if she hadn't known differently, she would have thought she was in love with him herself. A good friend was what he was, and a good friend was all he'd ever be.

She stood up. "Now that you've enlightened us about your love life, I'll go write."

"Now if we can just find you a Mormon man." He gave her a speculative look.

"With everything going on in my life right now, I'm in no hurry. Will you just keep this new relationship platonic for the time being? If you get involved with another woman, Gram wouldn't have company, the kids wouldn't be spoiled, and I wouldn't get my book finished. I don't want to sound selfish, but for our sakes, we need you free of romantic entanglements."

"You do sound selfish," he teased, "but that's okay because I can't think of any place I'd rather be than here."

Again, his smile assailed her heart, but she squared her shoulders. She was leaving. Somehow she thought she'd feel safer at her own home. Maggie entered the house and came back with her computer CD and her purse. "See you guys later."

* * *

The next morning Pat arrived early, filled with enthusiasm. How anyone got to be as wonderful a person as Pat was, Maggie didn't know. She was not only always helpful, but invariably upbeat.

"Any news to tell me?" Pat's voice had its usual mischievous quality.

"David has met an eligible Jewish woman." She couldn't wait to see Pat's reaction.

Pat's eyes grew big and her jaw dropped. "You're kidding."

Maggie nodded her head. "I'm not."

"I thought for sure you two would end up together." Pat still seemed in a state of shock.

"We're not. I'm not Jewish, and he's not LDS. How many times do I have to tell you? And all the wishing in the world won't make it otherwise." She didn't intend to tell Pat her own reaction to the news.

Pat's eyes narrowed. "Does that mean you're wishing?"

Maggie just laughed, then picked up her purse and left. As she drove along the leafy, tree-lined streets, she didn't know what she wished.

On her way home, she felt exhilarated. What a heavenly day it had been, alone with no interruptions. She'd managed to write ten pages, and she only had about thirty-five more and she'd be finished with her book. The end seemed so close that she could hardly wait.

* * *

Although David had wanted to arrive early, an emergency at the hospital had caught him. Going straight to the synagogue from the hospital, he managed to arrive only five minutes late. In the library were a group of nine or ten men surrounding an oblong table. Rabbi Weitzman stood at the head. "Welcome, David. I'm glad you made it this evening. Each week at the *parsha* we read from the Torah and discuss it. This gives each one a time to direct and reflect upon his life. Right now we are reading from Beraishis, or Genesis."

David was glad he'd come. He needed to reflect on his life, and maybe even some direction wouldn't be amiss. So, making himself comfortable, he settled back in his chair to listen.

"Tonight we begin with Genesis 24:1–4. *Abraham was old, well advanced in years, and God had blessed Abraham with everything. Abraham said to the senior servant of his household, who was in charge of all that he owned, 'Place your hand under my thigh. I will bind you by an oath to God, Lord of heaven and of earth, that you will not take a wife for my son from the daughters of the Canaanites among whom I live. Instead, you must go to my native land, to my birthplace, to obtain a wife for my son Isaac.'"*

Marriage. David wondered if this was the regular *parsha* or if the rabbi had been inspired to choose this topic because he was attending. He looked at the other men. The ones he knew were married, but all of them looked to be the age of fathers with marriageable children.

"The rabbis say that each person is given three *basherts*—their suitable, destined spouse. Some even say there are as many as ten. But there is always one who is the *richtige zivvug,* the optimal other half. God appoints the *basherts* forty days before the child is conceived. To find their *bashert,* children need the help of their parents. Parents must start by impressing their own good deeds and ethics on the hearts and in the minds of their children. It cannot be repeated too often." The rabbi's voice became stern. "Parents can only secure the well-being of the child and the future of their people by helping their children find their *bashert.*"

David knew that his suitable spouse had not been his ex-wife, Sarah. If the rabbis were correct, however, there were at least three destined for him. But where were they? His parents and grandparents had instilled their values on him and his brother Sam. Sam and his wife, Rachel, had definitely been meant for each other. Each one complemented the other perfectly. His parents were soul mates too. But somewhere they had messed up because they had been all for his marriage to Sarah. He smiled slightly. According to Rabbi Weitzman, he could blame them now because he hadn't found his *bashert.* After all the nagging his mother had done on the subject of his remarrying, David knew she'd be thrilled to learn that she hadn't done enough.

"But to find this person is not easy. The search requires perseverance, patience, fortitude, and trust in God."

Although he'd only been seriously looking for a wife the last three or four years, he believed he'd been more than patiently persevering. He did have faith that God would help him find his own soul mate, and that was what he wanted—a soul mate. Just thinking these words evoked an image of Maggie, and his heartbeat quickened. He frowned. Why hadn't it been Naomi? He thought surely his *bashert* would be Jewish, one of God's covenant people.

"Sometimes it might be necessary to engage a *shadkhan,* or matchmaker."

David shuddered. Now *that* sounded like his grandfather. He'd wanted a matchmaker for David's first marriage, and he'd been quick to point out that if they'd followed his direction, his grandson would have had his *richtige zivvug*. He smiled to himself. If his grandfather were still alive, the matchmaking would have been out of David's hands long ago and in the hands of a professional.

"In order to succeed, you must heighten your awareness of the Creator so you can be led to do what He wants, not necessarily what you might want for yourself."

After the lecture, the members gave their own ideas and experiences about *shadkhans* and *besherts*. David just listened. They concluded the evening with coffee and pastries that one of the wives had made.

On the way home, David's thoughts kept straying to Maggie. He didn't love her, but he found himself thinking about her a lot, and he figured it was because she and her family had embraced him fully, making him feel like one of them. He wondered if Maggie would ever convert to Judaism. It was a ridiculous thought because he knew she was firmly entrenched in her own religion. "Oh, God, giver of all blessings, whose care I am in, favor me that I might discover my *richtige zivvag*. Amen."

He looked forward to next week's *parsha*.

David's second meeting with Naomi was enjoyable. She was a good person, and they had a lot in common. Esther had told him on numerous occasions that companionship was enough, that physical attraction was highly overrated. But he'd wanted more. Esther considered him too picky, and he confessed he probably was. Naomi was a perfectly good woman, but he couldn't see her soul or feel it either. He wanted his soul mate, and he felt no affinity for Naomi. He felt sure there was someone God meant for him to marry.

David wanted to go to dinner with Maggie again, but finding an open night bordered on the impossible. One thing he knew for sure—if he invited her to his home, he'd have a chance to demonstrate his cooking skills. The thought made him grin, although why he felt it necessary to impress her was beyond him. He could also show her his bonsai. Then he considered that it didn't seem too wise to be asking her to dinner. He liked too many things about her, and he was involving himself in a relationship that could go nowhere. He'd better forget cooking dinner for her, and showing her the bonsai.

On Thursday he couldn't wait to get to Isabelle's. His mother's memoirs had arrived in the mail, and he was anxious to give them to Isabelle. She'd seemed enthused enough about reading them, and he thought that maybe getting her own copy would raise her spirits.

When he arrived, Robert was mowing the lawn and Caitlin was turning somersaults and trying to do cartwheels. Upon seeing him, they immediately stopped and ran to meet him, swinging on his arms all the way to the house.

"What's in the package?" Caitlin asked eagerly. "Is it for us?"

"Not this time, honey." He wished he'd thought to bring them something. "It's a present for your great-grandmother."

Caitlin seemed just as excited about the present being for Isabelle. "What is it?" she whispered, holding her head so he could whisper back in her ear.

Smiling, he bent his head down. "A book."

She eyed him curiously. "About Max?"

"No. About my mother."

"Your mother?" Her eyes opened wider, and she nodded her head as if she knew exactly what he was talking about. "Gram will like it."

Maggie met them at the door, and when she smiled at him, his heart jolted—a crazy reaction after the lectures he'd given himself about Jewish women.

"I've decided to write upstairs tonight on your nifty laptop, so if these two," she gave them a stern look, but her eyes twinkled, "give you any problems, just holler. I'll be right down to rescue you."

He grinned. "I can tell these two are terrors, so I won't hesitate to holler."

"We're not terrors, Uncle David." Robert gave him an indignant look.

"We're nice children." Caitlin frowned. "Tell him, Aunt Maggie." It was obvious the little girl was just as offended as her brother.

"You're the best children in the whole wide world. Now just act like it." She ruffled their hair.

"We will," Caitlin promised earnestly.

"See you later." Maggie vanished up the stairs.

They went on into the living room. "Gram, Uncle David brought you a present." Caitlin pointed to the book still in its white mailing folder.

"A present for you." Robert made sure he wasn't left out of the conversation.

"I brought you a copy of my mother's book." David handed her the package, and she eagerly opened it. "Every time I read this, I am grateful for my parents and their suffering so we could live safely in the United States."

"I can't wait to read about your mother, but," Isabelle warned, "I have such a hard time concentrating that it will take me awhile." She studied the book, skipping through it, reading pages here and there. "It looks interesting, and I look forward to reading it."

"Great. Mother sent that copy especially for you, and she wrote in the front of it."

Isabelle quickly turned to the inside cover. *For Isabelle. I hope you enjoy learning something of David's family history. You and your family mean a lot to him. Sincerely, Rebecca Rosenberg.* "How nice of her. I must give you something in return. On the shelf over there is a copy of the history of my great-grandfather, Parley P. Pratt." She pointed to a small bookshelf at the side of the room. "See right there on the next to the bottom shelf is a blue book with gold printing that says . . ."

"*Autobiography of Parley P. Pratt.*" He drew the book from the shelf and opened it to the first page. A picture of her great-grandfather stared up at him, and on the facing page, he read that this man had been one of the Twelve Apostles of The Church of Jesus Christ of Latter-day Saints. "Thanks, Isabelle. I'll be happy to read your book, but I'll return it when I'm finished. This is too expensive to be giving to me."

"No, it isn't!" She was determined to give it to him. "I want you to have it."

"Thank you, Isabelle. Since this book is from you, I'll cherish it." He could tell how proud she was of it and how much she wanted him to have it.

She beamed and turned back to his mother's book.

"Come on, Uncle David, let's play on the grass. You can help me do acrobats." Caitlin pulled on his arm.

Robert pulled on the other one. "Let's play."

The way the kids were pulling, David figured before too long he'd have arms six inches longer. "Let's go. Be back in a little while, Isabelle. We have to do acrobats."

"I mow the grass." Robert had definite plans.

"Okay." David helped Caitlin stand on her head and do cart-wheels. She had somersaults down pat, so she didn't need his help on them. Robert just mowed and mowed. Finally they went inside and got drinks of water.

Isabelle was engrossed in his mother's book, so he took the kids upstairs and got them ready for bed. Tonight they weren't too tired to brush their teeth. When they had their pajamas on, he said, "I'll read to you for a while. What book do you want to hear?"

"Max! Max!" they shouted in unison, running to get the book off the nightstand.

"Here," Robert said, shoving the book into David's hands and then crawling up onto the bed to snuggle close to him. Caitlin promptly scrambled up on the other side. They were satisfied at just hearing the story twice, although they had a myriad of questions about each picture. Finally all of them were tired. He tucked the kids in and then went downstairs for a little rest himself. Playing with Caitlin and Robert took its toll, and right now he felt every one of his thirty-eight years. He groaned. He needed to get married pretty soon. Otherwise he'd be too decrepit to do anything with his children but watch them from a wheelchair, a lap robe over his knees.

Isabelle looked up as he sat down on the couch. "I feel so bad for your mother. How sad to lose her entire family. No one got out of Germany but your mother and your grandmother?"

"Yes, the rest of her family ended up at Auschwitz, where they were exterminated." He couldn't hide the horror that he felt whenever he thought of the way they were treated.

"I can tell from your tone that you are still mourning their loss. How terrible for your mother." Isabelle shook her head sympathetically.

"Dad's uncles lost their lives in concentration camps also. Their wives and children were starving, but they managed to survive until the end of the war. My grandfather felt he had a responsibility to help them, and so he supported the families of his four brothers until the wives remarried." David considered this another admirable quality of his grandfather.

"Did they come to the United States too?"

"Yes, Europe was so ravaged by the war that there was nothing left for them there. All their property had been confiscated, and trying to get it back would have been a legal mess. Food was in short supply. Clothes were scarce, so Grandfather felt that the best thing he could do was help his sisters-in-law emigrate here. However, in 1950, two of them moved to Israel. And although they're very old now, they're still living."

Isabelle gave him a sassy look. "What do you mean by 'very old'? Are they as old as I am?"

He grinned. "No one is as young as you are, Isabelle, so I guess I'd have to say older than you." The old Isabelle was back, for a few minutes anyway.

He heard Maggie on the stairs, and she came in. "What are you two up to?"

He winked at her. "Just discussing how young your grandmother is."

Maggie slipped into the floral chair. "Nobody acts younger."

The look she gave Isabelle radiated so much love that David's heart turned over. Tenderness and kindness flowed from her entire being, beckoning his soul. How could this be? He thought of the rabbi's words last night about singles groups and chemistry. He suddenly realized that explained his feelings. He was confusing chemistry with soul mate. But he found it also wasn't easy to shake off those feelings.

Abruptly, David stood. "Well, I'd better get on my way." He smiled at Isabelle. "I'll see you Saturday."

"Are you sure this isn't too much? You have a demanding job, and then to spend two nights a week and Saturdays here is asking a lot on your part." Maggie rose from her chair. "Maybe you'd better hike on Saturday, or even," her mischievous smile lit up her face, "watch a little sports on television."

"Oh, no. I can't believe you said that." He leaned over and pressed his hand lightly against her forehead. "Do you have a fever?"

She laughed. Once again, the bewitching sound of her laughter resonated within him.

Then she gave him a disgusted look. "Can't I even be thoughtful without you thinking I have a fever?"

"You're an anomaly—the first person I've ever known who could be *thoughtful* about sports when she didn't like them." He gazed speculatively at her.

"Haven't you noticed?" She acted as if he were obtuse. "I'm just naturally thoughtful. But back to my question. Will you please take Saturday off?"

"No, I'm young enough to come here a couple times a week and not drop from exhaustion." Then he remembered how he'd felt an hour ago, and thought he might have been a little hasty with that last statement.

"Good-bye again, Isabelle. At the risk of being redundant, let me add, I'll see you Saturday." He waved his hand and started for the front door, Maggie right behind him.

"Thanks again for coming, David, and for giving Gram the book I can't wait to read it myself."

Maggie shut the door behind him and stood leaning against it. The more she saw David, the more she liked him, yet *like* was such a pallid word to describe what she felt. Every time she saw him, happiness bubbled up in her, and it was all she could do not to go around with a sappy smile on her face. But if she let herself fall in love with him, she knew she could forget eternal happiness. She simply couldn't be anything more than a good friend to him. She clenched her fists. She just had to keep reminding herself of that fact. Meanwhile, she had to finish her book quickly so he wouldn't be there all the time.

Chapter 13

After attending the synagogue Friday evening, David returned home. He enjoyed the peaceful feeling of the *Shabbat.* During services each week, when the rabbi recited the *Birkat Shalom,* the peace flowed into him like a physical presence. Hearing the Blessing of Peace over and over again had engraved it upon his heart. He sighed deeply. He loved the Jewish religion. It was a part of him.

He loved his profession, but his personal life didn't seem to be going anyplace. He looked around his study. He had a large condominium, decorated with favorite pieces of furniture he'd begged from his parents' apartment when they'd redecorated. His study had an antique Persian rug from his grandfather, leather furniture, and dark walnut bookcases. What his condo didn't have was a wife or children. Material things weren't enough. He shook himself and said aloud, "Snap out of it, David. You're becoming a whiner."

Relaxed in his most comfortable chair, his eyes caught sight of the book Isabelle had given him. He picked it up off the coffee table and leafed through it. Scattered throughout were pictures of the early West and Midwest, and even one of Joseph Smith. There were also pictures of Parley's wives. David thought *that* detail was intriguing. His curiosity drew him into the book immediately, and he began reading.

Both his mother's and Isabelle's great-grandfather's books started when the authors were six years old. Other than that, they didn't have much in common. His mother's parents had been well-to-do, whereas Parley Pratt's were poor, but both sets of parents had loved to read. It was surprising that a man with little formal education would turn out to be one of the Twelve Apostles of a church, but then, things were different in the nineteenth century.

He was particularly interested when Parley found the Book of Mormon. He thought it was funny how one book could affect two men so differently. Parley couldn't wait to read it, not wanting to stop to eat or sleep until he'd finished it. David himself had tossed it aside to read only when there were no ball games on television. There was no ball game on tonight, so he decided to start reading it. To his surprise, something about Parley's reaction to the book struck a note within him. Putting down the autobiography, he went in search of his copy of the Book of Mormon. He found it in his bedroom near the bottom of a pile of books he intended to get around to reading someday.

Going back to the living room, he settled down in his chair and opened the book. He hated prefaces. He usually skipped them and plunged right in. He doubted one was in the edition Parley read, so that man probably hadn't had to wade through it before getting to the meat of the book. If he were going to be thorough, however, he'd better start on the very first page. He stopped on the second title page when he read, "Another Testament of Jesus Christ." His grandfather would have been aghast to see David reading it, but David decided his own faith was strong enough, and he was liberal enough to go ahead and read the book.

"Written to the Lamanites, who are a remnant of the house of Israel; and also to Jew and Gentile." David frowned. Who were the Lamanites? What were they talking about? How could they be of the House of Israel? He found it interesting that this book would also be written to the Jews. His questions were answered in the next paragraph.

He skimmed over the testimonies of the witnesses because he found them difficult to believe. He hated to be cynical, but he figured people would swear to anything if they were paid enough. The testimony of the Prophet Joseph Smith was a different matter. He found it fascinating. The visitation of angels was reminiscent of the ancient prophets' experiences in the Bible.

He liked the explanation about the book, hoping it would make what he read easier to understand. He read the first page of 1 Nephi, and it sounded credible enough to him. *How could an eighteen-year-*

old boy in the nineteenth century throw in something like "reformed Egyptian"? he wondered.

As he continued reading, a good feeling welled up in him. He reread chapter ten of Nephi several times. He'd never heard of the Holy Ghost, and he decided what this book needed was a glossary. Later his eyes started blinking shut, and he glanced at his watch. Midnight! He was no Parley Pratt. He *did* desire sleep. Yawning, he put the book down and crawled into bed. He was anxious to read more tomorrow. Putting his right hand over his eyes, he repeated the *sh'ma*.

Saturday morning David rose early, and after the ritual of the *talit*, he started reading the Book of Mormon again.

As soon as he began reading, the same warm feeling that he had felt the night before filled his body, compelling him to continue. The main character in this book, Lehi, blessed his children before he died. Abraham had also. David wondered when had this custom died out among the Jews? He thought it a wonderful idea, and wanted to know if the LDS people still gave blessings to their children. Parts of 2 Nephi reminded him of the psalms, and the beautiful language resonated within him. Other parts of it were the words of Isaiah taken from the brass plates. They had the same rhythm as Isaiah in the Bible. He had to stop reading to absorb this. Would a teenager think of paraphrasing Isaiah? He thought not.

He discovered an affinity for this book, and he hated to put it down to go over to Isabelle's. Then he laughed, noting his behavior showed shades of Parley Pratt's! Just like him, he wanted to continue reading. What with doing the yard work and the demands of Caitlin and Robert, he'd probably have little time to read once he arrived there. But he'd take the book with him, just in case.

He parked in front of the house and Caitlin and Robert dashed out to meet him.

Glancing at the sack in his arms, Caitlin said, "What did you bring us?"

Before he could answer, Robert spoke up, "Let's play, Uncle David."

"That sounds fun. But how about mowing the grass first, then having some of this lemonade," he tapped the side of the sack, "and then we'll play."

"Okay." They both nodded agreeably.

"Let me put this in the refrigerator and talk to your Aunt Maggie, then we can start mowing." He grinned down at the two kids.

"I'll start mowing now." Robert purposefully went onto the porch and got his lawn mower. Caitlin headed for her dolls.

At that point Maggie came out, smiling as usual, which added to the tender feelings already flooding him.

Her eyes met his. "I'm going to my condo, but I'll be back early, so you can have some free time today."

"That suits me fine. I'm involved in another project, so getting home early will be a big help." Ordinarily, he'd have refused to let her sacrifice her writing time, but he wanted to continue reading.

Her eyes sparkling, she frowned and shook her finger at him. "And you weren't even going to mention it, just letting me selfishly keep you here all day."

He shook his head in mock disbelief. "The day you're selfish, is the day that I . . ." He laughed. "I can't think of anything drastic enough. But suffice it to say, selfish you are not! So there! I don't ever want to hear such foolish words from you again."

Maggie laughed with such warmth and joy that he couldn't stop the response darting through him. Each time he saw her he realized even more what a wonderful person she was and what a delight she was to be around.

"Don't get carried away." Her tone was firm, but a smile still clung to her lips. "By the way, I've read about half of your mother's story. What a remarkable person your grandmother must have been."

"She was. Very driven to make a good life for her daughter, and she succeeded. I started Parley Pratt's history, although I haven't read half of it yet. But I will. What an exceptional person he was. I can see why Isabelle is proud to be his great-granddaughter." He shifted the sack to his other arm.

"He was also a poet." Pride flickered across her face, but she said modestly, "I like to think that any talent I have came from him."

He nodded. "Undoubtedly."

"See you later." Stopping to kiss each of the kids, she made her way to her car.

David continued on into the house, going first to the kitchen to put the lemonade in the refrigerator, then into the living room to greet Isabelle.

"How're you doing?" She looked so dejected, he could tell without asking.

"Oh, all right, I guess." Her inflection only emphasized how miserable she was.

He went closer and grasped her small, wrinkled hands in his. "I hate seeing my favorite girl unhappy. What can I do to lift your spirits?" He looked into her faded blue eyes. Her age seemed to have settled firmly on her, not letting a spark of the old Isabelle free.

"Give me a new body—one at least thirty years younger." Her hopelessness came through in her voice.

"I wish I could." He smiled encouragingly. "I'd do anything to make you better, but it's out of my realm of expertise."

Isabelle remained silent.

"Are you still using your wheelchair?" He squeezed her hands gently and laid them in her lap. Moving a step back, he continued to study her.

"Yes. My legs are even weaker." She sounded as if she'd given up hope.

Concerned not only about her physically but mentally as well, he said, "I think we'd better have you come in Monday. Something is wrong that we need to fix.

"I hope you're up to watching the game today," he continued. "The Arizona Diamondbacks are playing the Dodgers. Randy Johnson is pitching, so I'm looking forward to it." Johnson was David's favorite pitcher.

She looked slightly interested. "Are you talking about that guy with the mustache?"

"Yes," he said, hoping the game would divert her after all.

"Okay." She gave a tired sigh, as if her body were depleted of all energy.

"I'll go mow the lawn, and then I should have time to feed us and play awhile with Caitlin and Robert before the game. Once they're down for their naps, we'll have the living room to ourselves and can watch baseball to our heart's content." He gave her a cheery smile to which she made no response.

When David got outside, Robert was mowing away in the corner, and Caitlin had her dolls all undressed, giving them each new outfits to wear. He went around the house to the garage and got the mower out. After two weeks of this, he hadn't decided if he was a yard man or not. Something could be said for hiring someone to do it and resting in the living room, but he better not let that on to Maggie. He started the engine and, cutting a swath behind him, headed for the front of the house where he would be able to keep an eye on the kids.

Finishing the front yard, he called to Caitlin and Robert to come around to the back. After he had them settled at the wooden table on the patio, he went in and got their lemonade. The sun was shining and a slight breeze was blowing, making it the perfect spot for a break.

After their break, Caitlin went back to dressing her dolls again, and Robert started mowing with his own mower in a corner of the backyard. David went back to work on the yard.

Before starting the mower for the final part of the lawn, David checked on Isabelle, whom he found asleep in her chair, so he silently returned to the yard. He didn't know how professionals mowed, but he'd found that it went faster if he cut the lawn into squares and triangles and mowed each one separately. Cutting just one long strip back and forth across the lawn was, in his estimation, a boring way to mow grass. He smiled to himself.

He played with Caitlin and Robert for a while before he fixed their lunch. Once they were down for their naps, he joined Isabelle in the kitchen. The first inning had just ended and the Diamondbacks had scored two runs, the Dodgers, none.

* * *

As she left the house, Maggie almost hated to go. While she wanted to get her book finished, she would have much preferred to hang out with David even if it meant a ball game on TV. The more often she saw him, the more she found herself wanting to be with him. When he turned his captivating smile on her, her pulse picked up speed. But at the moment, she needed to think about something else—like Blanche and Ruby.

She'd completed twenty pages of her manuscript already this week, and she hoped to have five more finished today. Then, next week at this time, she could be polishing her manuscript and hopefully sending it on its way to New York City. She took a deep breath. At last she'd be free to relax. Only how could she relax until she'd heard from the editor at Mystery, Inc? She couldn't.

Just being alone in her condo and knowing she had only a few pages to go lifted her spirits even higher. She wasted no time in settling down at her computer and transferring yesterday's pages from the CD onto the hard drive. She reread the paragraphs she'd already written so that, once more, she was in Blanche and Ruby's world. Then she started to write.

"Ruby, you watch out the door and tell me if anyone comes. I'm going to climb up that ladder and check on that loose ceiling tile. I bet it's drugs, just like Victor found." Blanche pushed the ladder against the wall and started up it.

Nervously, Ruby looked out the door. "You do know, Blanche, that we wouldn't recognize dope if we were hit in the face with it." She looked at her friend and said critically, "And that's exactly what's likely to happen to you up there." Turning around, she glanced out the door and screamed.

Maggie grinned. She loved these two old ladies.

By two o'clock, she'd finished five pages and left to go home and relieve David.

At Gram's house, she found him watching a baseball game while the kids napped and her grandmother dozed in her recliner.

When he looked up at her, David's smile gave her pulse a charge, which started it beating madly. Furtively, she tried to take a deep breath to calm herself. She didn't want him to realize he was having any effect on her. Having this reaction to a man who would never be more than a good friend to her was utterly ridiculous, she told herself. In fact, she was having the same sensations that she had in high school when she was around a boy she had a crush on. To be thirty-one years old and having the same response was absurd. She had to get over her ridiculous teenage reaction to him.

David stood and motioned for her to go into the dining room. "I don't know if Isabelle can't walk because she has had another small stroke or if it's a general deterioration of her muscle tone. Anyway, bring her in Monday, and we'll run some tests. I'll speak to her physical therapist and ask her how she sees the deterioration of Isabelle's walking ability."

"Lots of luck finding a therapist who knows anything. The last one walked out in a well-deserved huff, and they haven't gotten a new one assigned to her."

"What?" He looked astonished.

"Gram treated the last one really rotten, and she wouldn't come back. The one before her quit to do something else." Maggie sighed deeply.

"I know this will be difficult," he said, as if he hated to burden her with more, "but if I get an appointment for a therapist at the hospital, could you take Isabelle?"

Between her own worry over Gram and the proximity of David, it was difficult for her to act normal. "I'll get her there, but it would be easier if it could be before noon. Then I won't have to find someone to stay with Caitlin and Robert."

"I'm sure that won't be a problem. I'll have my nurse set up the appointments and give you a call." His voice was gentle. "We'll do our best to help get Isabelle back on her feet," he smiled, "literally and figuratively."

His piercing hazel eyes sent a warmth radiating through her, reminding her just how caring he was and just how much she cared for him. "Thank you." She couldn't seem to raise her voice above a whisper.

He flipped some hair out of her eyes. "See you tomorrow for church."

"Give me your home phone number, and I'll call you in the morning. I don't know if Gram will be up to going or not." Maggie doubted it.

"I could always stay with her while you take Caitlin and Robert."

She gave him a probing glance. "No, you deserve a day of rest from us. If Gram isn't going, we'll all stay home."

"Okay." He took out his wallet. "I'll write my number on the back of one of my cards. Let me know what the plan is. Remember, I'm always willing to give up a day of rest to take you to church." Now his gaze was so tender she felt as if he were speaking directly to her and not to the family collectively. She shivered.

* * *

Even after David drove away from Isabelle's, the sensation of Maggie's soft curls continued to linger on his fingertips. He was insane to have touched her hair, but all those curls captivated him, and when one drifted across her eye, he couldn't help himself.

What would Maggie's reaction be if they couldn't help her grandmother? Would she be ready for an assisted-living home? He didn't think she realized how demanding it could be to care for a helpless person. He thought Barbara would probably be all for it since she had wanted to place her in one earlier. Maggie had some big decisions to make. Soon she'd need to start teaching again. He couldn't see any way that Isabelle could possibly stay alone, and in his heart of hearts, he thought she'd continue to decline.

When he arrived home, he turned on the game. There were three innings left, and, in the end, the Diamondbacks won. David enjoyed watching good pitching, and Randy Johnson had kept the Dodgers scoreless.

Next he wanted to continue reading the Book of Mormon. Making himself comfortable in his leather chair, he picked up the book and found his place. Once again, the impression he'd previously had when he read settled on him. The Book of Mormon sounded true to him, but what did he know? And if this were an account of God's interaction with these people, where did that leave the Jews? They couldn't both be correct, and his money was on Judaism. But he still had the feeling that Lehi and his family had actually lived, that they weren't a figment of someone's imagination.

At seven o'clock, David stopped for a snack before reading on. Why did this book fascinate him? Finally his eyes were burning so fiercely from eyestrain that he decided to give them a rest. Marking his place at the beginning of Alma, he laid the book on the coffee table, then stretched out on the couch and closed his eyes to rest them. When he awoke it was midnight. Again! He was beginning to feel like Cinderella.

He made his way to his bedroom. When he had crawled in bed, he put his right hand over his eyes and repeated the *sh'ma, Praise to Adonai.* He turned onto his side and fell back asleep.

Sunday after Maggie called and said Isabelle didn't feel like going to church, David decided to get out and exercise. He had no idea where the hiking club would be today, but it didn't matter because he felt like being alone. Then he remembered Estes Park, and decided that's where he would go. Beautiful scenery lined the entire route, and the planners had laid out numerous hiking trails in the park. It was just what he needed today. Getting his hiking gear, he set out.

* * *

After she got the kids to bed Monday evening, Maggie went back to the living room and slumped down in the easy chair, stretching her legs out in front of her. What a day it had been. Medical tests and physical therapy had worn Gram out. She had come home and gone straight to bed exhausted.

None of the news had been good. The CAT scan had shown another stroke. The therapist was doubtful Gram would ever be able to get around without her walker, and only by exercising daily would she be able to even get back to using the walker. The therapist had scheduled daily appointments for her this week. Maggie wondered if Gram would even be up to going tomorrow.

After studying the reports, David also told her he thought Gram would continue to deteriorate until she was gone. He had no idea how long it would be—whether a month or a year. And he said pneumonia was always a threat to the elderly. Maggie took a deep breath, trying to clear her mind.

She decided she'd better call Barbara in the morning and give her the news, wondering what she would advise doing. David had told Maggie she needed to take a good look at a nursing facility. He said in that environment, Isabelle could get skilled nursing care and physical therapy. Maggie considered that maybe that was the best idea, although she knew Barbara wouldn't like that because it would eat up the money. But if Gram's time was limited here on earth, she deserved the best care possible, and that couldn't come from Maggie, who felt totally inept at helping sick people.

Brad had called the previous day and said he would arrive home the next. His house had sold, and he'd be closing on it, packing everything up, and moving to Memphis. Maggie had already started to miss Caitlin and Robert just knowing they would be gone in another four days, but right then all she could think of was that it would be one less problem to deal with. She'd pack their things in the morning.

School started in a little over two weeks, and she hadn't even given it a thought this summer. Usually by this time in the summer, she had oodles of new ideas and plans for activities, but not this year. She hated even to think of going back She wished she could sell her condo, live off the proceeds, and write mysteries. But Pat had warned, "Don't give up your day job."

Wearily, Maggie made her way up the stairs. She checked on the kids, turned them straight in their bed, and kissed their soft little cheeks good night.

In her own bedroom she knelt and poured her heart out to Heavenly Father, asking for guidance through these difficult times. Tears flooded down her cheeks as she pleaded with Him to take away her feelings for David, to help her find a worthy member of the Church to marry. She didn't want to spend her life without a companion and children. She told the Lord that she didn't seek to counsel Him, but wanted His wisdom to know what to do.

Slowly she rose to her feet and undressed, getting ready for bed. Her mind was such a jumble of worries that sleep didn't come readily.

As Maggie dialed Barbara the next morning, apprehension filled her. She had no idea what her aunt's response would be to the news about Gram, but she didn't have long to wait.

After she'd recounted the information she'd received Monday, Barbara spoke right up. "If she doesn't have long to live, we should have plenty of money to put her in a nice care center."

The words sounded callous hearing them aloud, but Maggie agreed with Barbara. "That's what I was thinking. Do you want to come out and we'll look for a place?"

"No. I can't get time off right now. You just go ahead and find some place. I trust your judgment."

Barbara's casually casting the burden of finding a suitable residence for her mother onto Maggie sent angry tears burning down Maggie's cheeks. "Barbara, I don't have extra time myself. Remember, school starts for me soon."

"But you're right there. It won't take much effort to find some-place." She made it sound simple.

"I'll tell you what. I'll put Gram on a nonstop flight to Atlanta, and you find her a place in your spare time."

Barbara sputtered a moment and then said, "Now, Maggie, you're Mom's favorite grandchild, and you wouldn't want to send her across the country where you couldn't see her often. I'm sure you can manage. Try to find a residence for not over three thousand a month, and when she's moved in, list her house for sale."

Maggie felt like saying, "Yes, master." But she didn't. "All this will take awhile, but I'll let you know when everything is settled."

She hung up as irritated as she'd expected to be. When Barbara had left after her last visit, Maggie thought she'd changed. Today she sounded like the same old Barbara, and that wasn't a compliment.

"Maggie, Maggie! Come here!" Gram sounded terror-stricken.

Maggie rushed into the bedroom. "What's happening?"

"I've just had a horrible dream. It woke me up." Tears filled Gram's eyes, and she appeared frightened.

Maggie put her arm under her grandmother's shoulders and hugged her close to her body. She patted her hands and reached for a tissue to wipe her eyes. "Tell me about it," she said gently.

"I dreamed movers came to take me to a rest home. They were taking all my furniture too." Tears filled her eyes again, and she sobbed, "Maggie, don't let them take me away. I've lived in this house sixty years, and I want to die here. I can't live somewhere else." Sobs wracked her body.

"Gram, you don't have to move. You can stay here forever." Maggie couldn't help but think of the odd timing of her dream.

"Maggie, promise me you won't let anyone move me out of my home," she begged, clinging desperately to her granddaughter.

"Oh, honey, now calm down." She rubbed Gram's back. "I promise. You'll never leave here while I'm alive." Maggie couldn't stand the thought of hurting Gram so badly in this way. But what did she do now?

Finally Gram stopped crying, and minutes later she was asleep again. Maggie gently laid her back on the bed.

She delivered Caitlin and Robert to preschool. She hadn't told them their dad was coming tonight in case something happened and he couldn't make it.

When she returned home, she found Gram still sleeping. Taking the phone into the living room, she called Pat. "Do you have time to come over here for thirty minutes or so? I need to talk to someone."

"What's happened now?" Pat said sympathetically.

Now the tears filled Maggie's eyes. "Gram's worse, and there isn't much hope she'll ever be any better." She felt desperate.

"I'll be right over." Pat hung up.

Maggie slowly put down the receiver on the coffee table. She knew she couldn't go back to school in a few weeks. This summer's problems had torn her into so many pieces that she didn't have a coherent thought about getting organized for teaching.

She checked on Gram and then went out to the porch to wait for Pat.

A few minutes later Pat drove up and hurried to the porch. She sat in the other Adirondack chair and looked at Maggie. "I'm worried about you. Did you sleep at all last night? You look terrible."

"Not much," Maggie admitted, giving Pat a grim smile. "That compliment lifts my spirits."

Pat smiled. "Now give me all the details."

Maggie told her about the weekend and the test results from the day before. She concluded with her call to Barbara, Gram's dream, and the resultant panic attack.

Pat grasped her arm. "Before we plunge into the heavy stuff, I have a couple of questions. Any idea when Brad is coming after Caitlin and Robert? And when are you going to have your book finished?"

"If those were my only two worries, I'd be in seventh heaven. Brad's coming tonight, and I should have my book in the mail by next Monday." She knew these were answers Pat would love.

"Great." Pat sat up straight, all business. "We can check off the least of your worries. You promised Isabelle you wouldn't let her go to a nursing home. Have you come up with any ideas about something else?"

"A couple of thoughts have come to my mind, but I want your input. I don't want to return to teaching this year." She shook her head. "Mentally, I'm drained, and I don't think I'm up to it." She sighed, sinking even deeper against the chair back.

"Quit or take a leave of absence," Pat offered.

"If I take a leave of absence, I won't have any money to live on. If I outright quit, I can collect my retirement pay, which I feel would be stupid. I certainly want something saved for my old age." *If I live that long.*

"Sell your condo. Invest the earnings. Live off them. Or rent out your condo and live off the income." When it came to advice on money, Pat was never at a loss.

"The income would be eaten up by my payments on it." She grabbed her head in frustration. "There isn't an easy solution."

"But I firmly believe there is a solution." Pat leaned forward in the chair. "I'm thinking you want to stay here with your grandmother."

"Yes, I'd like to, but I couldn't manage by myself. I'm not a skilled nurse." Maggie felt totally inadequate when it came to such skills.

"Your obvious love for her goes a long way, but I think you would need help so that you weren't worn out." Pat reached out and comfortingly touched her arm.

Maggie nodded in agreement. Pat was good at cutting through the chaff and getting down to the grain.

"What about applying for a leave of absence, and if that is denied, asking to teach part-time? Sell your condo, and I'll help you invest the proceeds. But first take out enough to live on for a year. Move in here with Isabelle rent free. Your only expenses would be food and storing your furniture." Pat laid out some possible alternatives.

"I wonder what Barbara's reaction would be to me living off Gram." Maggie gave Pat a quizzical glance.

"Who cares! You're here. She's there, making no effort to be of any help herself." Pat spoke vehemently.

"That sounds scary. What if my condo doesn't sell for months? What do I do in the meantime? What if I can't get a leave or a part-time position? Barbara could just throw me out if she decided to. She's co-owner of the house." While Pat's ideas were good, Maggie didn't have a positive feeling about them.

"I wouldn't worry about any problem from her as long as she doesn't have to exert herself. But I do think you shouldn't do anything until you've given it more thought and prayed about it." Pat's tone soothed Maggie.

"I wouldn't." Heavenly Father had always been her refuge, and He was now.

"Why don't we go to the temple tomorrow? Mimi is off, and I know she would be happy to stay with Isabelle while we're gone."

Maggie felt light, as if a load had been removed from her shoulders. "A wonderful idea. I haven't been all summer. Let's do it."

Pat smiled. "I knew you'd want to." Then her eyes twinkled with mischief. "What's happening with you and David the Doctor?"

"Maggie! Maggie! Come here!" Isabelle sounded as terrified as before.

Chapter 14

Her heart racing, Maggie dashed into the bedroom, Pat following close behind. "What's the matter?"

Gram appeared wild-eyed and scared. Her words sputtered out. "I've had . . ." She stared at Pat. "Who are you?" Fear sharpened her voice.

Smiling, Pat moved toward Gram, who immediately shrank back against the pillows, pulling the covers tight around her neck. Pat stepped back and then said gently, "I'm Maggie's friend Pat. I've known you for a long time. In fact, we spent last Wednesday together."

Gram's eyes narrowed, and she glared. "No, we didn't. I don't remember that, and I have a good memory." She turned to Maggie. "Tell her to leave. I don't want her in my house."

Pat said pleasantly, "Good-bye, Isabelle. I hope you feel better soon." She motioned to Maggie that she'd wait in the dining room.

When she had left, Maggie sat down on the edge of the bed and smoothed back her grandmother's white hair. "What's troubling you, dearest Gram?"

She shook her head sadly. "I don't remember."

Maggie's heart fell. What was happening to Gram now?

Gram grabbed for Maggie's hands and gripped them with all her strength. "Something's going to happen to me, and you've got to keep me safe. Promise?"

"Promise." Maggie nodded her head firmly. "I won't let anything happen to you." She wished she could be more comforting, but she didn't know what else to do.

Gram sighed with relief.

Maggie continued in a soothing tone. "Do you feel like physical therapy again today?"

Her grandmother seemed to shrivel up right before her eyes, becoming even smaller and more defenseless. "No."

"Do you want to get up now?" Her appearance worried Maggie. She looked as if even the smallest breeze would blow her away.

"No. Help me to the bathroom, and then I want to stay in bed today." Gram made little effort to get up.

As Maggie picked her up, she realized Gram was virtually a dead weight, but she didn't dare call Pat to help her. Finally, with a great deal of effort, she managed to get Gram into the wheelchair and to the bathroom. Then she joined Pat in the dining room.

"Is Isabelle this forgetful often?" Pat eyed her with concern.

"No, and I'm hoping this episode won't last long." She slumped down into a chair, depleted of all energy.

"Me too." For the first time, Pat didn't have a ready solution. She stood up. "Why don't I pick up the kids for you at noon? Meanwhile, I'll make the arrangements for tomorrow, and we can discuss them when I bring Caitlin and Robert home."

"That would be great. I'm afraid to leave Gram for even a few minutes when she's this weak." Then a thought struck her. "What if she doesn't remember Mimi? If she reacts to her like she did to you, poor Mimi could never handle her."

"Why don't we just wait and see? If she doesn't recognize Mimi, we won't go." She turned to leave. "Hang in there, kiddo. See you later."

"Bye." Maggie watched her leave, wondering what would happen next. After she got her grandmother settled back in bed, she called the physical therapy department at the hospital and canceled all the appointments. She didn't think Gram would be able to go out for at least another week—if then. Reluctantly, she went to the garage to find boxes to put the kids' things in. Packing their belongings only confirmed to Maggie that soon her darling niece and nephew would be gone. It was a sad twenty minutes, and she didn't feel any better when she went into the living room.

All she could do was sit and reflect on the decisions she needed to make. She wished she could be like Paul and Alma and have an angel appear and tell her what to do. On the other hand, she thought wryly, she wasn't in the mood to be struck down for three days either. But she valued Pat's insight, and decided her advice would be worth following. She desperately wanted to go to the temple tomorrow. She felt a deep need to feel the peace and love that filled that holy place. She closed her eyes. *O Father, please bless Gram that she will recognize Mimi tomorrow so that I might go to Thy house and worship Thee.*

Pat brought Caitlin and Robert home and told her that Mimi was set to come tomorrow and stay with Isabelle. Hoping that Gram would be back to normal tomorrow, Maggie waved good-bye and hustled the kids inside. Then she fed them and put them down for naps. Gram finally woke up and asked Maggie to turn on her television. She said she didn't feel like getting up yet, but she wanted something to distract her. Maggie fluffed up her pillows and helped her sit up more. Then she fixed her a chocolate milk shake. Gram seemed in good spirits.

While her grandmother sipped her milk shake, Maggie flipped through the channels with the remote. The movie channel was showing *The Way We Were,* with Barbra Streisand and Robert Redford. The movie was one of Maggie's all-time favorites. "What about watching *The Way We Were?*" Maggie suggested. "It'll be on in three minutes."

"Yes!" Gram said excitedly. "I loved that movie, and I can't wait to see it again."

Gram sounded like her old self, and Maggie marveled at the difference a couple of hours had made.

"I'll bring in the easy chair from the living room and watch it with you," she said.

"No. Don't waste your time watching movies. Write." Gram seemed determined for Maggie to write.

Maggie shook her head. "Not right now. I'm not in the mood. Maybe later." She dragged the heavy chair from the living room into the bedroom and plopped down in it.

Gram shook her head disapprovingly. "Maggie May, if authors wrote just when they felt like it, they'd get little accomplished."

She smiled with good humor. "Are you saying you don't want me to watch with you?"

"No," Gram said forcibly, "I'm saying *write*."

Maggie sighed. "Okay, if that's the way you want it, but I'm leaving the chair here just in case I want to take a break."

"When you get tired." Gram spelled out the terms, apparently wanting to make sure Maggie knew she didn't have permission to take a break for any other reason.

Maggie laughed. "Gram, have I told you lately how bossy you are?"

Gram replied with a satisfied smile.

Maggie figured it was just as good that she didn't watch *The Way We Were* which was about a Jew and a Christian who didn't end up together. She would have enough of that pain facing her in her own life if she let herself fall in love with David—something she'd never let happen.

She started writing, ecstatic to be on the last twenty pages. She knew she could finish this book this week.

Blanche's eyes narrowed. "I know what we should do."

Ruby looked apprehensive, as if she were unwilling to trust her friend's proposal. "What?"

"Invite all the suspects to lunch one at a time and tell each one that we know what he or she did. Perpetrators always confess to Jessica Fletcher when she does that." Blanche oozed confidence.

Maggie became lost in her writing, so when she heard Caitlin and Robert running down the stairs, she jumped. "I've got a snack for you. After you finish eating, why don't you play on the patio and," she glanced at her nephew, "you can mow the backyard." A twinge of sadness filtered through her body. She'd miss his sweeping and his mowing.

Robert's face lit up. "All right!"

Caitlin, cheerful as usual, said, "Can I get the snacks?"

"I'll help you get the cookies and milk out, and you can bring them in here to the table." Going into the kitchen, Maggie opened a package of Oreos and poured them each a glass of milk.

Caitlin carefully carried the glasses into the dining room and then came back for the cookies and napkins. By the time Maggie had taken cookies to Gram and gotten a handful for herself, the kids were nearly finished and ready to go outside.

"We're having pizza and sodas for supper." She watched as a smile filled Robert's face.

"Yes!" He pumped his arm.

Maggie felt tears at the corners of her eyes. How could she stand to have these two disappear out of her life? To think that Karen wasn't here to enjoy them increased her sadness.

Caitlin just as carefully cleared the table and put the glasses in the dishwasher. Then, laughing, both she and Robert ran outside.

"Maggie, there's a commercial on. Could you help me into the living room to finish watching this movie?" Gram smiled as Maggie came to the bedroom door. "Either my bones are getting old or this bed is hard, but I need to change positions."

"Probably a little of both. Let me move this chair back to the living room and then I'll take you in there."

When Maggie had her situated in her recliner, Gram asked if there were more cookies she could have.

"Plenty. I'll bring the package in and then you can eat to your heart's content."

"Good." Gram appeared satisfied.

Maggie was just cleaning up after their pizza when David arrived. Her heart skipped a beat when she saw him.

"What's happening?" His voice was sympathetic.

"Do you want some root beer first?" She smiled at him. "It's been a long, miserable day."

"Sure," he said easily, pulling out a chair and sitting down.

He always sounded so relaxed, but still capable of handling whatever might come his way. She wondered if he actually felt like that.

After she'd gotten the drinks, she sat down next to him and related the details of the day to him.

"So what are you going to do?" He took a sip of his drink.

"I wish I knew. I've been thinking of taking a leave of absence, selling my condo, and moving in here." To her own ears she sounded tentative, and while she could agree with all the arguments for doing it, she really didn't know if it was the right thing to do.

He frowned. "That's a major upheaval in your life. Are you sure you want to make that drastic a change?"

"I'm almost certain I don't want to go back to school this fall, and in order to live, I need the money from the sale of my condo." She wished she wasn't in this quandary.

"The accent is on 'almost certain,' and until you're absolutely positive, I wouldn't do anything. I don't think you fully understand the demands that caring for your grandmother would place on you." He spoke quietly. "Today was only a sample of things to come. I know you promised her you wouldn't, but maybe the best thing to do would be to arrange for her to move to an assisted-living home. Sometimes we have to break our promises to do what is best." He picked up her hand in a consoling gesture, and she didn't move her hand from the warmth of his.

Shaking her head, Maggie said, "No. I promised her that she wouldn't ever have to move, and the confusion she's had this morning just reinforces my commitment. It would break her heart. I couldn't do that." She blinked back the tears that were filling her eyes. She kept forgetting just how close to the surface her emotions were today.

He frowned. "What about Caitlin and Robert? Any word from their dad?"

"Brad called Sunday, and he should be here tonight. They'll be in Memphis by Saturday night." She tried to be brisk, but she could feel her chin quiver.

"I know that having them leave will be painful, but still it should make life easier for you." He squeezed her hand. "I'm not even around them that much, and already I hate to see them go. Do you think there's another child in the entire world who wants to sweep and mow the way Robert does?" His smile included his eyes, which were sparkling.

Maggie grinned through her tears. "No way. He's an original."

He released her hand. "I'll watch out for Brad, and you'd better write."

"That was a bit dictatorial, but I'll go." Picking up her laptop, Maggie headed upstairs.

David checked on the kids and found Robert vigorously sweeping the patio. Caitlin had her cups and saucers out and was cautiously filling them with water, as if the redwood table would be damaged if any water spilled on it.

David returned to the living room. "How are you doing tonight, Isabelle?"

"Just perfect." A broad smile crinkled her face.

"The kids are playing contentedly in the back, and Maggie is upstairs writing. That leaves just you and me to watch TV. Anything good on?" He rested against the back of the sofa. Isabelle seemed so much like her old self that he found it difficult to believe the incidents that happened this morning. But he knew they had, and he also knew she'd undoubtedly have more.

Isabelle held up the remote and grinned. "If there is, I'll find it."

After surfing the channels for a minute or so, she found a PBS special on elephants. They'd watched it for nearly twenty minutes when Caitlin and Robert came tearing in. "Come play, Uncle David!"

"Don't you want to watch the elephants on television?" To his surprise, he'd found the program enlightening. He'd never given a second thought to what happened to elephants when they couldn't perform for a circus anymore.

They nodded happily. Robert crawled up on his lap, and Caitlin snuggled against his arm, and their eyes never left the TV. They were totally fascinated by the elephants. When the show was nearly over, someone knocked at the front door. Carrying Robert in his arms and Caitlin walking in step with him, he answered the door.

On the front porch stood a smiling man whose expression quickly changed from one of surprise to one of irritation.

"Brad?" David questioned. This guy certainly didn't seem very happy, whoever he was.

Without bothering to answer, the man asked, "Who are you?"

"Daddy!" Caitlin dashed forward to hug his legs, and Robert leaped out of David's arms to his dad's.

"I take it you're the kids' dad." David gave him an easy smile. "We're sure going to miss these two." He stepped back. "Come on in."

"Who are you?" Brad repeated in a tone bordering on rudeness.

"David Rosenberg." He held out his hand. "I'm glad to meet you."

Brad reluctantly shook his hand. "Where's Maggie?"

David couldn't help but think that if he himself had just come back after being away for over a month, he would have been so glad to see his children that nothing else would bother him. "Upstairs writing. I'll run up and get her."

"Writing?" Brad looked amazed.

"She's finishing her book." David pitied these poor kids to have this guy as a father.

"Her book?" Brad sounded as though he'd never heard of Maggie writing.

"She didn't tell you that a publishing company was interested in her book?" David challenged him.

"Oh, she mentioned something about it, but I didn't realize she'd still be working on it." He continued to stare at David.

"Come on in, I know Caitlin wants a chance to sit on your lap." He held the screen door open for him.

"I don't think I need to be told what my own children want." Brad's indignation was apparent, and he seemed hesitant to enter the house.

"Come on, Daddy, let's go see Gram." Caitlin pulled on his pant leg and Brad followed her into the house.

As David ran up the stairs to get Maggie, he heard Brad say, "Darling Gram, how are you doing?" He sounded warm and loving, and to David's thinking, phony.

Isabelle's face brightened. "Brad, how nice to see you!" She glanced at Caitlin and Robert. "I see you've met Karen's children. Aren't they wonderful?" She made no mention that they were his children also.

Brad looked startled. "Of course I think they're wonderful, Gram. They're my kids too."

"No," she said definitely, "they're Karen's. How come we haven't seen you lately?"

"I've been in Memphis for over a month." He seated himself on the sofa, pulling Caitlin onto his lap followed by Robert.

"Why?" Isabelle words were pointed, as if he'd been crazy to go there.

"I've been working and finding somewhere to live. I've come back to get the kids and to move us down there." His tone was thoughtful.

"Well, you can't take the kids." Tears glistened in her eyes. "Maggie won't let you."

From the doorway, Maggie said warmly, "Brad, it's good to see you, but we're sure going to miss Caitlin and Robert."

He said coolly, "It looks like things have changed around here." He gave David a pointed look.

She smiled reassuringly at Brad. "We wouldn't have made it without David."

Brad's lips tightened.

Now David frowned. *What is Brad's problem anyway?*

Maggie continued. "I told you we'd moved in here with Gram because of her stroke. David has kept Gram company, played with your children, and best of all, mowed the lawn." Maggie's eyes sparkled happily as she recounted his good deeds, seemingly unaware of Brad's animosity.

David forced himself to be pleasant, but it was not without effort. He couldn't understand Brad's ungraciousness. After all Maggie'd done for him, he wondered how Brad dared to act that way.

"I expected you, not a stranger, to care for my children." He clasped the two in his lap even tighter.

David started to say something scathing when Isabelle broke in. "They are not your children. They're Karen's."

Maggie tensed. Evidently fearing another scene like the one this morning, she eyed David with apprehension. And he couldn't ignore her beseeching eyes. He put his arm across her shoulders to reassure her. He would have preferred to embrace her, but that would be unwise, just asking for trouble. He glanced at Brad, who stared at him, totally unaware of Maggie's turmoil.

Brad turned back to Isabelle, and to David's amazement, his manner changed completely. "Would you mind if I took them to stay with me tonight?" He sounded strained, but he made it clear he was ready to do whatever Isabelle asked of him.

This man amazed David. He acted impossible one moment and kind and generous to Isabelle the next.

"You can take them tonight, but Maggie won't like it if you don't bring them back in the morning," she warned sternly, her eyes narrowing.

"I'll bring them back in the morning, I promise." He leaned over and kissed Isabelle's soft cheek. "Come on kids, say good-bye to Gram and let's go." Caitlin and Robert reached their plump arms up and kissed and hugged Isabelle.

Maggie moved away from David and addressed Brad. "Where are you staying?"

"At our house. The movers are coming Thursday, and I'm closing on the house on Friday. Saturday morning we fly to Memphis."

"I've packed up the kids' things. Do you want to take them tonight?" Maggie spoke evenly, with no hint of how much she'd miss them.

"No, I'll get them tomorrow." He pushed Caitlin and Robert toward her. "Kids, give your aunt a kiss and let's go."

They both rushed to her, holding up their arms, saying, "Hugs and kisses." After she'd hugged and kissed them, they held their arms up to David.

Brad scowled. Before David could hug them, he grabbed their hands and they left, getting only as far as the front porch when Robert spoke up. "I take my mower."

"Your what?" Brad acted confused.

"My mower Uncle David gave me." Robert pointed to where it was leaning against the side of the porch.

Brad stared grimly at David. "I don't think so."

Robert broke away and ran over to get his lawn mower. "I take it."

"Leave it here." Brad made it obvious he didn't want anything from David. "And he isn't your Uncle David." The words poured out.

"Yes." Robert clutched the mower to him.

"No." Brad pulled it out of his arms and set it down.

Robert screamed, "I want my mower! I want my mower!" His sobs rang through the tranquil neighborhood. "I want my mower. I want my . . ."

"I think it would be easier and quieter to let him take it," Maggie pointed out, her teeth gritted.

Brad shrugged and picked up the mower, walking quickly to the car. Robert stopped crying immediately and followed him. Caitlin trailed behind.

After they'd driven off, David and Maggie returned to the living room and made themselves comfortable on the sofa. "He's not the most friendly person in the world, is he?"

"You're asking the wrong person. I've never liked him, so I could not give you a fair and impartial report." She smiled at him. "I actually thought he'd changed, but evidently it was only skin-deep. Tonight he was only slightly less irritating than usual."

"How did you manage to be so pleasant?"

"Sheer grit." She gazed around the room. "Can you feel the emptiness? I'll enjoy the quiet, but I miss them already."

"I know what you mean," he said softly, again wanting to hug her and relieve her of her burdens. He stood up before he did something foolish. "I'll be on my way. Do you realize my time here is getting short? Caitlin and Robert are gone, and you'll finish your book this week. I, unfortunately, won't be needed anymore."

A glimmer of a smile touched her lips. "Don't be in such a big hurry to get rid of us."

"Just tonight. I'll see you Thursday." He turned to her grandmother. "Good night, Isabelle. See you Thursday."

She frowned. "You're leaving this soon?"

"I'm afraid so." Actually, he hated to leave Maggie, but being a prudent person, he said good-bye and left.

He wondered what would happen tomorrow with Brad. He couldn't figure out why the man was so hostile toward him. He smiled to himself. After all, wasn't he one of the good guys?

What a week it had turned out to be. He found himself more and more attracted to Maggie, so it was a good thing that his visits at her place were ending. He worried that she was undertaking too big a job. He seldom saw people in his practice who had such a devoted family. Most of them cared about their aged parents, but a lot of them were more like Barbara than Maggie. She was a special person, and he wondered if he'd ever meet a Jewish woman like her. Then he stopped himself. He knew plenty of caring women, and he felt sure God would see that he found his *richtige zivvug*.

Reading the Book of Mormon that week had also turned out to be addictive. Usually all he found time to read were medical journals, but not now. He made time to read it. He'd been determined not to read any more on Sunday, but after his hike, he went right back to reading The Book, as he called it. He wanted to discuss it with someone, but wondered who. Maggie would be biased, and so would Pete. Maybe he'd ask the rabbi tomorrow night what he knew about it. Maybe Fred Scott would know of a meeting that he could attend like the synagogues's Torah class. He'd written his address and phone number in the front of The Book. That would be the answer. He'd give Fred a call tomorrow. This way Maggie and Pete would never need to know anything about his study of The Book.

When David had read King Lamoni's father's plea to God, he felt a wrenching inside him. The plaintive entreaty touched David deeply, and he could absolutely feel the king's humility and his hunger for the truth. He could understand it because he had the same yearning within him. The beginning of The Book said to pray to know if it were true. David didn't know how to pray if he weren't reciting a Jewish prayer. He wracked his mind to think of a Jewish prayer on the subject of truth. When he couldn't think of one, he got up and checked his prayer book. He did find a blessing for truth, but it didn't say what he wanted to ask.

Tomorrow he'd check with the rabbi.

* * *

Maggie woke up late on Wednesday morning. For a moment she panicked, thinking she'd overslept and she needed to be getting Caitlin and Robert dressed for school, and then she sadly remembered they were gone. She'd miss their delightful personalities, but even through all the sadness, she felt as though she'd had a burden lifted from her. She prayed Gram would recognize Mimi so she and Pat could go to the temple.

When she got downstairs, she found Gram awake and watching a morning television program. "How's my favorite grandmother today?"

Gram turned down the sound. "Better. But I still think I'll stay in bed this morning, if you don't mind helping me."

"Of course I'll help you." She laughed. "What kind of a granddaughter do you think I am?"

Gram smiled lovingly at her. "The best. Heavenly Father blessed me when He gave me you."

Maggie leaned over and hugged her. "Thank you for that vote of confidence. Do you remember Pat's daughter Mimi?"

Gram sighed. "How could I forget someone who used to visit me practically every other week with little presents she'd made just for me? No one forgets teenagers like Mimi."

Maggie sighed a silent breath of relief.

Pat and Mimi arrived just as she finished getting Gram ready for the day. Pat gave her a quizzical glance when she answered the door. Maggie shrugged and led them back to the bedroom.

Gram glanced up. "Mimi, my dear! I'm glad you're here. Come over and sit down so I can see you." She patted the side of the bed.

Mimi's love for Gram radiated from her, and she perched on the edge of the bed and hugged the elderly lady. "I've been so busy working this summer that I haven't gotten over to see you at all. Do you forgive me?"

Gram beamed at her. "What's to forgive?"

"I'm glad I got to come this morning, and," Mimi's eyes twinkled, "I've brought you a little something."

"What?" Gram's face became even more animated. Her enthusiasm for a present reminded Maggie of Caitlin and Robert.

"A book of Parley P. Pratt's poems and songs." Mimi handed her a gold bag.

Gram eagerly pulled out a small, leather-bound book. Her eyes widened as she looked at the title page, and then she read aloud, *"The Songs and Poems of Parley P. Pratt, compiled by Mimi Wilson for Isabelle Hughes.* You did this just for me? How?" Her astonishment was apparent.

"Besides working this summer, I've been taking a bookbinding class. With a lot of help from the instructor and my computer, I finished this."

"Don't I have a marvelous daughter?" Pat glowed with pride.

"In just about every way I can think of." Maggie smiled at Pat and Mimi. It felt good to see Gram happier and livelier than she'd been in a long time. "I know you've made Gram's day."

"You deserve another hug." Gram laid the book down and held out her arms. Mimi slipped her hands under her shoulders and hugged her. Then Gram ran her fingers over the smooth, golden-brown leather and leafed through the brightly illustrated pages. "It reminds me of a medieval Book of Days, except this is my own great-grandfather's writings." She held the book to her chest. "I'll cherish this the rest of my life."

Pat turned to Maggie. "Now that you've admired my talented daughter's handiwork, I think we'd better be leaving if we want to make the 9:30 temple session."

Maggie kissed her grandmother good-bye, and they left. This was turning into a glorious day, and if she'd known what decision to make about Gram, the day would have been perfect. Thirty minutes later they drove onto Phillips Circle. When she sighted the white gleaming temple and the beautiful gardens surrounding it, Maggie could feel a calm inundating her entire being, and she felt the assurance that this was the right place to find the answers to her problems.

After the session, Maggie and Pat sat in the celestial room to pray and meditate. Maggie relaxed her body in an effort to absorb the spirit of this incredibly beautiful room. Even the word *magnificent* did not do it justice. Light from the large chandelier and the crystal side sconces illuminated the area, with the focal point a stunning lead crystal table. The room was bathed in light. Maggie loved the word *light* in the scriptures. *The light of Christ, the light of everlasting life.* She didn't see how the celestial kingdom could be any more beautiful than this room. The white and creme colors of the furnishings, along with everyone's white clothes, only added to the stillness.

After praying once more for guidance and enlightenment in solving her problems, she felt open to the Spirit. As she contemplated Gram and the way she'd always eagerly served others, Maggie thought of the love and support Gram had showered on her when she'd lost her parents and Karen. Gram had always been a rock to lean on—not only for her but for others in their time of need. She loved Gram deeply, and she yearned to know the best way to help her now. Was taking a leave of absence and moving in with Gram the right direction to go? As she sat mulling these thoughts, a warmth enveloped her, and she knew her course of action was right. She thought of Lehi being encircled in the arms of God's love. And then again, an even stronger impression came into her mind. *The Lord loves you and is aware of what you are going through.*

As they walked on the temple grounds to the car, Maggie said to Pat, "I know your advice was right. I'm going to the school district office this afternoon to apply for a leave of absence." She had total confidence that this was the right move.

Pat raised her eyebrows. "What will you do if they don't give you one?"

"Quit," she said firmly. "I know what the Lord wants me to do. Later this afternoon, I'll call a real estate office and list my condo."

Pat smiled reassuringly. "For someone who was indecisive yesterday, you've certainly become determined today. I'm glad. For all you know, your writing career will take off and you'll never have to teach again."

Maggie laughed. "Wasn't it you who said, and I quote, 'Don't quit your day job'?"

"Just quoting others, my dear. I think you are making exactly the right move."

She still felt a glow about her. The Spirit was so strong, leaving no doubt in her mind that the Lord did love her, and she had faith in Him.

When they arrived back at the house, Pat said, "I'll run Mimi home, and then I'll stay with Isabelle while you go to the district office."

"Thanks." Happiness emanated from her heart. What an incredibly spiritual morning this had been.

Chapter 15

"Well, that was quick," Pat said as Maggie walked in the house later that afternoon. "What did they say? Did you get the leave of absence?"

"Yes. They talked to my principal, who gave me a glowing recommendation and told them by all means to give me the leave because he didn't want to lose me. Otherwise I'd have had to resign, since the date for leave approval was in April." Maggie hung her purse over the back of a dining room chair and sat down, facing Pat.

"I knew it would work out." A wide smile brightened Pat's face. "Now, did you get your condo listed?"

"That was the best news of all. Do you know that my unit has appreciated immensely? If I get the asking price—or even close to it—I will make a $30,000 profit." Her words tumbled out. "Can you believe it?"

"You'll have even more money to invest." Pat gave Maggie a self-satisfied smile. "Aren't you glad I urged you to buy it when your parents passed away?"

Maggie matched her smile. "Yes. If I'd only followed your advice on all my money matters, I'd be on easy street today."

"What did Isabelle say about your moving in here?"

"I haven't discussed it with her yet. I wanted to take care of the business matters first. If she says no," she gave Pat an impish grin, "I'll move in with you."

Her friend rolled her eyes. "I don't think I'll need to clean out the guest room anytime soon. Isabelle will be thrilled."

Maggie sighed. "I wish it were easy, but all these changes mean hard work for me. I'll need to decide which of my belongings to store and which to bring here. I'll have to clean out my classroom for the new teacher, and six years of teaching stuff will needed to be sorted through—and some discarded and some stored. I hate to think of it."

"Well, just listening to you is making me tired. When you have a date set, let me know," Pat teased. "I plan on being out of town."

Maggie shook her head in mock disgust. "If that isn't just like you."

Gram's weak voice interrupted them. "Is that you, Maggie?"

"Yes, Gram." She and Pat both stood up and started for the bedroom.

"She was asleep the entire time you were gone," Pat whispered.

When they entered her room, they found a cheerful Gram. "I think I'll sit up for a while in the living room, if you'll help me."

Maggie slipped Gram's robe on her and helped her into the bathroom to wash up.

After they'd settled her in her chair, Pat said, "I'd better be off. Keep me posted on the latest happenings."

"Will do." Maggie walked her friend to the door. "Thanks. That's such a paltry word for all you do for me. I hope you know how grateful I am."

Pat nodded and walked to her car, waving at Maggie as she drove away.

"Well, Gram," she said as she seated herself on the sofa. "How would you like me to move in here with you?"

Gram's eyes widened and she became excited. "I'd love it! When?"

"As soon as I can get packed. I've decided to sell my condo and store my furniture."

"So this will be permanent?"

"Afraid so. You might get tired of me."

"Never! I just wish you could be here all day and not have to teach."

"You know what they say, 'Be careful what you wish for.' I'm taking a leave of absence."

"Now you can write full-time." A sly expression crossed Gram's face. "I'll still need David to visit while you write."

Maggie laughed. "Sorry, trickster, but I plan on writing in the morning, and he's working then."

"I'll think of something." Although Gram was eighty years old, she apparently wasn't giving in.

This sounded to Maggie suspiciously like matchmaking. "Not on my account," she said briskly. She wanted to leave no doubt in Gram's mind how she felt about Gram's determination to get David and her together.

"Don't be so distrustful." She gave Maggie a disdainful look. "I want him over here to visit with me." Then her sly expression returned. "I noticed how quickly he put his arm around you when Brad was here, and when he glances at you, his eyes are brimming with love."

"For heaven sakes, Gram. You've been reading too many of Pat's books. It's the power of suggestion." Gram shrugged off her comments.

"No, it isn't." Gram picked up the remote and clicked the television on, adroitly changing the subject. "It's time for Tom Brokaw."

Maggie walked into the kitchen to get supper. As she crossed the dining room, she heard, "Aunt Maggie, let us in."

She glanced at the door to see two little faces pressed up against the screen, their hands framing their faces, Brad standing behind them. Delighted to see Caitlin and Robert, she walked over to unlock the door. "How are you kids? I've missed you all day."

They grabbed at her and eagerly wrapped their arms around her legs.

"Is David here?" Brad's tone made it clear he didn't relish seeing him again.

"No. He only comes over a couple of times a week to watch the kids and Gram so I can write." She didn't want any arguments with him.

Brad looked genuinely puzzled. "I didn't realize your writing was such a big deal."

Maggie frowned, irritated by his obtuseness. "If I've told you once, I've told you a dozen times. An editor is interested in my mystery, and I need to finish it."

"Oh, that." He dismissed her words as if writing were insignificant.

At this comment Maggie could feel anger tighten her throat and redden her cheeks. "Yes, *that*," she said coldly, her words like chips of ice.

Brad quickly moved on. "With a name like Rosenberg, he sounds Jewish."

"He is." She made little attempt to be pleasant.

"I'm surprised you'd let yourself get involved with him." The expression on his face only confirmed his negative feelings.

She gritted her teeth. "I'm not involved with him."

He rolled his eyes in response. "Who do you think you're kidding?"

Maggie glanced down at Caitlin and Robert, who looked scared. "Why don't you two run in and see Gram?" They scurried into the living room.

Brad continued, "I saw the way you looked at each other last night. You're in love with him. Don't deny it."

She opened her mouth to deny it anyway, and he rushed on. "I offered to marry you in the temple, and you refused. Now you're in love with a man who isn't even a Latter-day Saint. How could you?"

Maggie closed her eyes and took a deep breath. "I don't have to explain a thing to you. It's none of your business." She didn't know how she could make it any clearer.

His face stiffened. "Since I'm the only priesthood bearer in the family, I need to look out for you."

"No, you don't, and you're not. Aunt Barbara's husband, Steve, and her sons also hold the priesthood. So relax. I've managed for thirty-one years, and I can manage for thirty-one more." By sheer willpower she kept her words matter-of-fact and not vehemently spit out.

"I don't think you've *managed* well at all. You've *managed* to fall in love with a Jewish man. Are you giving up a temple marriage for him?"

"You're certainly reading a lot into one ten-minute meeting. Let me repeat: It's none of your business." She wouldn't dignify his accusations with a rational discussion, although she wondered if *rational* would ever describe a conversation with him.

Turning abruptly toward the door into the living room, Brad left Maggie standing there. Still seething, she waited a couple of minutes to cool down before she joined them. In the living room, Brad was explaining the move to Memphis to Gram, who apparently knew exactly who he was today. Somewhere along the way, the peaceful feelings Maggie had had at the temple that morning had dissipated, but she refused to let Brad further destroy the spirit of this marvelous day.

Going into the kitchen, she poured herself a glass of cold water and again took some slow deep breaths to let the anger dissolve before joining the family in the other room.

* * *

David arrived early at the synagogue on Wednesday, eager to find answers from Rabbi Weitzman.

After welcoming the men, the rabbi said, "Tonight our *parsha* is Genesis 12:1. *The Lord said to Abram, Go out, from your land, from your birthplace, and from your father's house, to the land that I will show you. I will make you into a great nation. You shall become a blessing.*"

He closed the Torah. "The secret of Abraham's strength was to go beyond his own limitations to recognize and connect with the Creator."

David wanted to do that. But he didn't know how when he didn't know the words to say.

The rabbi continued. "His connection with God was so strong that his name was changed to Abraham."

David shifted in his seat. Always devout, he had recited all the daily prayers his entire life, and had gone to the synagogue often. But he'd never felt this connection to God that Abraham had. Of course, Abraham was a prophet, but wasn't God the Creator of all mankind? David thought he should feel something.

The rabbi concluded, "Because of their relationship, Abraham remained loyal to God when he was with idol-worshiping peoples."

Who were idol worshipers today? Did he mean non-Jewish people, or those people who laughingly said they belonged to the church of the NFL? David found the scripture thought-provoking. It stirred in him a desire to be closer to God, to feel His presence.

After the discussion, David stood up, then asked, "Is there a Hebrew prayer for truth?"

The rabbi nodded agreeably. "You will find one in the prayer book."

"I found a blessing, but it doesn't say what I want to ask God." David's confusion must have shown because the rabbi moved closer to him.

"Truth isn't just a prayer, but a journey of discovery, for each of us believes whatever we have inherited or been taught is true. In order to affirm whether or not our beliefs are all there is, we must be willing to search for truth wherever it leads us, even into uncharted country. Some will actually have to leave their homes and families. Finding truth is a spiritual quest. We must study, have faith, and trust. We must become open to new ideas."

"But how do we know what is true?" David's eyes had been opened to new ideas in the Book of Mormon, but how did he know they were true? He wasn't about to divulge to the rabbi what he'd been reading because that wasn't the question. Instead, he wanted to know how to find out whether or not something was true.

The rabbi had a kindly manner, and his affection for David was evident in his answers. "There are many truths out there. You just need to find yours. God created many paths that all lead back to him. Does that answer your question, David?"

"Yes." But David didn't know if it did. He resolved to give Fred Scott a call when he got home and see if the Mormons had a meeting like this one, where he could get his questions answered.

Once he arrived home, he picked up the phone and called Fred Scott, who answered immediately. David identified himself and then asked, "Does your church have a discussion meeting that I could attend and have my questions answered?"

Fred never hesitated. "No, but I'll send the elders over. When would be a good time?"

David guessed this man must be a salesman because he definitely wasn't leaving any wiggle room. "Are the elders missionaries?" He just wanted to discuss the Book of Mormon, not have missionaries try to convert him.

"Yes, they've been set apart to teach people about the Church," Fred said firmly.

David wondered what *set apart* meant, but he wasn't about to ask. "I have a busy schedule this week." He checked his watch and saw that it was only eight-thirty. "Is it possible for them to come over now?"

"I'll check and see, then call you back." Fred's eagerness was evident. "Give me your phone number and your address." He called back a few minutes later. "They're on their way."

David started having regrets the moment he hung up, telling himself this was a harebrained idea. The rabbi had given him an explanation, and he ought to be satisfied with that.

When David answered the door and saw what looked like two teenagers dressed in suits, he groaned inwardly. What had he gotten himself into? He didn't think these kids could discuss The Book intelligently, even if they were "set apart," and if they were anything like Fred, he'd probably never get rid of them tonight.

The tall, blond-haired one held out his hand. "I'm Elder Douglas and," he nodded towards the dark-haired kid, "he's Elder Michaels." The other one clasped David's hand firmly. "It's good to meet you, Dr. Rosenberg." Elder Michaels's handshake turned out to be every bit as strong as Elder Douglas's. David wondered if they spent their spare time arm wrestling.

"Make yourselves comfortable." David pointed to the couch.

They sat down, placing their backpacks on the floor next to them. "Brother Scott said you had some questions you wanted answered." Elder Douglas looked him straight in the eyes.

"Well." He hesitated, wondering if he really wanted to discuss anything with these two boys. They seemed sincere, but David didn't think sincerity was enough. He wanted someone with a depth of knowledge. Smothering his reservations, he plunged on. "I've been reading the Book of Mormon." The elders glanced at each other. "I think the gold plates actually existed, and that Lehi, Nephi, Alma, and the other prophets were real people, but how do I know for sure? How do I prove it?" Before either one of the missionaries could answer, he went on, "The Book says to pray about it, but how do you do that? Do you have a prayer for knowing truth?"

Elder Douglas spoke up. "We have answers to your questions, but we need to give you some background before we answer."

David nodded his head for them to proceed.

"Our Heavenly Father has developed a plan for us to follow so that we might be with Him again. The first principal of His plan is to have faith in Him—that He is, and that He loves us." Elder Douglas's voice was warm and convincing.

"I believe that. I've always known God existed, unlike King Lamoni's father." When he said *King Lamoni,* the elders looked at each other again. "But in what shape or form, I don't know." David shrugged. "I doubt it's important."

Elder Michaels smiled. "We'll discuss that later too. Another part of the plan is to know of the Sonship of Jesus Christ, and how God has revealed this to us. He has witnesses, the prophets. Are you familiar with Amos 3:7?"

David nodded.

Elder Douglas spoke up, "This scripture from the Old Testament tells us that God does nothing except He reveals it to His servants the prophets. We've had prophets throughout the ages, and in modern times, Heavenly Father has given us another prophet, Joseph Smith, to be a witness to the truth."

"I read the story of his vision in the Book of Mormon," David spoke up. "My grandfather was a rabbi, and he believed in angels, so I found this credible." It was credible, but was it true? That was what David wanted to find out.

"I know Joseph Smith was a prophet of God. The Holy Ghost has borne witness to me." Elder Douglas spoke with the calm assurance of someone who comprehended the works of God.

"Before Jesus was crucified, He told his followers He would send a comforter, the Holy Ghost. The Holy Ghost's job was to bear witness to the truthfulness of the mission of Jesus Christ and His work, and to enlighten people's minds to the truth. In the Book of Mormon, sometimes He is called the Spirit of God," Elder Michaels said. "Have you ever read or heard something that made your bosom burn?" When David shook his head, Elder Michaels continued. "That is one way the Holy Ghost bears witness to us of the truth."

"When I've read the Book of Mormon, a warm feeling has enveloped me. Is this what you're talking about?" The fact that these missionaries had everything down pat, unlike the rabbi's philosophical discussion, troubled him.

"Yes. The Book of Mormon is another testament of Jesus Christ, and I believe that the warm feelings you've had are the Holy Ghost witnessing to you that Jesus is the Christ, the Messiah." The earnest conviction of Elder Michaels reassured David.

"When you pray, you thank God for all the things He has blessed you with, ask for the things you need, and close in the name of Jesus Christ. We have a study guide we'll leave with you." Elder Douglas reached into his backpack and handed a small pamphlet to David.

"Have we answered your questions?" Elder Michaels said earnestly.

"Yes, you've given me a lot to think about." In fact, David felt overwhelmed.

Then, to David's surprise, Elder Douglas said, "We'd like to have a word of prayer with you before we leave. Would that be all right?"

"Yes." David wanted to know how they actually prayed.

Elder Michaels said, "Do you mind kneeling?"

"No," he said, but he watched to see what the elders did first before making a move himself.

Once David was kneeling, Elder Michaels said, "Our Father in Heaven, we want to thank Thee for this beautiful day and for the opportunity we've had to meet with Dr. Rosenberg and teach him about Thy plan. We're grateful for the Prophet Joseph Smith, and for having a prophet upon the earth at this time. Please bless Thy son, Dr. Rosenberg, that he might know for himself the truth of our message and of the Book of Mormon. We ask this blessing in the name of Thy Son, Jesus Christ, amen."

As David heard the words of the prayer, a peaceful feeling once again spread over him. They all stood, and then Elder Douglas took out a day planner. "When would you like to meet with us again?"

David hadn't planned on a second meeting, but he said, "What about tomorrow night at the same time?" He estimated he'd be home from Isabelle's by then. Evidently they had more to tell him, and David didn't think there would be any harm in listening to them.

"Fine. We'll see you then." They picked up their backpacks, and David followed them to the door. "Good night." He watched them walk down the hall to the elevator.

Shutting the door, he glanced at his watch. It wasn't even ten o'clock yet. These elders certainly didn't hang around. They said what they had to say and they left. Even though they were gone, he felt within himself something he couldn't deny, and he wondered if it was the Holy Ghost bearing witness, as the elders had said.

When he had finished getting ready for bed, he knelt and virtually repeated the elders' prayer word for word. Then he crawled into bed and, putting his right hand over his eyes, recited the *sh'ma*.

When he awoke on Thursday, he felt wonderful. The good feeling he'd had with the elders continued to fill his soul. He said his daily prayers upon rising, and when he was ready to leave for the clinic, he knelt and tried to remember the prayer the elder had said. Only the essence of it remained in his mind, and so he considered his own prayer to be a stumbling rendition of the one he'd heard. To his amazement, the feeling lasted all day. He hurried home to grab a bite to eat and to change clothes, before he headed to Isabelle's. An excited sensation that something good was about to happen flooded over him.

Maggie was watering the flowers when he drove up. She turned at the sound of the car and waved to him. He waved back, calling out, "Hi, how's it going?"

As he approached, she laughed, once again sending shivers of happiness through him.

"Just fine." She put the hose down, letting it run on the petunias. "Come in, and I'll tell you all about it." She paused to shut the water off at the edge of the porch, and then led him up the stairs and into the house. Isabelle sat in the dimly lit room, watching television, which she snapped off as soon as she saw him. Maggie flipped on the overhead light as they entered.

After they situated themselves on the sofa, Maggie looked at David and said, "To begin with, I'm taking a year's leave of absence from school. Also, I've listed my condo for sale, and I'm moving in here with Gram." She grinned at her grandmother. "She's thrilled to have me, aren't you?"

"You know I am. This is the best news I've had in the last ten years," she said eagerly.

"We're also having someone come in five or six hours a day to help Gram and to do the housework. Gram's choosing her. We're not getting another person like the physical therapist, are we?" Her eyes sparkled with amusement.

Isabelle looked confused, as if she had no idea what Maggie was talking about. "Who?"

Maggie reached over and patted her hands. "Don't worry, I've taken care of everything."

Isabelle relaxed and smiled contentedly.

"I'm glad to hear that you're getting some help. Otherwise, I'm afraid you'd wear yourself out," David said. She was one of the most selfless individuals he'd ever met, but she deserved a life of her own.

"Believe me, nothing is more wearing than fourth-grade students." Her tone was light.

Everything about Maggie delighted him. Joy radiated from her, encircling everyone in her presence in its glow. The quirk of her smile and the sparkle in her eyes captivated him. It amazed him how she showered her kindness and thoughtfulness on everyone who needed it. He wanted a closer relationship with her, but since she wasn't Jewish, it was idiocy to even think about it. He needed to stay far away from her. Then he heard himself saying, "Do you have plans for Saturday night?"

She looked amazed. "No."

Shut up, David, he said to himself. *Don't do this.* But he went right on. "You need a break, and I think the ideal one is to come to my condo. I'll demonstrate my French cooking expertise." His heart pounded, and he found himself as nervous as he'd been the first time he ever asked a girl for a date. He couldn't believe how much he wanted her to come. His breath caught in his throat as he waited for her reply.

Maggie hesitated, and he could see the refusal in her eyes. "I don't know if I can," she nodded toward Isabelle, who was watching TV intently, "but I'd like to."

He wanted to touch her, to reassure her, and he picked up her hand. Speaking quietly, he said, "What about Pat?"

"I can't keep asking her for help." She looked into his eyes and smiled. "But I'll figure out something."

How did he resist her? She was coming to dinner Saturday night, and she wasn't Jewish. He released her hand. "Run on, Maggie, and write so you can keep to your schedule."

"I'll go and write, but you don't need to stay. I'll just be in the dining room, and if Gram wants anything she can holler." She stood up.

"Yes," Isabelle said, looking up. "You go on. I'll be okay with my darling granddaughter right here."

"Gee, you two are saying, 'Here's your hat, what's your hurry.' You could make me almost feel unwanted." He got up and followed Maggie to the dining room. "I'll see you Saturday to mow your lawn." He shushed her protests. "Now write."

* * *

David had no more than left when the phone rang. It turned out to be Susan Thompson, Maggie's Relief Society president. "I just heard about your grandmother, and I'm so sorry. I've been in Europe for three weeks chaperoning my daughter's high school drill team, so I've been out of the loop. Now what can I do for you?" She sounded cheerful and eager to be of service.

"Thanks for the offer, but everything's under control. But I do have sad news for me. I'll be moving out of the ward in a few weeks and in here with Gram." Maggie liked the people in Gram's ward, but she loved the ones in her own, so she wasn't excited about this change.

"I hate to hear that we're losing you. The whole ward will miss your Sunday School lessons. You're such a good teacher." Susan actually sounded sad. "If I can't do anything to help you, will you do something for me?"

Silently, Maggie took a deep breath. It was just what she needed—one more thing to do. "Sure. What do you have in mind?" She was such a weakling at turning people down.

"I want you to let me come and stay with your grandmother so you can have a break. I know you're dedicated beyond reasonableness."

Maggie couldn't help laughing. She might have known that was what Susan would want. "You're an answer to my prayers that I hadn't even said yet. What about Saturday night? I've been invited to dinner, and I need someone to stay here."

"I'm thrilled that you're letting me do something for you for a change. Just tell me what time and I'll be there." Enthusiasm was infused in her words.

"That's one thing I don't know. As soon as I find out I'll give you a call. Thanks again." They said good-bye and Maggie hung up, dazed by what had just happened. She loved being in David's company, and she could barely wait until Saturday night. Best of all, she'd also have her book finished. Best of all? Then she corrected herself. Best of all was going to be tasting David's French cooking.

Chapter 16

Butterflies flitted through Maggie's stomach, and then she found herself tapping her fingers on the arm of the sofa. Taking a deep breath to ease the increasing tension, she wished David would hurry and get there, hoping that maybe then she could relax. Waiting drove her crazy. While she watched Susan visit with Gram, she tapped some more. Finally she heard David's car, and like a teenager who was trying to avoid introducing her date to her parents, she said, "David's here. See you later." She ran out to meet him.

"Hi." His eyes lit up when he saw her, sending a jolt of excitement spinning through her, replacing the butterflies. A smile teased the corners of his mouth, causing her to respond the same way. He met her at the passenger-side door and helped her in. His easy manner settled her nerves immediately, and she was grateful she wouldn't spend the whole evening as nervous as a girl on her first date.

When he got in on his side, he looked at her and said, "Ready for some good food?"

She raised her eyebrows. "Are you sure that's what you fix?"

He chuckled. "Pretty sure. I think I at least do a reasonable facsimile of what they demonstrated at the Jewish Community Center, but a real Frenchman might disagree."

"I'm one step a head of you then. A real Frenchwoman taught our class, Madame Viret, straight from Paris," she boasted, a grin on her face.

He gave her an amazed look. "She's the one who taught our class."

"You're kidding!"

"Yes, I am," he admitted. "We had a man, whose name escapes me at the moment."

She turned sideways in her seat so she could observe him better. "I've noticed that Julia Child and Jacques Pepin don't agree on recipes for the same dish, so it will be interesting to see if what you make is anything like what we learned."

"Just wait and see!" They arrived at a high-rise condominium in the Cherry Creek area, and David pulled into the parking garage. He helped her out, and they took the elevator to the tenth floor. When the elevator doors opened, Maggie's eyes widened upon seeing the opulence of the hallway. A metallic Chinese wallpaper of a bridge scene covered the wall in front of them. The paper continued along the bottom third of the walls, with the upper walls and the ceiling being painted a light melon color. The carpeting was a deeper shade of melon. "Wow! All I can say is, this place is gorgeous!" Her eyes sparkled. "How do you stand living here?"

"It isn't easy, but I've made the sacrifice."

"What nobility! You're to be admired." She didn't think she'd ever seen a more beautiful hallway in her life, and she'd read a lot of home-decorating magazines.

David's unit opened up into an entry hall that had a harlequin black-and-white marble floor, an elegant crystal chandelier, and a glossy white-lacquer half-table with matching chairs on either side of it. The seats were covered in black silk. A huge, black-framed mirror rested on the floor behind the table. The facing wall held three bold, modern paintings. She stepped closer and saw that they were prints by Jackson Pollack. "I love it!" she couldn't help exclaiming.

The large living room was decorated beautifully. The walls were painted taupe, with cream crown molding. A thick, cream-colored rug covered most of the dark plank floor. The sofa and chairs all had the same ebony wood, but the upholstery was different. A burgundy, cream, and black silk stripe covered the sofa, and a solid burgundy silk covered two chairs. A cream silk fabric covered the other one. An imposing marble fireplace stood at one end. A large grandfather clock stood at the other end. Black-shaded brass lamps rested on antique tables, each of which had a small bonsai on them.

"Bonsai! Samples of your work?" She loved the charming effect they gave the room, and bent down to get a closer look. "Are these miniature plum trees?"

"Yes and yes. These are my smallest ones. I have them everywhere. As a matter of fact, after I filled my terrace, I ran out of places to put them. I now load unsuspecting guests with them. Interested?"

"Sure. I've always liked bonsai, but I was afraid I'd kill them, so I never bought any. Now that I'm acquainted with an expert, I ought to be able to keep one alive." She grinned at him.

"After we eat, you can go out on the terrace and choose whichever one you want."

"I love magnanimous people!" Maggie glanced around the room again. "I don't call living in this gorgeous place a sacrifice." She shook her head, still smiling at him. "I'm green with envy!"

"I love this room too. The furniture came from my parents' apartment. To use your words, I was green with envy of them. About the time I bought this, my mother redecorated, and I begged her old furniture off her. Thankfully, my brother Sam didn't want it."

The room was elegant, but it also exuded an inviting warmth that Maggie seldom associated with formal living rooms.

"I've been lucky with furniture," David continued. "My grandfather left me the brown leather furniture in my study, along with a Persian rug. So when I work or relax in there, I'm always reminded of him."

"From the things you've said, I can tell he had a great influence on you, like Gram had on me." People who felt a closeness to their grandparents had always impressed Maggie, and her appreciation of David increased.

"I admired everything about him, and he still influences me. I always try to look at things through his eyes." He started down the hall at the right of the room. "The kitchen is this way."

They passed through the dining room. "My mother's castoffs again." He shrugged appreciatively. "I've always liked this furniture, so she gave it to me as a bonus." A black, rectangular table with vibrantly striped gold-and-white side chairs centered the room. At one end of the table, David had set places for two with a bouquet of yellow roses and two candles in the middle. At each setting was a wine glass, and a wine bottle sat in a bucket of ice. "Wine?" she asked lightly.

He smiled reassuringly. "In the Jewish culture we drink plenty of red wine, but in your honor, we're having sparkling grape juice. Nonalcoholic."

When they reached the kitchen, Maggie looked enviously at the large space. One thing she disliked about her condo kitchen was its size—too small for serious cooking. "I take it you put your cooking classes to good use."

He helped her up on a chrome stool at the island.

"The man I bought my condo from was a gourmet cook. Look at this," he pointed to the stove, "a professional cook stove, imported from Canada. It has everything—a grill, a griddle, a warming oven, two regular ovens, one small and one large. The best thing about it is its bright blue color." He flashed her one of his easy smiles, and her heart turned over. "The floor tile matches the color, and even the backs of the cupboards are that color. He had everything imaginable built in—a pantry, two dishwashers, a vegetable preparation sink, recycling bins, even a wine rack and refrigerated drawers. Actually, there is enough room to keep a kosher kitchen."

Maggie wondered just how observant a Jew he was. "Do you observe the Jewish dietary laws?" she asked.

"No, not after my grandfather passed away. I attend Conservative services, and that isn't required." He put on an apron and took the meat out of the refrigerator. "We're having *chateaubriand* with *sauce béarnaise, haricots verts,* sliced asparagus, turned carrots and turnips, and the grand finale is *le gratin de framboises,* or raspberry gratin if you don't speak French. The trick is to get everything ready to serve at the same time."

"This I've got to see. Can I do anything to help?"

He looked shocked. "Absolutely not. How can I show off if you help?"

She laughed as she watched him maneuver handily around the kitchen. "You can't, so I'm happy to sit here and observe. Are you going to do the cooking for your Jewish wife?"

He frowned and appeared disgusted that she would ask such a silly question. Then he grinned. "Didn't I tell you? Gourmet French cooking is one of my prerequisites for a wife. The simple answer is no."

He took tongs and picked up some meat the size of a small roast. He burned grill marks into it on every side, then placed it in the oven.

"Well, that looks too easy to be gourmet cooking." Her eyes gleamed. "I would think gourmet," and she emphasized the last word, "would be more difficult to fix."

"Are you denigrating my efforts?" He scowled. "I just might not give you a bite of anything. But my next dish is more flamboyant." The vegetables were cut in two-inch pieces, and he placed them in a hot skillet with some butter. "Watch this." He held the skillet out in front of him and jerked it back. The vegetables all turned over, and he repeated the procedure.

Maggie clapped. "Excellent, monsieur."

David stopped for a moment and bowed to her. When he'd finished grilling the vegetables, he took out a platter from the warming oven, placed the meat on it, and poured the vegetables around it.

"Wow. Amazing that it all came together at the same time. Are you sure you want someone who can cook? You could get any woman you wanted with your own cooking skill." She got off the stool. "Now what can I do?"

"Would you get the salads from the refrigerator? I used Julia Child's very own dressing recipe, so I'm expecting them to be wonderful."

He placed the platter on the dining room table and went back for the hot bread and the sauce béarnaise. When they were seated, he said, "I always have a blessing before I eat." He bowed his head. "*N'vareykh et eyn hahayim harmotzi'ah léhem min ha'aretz.*" He looked up at her and smiled. "Anything like a Mormon prayer?"

"Not in Hebrew it isn't. What exactly did you say?" Her respect for him grew.

"Blessed art thou, Lord our God, King of the Universe, who bringeth forth bread from the earth."

"It isn't the way we pray, but I like it." She also appreciated him for being a religious person. He had a goodness about him she couldn't ever remember finding in sophisticated men.

"Good." He moved the platter to his plate and began cutting the meat diagonally. He put a couple of pieces on each of their plates, and then he handed her the vegetables. "I know a funny story about this blessing. In the Midwest, a football team was playing its first game of the season. Despite the Supreme Court's ban on school prayer, the team always had prayer before the game. Wanting to be ecumenical, the coach called on the only Jewish boy on the team to say it. He did, and they won the game. The team felt his prayer was lucky, so they had him pray each time. They won all their games, and at the end of the season, the coach asked him what the prayer was in English so they could all use it. The kid said, 'I only know one prayer, and that's the blessing on the bread. So that's what I've said all year.'"

Maggie laughed appreciatively. Then she took a bite of the meat and savored the wonderful taste in her mouth. "You're not bad. I could eat chateaubriand every meal." After she'd tasted everything, she said, "You do yourself proud with your cooking." She bent her head to the side and peered at him critically. "Now if you were only LDS, I'd marry you." Her eyes fastened on his, and the look she saw in his eyes caused her pulse to race. She decided to quit trying to be cute, and took a deep breath. She absolutely did not want him to think she was interested in him. She didn't want him interested in her.

"Now if that's a promise, I might take you up on it." His expression was pensive, and his eyes looked deadly serious. "What do I have to do to be a Mormon?"

"Too much probably." *Considering you'd have to change almost your entire life.* A ripple of pain exploded through her. Without saying anything else, she carefully went back to eating.

He placed his hand over hers, but he didn't say anything for a couple of minutes. Then he released her hand and stood up. "Time to whip up the dessert. Want to watch?"

"Of course." She followed him into the kitchen, where David pulled out some white sauce, raspberries, and cream from the refrigerator. At the island, she stood at his elbow while he mixed the cream and the sauce together, then poured half of it in a small casserole. He put most of berries on top of that, and then covered it with the rest of the cream mixture.

"This goes in the oven for exactly three minutes, and then we eat." He set the timer.

She checked her watch. "I don't think I can wait!"

When it came out of the oven, he scattered the remaining raspberries on the top and triumphantly carried it into the dining room.

"This meal has been fabulous," she raved. "And to think I fixed a pathetic little pot roast with potatoes and carrots cooked right along in the juice of the meat. How did you keep a straight face and not turn up your nose when you saw it?"

"It was easy," he said virtuously. "After all, I came for Isabelle's pie. I could have strangled down any main course, no matter how insipid."

"Thanks for the vote of confidence," she said dryly. "You'll never get another meal from me."

They finished the dessert and started to clear off the table, taking the dishes to the kitchen. While David took the last trayful, Maggie leaned over to blow out the candles. When she straightened up, he was right behind her. Startled, she turned around, and he cupped her face in his hands. She knew what she wanted him to do, and he did, bringing his lips down to meet hers. She stood for a moment before responding. When he lifted his head, his glittering eyes met hers, and then he kissed her again. This time she put her arms around his waist, and they moved closer together. Finally they parted. She hadn't wanted to stop. She stared at his cherished face, barely able to speak. "That was a mistake."

He nodded, and his words came softly. "I know it was, but I've wanted to kiss you for a long time. I love you, Maggie, more than I could ever love anyone else." At these words Maggie's pulse raced. "But any relationship between us is doomed. I'm Jewish, and I'm proud of my heritage. I don't want to become anything else." Heartbreak resonated through his voice. "Do you?"

Her heart breaking, she shook her head slowly. "I could never be anything else but a Latter-day Saint. My parents were, my grandparents were, and my great-great-grandparents were among the first to join The Church of Jesus Christ of Latter-day Saints. This is my heritage." She blinked back the tears.

He stared into her eyes. "Do you believe that it's true?"

"I know it's true." She spoke quietly, from the depths of her being.

He frowned and his eyes narrowed. "How?"

"When I was in the mission field, we always told people to study and pray about it and the Holy Ghost would bear witness to the truth." She managed to hold her voice steady.

"You've been a missionary?" He looked incredulous.

"Yes. Ten years ago in Romania. Just like you and Judaism, I've known all my life that what I believed was true. But I developed a deeper faith by studying the scriptures and praying. I read the Book of Mormon, and I prayed about its truthfulness. The Spirit bore witness by a powerful burning inside me. I know that Jesus Christ is the Messiah and that it's through His sacrifice that we can return to God's presence. I believe the Book of Mormon is another testimony that Jesus is the Son of God. I know that Joseph Smith was a latter-day prophet." Her chin trembled, and her hands shook. She wanted him to believe her so badly, but she was afraid it was all in vain. "I love you, but I could never give up the blessings of an eternal marriage for someone who didn't believe in it." She put her arms around him and held him close. "I do love you," she whispered, her words choked with tears.

"I love you," he whispered, his head nestled against hers. After a few moments they slowly pulled apart, still gazing at each other as if it took more effort than they had to look away.

In an attempt to break the mood, Maggie said, "I suppose you only wash this china by hand, and you expect your guests to do that little chore for you." But to her ears, her tone sounded artificial.

"I do," his smile was a total failure, "but tonight I'm making an exception. I'll do them. I think it's time we relieved Isabelle's senior-sitter."

She grabbed her purse, and they left. Since both of them were lost in their own thoughts, neither said a word the entire way home. When they arrived at Isabelle's, he walked her to the door. "I love you." He lifted his hands, smoothing back her hair before gently circling her lips with his fingertips. "You'll never know how sorry I am that our story couldn't have a happy ending."

At his touch, her heart seemed to shatter, and tears flooded her eyes. "I have an inkling. I keep thinking that nothing can be more difficult than what I'm going through at the moment, and then something even harder to endure comes along.

"Oh, David, parting from you is the hardest thing I've ever been faced with. I wish we'd never met, but we did, and I love you for all the caring things you've done for me." She stared at his face in an effort to engrave it on her heart forever.

He looked into her eyes and said, "I love you." Then he touched her shoulder and left.

She wanted to burst into tears and cry until the pain was gone, but she couldn't. Gram and Susan were in the next room, and she didn't want to talk about broken hearts right now.

Going into the living room, she pasted a smile on her face and struggled to keep her demeanor cheerful. "Hi, did you miss me?"

# Chapter 17

Driving away from Maggie, David felt as if he'd been kicked in the pit of his stomach and that his life force was being sucked away. He never thought he'd confess his love to Maggie. Warring emotions tore through him. He hated it. He didn't want to be in love with a Gentile. He didn't want to give up his Jewish heritage. He didn't want to be seeking the truth about whether or not the Book of Mormon was actually scripture. He wanted to have the peaceful existence he'd had a few weeks ago before Isabelle became his patient, before he'd ever met Fred Scott, before he'd ever heard of Parley Pratt, before he'd ever started to read the Book of Mormon, and before he'd fallen in love with Maggie. His life would never be the same, and he hated it.

The elders had come on Thursday night and told him about the gospel of Jesus Christ. He found Christ's teachings very profound. The trouble he had was accepting Jesus Christ as the Messiah. Many rabbis were profound thinkers also, but this didn't make any of them the Messiah.

At his invitation, the missionaries had arrived at eight o'clock that morning. They'd talked about Joseph Smith and the Restoration of the gospel of Jesus Christ. It sounded great, but David still wondered if the missionaries actually knew the truth. Their talk of "a burning in the bosom" sounded to him more like heartburn than a witness of the Spirit. Though he could feel something when they were with him, when they left, the feeling soon died away.

What was he going to do? He wanted to know God heard his prayers. He wanted an answer he could recognize. Praying was easier now, and he found himself thinking about what he was thankful for and what he wanted, and not just parroting the elders' prayers.

When he arrived home, he cleaned up in the kitchen, his mind on Maggie the entire time. He'd never felt this way about a woman before, and he recognized Maggie as someone whom he could be happy with—his ideal other half. He knew she loved him, and he wanted to marry her. But he also knew she would never leave the LDS Church, and he definitely didn't want a religiously split family. He wished God had given him a definite answer to his prayers. Then he would know what to do.

Afterward he settled down in his study and contemplated the changes in his life if he were to join the LDS Church. His parents would be devastated, and his brother, who was a rabbi, even more so. If his grandfather were still alive, David's decision would kill him. David had once considered being a rabbi, and now he was considering renouncing his religion—the core of his life. Was loving Maggie at the root of his even entertaining the notion of converting? That would never be a good enough reason to hurt his family and give up the beliefs he'd held sacred for an entire lifetime. He had to know for himself if the Mormon religion were true. He wondered how Pete had known. He'd always admired the way his friend could cut through the extraneous material to the heart of a matter. David had never known him to be taken in by something that appeared wonderful, but was in reality phony.

Picking up the phone, he dialed. Over two months had passed since he'd last talked to Pete. When he answered, David identified himself.

"David! It's good to hear from you. What's happening?" Pete sounded enthusiastic.

David didn't know how to phrase his questions, and he hesitated, then slowly admitted, "I've been reading the Book of Mormon."

"What!" Pete's shock reverberated through the lines. "Did I hear you correctly? You're reading the Book of Mormon?"

"Yes." He paused again. "Did you go ahead and get baptized?"

"Yes, nothing could have stopped me. Besides marrying Nikki, it's the best decision I ever made."

David could hear the conviction in Pete's tone which made him feel more confident in asking him for help. "I've got some questions, and I thought you might be the one to give me the answers."

"Would you like me to tell you what made me decide to join the Church?" Pete's voice was quiet and assured.

David squirmed in his chair, getting more comfortable. "Yes." He really did want to know what had convinced Pete to leave Judaism, and he hoped maybe this would help him.

"You know that after Nikki and I were married, I continued to attend the synagogue Friday evenings and Saturdays. Nikki went to her church on Sundays. I occasionally went with her just so we could be together more on the weekend. Even when the church was noisy, I could feel a good spirit there." Then he added, "Our children were blessed in the Mormon Church."

David was dismayed. "What did you think of it?"

"When a baby is blessed in the Mormon Church, he or she receives a name, and then a blessing is pronounced on him or her. In our case, Nikki's father gave it. I found the ceremony very moving, and my soul was again touched by the Spirit." His voice was filled with reverence.

David spoke up. "I attended services one Sunday when a baby was blessed, and all I felt was that it lacked the significance of a *Brit milah*." He still didn't understand what it meant to be touched by the Spirit.

"Maybe to you, but trust me, when it's your own child, you'll find the ceremony moving.

"When I read the Book of Mormon, I knew that Jesus wasn't just a teacher, but the Messiah. But while intellectually I knew the gospel of Jesus Christ was true, that wasn't enough. Then I had such a strong spiritual witness—a burning in my bosom, if you will. Afterward nothing could convince me otherwise."

David didn't hide how forlorn he felt. "Sometimes I feel like I know for sure, but then the feeling leaves me. I don't know if God is even hearing my prayers." More than anything, he wanted to feel that God heard his pleas.

Then Pete spoke again. "When I read 3 Nephi, an overwhelming feeling of the truth of it consumed me. I know it might sound bogus, but it was real. I had no doubts."

"That's my problem. I want to know the truth. Sometimes I feel that the Book of Mormon is a true account and that Jesus Christ was the Messiah, but the feeling doesn't stay with me. Frankly, I've never had a 'burning in my bosom.'

"I've also fallen in love with an LDS woman. She will only marry me if I am a member of her church." His next words came slowly. "No matter how much I might love Maggie, I would never join a church in order to marry her. In fact, she has no idea that I'm even reading the Book of Mormon. I have to *know* for myself that I would be giving up Judaism for the truth, and I have never had a burning feeling of truthfulness about it. I've had a quiet feeling, but no overwhelming burning."

"Have you knelt and prayed from your heart to know the truth?"

David could tell from his friend's question that he wanted to help him. "Yes. I don't think I've ever wanted to know anything so badly in my life."

"I know it sounds simplistic, but God loves us and wants us to know the truth, and trust me, you will," Pete said confidently.

David found his comments heartfelt and, at this moment, inspiring. "I hope so. I've found myself consumed by the Book of Mormon and the desire to know the truthfulness of it. But," his throat tightened, "haven't you found it hard to give up your Jewish heritage?"

"I don't think it's ever easy for anyone to give up strong religious beliefs, and especially when you know people you love dearly will suffer, but it's just something I had to do. My parents are still warm to me. They love Nikki and the kids. It may be difficult and it may take time, but I think your parents will come around in the end. Even my grandmother is more accepting."

"I hope so. I know it will be particularly hard for Sam. We've always been close, and I hope he doesn't see this as betrayal." At the thought of wounding his family so deeply, a sharp pain scissored across David's chest.

"You probably never thought you would be hearing this from me, but I know God has heard your prayers. Somewhere in the scriptures it says to wait upon the Lord. I know for a certainty that in His time and in His way, you will receive an answer that you will recognize as being from Him. God is truth. He cannot fail us." Pete's voice was quiet, but commanding.

His words resonated in David, giving him more confidence in God. They continued to discuss baptism and leaving Judaism. When they hung up, David had a conviction that it was possible for him to make the right decision, but doubts that he could hurt his parents and brother this way still lingered.

Rabbi Weitzman had said, however, that in seeking truth, a person often had to leave their home and family and follow other paths to find it. David knew he would certainly be doing this. The rabbi had stressed that to know the truth took sacrifice. His close-knit family always rejoiced in each other's victories and wept together when sorrow came, and it would be hard for him to hurt them with this news. But if he found the truth in the Mormon Church, he would find some way to tell them. In order to be a Mormon, he'd have to find the strength to give up his grandfather's prayer *talit* and all the Jewish practices that were sacred to him. When he thought of the specifics of his heritage, it brought home to him just how much he would be giving up. But, he kept reminding himself, if he knew the Mormon Church was where God wanted him, he would manage.

The next day the missionaries came again. He asked them to explain eternal marriage. Essentially they told him it was being married in an LDS temple for time and all eternity, not "till death do you part." They explained that the husband also needed to hold the Melchizedek Priesthood to be married in the temple. In David's case it would take a year of membership in the Church before he could go to the temple. He didn't mention it to the elders, but the prospect of waiting raised more questions. Would he need to delay marrying Maggie? He'd found his other half, and he didn't want to wait a year. After the missionaries left, David finished reading the Book of Mormon. He could tangibly feel Moroni's devastation at being alone and separated from his family for so many years. Sorrow filled David as he recognized the distinct possibility that isolation from his own family might be what he had to look forward to.

* * *

Her heart heavy from her discussion with David, Maggie moped around the house on Sunday. She couldn't keep her mind off him. He was such a good person—and religious—everything she'd ever wanted in a husband. She couldn't think of anything she didn't love about him.

She knew she could do worse than marry him. What if she never found anyone else? She couldn't help but wonder if holding out for a temple marriage was worth going through life alone. And once Gram was gone, she would be alone. She wanted to be a mother, to have children as darling as Caitlin and Robert. David wanted children, and just watching him with Karen's kids convinced her he'd be a good father.

She knew he would be supportive of her activity in the Church, but she doubted he would want his children raised as Latter-day Saints. He'd want them raised in his faith, with his heritage, and she felt the same about the Church and her beliefs. If he married her, he'd be giving up his goal to marry a Jewish woman. She sighed deeply. They might love each other, but was it enough? She shook her head. She didn't think so. Her face crumpled, and she could feel tears cascade down her cheeks. She loved David. She admired him. She wanted to marry him. But for any marriage to work between them, they'd both have to sacrifice too much. No matter how much her heart ached, she couldn't marry him. But oh, how she wanted to.

The next day she couldn't shake the grief that permeated her body, and she wondered if she'd ever be happy again. She managed to work on her mystery, proofing and polishing the manuscript and writing the dedication, *For Dr. David Rosenberg. Without your help, this book couldn't have been written. Thanks.* Early Tuesday she got it in the mail.

Although she still felt weighed down by the chores ahead of her, she was glad she could start on sorting and moving. She had asked two teens from her ward to help her dismantle her classroom. The principal had hired a first-year teacher to take over Maggie's class. She was twenty-two years old, fresh out of college, and bursting with enthusiasm. The new teacher wanted to keep everything that Maggie didn't want, which saved a lot of emptying out of boxes and files. She also bought many of Maggie's teaching manuals. She had so many ideas for things to do during the coming year that she was stymied over which ones to choose. In the end, Maggie and the girls only had to pack six boxes, but Maggie was glad she'd had help.

* * *

Elder Douglas and Elder Michaels came every day the next week, and David decided for kids, they were pretty knowledgeable. Then he thought back to when he was their age. He had graduated from Hebrew school, and he had an equal depth of knowledge himself about his own religion.

They taught him about tithing, which he found not to be a problem. He also learned of the Word of Wisdom, and although he had drunk wine from the time he was a child, he did very little social drinking. He didn't smoke, and the only time he drank coffee was at the synagogue, so that law would be easy to keep.

He believed in observing the Sabbath, but he wished the Mormons observed the Jewish Sabbath—Saturday—because he hated giving up his Broncos tickets. If he joined the Church, Isabelle would never get to an actual game. He smiled at the thought.

He'd discussed with them his lack of an answer to his prayers. On Thursday evening, they brought him a copy of the Doctrine and Covenants. Elder Douglas opened his own copy to section six. "This section of the book is a revelation given to Joseph Smith and Oliver Cowdery. The revelations in this book are not only for them, but for all the members of the Church. In reading this part myself last night, I thought it answered some of your questions. Verse sixteen reads, *'Yea, I tell thee, that thou mayest know that there is none else save God that knowest thy thoughts and the intents of thy heart.'*

"In verses nineteen and twenty the Lord says, *'Be patient; be sober; be temperate; have patience, faith, hope and charity. . . . Be faithful and diligent in keeping the commandments of God, and I will encircle thee in the arms of my love.'*" Elder Douglas paused and looked at David, letting the message sink in.

The beautiful text stirred something deep within David, and he blinked back the tears that pricked the edges of his eyes. He followed along in his book, listening intently.

Elder Douglas continued. "In verse twenty-one, the Lord says, *'I am the light which shineth in darkness, and the darkness comprehendeth it not.'*"

Elder Michaels interrupted, "These next two verses might as well begin with, *'For my son, David.'* See if they strike you the same way."

Elder Douglas earnestly proceeded. "*'Verily, verily, I say unto you, if you desire a further witness, cast your mind upon the night that you cried unto me in your heart, that you might know concerning the truth of these things.*

"*'Did I not speak peace to your mind concerning the matter? What greater witness can you have than from God?'*"

Once again, peace spread over David, powerfully filling his entire being. His doubts were swept away, and he knew that what he'd read and what the elders had taught him was true. "I'm glad you found those scriptures. They've clarified God's answers to me, and . . ." His feelings surfaced, and he found it difficult to speak. Taking a deep breath, he slowly continued, "I know that what you've taught me is true."

The elders smiled. "So you're going to be baptized," Elder Michaels said. His statement was just a calm declaration of what he expected to happen.

David hesitated. Then took a deep breath. Could he actually take that step and deeply hurt his family? Despite what Pete said, he didn't know if he could be baptized and leave everything he'd ever known. But he'd told himself if God showed him the truth, he would follow it. Remembering this, his heart leaped and he said, "Yes."

Elder Douglas reassured him, "You've made the right decision, Brother Rosenberg. I know this is what Heavenly Father wants you to do."

"We usually hold baptisms on Saturday morning at the stake center. Would this Saturday be all right?" Elder Michaels took out his day planner.

David hesitated. He wanted to tell his family first, and he wanted Maggie present at the baptism. He knew she'd be thrilled. "I'd prefer to wait until the following Saturday, if that would be all right. There are some things I need to take care of first."

Elder Michaels began writing. "We'll schedule your baptism for ten o'clock in the morning a week from Saturday. There are several things we need to do before then. You will need to be interviewed, and we'd like you to attend church with us on Sunday."

* * *

David attended services at the synagogue on Friday to thank the rabbi for his insight into searching for truth. Observing Jewish rituals had played a major part of his entire life, and he couldn't help but miss them, so he felt a twinge of regret when he told Rabbi Weitzman he was joining The Church of Jesus Christ of Latter-day Saints. The rabbi merely said, "I hope you've found the truth, David. You're giving up all the traditions of your Jewish heritage, the laws you've lived by your entire life."

He called his parents on Sunday morning, wanting them to be able to observe their Sabbath in peace. They were deeply disturbed at his news, and it was distressing to him to know how badly he hurt them. Through their tears they told him that they felt as if they were losing their son. But they repeatedly told him how much they loved him, and if he had discovered the truth, he should pursue it—if it was the truth. Their tone told him how much they doubted he had found it. When he told his brother Sam, he could hear the anguish in his voice, but Sam said little, and they hung up.

He attended church with the missionaries. While there, David knew what Pete had been talking about when he'd told him of the overwhelming feeling that possessed someone when he had a knowledge of the truth. He, too, could feel the burning sensation within him that he had made the right decision.

The bishop and his wife had invited the missionaries and him to Sunday dinner. The bishop was an affable man about his own age, someone David felt that he could relate to. All in all, the events of the day were positive, further convincing him he'd made the correct choice.

David had just returned home and taken off his suit coat when the phone rang. He wasn't surprised to hear from his brother. He'd known that Sam would never accept his joining another church without trying to dissuade him. "Sam, I'm glad you called. We need to talk."

"I thought so too, so if you'll buzz me in, I'll come right up."

Startled, David said, "You're here?" He'd never thought Sam would come to Denver. He'd just talked to him that morning. He pressed zero on the phone and then walked down to the elevators to meet him.

"David." Sam's normally twinkling eyes and good-natured demeanor were gone, replaced by a serious manner totally foreign to him.

"It's good to see you." David searched his brother's face for a moment and then reached out and gave him a bear hug. He could tell his decision to be a Mormon was taking its toll on his brother, and he could see the strain in his face. Heartache welled up in him at the grief he was causing his family. But he had no other option because he knew that Jesus Christ was the Son of God and that His Church was on the earth. He couldn't deny it.

They walked down the hall to his condo in silence. Once in the living room, David said, "Let's go into the study. It's more comfortable. You know where everything is, so make yourself comfortable while I stow your suitcase in the spare bedroom."

Once they were settled in the den's leather chairs, Sam looked at the Persian rug and said, "I feel like I'm back in Grandfather's study. I can practically feel his presence."

David eyed the room that made him recall scenes from his childhood. "I know what you mean. This is my favorite spot in the entire condo."

Sam frowned. "I don't understand how could you give up Judaism when you're surrounded by all this. It brings back many memories to me, reaffirming who I am, and that I am a Jew." His words were quiet.

The plaintive cry in them wrenched David's heart. He didn't want to cause such misery to his brother or his parents, and yet there was no way he could renounce his faith and join a Christian church without wounding them deeply.

"I am still a Jew by birth. I can't give that up. Don't you know how this hurts me?" David's voice broke. "I love my Jewish roots. I love my family." He strained to hold back the tears. "But I know that Jesus is the Messiah, and that His Church is on the earth."

A stunned silence followed.

Then David said quietly, "Remember the hut Grandfather built each fall in his backyard when he lived in Brooklyn? We had some great times there, didn't we?"

Sam smiled briefly at the recollection. "Yes. It was like camping. We lived in that three-sided hut for a week each year during *Sukot* to commemorate the Israelites wandering for forty years in the desert. It was fun."

David leaned back in the chair. "By the end of the week I always felt as if I'd just spent forty years in the wilderness myself, eating only vegetables and sleeping on the ground. When we were kids it wasn't too bad, but the older we got, the harder the ground seemed to get. One good thing about it was Grandmother's cooking."

Sam nodded. "I don't think I've ever eaten any better food than what she fixed. I've said so to Rachel a couple of times, and now she's really sensitive about her cooking." Sam gave David a rueful look.

"Do you still celebrate *Sukot?*" David asked. He could have built a hut on his own veranda, but being alone he hadn't bothered. One was always constructed in front of the synagogue anyway.

"Yes. The kids love it, and it's one of the ways for them to preserve their history." Sam's expression evidenced his heartache. "Remember all the *seders* we had at Grandmother's? I think Mom was always a little jealous not to be observing Passover dinner at our house. Now Rachel and I switch between her home and ours every other year."

Regret at missing such joyous times with his family pierced him. Moving to Denver had separated him from them, and now, if he joined the LDS Church, he would truly be isolated. Could he do it? Reminiscing about their past brought up all the memories he shared with his family involving Judaism. "Now Chanukah has become a major gift-giving holiday. When we were growing up, we lit the menorah each day, but never received any presents." Although it was a minor festival, the entire family had enjoyed it.

"We give gold-wrapped chocolate coins to our children, but that's all. We do eat potato pancakes and jelly donuts." Sam smiled.

"Now those I remember Mom making. Delicious. I think Grandmother's cooking always intimidated her, but she is no slouch in that department herself." David practically salivated thinking about her cooking.

Sam stared at him, an earnest look on his face. "Thinking about what the Jewish rituals have meant to us throughout our lives, how can you deny these experiences to your own children?" He shook his head morosely. "Of course, since the children follow the mother's line, your children won't be considered Jews."

David considered this salient point. He wanted his children to consider themselves Jews. He considered it a noble lineage. He said slowly, "I want my children to know their history. I consider Judaism a birthright. My children will know they are Jewish, and they will know of our culture."

"Are you joining the Mormon Church because you're in love with a Mormon woman?" Sam's voice was filled with scorn.

"No. I know I've found the truth about God and His plan for us, so I can't do anything else but be baptized. Yes, I am in love with a woman who is LDS, but I'm not joining because of her. In fact, Maggie doesn't even know anything about my search for truth," David said gently, trying to ease the pain he was causing his brother.

"But would she have married you if you hadn't converted?" Sam's words were sharp.

"That isn't the point. I was seeking the truth, and I found it. In fact, Rabbi Weitzman said that finding truth often meant leaving our families. I have found the truth, but I don't want to leave my family. You're the very foundation of my life, and I love you and depend on you." David hoped he conveyed his deep feelings for his parents and brother.

"You'll never lose us." Sam's smile was crooked, as if his grief were so heavy that this was all he could manage. "But the pain of your giving up Judaism will take time to get over."

They talked until one in the morning before they turned in. Sam regaled him with stories of his congregation and gave David the latest news about his parents. David wished Sam could spend more time in Denver, but he had a noon reservation to fly home. As he went to bed, David felt better. The worry of losing his family had lifted. The next morning, Sam seemed to be his old self. While David thought it was probably a facade, he knew there was hope for the future.

* * *

Gram and Maggie found the perfect girl to help them. Sandy was nineteen, vivacious, and she had a real knack for caring for the elderly. She was going to night school in order to be an assistant in a forensic lab. Best of all, she was a whiz at housework. Gram loved her. Sandy confided in Gram every minute of her social life, and Gram, of course, loved being her confidant.

Sandy also made it possible for Maggie to have free time. The first day at her condo, Maggie spent most of her time relaxing in her easy chair and absorbing the feeling of being in her own home. She would be giving up this, and while she didn't bemoan her choice, she did look forward to having another home of her own.

Maggie walked through her unit deciding which things to store and which things to move to Gram's house. The kitchen was easy— she'd store everything. Her office was easy—she'd take everything. Her personal belongings were a different matter. She wondered if she really did need all her clothes. Then she had to choose which pieces to keep of the furniture her mother had given her over the years. She wanted a constant reminder of her mother's delightful personality and of what wonderful parents she'd had.

Caitlin and Robert called her that evening. They excitedly told her about their new house, their new school, and that Caitlin would start the first grade in another week. The little girl had met her teacher, Miss Johnson, who she said looked just like a Barbie doll. Maggie had to laugh at that, but when she hung up, she was depressed. The kids were gone—maybe forever—and they didn't even seem to miss her. She shook her head dismally.

Two weeks from the Wednesday she'd made the fateful decision to change her life, she was rearranging the furniture in Gram's upstairs bedrooms. The movers had just left and she'd gone back to her bedroom when the telephone rang, causing her to run back down to the dining room to answer it.

Breathless, she said, "Hello?"

The woman on the other end said, "This is Connie Freed, from Mystery, Inc. I'd like to speak to Maggie Summers."

When the editor identified herself, Maggie's heart caught in her throat, leaving her both breathless and speechless. Finally she mumbled, "Yes. This is she."

"I've read your manuscript, and I love Blanche and Ruby. We want to buy *Murder at the Berkeley*, and we're also interested in doing a series with these characters. I like your ideas for the next two books. What do you say?"

The words swirled around her. "I think I'm hyperventilating!" She tried to control her rapid breathing. "I'm thrilled that you want to buy it."

"We're thrilled that you sent it to us. The legal department is drawing up your contract, and when you receive it, call me, and I'll go over it with you. You should probably have it in a week or ten days. The marketing department is sending you an information packet to fill out for publicity purposes."

"I feel like I'm dreaming. Are you sure you want to buy it?" She had a hard time comprehending Connie Freed's words.

The editor laughed. "I'm sure."

"Any idea when it will be published?"

"It hasn't been slotted yet, but it'll probably be at least a year. You'll be glad to know that you'll get an advance of $5000—half of it when we receive your revisions, and the last half when it's published. We can discuss it more when we go over your contract. Your manuscript hasn't been edited yet, so you won't get your revision letter for about six weeks or so."

"Okay." Maggie was embarrassed she couldn't come up with something a bit more clever to say.

"Get started on your next book. I can't wait to read it. Any questions?" Connie sounded so warm and enthusiastic that Maggie thought it would be great working with her.

"I'm still trying to take it all in. But needless to say, you've made my day." *As well as my week, my month, and my year.*

"It's always exciting for me to call a new author with an offer for her book. I look forward to working with you, Maggie. We'll be in touch."

Her pulse still racing, Maggie made what she considered a few more inane remarks and they hung up. "Gram!" she yelled as she tore into the living room, "Mystery, Inc. wants to buy my book!" She ran over and hugged her grandmother. "They want to buy my book! Can you believe it?"

"Of course I can believe it. No one has worked harder than you have, and you deserve to be published," Gram said in a no-nonsense tone.

"Oh, Gram, you're wonderful. There are probably grandmothers all over the world who are saying the same thing to their granddaughters today." She stood up. "I've got to call Pat."

Pat squealed when she heard the news. "Way to go, Maggie! I knew you'd sell it. Now no more teaching—you can write full-time. David was a big help. Have you told him?"

Even though Pat couldn't see her, Maggie shook her head. "No."

"What's that doleful sound I hear in your voice? Don't tell me something has happened to the match made in heaven?" While Pat's tone was light, her concern for Maggie shone through.

She hadn't spoken to David since she'd gone to his home for dinner. She hadn't confided in Pat because her emotions were still too tender to be exposed. "Actually, Pat, David and I discussed our feelings for each other and decided that nothing would work out. He's Jewish, I'm LDS." She could hear her voice tremble.

"You sound too rational. I'm thinking you're trying to hide a broken heart." Pat picked up on her hurt immediately.

Maggie sniffled.

"Just as I thought. Oh, Maggie, I'm sorry. I know how important the gospel is to you, and I think you've made the right decision. Regardless, I know it's a difficult time for you to get through. I think we should go out and celebrate to take your mind off your pain." Once again, Pat's warmth radiated across the distance and buoyed up Maggie.

"That's a marvelous idea. Let's go somewhere wildly expensive, and I'll pick up the check."

"What a deal." Pat chuckled. "Where shall we go and when? You choose."

Maggie thought for a moment. "I've got an idea. Why don't we go to the Wolfgang Puck Café at the Sixteenth Street mall? We'll pretend we're celebrities like the ones who eat at his L.A. restaurant," she said, getting into the spirit of things.

"Great idea. Let's wear dark glasses and four-inch high heels so we're stylish. We'll be as snooty, as if we're somebody they should recognize." Laughter welled up in Pat's voice.

"I'll call and see if I can get a reservation for tomorrow night. Can you go then? I think Thursdays Sandy is free, and she'll be happy to stay with Gram. If not, we'll just have to choose another date."

"I'm free. Get back to me with the plans, soon-to-be mystery writer of the year." Saying good-bye, Pat hung up.

Maggie turned from the phone, a smile on her face. She always felt better after talking to Pat, and she couldn't think of a better person to celebrate with and keep her mind off David. Now she had to buy some four-inch heels. She loved high-heeled shoes, but she usually stuck to two-inch ones. She was splurging. Red sling-back pumps would be perfect. After all, she told herself, wasn't she the soon-to-be mystery writer of the year?

Wolfgang Puck's food turned out to be yummy. The waiters were snooty, but Maggie and Pat acted as if they were rich and famous. Nobody had anything on them. Maggie found some three-inch, red sling-backs, which she wore with a red linen pantsuit and huge sunglasses that practically covered her whole face. Pat looked equally as stunning in her black silk pantsuit. She wore black-and-white four-inch-high designer shoes that she'd bought in New York City, and her sunglasses were the same size as Maggie's. They giggled all the way through dinner except when they were dealing with their surly waiter. Then they matched his patronizing tone.

Maggie felt wonderful. She couldn't remember when she'd been so lighthearted. The next day she started her new book, *Signing Off,* starring Blanche and Ruby. Some way, she told herself, she'd make it through the hurt of losing David, and she couldn't think of a better way than to be involved in these old ladies' antics.

She'd just gotten involved with Blanche and Ruby's new adventures when she heard a knock. Running downstairs, she found David at the door. Just seeing his beloved face started the pain churning through her all over again. She couldn't force the trembling muscles in her face to smile. She managed to say, "Hi, come on in." She assumed he had probably dropped by to visit with Gram.

David stepped into the hallway.

She sized him up, wondering what was going on. "By the way, I finished your mother's book. What a remarkable life she's led. No wonder you turned out so well."

A smile crinkled his eyes, and Maggie's heart leaped as he said, "Thank you. She'll be glad to know that someone besides her thinks I turned out well."

David looked around. "Is Isabelle in the living room?"

Maggie nodded. "Why are you acting so mysterious? Is something wrong?"

"Let's go out on the patio, where we won't be overheard. I've got some good news." He took her hand and guided her through the kitchen and out the back door.

She protested. "What's up? If it's good news, Gram will want to hear it too. I have some good news of my own. Mystery, Inc. bought my book."

"Fantastic!" His mouth curled into a loving smile that reached to his eyes and lit up his face.

Her breath caught. His was a smile so romantic that she thought she'd melt on the spot. She knew it was ridiculous, but it reinforced how much she loved David.

When they were on the patio, he helped her up onto the wooden picnic table and stood facing her, still holding her in his warm gaze.

Attempting to brush aside the emotions he generated in her, she adopted a quizzical attitude. "Tell me your good news." She found it difficult to speak with any composure.

"Are you busy Saturday morning?" The smile still played around his mouth.

The conversation wasn't going the way she expected. She frowned. "Why? What do you have in mind?"

"I've met a Mormon man who's just right for you. He's free Saturday morning, and I thought I'd introduce you." His eyes gleamed as if he'd just informed her of the most wonderful thing in the world.

"What?" His comments astonished her. He knew she loved him. Did he think she could turn her feelings off so quickly? Why at this point in her life did someone have to find the *right* Mormon man for her? She was already in love with the wrong person, but that didn't make it easy to fall in love with someone else. "How could you even find an LDS man?"

"He's a doctor at University Hospital." He continued smiling, looking deep into her eyes, the happiness radiating from him. He picked up her hand and squeezed it gently.

A sharp pain slashed through her, and she felt as if it had splintered her heart. How could she have been so wrong? He'd said he loved her, but evidently he hadn't been as much in love with her as she was with him. How could he find another man for her? If she'd found a Jewish woman for David, no matter how wonderful the woman might be, she certainly wouldn't be this happy about introducing them. She tried to smile, vowing not to let him see how he was wounding her. She could feel her mouth tremble, and her facial muscles refused to work. She just stared at him, willing her face to not reveal her hurt.

"I—I can't." Her voice faltered. "I—I don't have anyone to stay with Gram. Pat's busy Saturday." She took a deep breath in a vain attempt to steady herself.

"I've already talked to Pat, and she'll be happy to come over and stay while you're gone," he said resolutely, allowing no room for argument. "I think she wants to get you married off."

Those words were like a dash of cold water. "What! You've already talked to Pat?" Her eyes blazed. "I hate being manipulated, and I'm not going anywhere Saturday! I don't care how wonderful the *Mormon* man is!" Didn't anyone care how she felt?

He laughed, a gentle, caressing sound. "Not even if the man is me?"

"You!" Her disbelief was obvious. "You're not LDS! You're proud of being Jewish."

He said thoughtfully, "I am proud of my Jewish heritage. My family has suffered untold misery because of who they were. I can never forget their pain and sorrow. I want my children to celebrate their heritage, but Maggie, I can't give up the LDS Church either. I know that the Book of Mormon is true. I know that the Church is true. I've felt God's spirit when others bear their testimonies and when I read the scriptures. Nothing could stop me from being baptized."

She was astounded by his decision. "What about your parents?" She knew he was close to his family, and she didn't see how he could hurt them like this.

"They are suffering, and my brother came to Denver to talk me out of it. While his arguments were valid—ones I've made to myself over and over again—he couldn't win. I know the truth."

"You're getting baptized Saturday morning?" What a bizarre conversation this was. She'd gone from despair to hope in a matter of minutes.

"Yes. Isabelle knows, and she called Pat. They're coming—even Fred Scott is coming." He grinned at her. "After all, he's the one who gave me the Book of Mormon. Now all we have to do is convince you to be there."

Before Maggie could speak, she had to take a deep breath to steady the jumble of emotions that were threatening to overwhelm her. "Of course I'll go." Scowling, she looked at him. "How come you didn't tell me you were investigating the Church?"

"I needed to study, and as you say, *investigate* it on my own. I didn't want any outside influences, and I most certainly didn't want my family blaming you if I converted."

"Well, they won't, that's for sure. I never knew a thing about it, and in fact, I can still hardly believe that you, David Rosenberg, are getting baptized a member of The Church of Jesus Christ of Latter-day Saints. Miracles never cease."

"They don't, do they? Who made that appointment for Isabelle? No one in my office. The remarks you made the first time we went out have reverberated through my mind. God is aware of us, He loves us, and I believe He wanted us to meet. I want to marry you, and I believe you feel the same way." He cupped her face between his hands. "Will you marry me?"

Long ago she'd decided that she'd probably never hear those words, but now she had, and from the love of her life. Still, she hesitated. "I love you, David, but Gram is my responsibility, and I won't put her in a nursing home. I promised her she could stay at home, and I won't break my promise," she felt her lips quiver as she attempted to smile, "not even to marry the most wonderful man in the entire world."

"From the beginning, Maggie, one of the things I loved most about you was the caring concern you showed for Isabelle. I've seen enough families of the elderly to know that you are an exceptional granddaughter." His gaze penetrated her eyes, and he said with solemnity, "I'd never ask you to break your promise. We could move in here with her or hire a companion to live with her full-time. It doesn't make any difference to me, just as long as we can be together. Let's leave the decision up to Isabelle. We'll see what she wants to do."

Then, in a lighter vein, he said, "But my darling Maggie, if that's the only thing that is holding you back from agreeing to marry me, then I think we're all set! Just say it. 'I'll marry you!' I want to hear it from your lips."

The heaviness had lifted from her heart, and joy enveloped her. She stood up, and he put his arms around her. "I'll marry you." Her mouth curved into a smile. "For time and all eternity."

"Do you really think eternity will be long enough for us to be together?" His eyes pierced hers, and all the goodness, all the love, all of his spirituality shone from them, leaving her awestruck.

"Definitely not," she whispered. "It's only a beginning." He drew her closer, and she slipped her arms around his waist.

"I love you." His fervent tone emphasized the strength of his feelings.

"I love you too." Looking at his cherished face, she wished there were a stronger word than *love*.

His arms tightened their embrace, and then his lips met hers in a kiss that sent a rush of happiness winging its way through her entire being.

Epilogue

Thanksgiving Day
One Year Later

Brad leaned back against the sofa in David and Maggie's condo, his arm around Elizabeth Johnson, his fiancée. "I'm sorry I couldn't be here for Gram's funeral, but I knew she'd understand."

"I'm sure she did. She was ecstatic that David and I had gotten married. She took credit for the entire romance." Maggie glanced at David, and tears came to her eyes as she thought of the part Gram had played in it. "At my wedding, she placed my hand in David's and told him she trusted him to protect and to care for her most precious treasure.

"She supervised me while I made hot rolls for our reception—with her recipe—and it took a great deal of effort on her part because she was so weak. The next two weeks were such a happy time for her. It was as if she'd come to terms with her life and with what she had accomplished, and was anxious to be with Grandpa again. She knew she'd be free of her weak body and be able to do even more in the spirit world. Her funeral wasn't sad, except that we were missing her already, but the whole thing was really more of a celebration of her life."

As she thought back on it, Maggie smiled. "We'd frozen the leftover rolls from the wedding, and so the family had one last loving reminder of her at the dinner afterward."

"Did she leave you the house?" Brad asked. "You deserved it."

Maggie smiled at Brad again and shook her head. "No. She left it to Barbara, which is for the best. They have a missionary-age son, and they'd like to retire in a few years. She left me her personal items, which mean more to me." She'd even been surprised herself at how little it bothered her that Barbara had inherited the house. "I'm just going to have to become a rich and famous author and take care of myself."

"Now that I've met a published author, I wouldn't miss your book signing for anything. We'll see you again tomorrow at the Tattered Cover," Elizabeth said, looking at Brad. To Maggie's surprise, Elizabeth didn't seem to need Brad's permission to do things. They appeared to have a more equal relationship.

Brad said agreeably, "Absolutely. Sorry we have to run, but Mom is serving dinner exactly at 1:00 P.M., and you know her. Maybe we could get together tomorrow after your signing and eat."

"Sounds like a winner." David's voice was cordial. "We'll see you there."

Brad and Elizabeth stood up. "Time to go, kids."

"Hugs and kisses, Aunt Maggie." Caitlin held up her arms to Maggie, and Robert crowded right behind her, reaching up too.

Kneeling on the floor in front of them, Maggie tightly hugged each one. She smiled. "I've missed my favorite kids in the whole wide world so much this last year, and I hate to see you leave now." Then she seated herself back on the couch as they reached for David.

Caitlin and Robert clung to Elizabeth's hands as David showed them out. He returned to the living room and slumped down on the couch beside Maggie. "I never thought I'd live to see the day that Brad was pleasant to me."

Maggie grinned at him. "What does he have to be mad about? He's engaged to a woman who obviously adores him and his children, and to top everything off, she even looks like Barbie. You joined the Church and hold the priesthood, so he can't be angry over that. We went to the temple and were sealed, so he can't hold anything against me."

Putting his arm around her, he drew her close against him and whispered, "I love you, Maggie. I thank Heavenly Father every day that He directed me to my other half." He looked tenderly at her. "My *richige zivvug.*"

She traced the side of his face with her fingers. "This has been the best year of my life. I met you." She grinned. "We got married, yesterday we were sealed for time and all eternity, and in April, we'll be a family of three. I don't want you to get conceited, but you are the most wonderful man in the world." She ran her fingers across his mouth and then kissed him.

His lips met hers. "What more could you ask for?"

"Not much. However," her eyes sparkled, "while it's not on the same level, writing two more books, selling them, and having your parents happy would be quite impressive."

"The news of the baby softened their attitudes, just as Pete predicted." He glanced at his watch. "Time to leave for Pat's if we're going to give her a hand with the dinner."

David stood and pulled Maggie up beside him. "Like all good romances, as Isabelle would be happy to tell you, this one had a happy ending."

"And as Pat would point out, 'They lived happily ever after.'"

The End

About the Author

A native Idahoan, which she unabashedly considers the best state in the union, Beverly King currently resides in Salt Lake City. Bev loves to read, particularly mysteries, legal thrillers, and catalogs, although she never orders much. Her Saturdays are spent watching Bob Vila and Norm Abrams remodel houses, and with them as her inspiration, she is now planning to add architectural detail to an otherwise blah condominium.

She's busy reading travel books and planning trips to New York City, Athens, Rome, the British Isles, and Romania. Unfortunately, she won't be on the next plane!

Bev loves the gospel, and when you read a testimony in one of her books, it's coming straight from her heart.

She is the author of *Christmas by the Book,* and *Picture Perfect,* published by Covenant Communications.

Beverly enjoys corresponding with her readers, who can write to her in care of Covenant Communications, P.O. Box 416, American Fork, Utah 84003-0416, or e-mail her via Covenant at info@covenant-lds.com.

Excerpt from *Before the Dawn* by Carol Warburton

CHAPTER 1

Oregon Territory—1862

I did not come to love a man, needing him like sun and air and the soft Oregon rain, until I'd been married five years—and the man I loved was not my husband. Lest one might think me wanton, I'd best explain. Wantonness was never in my nature, though I confess there were times in my youth when I was inclined to flirt, knowing others thought me more than comely. I must also confess I was not above studying myself in the mirror to confirm the fact.

Although I was sometimes vain, I was never one who could be untrue to my marriage vows. Yet to understand how I came to love and be loved by another man, I must first explain why I married Jacob Mueller.

When I was thirteen years of age, I moved with my widowed mother and older sister to a farm near the village of Mickelboro, Massachusetts. Deacon Mickelson and his wife, Hester, took us in following the death of my father, letting us live in a cottage on their property. The deacon was inclined to spoil my sister Tamsin and me, his overbearing goodness putting him at odds with his wife, whose resentment of us was but barely concealed. Even so, we were happy. Tamsin and I spent many hours exploring a wooded headland towering over the Atlantic, its protecting height forming a little cove which we came to think of as our own. Our delight in tide pools, shells, and gulls skimming white-capped breakers vied with our enjoyment of evenings in the cottage. I can see us still, the two of us curled up close to Mother—Tamsin dark and angular, me fair and more rounded—listening while she read to us from Shakespeare or sometimes Tennyson. Often we would end the evening with music, me playing the pianoforte and singing while Mother and Tamsin listened, pleasure evident on their faces.

All went well until I approached my sixteenth birthday. Although Tamsin was a year and a half my senior, she was slower to mature, her slender frame still that of a girl, while mine took on the curves of womanhood. More than that, Tamsin was inclined to shyness, while my nature was more open. I dared while Tamsin hung back. I often took the lead, my confidence such that I never doubted I knew best. Perhaps it was my pertness and confidence that first attracted Deacon Mickelson, though my looks were a factor too. It was then that I first noticed him watching me in a manner that made me uncomfortable. For some months it was only looks and knowing glances. I tried without success to explain them away. Amos Mickelson was like a jovial, benevolent uncle. Surely I was mistaken in what I read in his eyes. But deep down I feared I was not.

Some months later, in fulfillment of a terrible premonition, Deacon Mickelson's looks progressed to a touch. A more timid girl might have looked away and pretended it hadn't happened. But I was not timid. To the deacon's surprise, I lifted my head and glared at him, taking satisfaction in the smear of red that came to his fleshy jowls, watching his gaze slide from me to Mother, who was in conversation with his wife.

That glare and my subsequent aloofness bought me time, months actually. Once again the deacon became a paragon of propriety when he came to call, which was frequent, for Mother's health wasn't good and he made it a practice to check on her almost daily. In time I relaxed my guard, laughing with Tamsin and Mother when he made a joke, convincing myself the deacon had learned his lesson and would not try his sly advances with me again. In this I erred.

The day it happened is still vivid in my mind. I had spent the afternoon with my friend Pru Steadman, the two of us giggling about boys and at the antics of her baby sister. My heart was light as I made my way home. I remember the song I hummed, the softness of the evening air, the smell of lilacs. Having stayed longer than planned, I entered the cottage with an apology on my lips. The spicy smell of brown Betty told me Tamsin had spent the afternoon baking. I hung my cloak on a peg by the back door and turned, expecting to see Mother and Tamsin lingering over supper. Instead, I found Amos Mickelson sitting at the kitchen table, his bulky legs stretching the fabric of his trousers, his arms folded across his barrel chest.

"Oh," I gasped, surprise making my voice breathless. "Where are Mother and Tamsin?"

"Gone to Wednesday prayer meeting with my wife and the servants."

"Why aren't you . . .?" I began.

"I told them I had other business to attend to." The deacon smiled and patted his leg while his eyes traveled over me in a hungry manner. "Come sit on my knee like you used to and I'll explain."

I tried to quell my nervousness with a smile. "I'm not a little girl anymore, Deacon Mickelson. Nor do I think it proper for you to be here when my mother and sister aren't present." As I spoke, I reached for the door and jerked it opened.

"Close the door," Amos commanded.

Heart pounding, my mind searched for escape. Could I outrun the bulky man? If only we lived closer to neighbors. If only . . .

The deacon's fist hit the table. "Close the door!" he shouted. He seemed to have read my thoughts, for before I could act, Amos was on his feet, the chair toppled, and the door slammed shut.

"There," he said. His features had lost their genial expression, his heavy jowls and face tightening, his blue eyes narrowing. "Lest you think to play any more tricks, let me inform you there's no one close enough to hear you if you scream." He paused and took a deep, satisfied breath. "I've planned this for days . . . though it took some talking to convince your mother that this evening's prayer meeting was the very thing to make her feel better."

Amos had hold of my arm, his fingers pressing into the tender flesh. "I don't want to hurt you," he went on, his voice softening. "Indeed, I hope this can be pleasurable for us both."

"*This?*" I demanded, striving to make my voice cold and steady. "Just what do you mean by *this?*"

"I think you know," Amos chuckled. "I've seen the way you look at the young men . . . how you smile and flirt. I want no more than what you've probably given to them. Only your company and a sweet kiss or two."

I won't attempt to describe what happened next, the fumbling and attempts to kiss me as he pulled me onto his knee. Instead of fighting off his advances, I sat stiff as a tree with my eyes closed, hoping that just as my glare had stopped his hungry looks before, so would my coldness stop him now. After several unsuccessful attempts to loosen my tight-pressed lips and force my stiff frame to curve against his neck and chest, he swore and pushed me off his lap. Rising to his feet, he glared down at me, his face tight and angry.

"Let me tell you, Miss High and Mighty—"

"Just what are you going to tell me?" Though I pretended bravado, my legs were shaking so hard I feared they'd collapse. *Please, help me . . . oh, please,* I prayed, for to faint or give way to tears would undo any advantage I held over the deacon.

"If you don't do just as I say, I'll stand up in church and denounce both you and your mother as harlots."

"That's a lie!" I cried. "No one will believe you."

"Ah, but they will." Amos waited, the satisfied smirk on his face telling me this had been long planned. "More than one of my friends has joked about the little house I keep right under my wife's nose . . . of my three doxies."

"You . . ." My control vanished and I flew at him, anger overriding fear, blind rage stilling good sense. For an instant my fingers found his face and raked the fleshy skin. Then he pinned me tight against him, his arms pressing so hard I feared he'd break my ribs. I couldn't breathe . . . couldn't think.

Just when I thought I would faint, the deacon's hold on me relaxed slightly. With my arms still pinned to my sides, he forced up my face, his fingers bruising and harsh like his voice when he spoke, "Do exactly as I say."

I closed my eyes and let his greedy mouth cover mine, but when his pudgy fingers began to work at the fastening of my bodice, I tried to twist away. *Please . . . oh, please.*

The barking of a dog broke through the wall of my fear. Amos stiffened and his head jerked up when a male voice called from the direction of his house. "Ho, there, Amos. Where are you?"

There was a moment of startled silence, the heavy pounding of the deacon's heart the only movement until his eyes flitted toward the door. "Meet me at the apple cellar on Friday afternoon. If you don't do exactly as I say, or if you breathe one word of what happened today, I swear I'll talk to the reverend and the two of us will denounce both you and your mother as harlots. Tamsin too."

Amos paused, his breathing ragged as if he'd been running, the scratch on the side of his face oozing blood. My breathing was as ragged as his, my starved lungs acting with a mind of their own. As he forced me to look into his narrowed eyes, I thought only of how much I loathed the man. *Pig eyes,* I thought. And he, like a huge boar who'd gone mad, could wipe out my life as I'd known it—Mother's and Tamsin's too. Unless I did as he said.

"Do you hear me, Clarissa? Do you understand?"

All of the fight had gone out of me. Even so, I had to force the words through my lips. "Yes," I whispered.

"Let me hear you say it again. This time louder."

"Yes."

"Good." Amos released me so suddenly I almost fell. I grabbed onto the table, only dimly aware he had gone to the door, wiping his bleeding face with the palm of his hand.

"I'll make you pay for this," he snarled. Then he closed the door and left.

* * *